REMEMBERING EVERLY

Also by J. L. Berg

Forgetting August

REMEMBERING EVERLY

J. L. BERG

FOREVER

New York   Boston

Copyright © 2016 by Jennifer Berg
Bonus chapter copyright © 2016 by Jennifer Berg
Excerpt from *Forgetting August* copyright © 2015 by Jennifer Berg
Cover design and hand lettering by Elizabeth Turner
Cover photograph by Claudio Marinesco
Cover copyright © 2016 by Hachette Book Group, Inc.

Forever
Hachette Book Group
1290 Avenue of the Americas
New York, NY 10104
hachettebookgroup.com
twitter.com/foreverromance

First published as an ebook
First trade paperback edition: July 2016

Printed in the United States of America

RRD-C

10 9 8 7 6 5 4 3 2 1

Forever is an imprint of Grand Central Publishing.
The Forever name and logo are trademarks of Hachette Book Group, Inc.

The Hachette Speakers Bureau provides a wide range of authors for speaking events. To find out more, go to www.hachettespeakersbureau.com or call (866) 376-6591.

The publisher is not responsible for websites (or their content) that are not owned by the publisher.

Library of Congress Cataloging-in-Publication Data is available upon request.

ISBN 978-1-4555-3677-1

For Hannah and Emily,
May you each find your own happily ever.

REMEMBERING
EVERLY

Prologue

Guilt, regret, dread.

Three simple words that had the power to strip a man bare.

To make him feel powerless in the most primitive of ways.

That was what my life had been reduced to. Surrounded by money, unlimited wealth, and affluence, and yet I couldn't protect her.

I couldn't keep her safe. It's all I'd ever wanted—to give her more...everything, protect her from the evil in the world. And yet, somehow, I'd managed to bring it right to our doorstep.

"Why aren't we taking a hired car?" Everly's voice cut through my spiraling thoughts as I turned to see her sitting next to me in the passenger seat, looking speculative and slightly suspicious. She was a vision tonight—the way the indigo blue of her dress contrasted against the fiery crimson of her hair. She'd worn the beaded emerald necklace I'd given her so many years ago—maybe as a peace offering, hoping to bridge the gap of silence that had grown between us.

Because of me, and all of my many failures.

"I thought it might be nice, if it were just the two of us tonight," I answered, sliding my hand across the center console to reach for hers. She didn't seek mine out, but she didn't resist my touch either. The thought of my embrace didn't make her draw back in fear. There was still hope in her eyes that I hadn't become the monster she feared.

If only she knew.

"I thought we were going to the art gala," she said in obvious disappointment.

"We were. But I know how much you hate those types of events, so I canceled and decided an evening alone would be much nicer."

Every word I uttered was total bullshit. I was still expected at that gala and when I didn't show...

Passing the small restaurant I'd picked out—the one that wouldn't require reservations on a Saturday night—I searched around the block for parking, to no avail.

Sometimes I really hated this city.

Three blocks up, I finally found a tight spot on a steep hill. Climbing out of the car, I ran around to the other side to help Everly out, taking note once again of how beautiful she looked. Her legs seemed to go on forever as she stepped out onto the dirty street, the deep blue fabric of her dress brushing over her lush thighs as she rose to meet me.

"Looks like we have a bit of a walk," I said, offering my hand.

She looked around, taking in the location. "Where are we? I don't think I've ever been to this part of town."

I shrugged, playing it off as best I could as we took a step onto the sidewalk side by side. "A guy at work said he'd taken his wife to this place last week and she still hasn't stopped talking about it. I thought it might be worth a try."

She glanced at me suspiciously as I tried not to let the stray graffiti and random bits of trash fluttering in the breeze distract me. I'd once sworn to myself I would always give her nothing but the best—nothing less, and here I was taking her to a ratty part of town, to a restaurant I'd never heard of, just so I could get her out of the house for the evening.

All because I needed to explain.

Everything.

And it needed to be done on neutral territory, without the threat of being interrupted or discovered. God only knew who was listening.

Soon, she would understand.

Soon, she would know why.

We continued to walk together in silence, until she stopped suddenly. I turned to see tears welling in her eyes as the dim streetlights cast a halo on her bright red hair.

"Why are you crying?" I asked hesitantly, stepping forward to offer my hand.

She pulled back, her expression wide with fright as she took in her surroundings. I hadn't been the only one to notice the less than stellar neighborhood.

"What's going on, August?" she asked, her tone filled with panic.

"What do you mean?" I said, trying to remain calm as I held my hands up in a gesture of peace.

"Canceling the art gala... taking me to a place like this? It's not like you. It doesn't make any sense."

Frustrated, I ran a hand through my hair, knowing she was right. None of it made sense, but it was the best I could do and I was hoping she would just go along for the ride. She used to trust me without thought, without reason, but somewhere along this crazy journey we'd created together, we'd somehow lost our way. I'd lost that precious connection with her.

"Maybe you don't know me as well as you think," I bit back, hating myself the instant I said it.

I just needed her to trust me once again. But trust was something that had to be earned and over the last few years, I'd slowly chipped away at that hard-earned treasure I'd once cherished more than anything. Now, when she looked at me, there was little left but doubt.

Doubt and fear.

A sob tore through her and I watched her turn and run down a dark alley.

"Fuck!" I cursed under my breath, chasing after her. The clicking of her heels echoed through the narrow passage, until the sound ceased altogether and I found her wrapped tightly around herself near a side entrance to a sandwich shop. The flickering light above gave me a glimpse of just how much damage I'd done to this poor woman.

The woman I'd loved for so long.

Mascara ran down her swollen red cheeks, puffy from the tears she'd shed over the hurtful words I'd uttered. How many tears had she cried over me?

A few buckets' worth, probably.

I wasn't worth it. But I would be. Starting tonight.

"Why don't you love me?" she asked, her gaze blank as she stared at the grimy wall beyond.

"I love you, Everly. I love you so much," I pleaded, taking her hand. It felt lifeless in mine, like everything had just been sucked out of her and she was just an empty shell standing before me.

Maybe she had been this way for a long time, and I'd been too stupid to notice.

"You don't," she replied, finally turning to look at me. *"You haven't for a long time, and I've just been too afraid to see it."*

"No, you don't understand—let me explain. But just not here," I said, looking around us. *"We have to go. We're not safe here,"* I insisted.

"No, I'm not safe with you!" she yelled, struggling out of my grasp. I tried to catch her as she moved erratically in my tight hold, but the slippery fabric of her dress fell out of my grasp and I lost my balance, sending us both flying. Her fist collided with my skull, and I felt myself falling . . . reaching . . .

Green stones fell around me like rain as I tumbled to the ground, and the last thing I saw was her tortured features as I tumbled into oblivion.

I could see it all written on her face: horror, pain, fear . . . but most of all—relief.

Complete and utter relief.

Chapter One

Everly

Secrets.

They had the ability to destroy lives, obliterate relationships and sabotage even the strongest partnerships. Big or small... it didn't matter. Even the tiniest white lie had the power to corrode—to shatter and dismantle everything you loved.

I'd carried a secret so big, for so long that sometimes I felt physically weak from its weight. I had thought I could carry its burden to my grave—that eventually its truth would die along with me.

But secrets never die.

They live on far longer than we do, and they always find their way to the surface.

Mine certainly did.

Sitting alone in the apartment I shared with my fiancé, I gently rolled the smooth green stone between my thumb and forefinger, over and over, remembering the day it was returned to me.

In all our years together, I'd never seen August so cold. So lifeless.

It frightened me to my core.

But I still hadn't told anyone. It had been three days and I had yet to tell my fiancé or best friend about the events that had taken place in that bridal shop. As far as Ryan and Sarah knew, August had rudely interrupted my bridal appointment to tell me he had his memories back—that was all.

Nothing more, nothing less.

Why hadn't I elaborated? I didn't want to admit my shame. I couldn't share this secret, my darkest lie. What would they think of me? I was the reason August had been in that hospital bed for two years. And the worst part? I'd lied about it—to everyone.

Even those closest to me. Even August.

I was the worst kind of human.

I knew Ryan would tell me the opposite. He would comfort me as I told him the truth, holding me as I shared my story about the awful truth from that night.

There was no mugger.

There was only me.

* * *

"911 Dispatch, what is your emergency?" The words rang clear through the speaker of my cell phone as I held it with both hands, looking down through blurry, tear-soaked eyes at August's lifeless body sprawled on the ground.

Oh God, what had I done?

"Is anyone there?" the woman asked again.

"Yes," I managed to say. "Please send help. My boyfriend has been injured." My voice cracked as the words fell from my lips, becoming reality.

"What happened? Was there an accident? Were you attacked?"

Glancing around at the dark alley, I felt my head nodding in agreement before I even said the words. "Yes, we were attacked. Please, come quickly."

*   *   *

It had all been so easy. No one had ever doubted me. And I never gave them reason to. I was a broken, sobbing mess as they took August away in the ambulance, and stood by him for weeks until they broke the news that he might never wake from his coma.

The coma I'd put him in. I'd sit with him in that lonely white room, watching him become increasingly frail as the days seemed to pass without end. His doctor mistook my guilt for grief and suggested I try to move on with my life. I was young. August would want me to carry on without him.

I remembered him rubbing my back as he delivered the ultimate truth.

"It would take a miracle for him to wake up at this point," he'd said with utmost care. I'd nodded, thanking him for his candor as I looked down at August, wondering whether I wanted a miracle.

Would he be the same? Or different?

I'd decided in that moment that I couldn't wait around to find out—it hurt too much. So I'd taken the doctor's advice and moved on, finding my own apartment and job. And eventually...Ryan.

Gentle Ryan.

Ryan would tell me that horrible night had been just an accident and I'd panicked—an intense moment of weakness. He'd soothe my tears and insist none of it was my fault. Everything would be forgotten and swept under the rug and life would go on as usual.

But I didn't want it to. I didn't deserve his kindness or empathy. I needed someone to scream and yell at me for all the suffering I'd caused. I needed to pay for the life I'd stolen.

Because when it came down to it, I'd taken a life.

And I'd walked away, allowing everyone to believe I was the victim of this story when in actuality, I was the criminal. The perpetrator.

The real monster.

"Hey, I was wondering where you were." Ryan's warm familiar voice filtered through the room as I closed my hand over the stone and slowly slid it beneath the blankets, meeting his friendly gaze.

"Hey," I answered, feigning sleepiness. I stretched my neck back and forth, making an elaborate show of my yawn for effect as the tiny green stone burned hot and bright in my hand. "I was just trying to take a nap."

"No luck?" he asked, leaning against the door frame, crossing his arms over his broad chest as he took me in.

"No. I don't know why I bothered. I can never sleep during the day. But I haven't been sleeping well since—" I stopped myself, regretting the words instantly.

"Since the bridal shop. I know. I feel you tossing and turning in the night," he said as his eyes lingered on me.

Nodding, I felt the silence settle between us, unsure of what to say next.

He pushed off from the door frame and walked toward me, taking the empty spot on the bed beside me. I felt the mattress dip as his large body crawled on top. It felt comforting, having his weight there next to mine.

Safe and real.

He took his time gathering his thoughts, and I could almost see the wheels turning in his head as he chose each word carefully.

"Do you regret your decision in choosing me? Now that he has his memories... does it change your answer?"

And there it was.

The seed of doubt that had sprouted and blossomed buds and blooms since I'd been away with August. Ryan had walked away— sent me into the arms of another man, and even though I'd come back willingly, he didn't always seem to feel confident in my choice. Would I ever be able to uproot the existence of this uncertainty or had the damage already been done?

Were we doomed from the start?

"No—God no," I answered, backpedaling. "That is not what I'm thinking at all," I explained, sitting up in bed to face him fully. "It startled me, yes. I'm still processing it—still trying to figure out what it means to us. But it doesn't change anything. I chose you. I chose this life. That hasn't changed, and it never will."

I'm really quite surprised how quickly Ryan welcomed you back with such open arms, considering how quickly you ran from them when given the chance to fall into mine.

My voice quivered as I spoke, betrayed by my raw emotions. Ryan saw this and mistook my still overwhelming feelings for passion. His lips met mine, a tender whisper of a kiss with a dangling question mark at the end, begging for more. Knowing he needed the reassurance only I could give, I answered with a kiss of my own, returning his tenderness with passion and fire as we fell back onto the mattress and forgot all about memories and choices and only thought about one thing.

Each other.

*   *   *

"Two months?" Sarah squeaked loudly in response to my surprising answer. "Two months?" she repeated as I just nodded, keeping my eyes straight ahead as I followed the signs to the first place on the list.

"You're not pregnant, are you?" she asked, and then before I had a chance to answer, lowered her voice and said, "Oh my God, you're not pregnant with... August's child, are you?"

"What kind of person do you take me for?" I questioned as I switched lanes, taking the exit the brochure had instructed. "I know my life may seem like a soap opera lately, but damn... it hasn't gotten that bad!" I laughed, feeling a little wounded that my best friend really had asked that question. I knew my life had been a little turbulent and I hadn't exactly made some of the best decisions in the last few months, but I did still remember how to prevent pregnancy.

"You haven't answered the question," she pointed out, crossing her arms over her chest.

"For fuck's sake! I'm not pregnant! With anyone's child! I just want to get married!" I hollered over the radio, shaking my head.

"In two months? Why so soon?" she asked, still pestering as she began looking around at the affluent neighborhood as we came to a red light. Mature old trees and meticulous landscaping stretched out as far as the eye could see. It was the kind of place you could picture raising a family—someday.

"Why not so soon?" I said, shaking the picket fence dream from my mind. I had a wedding to plan. "I've made my decision—and yes, I made a mess of it all—but now it's made and I want to start living my life, so I don't see any reason to wait."

Her eyes met mine a moment before I hit the gas to pass through the green light, and I saw her smirk and give a quick nod.

"Okay then. Let's get this thing planned. Good thing I had you shopping off the sales rack last week at the bridal shop." She giggled.

"You knew this would happen?"

"I figured you would either drag your heels or race to the altar. I was really hoping for some sprinting—it's a hell of a lot more fun."

I let out a gentle laugh as we pulled into the small parking lot of the first venue option, killing the engine and turning to her with a smile. Looking up at the beautiful white church, I smiled.

"Well, let's get this thing started."

⁂

"I need caffeine!" I whined, nearly falling into the quaint coffee shop that had served as my employer for nearly three years. The familiar scent that greeted me felt as if a warm, snug blanket was being wrapped around my senses. This place was, at times, tiring, and the hours sometimes sucked, but it had always felt like home.

"I need new legs!" Sarah cried out. "You're a slave driver!" She staggered into the nearest chair, her head falling to the table with a thud. "So tired," she mumbled against the hard wood.

"I didn't mention we were planning everything today?" I said with a wink as I walked up to the counter to greet my coworker Trudy.

"No—you definitely did not. If you had, I would have worn different shoes." To make her point, she held out her foot, displaying her very adorable, incredibly high-heeled wedged sandals. They were tan, with accents of lime green that perfectly matched the bright hues of her flowered sundress.

And she'd bought them on sale—a fact she'd told me with great pride this morning on the way to our first appointment.

But thanks to me and my ambitious schedule, she now hated them—with a passion.

Everything in the world was currently my fault, according to Sarah. But I'd had a plan when we'd left the house today, and I didn't want it ruined by her overachiever brain. So I'd left a few key items out of the agenda. Like the florist appointment... and the bakery appointment... and every other bridal-type duty you would need to accomplish before a wedding.

I'd finally decided to pick a wedding date—to get married and start my life. I'd been a runner for as long as I could remember, darting as soon as life got rough. When Ryan and I fought, I needed air. When things got too real with August, I made excuses and fled. It was why my own fiancé had been the one who helped me come to terms with my feelings for August.

It was wrong. So wrong. And it needed to stop.

From now on, I would have my feet firmly planted on the ground. No more running, starting with this wedding. To make sure I stayed where I was supposed to be, I'd plan the entire thing from start to finish, so help me God.

However, I wasn't stupid. I realized I would eventually need Sarah's assistance and expertise. There's a reason I work in a coffee shop. The work attire required jeans and T-shirts every day of the year, and I barely had to wear makeup. I was a low-maintenance girl. But usually, when I asked for Sarah's assistance, it came in overwhelming waves. So, I'd fibbed a little and told her we were meeting up today only to look at one or two venue options.

Okay, I'd lied a lot.

Did I feel bad? Looking at her hunched over the table, mumbling about her *pretty, pretty shoes...*

Maybe a little.

"Two of the usual?" Trudy asked, with a wink in Sarah's direction.

"Yeah, that'd be great. Maybe a small brownie, too," I added, biting my lip in indecision. Sweets were always a risk when Sarah was moody. With the strict stage diet she always followed when she was performing, and her lingering issues due to years of eating disorders, I always knew to tread lightly when it came to food. But I decided that for today, the chocolate was definitely needed, and today, I needed all the help I could get.

With coffee and chocolate in hand, I walked back to the table and placed the cups down on the table. The aroma immediately brought her face skyward, as she eyed the coffee first and then the brownie with a frown.

"That whole thing is mine. You don't get a single bite," she snarled, kicking her sandals loose underneath the table.

I grinned, nodding. "Deal."

"So, why didn't you tell me we were planning your entire wedding in a day?"

I shrugged. "I guess I wanted to be in charge of it."

"And you thought I wouldn't let you if I knew?" she asked, taking a long sip of coffee before breaking off a piece of the decadent brownie.

"I don't know. Part of me feels bad for the way I acted before. I never got involved—never played the happy bride."

"And so now you're overcompensating? Are you sure this isn't compensation for something else?" Her eyes met mine as our conversation took a turn toward the serious.

"What do you mean?" I asked, clutching my favorite ceramic coffee cup for warmth. It was the same cup I used on all my shifts. It had a cheesy one-liner that said "Meh." My customers loved it.

"Look, I know you are firm in this decision and I see you're happy, but no one is forcing you into marriage. You don't have to marry Ryan to prove you're over August."

"I know that," I answered defensively.

"I just want to make sure you're getting married for the right reasons."

Looking down at my coffee, I watched the steam rise from the cup, like a memory caught in time.

* * *

The last bit of coffee brewed, gurgling and steaming until the last drop was done. I quickly turned to grab the sugar and milk and returned ready to fix everything up.

Only to realize I had no idea how he took his coffee anymore.

Looking up at him, I opened my mouth to ask, but saw him smiling. "Just black," he answered.

I only nodded as I pivoted back toward the refrigerator to return the milk. I'd grabbed everything on impulse, ready to dump two spoonfuls of sugar and a splash of milk into a cup of coffee just like I always had.

How easily I'd fallen back into an old routine.

"I take it that's different?" He spoke up.

"Yes," I answered, "but a good different. Now you're a purist like me."

* * *

"It's for the right reasons," I answered quickly with an encouraging smile.

"As long as you're happy. You know that's all I ever want for you."

"I am. I really am."

"Good. Now about those flower arrangements..."

Oh God, here we go.

Chapter Two

August

"You're not happy," I said, not bothering to attach a question mark to the statement. I could see the disappointment in her eyes as we left the fifth in a string of shiny, upscale apartments we'd been touring.

"No, I'm fine—really."

We'd just left a sweet apartment building—a step up for both of us, really. A mansion compared to the shack I'd found her in, and so much nicer than the bachelor pad I'd been living in since college. I wanted to give her someplace to call home—someplace for both of us to, really. But after compiling a list of some of the nicest places I could afford in the city, and setting up several visits, I knew I'd come up short.

Elevators and doormen—this wasn't what she wanted.

Taking her hand as we walked toward the car, I stopped. The modern, sleek building had disappeared behind us.

"You're anything but fine. Talk to me, please."

Her eyes met mine for a single second and then lowered. Grasp-

ing her chin, I tilted her head back until her beautiful blue irises met mine.

"They're just so shiny and new," she said softly. "I'm afraid I might break something in there. Even the stove was shiny!"

A small puff of air escaped my lips as I tried to contain the laugh threatening to break through.

God, I loved this woman.

"Well, it's a good thing I saved the best for last," I exclaimed with a wolfish grin.

Her eyes widened with interest and surprise as I opened the passenger door and helped her in.

"I thought this was our last stop," she questioned, settling herself inside.

I'd thought so, too. Luckily, I had scheduled something on the off chance that this all went downhill.

And downhill it had gone.

"Nope. I have one more up my sleeve."

"Where?" she asked excitedly.

"Nope, not telling."

It took a while to get there, but I enjoyed every second, watching her knees bob up and down in anticipation. She gazed out the window as the high-rise apartment buildings gave way to small neighborhoods. This part of town wasn't nearly as trendy, and there were very few shops and restaurants within walking distance, but this last place had one thing the others didn't.

I pulled off the road, parking at the curb, and turned off the engine.

"I don't see an apartment building anywhere," she said, looking around.

Smiling, I turned and answered, "That's because this place is a house."

Her eyes grew wide as she looked around. "A house? Which one?"

Leaning in so our heads were close, I pointed to the small house across the street. "There."

I waited and watched for her response. She didn't breathe for what seemed like an eternity. And then, the tears came.

"There are flower boxes in the windows," she whispered as moisture fell from her eyes.

"Yeah," I said as happiness overwhelmed me.

"It's perfect," she said. "You're perfect."

"We're perfect. Together," I agreed.

* * *

Lies. I was drowning in them.

I'd told so many, done so much, I felt like I was swimming in an ocean of my own undoing.

My head continued to spin as I came out of the memory. This was how it always happened. They came without warning—without notice. At any time of the day or night—sometimes even in the form of dreams. I couldn't control them.

I'd told Everly I remembered everything.

Another lie.

Rising from the couch, I shook my head, hoping to disperse the remaining fog that lingered in my psyche. Looking down at my watch, I realized I'd lost an hour due to this latest travel down memory lane.

We're perfect. Together.

The words seemed to echo through the silent house as I walked to the kitchen to make myself a cup of coffee. Tossing a couple scoops of grounds into the pot, I leaned against the counter and waited for it to brew, thinking about the way her eyes had glistened with joy as she'd taken in that tiny shoebox of a house.

So happy, so alive. Why did it all have to end?

"I smell coffee." A familiar voice came booming through the hallway.

I swear, one of these days I was going to remember to lock my damn door.

"I don't remember inviting you over for any," I said as Brick walked into the kitchen. He opened the cupboard door that housed the many coffee mugs.

"If I waited for an invitation from you, I'd never see you."

"Maybe that's a hint," I replied gruffly. I watched him take the first cup as if he owned the place, then inhaled deeply as I followed his steps, taking in the smell as I poured my own cup, watching the dark liquid slowly fill the cup.

"Look, we are not carrying on this friendship through e-mail. If you want to talk to me—we're doing it like this."

Letting out a frustrated sigh, I turned to the fridge to pull out a pint of cream and stopped. The sudden onslaught of memories had me so completely disoriented and brain-fried that I couldn't even remember how I took my coffee anymore. Memories mixed with reality, leaving me hazy and confused.

Always so confused.

"You're having more blackouts, aren't you?" Brick asked. I was still turned away toward the refrigerator.

"You already know the answer to that question."

"Ah yes—the e-mail: 'Hey Brick—Is it normal to feel dizzy during one of these things?' Nothing else. No other information. Thanks for that."

I was pretty sure I'd elaborated a tad more than he'd alluded to, and I didn't recall using the word "thing." I chose not to respond and stared at my untouched coffee cup instead.

"I have a master's degree in psychology and a license to practice psychotherapy. I am not your damned doctor, August!" he boomed. "I'm not even your counselor anymore; otherwise I sure as hell would be reporting these *things* to your doctor. Someone certainly should."

That got my attention.

"I don't need a doctor. I'm fine," I argued, turning sharply to stalk to the other side of the kitchen for air, a move I'd learned from Everly.

"No, of course not. It's completely normal to black out for minutes on end without notice. In fact—keep driving, August. That sounds safe. Or take a jog on a busy road. Hell, why don't you—"

"Stop!" I roared, swiveling back around, my fists tight, ready to fight. "I need them," I gritted between my teeth. "It's the only way I can..."

"Be close to her again?" he finished.

My head fell as the fight fled my body.

"You could have chosen a different path. You could have included her—trusted your love," Brick insisted.

"No."

"So, now you just live amongst the web of lies you've spun?"

"As long as it keeps her safe," I answered with conviction, my gaze narrowed.

Everything I did. Every move—every lie and layer of deceit—I cast was for one single purpose. To keep Everly as far away as possible from me and the fucked-up mess I'd created in my former life. So far I'd only gathered a handful of memories of the formidable partnership that had been August Kincaid and Trent Lyons, and they were terrifying. There was something about Trent that just wasn't right. That feeling, coupled with what I'd learned in my dealings with him since he'd waltzed back into my life, made me realize my decision to push Everly away was completely justified. Trent was a sociopath, completely driven by power and money. Nothing ever got in his way and right now, I was a pawn in his game for achieving ultimate wealth.

There was no fucking way I was letting him anywhere near Everly. He might own me, but I wouldn't let her life be ruined by my mistakes ever again.

"Well, count me out," Brick said. "I can't sit by and watch you ruin your life. I won't lie for you again. I can't do it, August—"

"Then don't," I answered expressionlessly.

"When I saw her—that night by the bridge—she knew Trent was behind this. If you could have just explained…told her everything that had happened rather than letting her walk away."

"And what if he went after her for something I did wrong, Brick? I don't have all the clues, but I remember that night, before I blacked out. I was panicked, full of fear. Because of him."

He huffed out a frustrated breath.

"Exactly. I sent you there to find out how she felt about me. I got my answer."

"And so you retaliated by making her believe what? That you hate her—that you're this evil version of yourself? Why?" Brick asked.

"Because at least if she fears me, she'll stay away."

"You mean she'll stay with Ryan," he corrected, his hands running through his graying hair. Had his face always looked so aged? Or had I put those wrinkled, jagged creases in his forehead?

"Better there than here," I responded curtly.

"Someday you'll understand what you've given up. Someday, you'll realize that love like that only comes around once in a lifetime, and rather than fighting for it, you let it slip away." He put down his unfinished coffee.

"This is me fighting," I argued, watching him walk to the entrance of the kitchen.

He stopped briefly and turned to catch my eyes before he disappeared. "Then I guess you weren't the fighter I thought you were."

* * *

"It's showtime, jackass. Don't mess this up. Remember, this isn't one of those podunk clients you're used to. This is the big leagues now. Do Daddy proud," Trent growled under his breath as his white toothy grin lit up the room.

"Shut up," I seethed as we both stepped forward to greet the unknowing bastards who'd just stepped into our web. The elderly couple held hands as they slowly walked through our doorway. I immediately stepped forward to help, offering a welcoming hand as I ushered them to our meeting room. I was, after all, the trustworthy face of the partnership—or at least that was how it had been explained to me.

I had that look, Trent had said—that wholesome, save-the-world, hero-type face that made people believe anything was possible. Like this elderly couple, who owned a string of bakeries up and down the California coast, finally trusting someone enough to invest all of their hard-earned money so that their legacy could survive generations.

Mine was the face that made them believe that was possible.

And Trent would take that money and do God knows what with it—probably buy himself all sorts of shit while he faked documents and account records that stated the opposite, all while the poor couple believed they were making a fortune.

It appeared to be a seamless system and Trent and I seemed to do it well—a thought that disturbed me more and more with each passing day. Was this the type of person I'd been in the past? Stealing money from little old ladies without a second thought? I'd considered asking Trent, but one glance in his direction and I knew no good would come from asking that spineless snake for the truth. He was never too forthcoming with the details of anything that went on around here, but I definitely had my suspicions, and they weren't good. I wasn't about to speak up, especially since he'd finally seemed to turn his attention away from Everly.

"What was her name? Everly?" His bone-chilling question still haunted me and I had no doubt he'd do whatever it took to keep me here.

Even if it meant hurting the ones I loved.

Within minutes, I'd captivated the ancient couple and had them signing on the dotted line, giving us complete access to all of their hard-earned money—to do with what we pleased. After quickly explaining the risks of investing and the many happy endings of our successes, *wham bam*—several million dollars had been made even before our Starbucks cups went cold. That's how easy it all went down.

"That comes off my debt," I said as I returned from escorting our new clients out the door.

"No," Trent answered, his legs crossed casually in front of him.

"No?" I questioned.

"I found the Smiths," he explained with an easy smile. He sat back in the chair, holding his cup of coffee bought with someone else's money. "They are my clients—my commission, my money. You may have smiled and soothed their fears after they walked in the door, but I found them. So, no—you don't get shit for them."

I wasn't looking at him, but I could feel the sneer from his smile scorching into my back. He knew he'd pissed me off and I wouldn't give him the satisfaction of letting him see it.

"Fine," I answered. "I'll find someone else."

"Of course you will. It's going to take quite a few clients, though, to knock down fifty mil."

He was goading me, but I didn't bother answering. It had become his favorite pastime since I'd returned—pushing my buttons to see how I'd react. So far, I'd held my own, but I knew it was only a matter of time before I blew. Pushing off the edge of the wall I'd been leaning against, I made my way to my office. It was thankfully a safe distance from Trent's and right now, I needed all the space I could manage.

Fifty million dollars.

Arrogant prick. A part of me still didn't believe him, but the fear and dread that came rushing back when I relived that last night before I lost everything—I knew he wasn't lying.

I'd fucked up. I'd fucked up royally.

And Trent expected ultimate payback.

We'd just made a cool two million on the Smith couple. Even if he had handed them over to me toward the debt I owed him, I'd still be paying him back for this fucking mistake for the rest of eternity.

And he knew it.

He had his partner back and I was working for free.

He had the best of both worlds.

I hated him more now than I ever had, which was why I needed clients of my own. But every single lead I had, he'd manage to win over in the last second.

I needed to branch out on my own. Without his watchful, greedy eyes staring me down.

But how?

Moving around the mouse on my computer, I began to search the Internet—newspapers, gossip columns, business magazines. Hell, anything I could find. I needed leads. Asking to manage people's money was a subtle business, especially when you were dealing in the big leagues—which was where I needed to be if I ever planned on leveling the playing field with Trent. You couldn't simply walk up to some billionaire and say, "Hey, I'd like to dick around in your money...sound good?" With the exception of a notable few, the uber-rich were wealthy because they were smart. Earning their trust was a game of give and take that took patience, and I was out of practice and majorly out of my league. I may have still possessed a few wining-and-dining skills Trent found valuable, but when it came to actual number crunching and facts, I was clueless. That was a part of my memory that was still lost, and so far, I was seriously faking it.

Hours dragged on as I went through pages of web searches until I finally stumbled upon something worth looking into.

"Magnolia," I whispered softly. My eyes fell on a magazine article regarding her father and his multi-billion-dollar success story. A small picture had been included of his family, with the beautiful, leggy blonde I'd briefly dated a few months earlier when I'd convinced myself a life with Everly was hopeless and I'd be better off without her.

"Bingo," I said to myself, knowing exactly what I had to do. I picked up my phone to make the call that I knew would push me even further into the dark side.

No going back now.

Chapter Three

Everly

I groaned inwardly as I read the letter a second time.

"Why so serious?" Ryan asked, doing his best Joker impersonation. It came off sounding more like he had a horrible cold, rather than anything remotely close to Heath Ledger's iconic character, and I couldn't help the small grin that pulled at the corner of my lip.

"We got a letter from your mom," I answered, my head already falling in defeat.

"Oh yeah?" he replied, snatching up the personalized stationery from my fingers as he swooped past me on his way to the kitchen.

"This is a long list," he commented, grabbing an apple from the fruit bowl I desperately needed to replenish. Ryan was a fruit maniac, eating several bananas and apples a day. It was impossible to keep the bowl full.

"No kidding," I replied, moving like a zombie toward the coffeepot at the sheer thought of it all. Me? I didn't need much food as long as there was coffee around.

"Calligraphy? Is she mad?"

"She's your mother, and that was just a *suggestion*," I said, filling my cup as the long list of requirements came rushing back to me. Ryan was an only child. After several miscarriages, his parents had given up on the idea of children altogether and settled into the idea of living out the rest of their days as a family of two. At the ripe old age of thirty-nine, at an annual visit to her doctor, Ms. Sparrow found herself with child. The couple was delighted but it meant Ryan was blessed with parents from an era long since gone, where calligraphy was considered the norm and sending out electronic invitations for an event was definitely frowned upon.

Mr. Sparrow had passed away several years ago from a heart attack, and I'd only met Ryan's mother once. After her husband died, she'd chosen to move to Pennsylvania with her sister, who was now her primary caregiver. Ryan, being the faithful, loving son that he is, had offered to move back into his childhood home and tend to her, but she'd known better. Even though I was currently frustrated with the woman for the outrageous list of wedding duties she'd sent, I was grateful she'd denied his offer. Had he moved in with his mother, I don't think I would have ever found him visiting my coffee shop that day, patiently waiting for me to say yes to a date. Even though I'd only met her once, she struck me as a demanding little thing. He probably wouldn't have had time for coffee, stalking, or dating.

And then we might never have ended up here.

"How the hell are we going to get all of this done in time?" he remarked, chomping on a Granny Smith as he held out his own cup for me to fill with coffee. I took it from him and began to give it the same treatment I'd done to mine—filling it to the brim and handing it back to him.

He looked down and frowned. "You didn't leave any room for cream," he said.

Now you're a purist like me.

I realized my error almost immediately and took it back, taking a quick sip to make an inch or two for his cream and sugar. "I'm so sorry. I'm frazzled," I replied quickly as I stepped over to the kitchen table and took a seat, looking down at the worn wood as my heart beat frantically.

"No problem," he answered brightly, not seeming to notice my anxiety as I averted his gaze.

It wasn't the first time I'd slipped up since seeing August last week. Ryan hadn't said a thing. I didn't know if that was on purpose or just a general lack of knowledge.

He didn't know how August took his coffee, or what side of the bed he preferred.

I'd told myself over and over, this was just guilt: deeply buried guilt making its way back up to the surface in waves. It had been so long since I'd allowed myself to think about that night—so long since I'd even allowed myself to acknowledge that I'd been the cause of it, that of course—*of course*—I would have an overwhelming amount of emotions boiling to the surface now that I'd opened up that part of me again.

But part of me knew it was just another secret I was keeping from myself.

Because deep down, I knew that there was one thing far worse than the guilt and the anguish of knowing I'd caused so much pain to a man I'd once loved so completely.

It was knowing that August now knew the truth.

And hated me for it.

*   *   *

"Is this really your idea of fun on a Saturday afternoon?" I asked, looking around the upscale shopping mall in apprehension. It was a place I'd visited several times in my previous life with August. We'd dined at nearly every restaurant, shopped at almost every store, buying gifts and treasures that had long since lost their meaning and sentiment.

"My mother demanded we register somewhere," Ryan shrugged, taking my arm as he pulled me in the direction of a high-end department store.

I begrudgingly passed through the double doors. The sharp smell of expensive perfume hit my nose immediately, taking me back to black tie galas and formal dinner parties. Ryan always asked why I never wore a single ounce of perfume. This was why. Standing in those rooms night after night, smelling them all converge as I waited for August to return to my side, only to stagger to a lonely corner in silence while he wined and dined every person in the room but me, had been like a punch in the gut.

Now here was a sensory reminder of the life I'd left behind.

And the man I could never be enough for.

"Look, they have china and crystal. Both, according to mommy dearest, are the cornerstones to a perfect marriage."

"Right." I resisted the urge to roll my eyes. Barely.

His laughter filled the air. "Right? That's all the response I'm going to get? Come on, Ev, I need a comeback better than that."

We'd crossed through the men's section into the world of kitchen needs and I was fondly eyeing a stainless mixer I'd secretly had my eye on for years.

"I'm holding my tongue. Your mother will soon be mine, and well—I've never had a mom, so who am I to judge what does and does not count as motherly wisdom? Maybe she's right. Maybe expensive china and sparkly crystal will one day be important to our daily lives and we'll look back and thank her for the batshit crazy list she threw at us at the last moment before our wedding."

"Exactly," he grinned.

I tried not to join him as I schooled my expression. "All I know is that it's nice that you have a mother who cares so deeply for you. For us. And I don't want to upset her. I don't want to disappoint her. I'm sure I've already done a decent job of that, with everything before—"

"She knows nothing," he assured me. "I told her it was my decision to call it off. All she knows is we had some issues we needed to work out, and we have."

"Well, that's very gallant of you, but you shouldn't have done that."

"It was me who walked away," he reminded me.

"Only because I wasn't brave enough to do so," I added, feeling slightly odd talking about our breakup in the middle of the store, especially as we prepared to register for gifts for our wedding.

"We made it back to each other eventually." His fingers brushed against my chin, tilted it upward as his lips gently touched mine.

"Yes," I smiled. "We did."

"And now, we need to find some wedding gifts."

"Lead the way."

* * *

"That was actually kind of fun," Ryan said as we stepped out into the fresh California breeze. We'd just spent two long hours covering every inch of the store, scanning everything from the fancy Irish crystal Ryan's mother had suggested to the stainless mixer I really wanted. I couldn't imagine anyone attending our wedding actually buying such an extravagant gift, but I couldn't help but add it anyway. There were so many things on that registry added for the sake of tradition, I couldn't help but add in a touch of myself. Ryan had thankfully pulled me away before I embarrassed myself and started petting the polished steel and shiny blue exterior.

"You just liked using the scanners," I commented as we went in search of sustenance. It had been a long two hours, and I was starving.

He grinned in agreement. "Yeah, those were awesome. They made me feel so powerful. They should really advertise that little tidbit as a perk. It would get the men more involved."

"And then every bride-to-be could have three different grills on her list."

"Hey—I just wanted to give our guests an option," he challenged, holding up his free hand in surrender.

"We don't have a balcony!" I giggled.

"We could. One day. And when we do, we'll be prepared—with our three amazing grills. Did I mention one did charcoal and gas? At the same time?"

I rolled my eyes, the laughter warming my belly as we strolled down the crowded path.

"Where do you want to eat?" I asked, looking around at several options. It was a beautiful day, and there were a few places that offered outside dining. The smell from one of my favorite Italian bistros wafted over, luring me in that direction.

"I think you've already decided," he replied. My feet were starting to move toward the heavenly scents of garlic and freshly baked bread.

"I'm just looking," I stated, taking a few paces closer so I could peek at the menu. It had been a while since I'd been here, and I wanted to make sure they still had one of my favorite items—eggplant parmesan.

A deep laugh halted me in my tracks.

My eyes darted to the left and there he was, tucked into a corner table with a gorgeous blonde. Even from this angle, I could see the designer labels I'd once become so familiar with adorning her from head to toe. She was everything I was not.

Everything he'd wanted me to be.

Manicured, primped to perfection without a hair out of place, she was every man's fantasy. Sitting there together, they truly made the perfect couple. He'd cut his hair short again, matching the razor edge precision of his tailored suit. He screamed money and class, and with her by his side, it looked like the missing piece of the puzzle had finally been found.

It shouldn't matter.

I shouldn't care.

But God, I did.

Look away, Everly. Look away.

As if he heard the silent mantra screaming inside my head, his attention turned and his eyes widened slightly, his gaze colliding with mine.

Time froze. The world melted away and there was only him, me, and the swirling sea of emotions between us. His jaw ticked as my heart leapt into high gear. And as quickly as he found me again, his eyes slid away as if I'd never existed.

Like I'd never meant anything.

His focus returned to his date and I was left shaking like a leaf. Forgotten. Again.

"Did you decide?" Ryan asked, his hand sliding around my waist as I blew out a breath and looked up with a fake, strained smile.

"Yes. Yes, I've decided," I answered, wrapping my arms around him tightly. "Let's go home to eat. It's too crowded here."

We walked away arm in arm as I forced myself to never ever look behind me.

There was nothing waiting for me back there anyway.

Chapter Four
August

"So, why am I here, August?" Magnolia asked, leaning forward in her seat. I watched as she slid one silky smooth leg slowly over the other and rested her chin casually on her upturned palm.

"Would you believe me if I said I missed you?" I answered, trying not to notice each and every detail that differentiated her from Everly. From the diamond tennis bracelet that adorned her dainty wrist to the platinum blond extensions she'd added to her hair since we'd last seen each other, she was a vast contrast to the flip-flop-wearing, tree-hugging girl I'd let walk away.

Not to say Magnolia didn't come with her own set of charms.

Like a father worth billions.

"Maybe," she answered. "But, considering our last encounter and the way you left me high and dry without a single word since, I'm finding that hard to believe." There was no hurt feeling in her tone, but I could see it in the way she turned away, not wanting to meet my gaze. She was playing it cool, trying to appear confident and self-assured, but I knew better. I'd wounded this woman—maybe only a little, but it showed.

I was starting to realize I'd hurt a lot of people over the years.

"I needed time to get myself straightened out," I lied, each word coming out easier than the last. When had it become so easy? "I realized I wasn't the type of man you needed. Hell—I wasn't any type of man at that point and before I took that crucial step with anyone, I needed to figure out who I was."

More lies. More bullshit. When would it stop?

A small smile played across her painted red lips. "And did you?" she asked, looking appreciatively at my new, polished appearance. Magnolia might have approached the casual-looking amateur photographer that night in the bar, but this man sitting before her would always be her top choice. The power-hungry, dominant type who could sweep her off her feet and give her the world.

The guy with the camera, she'd dated for just a fun run and nothing to get too upset over. A bruised ego and a pint of Ben and Jerry's and she'd probably thrown me into the "What was I thinking?" category. Looking at me now, she saw something worth keeping.

Something worth fighting for, and that made me nervous.

Because there was nothing left of me to give. I was an empty, broken shell.

"Well, I'm interested in discovering the man you've become," she said with a note of seduction in her voice.

I smiled darkly, hiding the pain in my voice and answered with a playful laugh. "I bet you are." As her gaze met mine, a wisp of fiery red hair caught my attention and I turned.

Everly.

Her eyes crashed into mine, and she froze mid-step.

In fear? Disgust? Remorse?

God, she looked beautiful.

Look away, August, look away.

It caused me physical pain to turn away from her. To cast her aside as if she were nothing more than a momentary distraction, but I had to. To do anything else would ruin everything.

Run, Everly, I silently pleaded.

As I saw her walk away in the arms of her fiancé—the man she would safely spend the rest of her life with, I knew I'd made the right decision. No good could come from me. She was exactly where she was supposed to be, and unfortunately, so was I.

"So, you'll give me a second chance?" I asked, forcing a smile to my lips as I focused all my attention on Magnolia and the road again.

I had a goal and there was no looking backward.

Only forward.

* * *

I was in a foul mood when I entered the office the following Monday. The tie around my neck felt too tight, too restrictive...too everything. The expensive Italian leather shoes I wore felt heavy and uncomfortable. Every step I took brought me closer and closer to that small, confined space of a prison that reminded me of the person I had become.

Again.

Recovering my memories was something I'd thought would

never happen. The doctors at the hospital had warned me that with each day that passed since my reawakening, the likelihood of retrieving them became slimmer.

So what did I do with the rest of my life?

I moved on; that's exactly what I'd done. But in the opposite direction. I'd become a different person altogether, and with Everly back in my life, I hadn't missed the memories. I hadn't needed them because I was making new ones with her.

A new start.

But now, as the memories tumbled back and my old life threatened to take over, I felt as if I was being torn in two very different directions.

The life I had once led was vastly different than the one I'd begun to make for myself. How did I navigate? How did I find a path when my memories showed me one person and I wanted another?

I didn't.

As soon as Trent reentered my life, I'd lost the capability of choice and everything had come down to one driving force.

Keeping Everly safe.

I'd taken a turn . . . gone down a dark path with my lunch date intending to rekindle things with Magnolia.

Was that really the man I wanted to be? Using someone to save my own ass? I'd sat across from her for two hours, and it made me remember what had drawn me to her in the first place. Once you got past the obvious beauty and flawless package, she really was fun to be around. Because I knew she'd been raised around that much affluence, I would have thought she'd be more of a demanding brat than a sweet girl next door.

After we'd said our good-byes, I knew I couldn't go through

with it. Keeping Everly out of Trent's reach was my main goal. No one else needed to suffer at my expense.

If there was anything I'd learned over the last few months, it was that Trent was a crazy, manipulating asshole and would do anything to get his way. He'd had an entire waitstaff fired last week because his steak wasn't rare enough. He treated women like they were disposable—breaking them one at a time. He never used his real name and he kept the drama far from the office, but I'd caught on swiftly when our late night meetings got too boring for him and he'd order entertainment.

God only knows what he did when I wasn't around, when he didn't need to hold up appearances and pretend to have a sliver of humanity left in that lifeless body of his. He wanted my penitence for the last two years I'd left him hanging, and right now I believed he'd do anything to keep me on that hook he'd left dangling out in front of him.

Including getting rid of any and all distractions I may have in my life, which was why I decided to let go of them myself. Better for him to think Everly had left me of her own accord than to assume she still had feelings for me. It was safer this way.

Seeing her arms wrapped around Ryan, though? Knowing his arms, his hands, and his body would always be what she reached for in the middle of the night?

It was the worst kind of pain imaginable.

I staggered to my desk, keeping my head low and my emotions in check. The last thing I needed was Trent on my ass at this crazy hour. It was too damn early in the morning for that. I just wanted to drown myself in a cup of coffee and the stack of papers on my desk and not talk to a single soul.

"Good morning, Mr. Kincaid." A friendly voice brought my attention forward. Next to the little desk outside my office stood my elderly secretary, Cheryl.

She looked more like a cheery librarian, ready to help you figure out the Dewey decimal system, than a woman working for one of the most successful financial firms in San Francisco. But then, I was beginning to wonder if that was Trent's strategy all along—keep the supporting staff small and stupid.

My secretary had been with us since the beginning and was old enough to be my grandmother. Her gray, stringy hair and wool pantsuits reminded me of old sitcoms, where the only place women worked were either in the home or at a desk much like the one she sat at.

Cheryl didn't ask many questions and she kept to herself—qualities she probably carried forward from another generation. In this office it was, no doubt, a good skill to have.

"Good morning, Cheryl. Have a good week with the grandkids?" I asked, remembering today was the day she was returning from her week-long vacation. With Trent breathing down my neck, I'd barely noticed she had been gone. At least someone would be around now to field my calls again. If only she could keep Trent from darkening my door like a creepy stalker every fucking hour.

"I did." She smiled sweetly, a hint of sadness touching the corners of her wrinkled eyes. "They grow so much when I'm not around. Makes my heart ache, but I understand. Jobs are important."

I nodded in agreement. I'd gotten to re-know several things about my charming secretary over the last couple of months in the few conversations we'd had. When I'd first met her, my immediate thought was to wonder what the hell she was doing still working. She had to be pushing seventy-five and was still the first person to show up to work. While most people her age were long since retired, making quilts and traveling to Florida or Europe, she was still working forty plus hours a week along with the rest of us who were more than half her age.

I'd then learned, as she'd rambled on over a cup of coffee, that her only son, Brogan, had moved away several years earlier, due to a job transfer in the software industry. His move left her alone in a large family house she was unwilling to part with, with no one to look after her since her husband had passed away ten years prior. The work she did here, I think, gave her something to do—someone to care for.

I guess I was that someone for her.

This poor woman.

"I'm going to head in and work on some things," I said, effectively ending our morning chatter as I took the last remaining steps toward the door that separated my little circle of hell from everywhere else.

"Okay, sure," she answered, turning away in disappointment. I knew she was hoping to talk more—to catch up and tell me more about her vacation, but I just couldn't. I didn't have it in me today—to be happy for others when my life was the exact opposite. Not so closely after seeing Everly in the arms of another, knowing soon she would be his . . . forever.

I just needed time. Time to heal and process. Time to refocus my priorities and shove away the sight of her body wrapped around his. Time to remember what I was doing and why I was doing it.

But today, I just wanted to sulk and loathe the life fate had given me.

"Mr. Kincaid?" Cheryl's timid voice stopped me from taking the last step into my office.

"Yes?" I turned around.

"Before you go, I forgot to mention...there was a message for you on the voicemail over the weekend. Someone named Roger from an art gallery downtown? He said he sold one of your—"

"Thank you," I said, quickly cutting her off before she could finish her sentence. I didn't need her to say any more. God knows Trent had ears everywhere.

How Roger had managed to get my work number was beyond me. It was something I needed to change, and quickly. Having him call here was not wise.

Walking back to her desk, I gave her a confident smile as I snatched the pink message slip from her hands and swiftly walked into my office, shutting the door behind me. Leaning against it, I took a deep breath and let my back slowly melt into the solid grain.

Looking over the message, I felt my eyes widen in surprise. I read it over and over in disbelief.

One of my photographs had sold.

Mine.

It was a day I'd been waiting for for months. I looked around the room, the excitement bubbling up inside of me like a newly opened bottle of champagne. My heart beat loudly in my chest.

Pulling out my phone, I touched the keypad and paused, the harsh reality stopping me cold.

I had no one to celebrate this with. There was no one in my life I could call and tell this news to. There would be no celebratory night out. No happy phone calls or excited shouts of congratulations.

Because I had no one, and I could blame it all on one single person.

Trent.

Ambling across the floor I slumped into my desk chair, the perky pink note tumbling from my fingers as it fell to the desk—a reminder of everything my life could have been if Trent had just left me the hell alone.

I could have had everything.

Everly, a new career, and my memories.

I stared down at that single piece of paper, the rage and anger building inside of me, and felt it:

The all-too-familiar feeling of my past resurfacing.

My eyes started to blur, and the world tilted on its axis. Suddenly I was falling.

* * *

The music boomed as the bass vibrated down to my very bones, shaking nearly everything that wasn't nailed down in the small house. Haphazard streamers and pink flamingos littered the walls and floor, as half-naked girls danced around carrying red Solo cups in their hands, while guys tried to decide which ones looked hottest in a bikini.

My first college party.

It was fucking awesome.

Having been raised by two scholarly bookworms, the idea of a Friday night out in high school had mostly consisted of making my way to a football game or two—assuming all of my homework for the following week had been completed. I'd never complained, though. I understood the value of an education, and all that hard work and dedication had paid off in the end, earning me a full-ride scholarship to Stanford, but damn if I didn't finally deserve a break.

"Hey man, aren't you in my economics class?" I turned to my left to find a tall, familiar-looking guy walking up to me. He held out a red cup filled to the top with frothy golden liquid and I took it with thanks, as he continued to shout over the popular music that roared through the sound system while people danced around us.

"Did you make it through that last quiz? I'm pretty sure I left with my balls shoved firmly up my ass."

Nearly choking on my beer, I laughed at his vivid analogy of our recent pop quiz. I had no idea what he was talking about. I'd walked out of there in record time, barely breaking a sweat, but I nodded, chuckling in agreement like I completely understood his pain.

"The name's Trent. I'm a junior." He held out his free hand.

I took it, shaking it firmly. "August. Freshman."

He grinned, a knowing look in his eyes as we surveyed the crowd.

"Have you pledged yet?"

"To a fraternity?" I asked, as my eyes fell on a group of girls huddled around each other. I recognized a few from classes—one especially. She sat a few rows in front of me in English and I think I'd spent the majority of the semester observing the way her sweater always seemed to fall off her beautiful shoulder more than anything the professor had said.

My parents would not approve.

"Yeah—I'm a brother of Kappa Sig and we're always looking for new members, if they're the right kind, that is," he said with a laugh. "Someone like you? You might be just the kind of guy we're looking for."

"I'm not sure I'm the frat boy type," I answered honestly, my eyes never leaving the group of girls I'd discovered. He'd obviously caught on to my new fascination because at that moment he leaned over, pointing to the long-legged girl of my dreams.

"If you were—a frat boy, that is—you wouldn't have to be sitting here on the sidelines wondering what a night with her would be like. You could just have it. You could have it all."

My eyes widened as I turned to him.

"Seriously?"

"Seriously. Go over there. Introduce yourself and tell her you're a pledge. It's going to change your life, August."

Trent disappeared into the crowd as I downed the rest of the beer he'd given me. Liquid courage. I hadn't had much experience with girls in high school. A few steady girlfriends, but actual dating and flirting? I had no clue. I was just the good-looking smart guy, like Trent had pegged me for. I had no game, no angle, and absolutely no idea what I was doing. The girls I'd dated in the past had always made the first move.

You could have it all.

I guess it was my turn to step up to the plate.

Feeling a bit brave, with the cheap beer running through my system and after the pep talk from Trent, I made my way to the other side of the room. Her back was turned as I approached and I took those last remaining moments to appreciate the way her bikini bottom hugged her round, curvy ass. Her long legs definitely still held my attention, going on for days as she stood among her friends in a large circle, drinking beer and bouncing around a beach ball.

A beach party in winter.

Fucking brilliant.

One of her friends caught sight of me first, and signaled my approach, causing her to turn as I took the last few steps toward her.

Shit, what do I say?

"I'm August. I think we have a class together," I tossed out in a rush, the courage I'd brought with me fleeing faster than a dog with its tail between its legs.

She smiled, amusement painting her delicate features as she casually looked me over. She must have liked what she saw because she took a slow, sensual sip of her drink and replied, "Oh yeah? Which class might that be, August?"

"English."

Her smile widened, as recognition washed over her. "You're the one with all the answers."

"Well, not all of them," I admitted. "I've been a bit distracted."

"Why's that?"

"I can't seem to keep my eyes off you," I answered honestly, a blush creeping up my heated complexion.

"Aren't you a sweet talker, August. What's your last name?"

"Kincaid. I'm a freshman. From the city—on a full ride and…" I hesitated before deciding my fate. *"I'm pledging to Kappa Sig."*

Her eyes widened in interest as she slowly wrapped an arm around mine. "Smart and sexy. Well, I'm Jodi and if you're good, maybe I'll give you my number by the end of the night."

"Deal."

We spent the next two hours laughing by the pool over old childhood antics, sharing high school stories, and just getting to know one another. It was easy, and natural. The heat and passion I felt for her all those days I'd spent staring at her from across the room was still there—in spades, but now I saw her as the full package. A girl I could date, and someday really care for.

The night held possibility.

"I'm going to go refill my drink," she announced, rising from our spot by the pool.

"Do you want me to come with you?" I offered, beginning to rise.

"No way. Save our spot. With all the crazies around here, it will be taken in seconds and then we'll be standing for the rest of the night."

Chuckling, I nodded. "No problem."

"I'll be back," she promised.

I started to worry when thirty minutes passed and she still hadn't returned. Self-doubt kicked in ten minutes later when there was still no sight of her. Had I misinterpreted the last couple of hours? Had she been bored? Was she just dying for an opportunity to escape me?

I got up and decided to search for answers. For all I knew, she could have fallen and twisted an ankle and I was out here, sitting around like a dumb ass while everyone rushed to her aid.

Or she could have bailed on me...

Passing through the living room and kitchen with no luck, I headed into the front room where I'd introduced myself, finding her group of friends in the same spot where we'd started.

Jodi wasn't there.

Feeling frustrated and defeated, I went in search of my coat. It was California, but walking across campus in my shorts and flip-flops in fifty-degree weather didn't sound very appealing. I'd been told our coats would be dumped in an empty bedroom at the end of the hall, so I was surprised to hear voices as I turned the door handle and entered.

Not as surprised as Jodi was when her eyes met mine.

Shoved against a wall, her bathing suit top was askew. A large male hand covered her naked breast. She rushed to cover herself as her partner adjusted himself and turned to greet me.

"Hey August." A sly smile spread across his face.

"Trent?"

"I'm so sorry, August. I don't know—" Jodi stumbled over her words.

Turning, Trent gave her a gentle pat on the shoulder. "Why don't you give us a minute or two alone, sweetheart?"

She nodded, her eyes rounding at the near sight of him as she quickly fled the room.

"What the hell, Trent?" I said angrily.

He held his hands up in surrender, a gentle chuckle falling from his lips. "Easy, brother."

"I am not your brother," I gritted through my teeth, beginning to stalk from corner to corner.

"No, but you will be if I have anything to say about it."

Silence followed as I paced.

"You know, I did you a service here tonight."

Trying to keep my chin from falling to the floor, I looked up at him in curiosity, waiting for him to explain.

"She wasn't good enough for you—for a brother of Kappa Sig. I saw the way you looked at her—you were already falling for her. I only did what any other brother would do for another. I put her to the test, and she failed miserably. Would I let a girl like that date any little brother of mine?"

I had no words. Was he for real?

His arm wrapped around my shoulder as he laughed. "Welcome to my world, August."

* * *

"August!" Trent's voice pulled me from the abyss. The normal gradual return I felt when tumbling back to reality was more like a free fall, and I suddenly felt nauseated and sick.

"What?" I answered as I quickly tried to get my bearings, looking around the office as my vision came back onboard along with the rest of my senses.

"Where the fuck were you, man?" he asked, taking a seat in front of me as he fiddled with his phone. His fingers hitting the screen made a sharp sound as he tapped a message or e-mail. He'd made it a habit to never give one hundred percent of his attention to any one person or thing, unless you were a client and money was on the line. Then, you got the fucking world.

"Sorry, didn't sleep well last night," I lied, still blinking several times to adjust to the bright overhead lights.

"Well, do it somewhere else. This isn't your fucking bedroom. I don't pay you to sit around."

I ignored those comments.

It was hard, but I did.

This business was a partnership. Trent had started this company and brought me in as an equal to build it from the ground up. I'd worked my ass off for this company, and because of my two-year *vacation,* I was now thought of as an employee. Nothing more than a peon. Someone he could maneuver and boss around. I was starting to wonder if I'd been that all along and just hadn't realized.

"So," he began, setting his phone down on the desk in front of him. He sat back in the seat, making himself comfortable. Suddenly I had his full attention.

Shit.

"Did you think you could get away with seeing Magnolia Yorke without me knowing?"

"How did you?"

He just smiled. The little shit had had me followed.

"We're just friends," I answered, keeping my expression blank.

"You're just friends with the daughter of a multibillionaire?"

Shrugging my shoulders, I replied, "We met at a bar several months ago. Went on a few dates."

"And you never thought about all that money...just ripe for the taking?"

"It's not like that," I answered firmly.

His expression hardened as his eyes locked on mine. "Then make it. Jesus fuck, August, don't you get it? An account like that could set us up for the rest of our entire lives. Stop pussyfooting around and do what you have to do."

He pushed off the chair and stalked toward the door, pausing before he exited. "Or I will."

His haunting last words echoed through the small space long after he left.

I should never have called her.

I should have never gotten her involved. Because now, whether I liked it or not, Magnolia was going to end up smack dab in the middle of my shitty mess.

Welcome to my world, August, I remembered Trent saying during that party in college.

He'd been ruling over my life for well over a decade.

Somehow, some way, he had to be stopped.

Chapter Five
Everly

It had been a quiet day at work so far, but that didn't keep my feet and back from aching more and more over the hours of endless standing. I was the commander of the coffee today—barista extraordinaire, so in addition to my sore, tired feet and aching back, I was also a sweaty mess from the steamer. I was pretty sure my half-assed attempt at vanity this morning, when I'd tried to apply makeup at 5 a.m., was currently running down the sides of my face. I probably resembled something close to one of those women in the horror flicks right before she bites the dust. I kind of felt that way, too.

We hadn't had a new customer in over thirty minutes, though, and after cleaning every piece of equipment to a high polish, I decided to reward myself with a double espresso. In my current sweaty state, something iced probably would have been a better choice, but I was jonesing for something with a little extra buzz.

As Trudy refilled the bakery case and jabbered on about her latest conquest—a waiter down the street at one of the restaurants we liked to frequent—I danced slowly from one foot to the other, waiting for my espresso to brew.

"So, I look at him and go, 'Wouldn't you like to know?' and he just glances down at me with this goofy smile. Was that not clear enough? How dumb are men?"

Shaking my head, I snorted out a laugh. Trudy was always hopeless when it came to dating. Always moving from one man to the next, she was notorious for hopping into bed too soon, latching on too quickly, and finding out she'd picked the wrong one just as fast.

"Have you ever considered not laying it all out there, Trudy? Maybe just a little flirting to let him know you're interested and then seeing where it goes?"

"Like, go on a date or something?"

As the last drop of my double shot trickled from the espresso machine, I tried not to giggle.

"Yes, like a date. One that doesn't end in your bed. Or his," I clarified.

"So, how will I know if I like him?"

The sad part was she was asking this question with sincerity. The even sadder part was I was the orphan girl, who'd practically raised myself because my dozen or so foster parents had been too self-involved to do so themselves. Trudy? Her parents were amazing. They came in every weekend like clockwork to visit her at work, give her money if she needed it, and pat her on the head on their way out, affirming their love and affection for their only daughter.

How she'd managed to come to the conclusion that sex was the only way to a man's heart was beyond me. The fact that I was the one trying to set her straight was slightly ironic.

Grabbing my cup of liquid fuel, I made my way up to the front so we could speak face to face. Her lovely bright eyes found mine as she rose from the bakery case, closing it tightly as she brushed off her apron. "You talk to him—he'll hopefully listen, assuming he's not a jackass. Then you do this same process, in reverse. He'll talk, you listen. Somewhere in between all this, you'll eat, and worry about every piece of food you put into your mouth, wondering if you have bits of lettuce in your teeth or if there's sauce around your lips."

"That sounds horrible."

"It can be," I answered honestly. "But if you're with the right person, it can be absolutely amazing."

"Amazing enough to give you that dopey smile you've got right now?" she laughed.

Grabbing the towel I had slung over my shoulder, I threw it at her, snickering. "Yes, exactly. Just admit it—you want the dopey smile, don't you?"

"Maybe..." she began to answer, but stopped abruptly when we heard a rumble race through the shop.

"What was—" I said.

"Earthquake!" she yelled. Like trained soldiers, the few locals we had inside jumped under tables, some moving away from the windows to seek shelter together. Earthquakes weren't everyday occurrences for Californians, but happened often enough that we knew what to do when that familiar roar came tearing through a building.

Trudy and I ducked beneath the front counter, covering our heads as we huddled next to each other. The quake wasn't major and barely lasted the time it took for us to find a safe spot to hide. As soon as the ground fell quiet, we waited, wondering if it would come alive again.

A minute or two passed in silence before we rose.

"Everyone okay?" I asked, looking around to see our loyal patrons rising from the floor.

Each nodded, standing and brushing their pants and bare knees.

"How about another round of coffee for everyone?" Trudy offered. "On the house?"

Of course this perked everyone up and helped ease the jitters as they settled back into their normal spots. Some pulled out cell phones to check in with loved ones, while others just carried on with what they were doing before all the commotion had started.

After a quick hand rinsing, I got started on everyone's coffee. These were my customers, so I knew what they liked. A half-caff cappuccino, a caramel macchiato, and an Americano with room. Easy.

I noticed Trudy was busy in the front, pulling a few things out of the case, and I smiled. She may not have the whole dating thing down, but her heart was always in the right place.

Tiptoeing out from behind the counter, she carefully began setting down little treats in front of each customer, with a little kiss and hug to top it off. While some of us might retreat into our shells after a startling event, she did the opposite, stretching out wide to help anyone within reach.

Maybe that's why she couldn't find love. Perhaps her overeagerness was always placing her in a false path—always causing her to seek love in the wrong way. I only hoped that one day she would find someone lucky enough to be deserving of everything she had to offer.

"Well, that was something, huh?" Trudy commented as she came up beside me to help finish up. She grabbed the whipped cream and topped off the macchiato, adding a touch of caramel drizzle for decoration.

"Yeah, definitely didn't expect that when I woke up this morning."

"We never do. But they come anyway. Really makes you think, doesn't it?" she said as I watched a shot of espresso brew.

"About what?"

"Life, I guess. I mean, if this had been the big one—the end. It would have been just me and you," she smiled.

"Is that a good thing?" I asked.

She laughed. "It's a great thing, but it definitely makes me think more about your dating comments. It's time I start doing things differently. God knows, when and if the big one comes, I want to know I have more than just you to reach for at the end of the world."

I handed her the cup of coffee as she sauntered off to serve everything, leaving me reeling in thought. I knew she was just thinking theoretically, but it sent my mind in a tailspin.

When those tremors had started, I hadn't thought about Ryan at all. For one brief second, when the shop shook and tremors shook my bones, there was only one face I saw.

August.

I shook my head, realizing I was probably making a big deal of nothing.

If it had been something major, surely I would have reached out for Ryan—called out his name as the world crumbled around us?

Right?

Or was I giving my love away for all the wrong reasons...just like Trudy?

*   *   *

I felt in a bit of a daze the rest of the day, as I tried to process everything.

The news said it was a minor earthquake—nothing to worry about.

Yet, in my mind, it felt anything but.

Was I marrying Ryan for the right reasons? Looking back, I remember believing I was making the right choice when I'd asked him to take me back.

It had all seemed so clear. But was it?

My head was swimming with a million different emotions as I drove toward the bridal shop. I felt like I was going through the motions rather than living them as I parked a few blocks away and just sat there, still and silent, trying to muster the courage to get out of the car.

Go pick up your wedding dress, Everly, I chanted in my mind, and yet my feet stayed firmly planted on the floor of the car.

Dear God, what was wrong with me?

Tears formed in the corners of my eyes as the air left my lungs. I could feel the sobs just about to break through. I would not do this.

Not again. I couldn't. I'd made a promise. I'd said yes and given this man my heart.

I couldn't walk away again.

Just as I was choking back tears, fighting myself for control, I saw a sign that stopped me dead in my tracks.

Grand Opening.

Squinting, I tried to make out the letters through my blurry, tear-soaked eyes.

"He did it," I whispered, a smile replacing the tortured frown I'd had.

Getting out of the car, I quickly wiped away my tears and jogged across the street, the familiar smell of burgers and fries lulling me into a wonderful feeling of security as I pushed open the door and looked around.

Everything looked different yet oddly the same.

The location had obviously changed, which was a vast improvement. This part of town was known for its vibrant young crowd of shoppers and tourists. With the updated decor he'd chosen, I knew he'd do well this time around.

"Hey, hey—there's my girl!" Joey exclaimed, his familiar Boston accent full and thick, as he came out from what I assumed was the kitchen. He looked different, but again, the same. There was a vibrancy in his eyes that hadn't been there that long ago afternoon when he'd made me my favorite birthday burger as a favor to August. He'd cleaned up since the last time I'd seen him, too—gotten a haircut—but was back in chef gear, ready to grill and fry in his own kitchen again.

"I can't believe this!" I said, giving him a big hug.

"Fancy, huh?" he said, smiling widely, pride beaming from his eyes.

"How did you manage this?"

"You, and your wealthy boyfriend," he explained.

I looked at him oddly, ignoring the boyfriend comment, and waited for him to explain.

"The designer watch and the huge chunk of cash August gave me was enough to convince the suits over at the bank to give me a business loan."

"That's fantastic. I'm so happy for you!"

"Well, I wouldn't be here without your help. So, why don't you take a seat and I'll make you a burger?" he offered, pointing to a sleek corner booth near my right.

My mouth watered just thinking about eating a burger and a pile of fries.

"I would love to, but I actually have an appointment down the street to pick up my wedding dress. Can I take a rain check?"

His eyes lit up and he smiled. "August didn't mention you two were getting hitched. I guess you'll be coming in for an anniversary burger once a year too?"

I gave him a sad smile. "Actually, August and I broke up a few months ago. I'm marrying my former fiancé Ryan. It's all a little complicated," I explained. My focus fell to the polished floor, rather than to his falling expression.

"Oh. Okay. Well, that's just too bad. I didn't know," he answered, clearly embarrassed.

"Wait," I interrupted his mumbling as my head shot back up. "You said August didn't tell you? Are you still talking to him?"

"What? Oh yeah. All the time. He helped me set this all up. Went to the bank with me and everything—even bought me a suit for the meeting. He's been my lifesaver."

I was stunned.

"I see." I had no idea what else to say.

"You two are really over, huh?" he asked softly.

"Yeah."

"Can I ask why? I mean, if you don't mind. It's just that a guy who would do something as crazy as what he did for you—you just didn't seem like the type to fall apart."

Taking a deep breath, I gave a ghost of a smile as I tried to steady my emotions. "He didn't love me enough to stay."

"Or maybe he loved you enough to let go?" Joey offered with a friendly pat on my shoulder. I gave him one last hug before leaving as I made my way down the street.

If only that were true, Joey.

If only that were true.

*   *   *

I'd just finished stuffing the giant white garment bag in our closet when I heard Ryan shout his arrival.

"Honey, I'm home!" he said playfully from the living room.

I hid the ivory satin shoes I'd bought to go with my dress and promptly closed the closet door, feeling like I'd just hidden away some deep dark secret in the belly of our closet.

"Hey!" he said from the doorway. "Whatcha doing in here?"

"Secret wedding stuff," I answered with a smile.

"So, shoving your wedding dress in the closet, then?"

"Hey, how did you guess?" I exclaimed, folding my arms across my chest.

"Because you had an appointment to pick up said wedding dress today. It doesn't take a genius to figure out that you'd need someplace to put it."

"Oh. Right." Looking around, I bit my lip and finally said, "Well, don't peek at it. It will give us seven years' bad luck in bed or something."

He chuckled, shaking his head. "I'm pretty sure that's not true. But, don't worry. I want to be surprised when you walk down that aisle."

"Oh, you will be. Especially when you find out I'm wearing a burlap sack. So sexy."

"Oh yeah?" He took a few steps closer, until we were nearly touching. "And how does this burlap sack fit? Is it really tight around here?" His hands wrapped around my backside, curving around each shapely, round cheek.

"Totally. Chafes like a bitch, but fits me like a glove."

"I'm trying to woo you here," he laughed, shaking his head as his shoulders shook.

"Oh, okay. My bad. I'll try to be more accommodating. Try again." I immediately went blank in the face, looking up at him with doe-like eyes.

His deep, unfiltered laughter was all I heard as he threw me over his shoulder and we both toppled onto the bed.

"You're insane, you know that?" he said as his fingers gently swept away the few pieces of hair that fell in my face.

"Yeah, I know. But you love me," I said.

"Yes. I do."

I froze, instantly. The words coming back to me, as quickly as the memory. The smell of thousand-year-old trees and the sound of laughter as August repeated the same exact words to me beneath the redwoods.

My heart tightened a little as I fought off the pain. Brick had reminded me it would never stop hurting. He was right. Some days, it only hurt a little—barely enough to notice. Other days, I'd agonize over what I'd done, where I'd gone wrong. Those days, sometimes it hurt to breathe.

It made me second-guess everything.

"Hey, the earthquake," I said. "You never called me. Were you okay?"

Obviously he was fine since he was lying beside me, but as I remembered watching the coffee shop patrons call their loved ones, I realized I'd never once reached for my own phone.

And Ryan hadn't reached for his.

Wasn't there something to be said about that?

"It was such a small one, I figured if you needed me, you'd call." He shrugged, pushing off the bed. I watched him walk down the hallway toward the kitchen and wondered.

If the end of the world came, would I be the one he reached out for?

Chapter Six

August

It was nearing eight long hours at the office, and I was currently waiting for my sixth—possibly seventh—cup of coffee to brew in the break room.

When I'd returned back to this hellhole, Cheryl had practically begged to do this simple task for me, saying it was a secretary's pride and duty to make her boss's coffee throughout the day, but she didn't understand the significance this darkly scented beverage held for me.

It was in these few silent moments, when the single-serve, fancy coffeepot in the break room would gurgle out my java, that I'd let my mind wander back to those precious few weeks when I'd had everything. When life was simple and easy, and coffee was made in the morning by the only woman who'd ever managed to steal my heart.

Now it just tasted like watered-down tar. It didn't matter who made it, or where I went to buy it; nothing would ever be the same and this simple cup of coffee was just a physical reminder of her absence in my life. And of all the ways I'd failed.

Leaning back against the counter, I slowly sipped my coffee, letting the caffeine do its work as I surveyed the office through the broad windows that opened out onto the lobby. Trent was busy flirting with his secretary.

Again.

A faint blush stained her cheeks as she held back a laugh. His infectious personality was overwhelming and soon she couldn't contain herself, and the entire office space was filled with her melodic giggles. He said people couldn't stand him, and that was mostly true—except for women. He seemed to have a power over women that was electric. It unnerved me.

I watched him closely, knowing his attention was elsewhere.

I'd dreamed about him last night, another memory to add to the growing pile. Much like Trent's secretary, I'd fallen prey to the charms and false promises of my longtime friend and partner. My former self had once believed he could make or do anything—and I took everything he said as truth. A mistake I would regret to this very day.

*   *   *

"A toast to August!" Trent hollered with enthusiasm, thrusting his champagne flute high in the air. Feeling mightier than a fucking oak tree at that particular moment, I joined in, seeing Everly do the same right next to me.

"To August!" she parroted, her eyes full of pride.

Several diners from other tables looked over with a mixture of annoyance and curiosity, but we just carried on, still high from my success.

My first big deal.

I'd been a stockbroker for years now, doing my due diligence, working my way up in hopes that one day I'd finally make something of myself. Randomly running into my old buddy Trent from college had been the best accident of my life. He'd shown me a way to the top, without the wait.

Now I was making deals I'd once only dreamed of. And I was a partner of my own firm.

"Hey," I said, turning to Everly, my eyes wide with excitement. "I got you something."

She watched as I pulled a long blue velvet jewelry box from under the table.

"You know I don't expect anything. Tonight is about you!"

"I know, but I couldn't help it. I wanted to show you how much you mean to me," I explained, antsy for her to open the gift I'd picked out for her. In all our time together, I'd never been able to go to a store and shop for something so extravagant. It was exhilarating and addictive. I couldn't wait to cover her in jewels and fine things.

A small gasp escaped her throat as the lid popped open and her gaze locked with the beaded necklace.

"Oh August—it's gorgeous."

"They're emeralds," I explained as her fingers brushed over the smooth round stones. "I saw it and just knew it would be spectacular on you."

Her eyes glistened as she looked up at me. "I don't know what to say."

"Say you like it," I smiled. *I pulled the necklace out of the box and slowly placed it on her smooth, porcelain skin.*

"I love it," she answered, leaning forward to kiss my lips.

As she pulled away, the tiny stones from her necklace almost seemed to wink at me, catching light from above as she turned.

Trent, silently watching our exchange, just smiled and looked at me with hungry eyes. "You ready for more?" he asked.

"Yes," I answered, catching Everly's happy smile once again. *The smile I'd put there. I was hooked now.*

"Let's make more money."

* * *

Trent was exactly what he needed to be when the time called for it—completely malleable for every unique situation. He'd used me to do his bidding—just like everyone else. Like now, he was the charming boss, who made his secretary feel at ease and secure in her position. When the time arose and he needed her to do something questionable, she would, without question. Why? Because she trusted him.

Even though he probably couldn't remember the woman's last name or anything about her. Alice Towers had been working for us since we'd opened. She was middle-aged, had two teenage sons, and loved the Giants. She also had an epic-size crush on her boss. That last tidbit was the only piece of information Trent cared about and he used it to his advantage, playing off her emotions to get her to do everything and anything without knowing why.

This was what Trent did. He wooed people into giving him what he wanted, and then he walked away. But like I said, wealthy men tended to be that way because they were smart, and they could sniff out Trent and his crooked ways in seconds.

Me and my honest face—we legitimized him. We gave him credit.

And I hated the fact that it was all just another fucking lie.

Everything Trent touched became tainted. He was on a destructive path to disaster, and it was just a matter of time before every single one of us in this office was sitting behind bars for the crimes we'd committed because of this man.

How many others would suffer the same fate? Or worse?

*   *   *

I was like a cannon ready to explode as I raced home that evening.

Caffeine and a shitload of anxicty raced through my system as I pulled the car into the garage and jumped out, knowing I was already running late for my date with Magnolia.

I couldn't screw this up.

Not now that Trent knew.

Alice laughed at his jokes while Cheryl showed him pictures of her grandkids. Brick told me I should have let Everly know what had happened between Trent and me. He thought I was being overly paranoid.

No one else saw it, but I did.

Trent was dangerous. I could see it in his eyes, feel it in my bones, and damn if I was going to let him ruin anyone else's life on my account.

Quickly stepping into the garage and unlocking the door, I ran inside, pulling my tie off as I went. Taking the stairs two at a time, I had every intention of making it to the bathroom for a quick shower. But my feet had other plans. My toe hit the edge of one of the last steps, and as gracefully as a six-foot man can go, I fell, collapsing onto the stairs with a loud, audible bang.

As I went, the stars and blurs began and by the time I hit, I knew I was falling—not just to the ground, but out of time.

Back into a memory.

"Ah fuck—" I mumbled as the lights went out.

*   *   *

Must get home.

Driving like a bat out of hell, those were the only words that repeated over and over in my head as I swerved through traffic, trying to maintain my erratic, high speed down the freeway.

Must get home.

Raw, deep, unbridled fear coursed through my veins as I barreled down the streets trying to get to her.

God, what have I done?

I need her to be ready to go.

Taking a deep breath, I tried to calm my shaking nerves as I pressed the speed dial on my phone. She answered almost immediately. She sounded sad. How long had she sounded that way?

It didn't matter.

None of it mattered after tonight.

"Hey, gorgeous," I greeted her cheerfully. That piqued her interest.

"Hi," she answered, her mood sounding slightly lifted.

"I was thinking tonight would be the perfect night out. Just the two of us?"

Silence followed, and I waited. My heart pounded in my chest, fearing she'd already seen through my lie.

"Really?" she replied, her breathy voice filled with glee.

"Really. Can you be ready in thirty minutes?"

"Absolutely!" she squealed, the excitement palpable over the airwaves.

"Fantastic. I'll see you soon."

"Okay, sounds great!"

"Oh, and Everly," I said quickly, before she hung up the phone, "I love you."

I could feel her smile from across the city.

"I love you too."

The line went dead and I was alone again. The fear and regret came rushing back like a flood. As I pulled off the freeway, I passed a row of houses. They were simple and well kept. A flower box sat perched on one of the windowsills, reminding me of the days when something so simple used to bring us so much joy.

When did it all change?

Driving farther, I noticed the houses becoming larger. Everything became more grand and outrageous until I pulled into the house that was ours.

The one I'd given to her with a giant red bow wrapped around the front.

She'd never asked for it, but I'd given it anyway.

I'd have given her the moon if I could. But somehow, I had lost my way and in the process of giving her the world, I'd neglected the one person that had given me everything.

Tonight, I would make it right.
Tonight, I would tell her everything.

* * *

Coming back to reality, I rubbed my sore limbs and head and pushed myself up off the floor. Frustration replaced every other emotion I'd once had as I replayed the memory in my head.

What was I going to tell her?

I could only recall the intense need to get home to her and finally lay everything out on the table. But why couldn't I remember what that was?

Would I have left any clues?

Suddenly remembering piles of paperwork on the desk I had yet to sort through, I raced back down the steps, careful not to fall this time, and made my way to the darkroom that had once been my home office.

When I'd decided to transform this into a darkroom I hadn't worked through the details all that well. Basically I'd just shoved everything that had been in the room to the outside corners and set up my makeshift table in the center. I'd had plans to go back and do everything properly at a later date, but obviously life had taken a turn and my days in the darkroom had dwindled to next to nothing.

I had no desire to be in here anymore—not when there wasn't anything left to photograph.

I tried not to look at the dusty equipment, reminders of Everly walking around in this space—haunting me as I pushed past everything to make my way to the large desk in the corner. I'd covered the heavy wood top with a white sheet to protect it from any chemicals that might contact it from the print processing.

I may not have been much into the home office, but it didn't mean I couldn't appreciate fine furniture.

Lifting the sheet, I found everything exactly where it had been left. I'd once taken a stack of bills in here, trying on the room for fit, but decided I hated the drafty place. Now, I paid bills over morning coffee out on the deck.

It was much less dreary and the view was a hell of a lot better.

I spent enough of my life seated at a desk.

Sitting on the edge of the desk, I picked up a stack of old papers and began rifling through them, not sure what I was looking for, but sure I needed answers.

I went through everything twice.

Nothing.

Just old party invitations, bank statements, and other junk mail. Nothing that had a big red arrow on it that screamed, "This is what you're looking for, August!"

I shook my head as it fell into my palms.

There was a time when I'd wanted nothing more than to have every minute of my life back—to swim in the stream of my own consciousness.

But now that it was a reality, that old saying about the grass being greener was definitely starting to bite me in the ass. My head was constantly swirling. I never knew when a memory would come and when one did, half the time it didn't make sense. One day I'd have a flashback from childhood—something random like a trip to the grocery store with my mom. Two days later, I'd remember opening my locker in high school or going to lunch with Everly.

It was as if my life was an endless roll of film, and someone had come along, spliced it all up and tossed it to the floor. Now every film cell, or memory, was out of order. I didn't understand how they all fit and I was beginning to fear I might never put them all back together again.

I needed answers. I needed everything lined up in a nice neat row so I could see the timeline of my life and understand the barrage of memories that kept assailing me. Nothing made sense. Hell, I still barely understood the job I went to on a daily basis. A few memories of a financing class would be helpful.

Part of me still held out hope that if I could just shuffle through the right memories and find the clues I needed to somehow get out from under Trent's tight grasp, everything could go back to the way it was.

Everly could be mine again.

But she wasn't.

She'd chosen someone else, and there wasn't a damn thing I could do about that.

*   *   *

I was over an hour late when I pulled out of my driveway in a rush and headed for Magnolia's high-rise apartment downtown.

She'd already left two voicemails and several text messages. I hadn't responded to either.

This level of groveling needed to be done in person.

She'd invited me over for a casual night at her place tonight. With the promise of a cooked meal and a movie, she'd reinforced that her five-date rule was back in full force and we were definitely starting over from the very beginning.

I'd happily smiled and told her that was absolutely fine with me. I was in no rush.

She thought I was being a gentleman, but honestly the idea of moving on beyond Everly seemed unimaginable. The mere thought of taking another woman to bed had me nearly nauseated.

I knew eventually it would happen. I wasn't planning on joining a monastery any time soon, but I just had this romantic notion that if I held on to that last night with Everly for as long as possible, a part of her would always belong to me—only me.

Knowing her lips had been the last I'd tasted, and her body had been the last I'd touched? It centered me. Grounded me. Realizing that could soon come to an end was like drilling the final nail in my coffin.

Parking in the garage below, I took the elevator up to Magnolia's apartment and walked down the lavish hallway until I reached her door. Knocking gently, I waited for her to answer.

The look on her face was anything but happy when the door slowly creaked open.

"You're late," she said, the look of disappointment written clear across her perfect complexion.

"I'm sorry," I said, feeling like the worst kind of asshole on the planet. She quietly studied my features, clearly weighing the sincerity of my apology. After a moment or two, the door opened, an obvious invitation that I was now welcome inside.

I followed her as she turned, letting the door shut behind us. She was dressed down, something I'd never seen before. Every other time we'd seen each other, she'd always been in smart dresses and heels, or something equally impressive. Tonight, she was in simple jeans and a cute T-shirt. Her hair and makeup were much less grand as well, but she was still beautiful. Just different—more vulnerable looking.

I glanced over and noticed her small dining table set for two, the candles long since burned out. Guilt slowly began to set in, but not just for the dinner I'd ruined.

Was I any different than Trent in this situation?

Wasn't I just manipulating someone in order to get something I needed?

Magnolia obviously had feelings for me, and I was going to use those to my advantage. It was exactly what Trent wanted me to do.

How quickly the student had become just like the master.

But I couldn't stop now. The only way to protect her was to use her, because if I didn't Trent would, and I'd seen the way she responded to powerful men. She didn't deserve to be screwed over by someone like Trent. She might never recover.

She took a seat on the plush sofa in the living room, tucking her legs beneath her as she waited for me to join her. Feeling like she might need some space, I chose the seat adjacent to the sofa and placed my elbows on my knees, letting out a frustrated sigh. The growing silence between us was almost deafening as she patiently waited for me to explain myself.

Fuck, where do I even start?

I could tell her another lie; I could go with the actual truth for a change. My life was filled with a hundred different lies, so many that sometimes it seemed difficult to see where one ended and the next began. Right now I just wanted to be honest with someone.

"About six months ago, I woke up in a hospital with absolutely no memory of my past. When we met and you asked if I'd worked at that bar, I honestly didn't know how to answer. I'd been in a coma and it did something to my memory."

Her brows furrowed in confusion, "A coma?" she asked. "How long?"

"A little over two years."

"My God, August. Why did you never mention this?"

She leaned forward, and I could see she wanted to take my hand, offer me comfort of some sort, but I couldn't. I wasn't going to play her affections that way. I knew which way this was going, but I wouldn't use her sympathy of my situation to my advantage.

I had to keep some of my integrity intact.

"It's not exactly the greatest pick-up line," I replied. "And besides, I haven't made it my business to tell many people. The few I have told usually react with a mixture of false sympathy and awkward remorse. It's something no one can possibly comprehend, so why try to make them?"

"I guess, but it must be an awfully lonely existence," she commented, her eyes full of concern.

My thoughts drifted to Everly—of Everly as she stood on a platform surrounded by mirrors in a beautiful white wedding dress. Her happy, tearful smile as she turned, admiring herself from every angle as she pictured herself walking down the aisle.

With another man. The man I'd pushed her toward.

"Yes, it can be," I said, rising abruptly. I turned toward the large windows, pinching the bridge of my nose to keep the rising emotions at bay.

"Well, now you have me. You don't have to explain yourself. I get it. I mean—I don't, but I can see the struggle in your eyes. I know it must be hard to have lost everything you had."

"I'm getting them back," I tried to explain, turning back toward her. "The memories. That's why I was late. They come without warning. Sometimes I black out for minutes...once it was an hour."

Her empathetic face turned to something closer to concern, mixed with a bit of horror.

"How long has this been going on, August?" she asked, rising from the sofa. Her fingers hesitantly touched my shoulder and I glanced down to see her manicured hand resting there. I could feel the warmth of her touch. It felt foreign, different, but my stomach didn't roll at the thought of it being there.

I shrugged. "A few months," I answered.

Her eyes widened. "Have you seen a doctor?"

I just shook my head. "No, and I won't."

She opened her mouth to debate, but I interrupted. "I won't lose my freedom again, and I will not end up back in that hospital."

My words seemed to cease all further discussion as she wrapped her arms tightly around me and just nodded, saying, "Okay, okay..."

It was the first time I'd felt the touch of another human in months. My arms slid around her waist and I held on to her like a lifeline, letting her compassionate spirit breathe life into my tired body.

For the first time in ages, I didn't feel alone, and that scared me more than anything.

My eyes slid closed and I saw Everly walking away, her arms wrapped around Ryan.

Magnolia's hold on me tightened.

It really was over.

Chapter Seven

Everly

I was getting married in two weeks.

In fourteen days, my name would change.

My life would change.

It was the beginning of the end of a very long chapter of my life. Soon I would be Mrs. Everly Sparrow. Everly Adams would be gone, and I secretly wondered if a part of me would be gone with her.

"Are you ready?" Sarah hollered as she flew through the door of my apartment, a flurry of activity. She was dressed fairly conservatively today, a change from her usual vibrant look. She wore a modest plum-colored A-line dress and nude peep-toe heels adorned her feet. She'd pulled her hair into a neat, sophisticated little braid gathered at the side of her head. It was almost startling—seeing the difference the lack of color and accessories did to her striking frame.

"Are we going to a funeral or a bridal shower?" I asked as I grabbed the sweater I'd laid out on the sofa beside my purse and keys.

"What?" She looked down at her attire before sticking out her tongue in my direction. "I just wanted to look nice in front of all of Ryan's mother's friends," she admitted, snatching my keys from my hand and shoving them deep in my purse. "It's your day. I'm driving."

I gave her a smug grin as tiny butterflies came to life in my stomach at the mere mention of the wedding day. "Well, it's not actually—my day, you know."

"Shut up and let me drive. I'm trying to be nice."

"Okay," I laughed.

"Hey, where's the groom-to-be?" she asked as we headed out the door toward the elevator. I caught her admiring my dress, and I mentally patted myself on the back for my shopping success. It was the first time I'd bought anything full price since my days living at the Cliffs. When I went into a store, I normally headed straight for the clearance rack and did all of my decision-making there. If I couldn't find something I liked, I went on to another store and so on. It was exhausting, but I was frugal and had a secret obsession with those little red stickers boasting a new, lower price.

Today, I'd just wanted to look nice. Ryan's mother had flown in two weeks early for this specific event and I had to make a good impression on my future mother-in-law.

In my mind, clearance items just didn't do that moment justice.

"He went out paint-balling with a couple of guys from work. He thought it would be good to stay as far away from the female ritual as possible, just in case someone decided to rope him into it."

She nodded, a grin forming across her face. "Smart man. Now he'll be covered in neon-colored paint and sweaty. Totally gross—no one will come near him."

"That was his plan."

"Have you seen his mother since she arrived?" she asked as we made our way to her car, parked across the street. I caught my reflection in the window of her little yellow Beetle and smiled. The light dusty blue fabric I wore matched my eyes perfectly and thankfully didn't clash with the vibrant color of my hair.

Having such a unique hair color was great, most of the time… until you went to the store and realized the hot new color for the season was hot pink, and your flaming ginger hair looked hideous against anything even remotely pink.

"No. She flew in yesterday while I was at work, and Ryan picked her up and helped her get settled at her hotel, but she was so tired from jet lag that we just let her rest for the evening."

"So, are you nervous?"

"About what?" I asked. I lowered myself carefully into the tiny car, smoothing my skirt out over my knees as she started the engine.

"About today! About hanging out with your future mother-in-law and all her geriatric friends!"

"Oh my God, I can't believe you just said the word *geriatric*!" I scoffed, trying to keep from laughing at my best friend's lack of tact.

"Well, they are—old, I mean," she laughed. "One lady called me to ask what types of food would be served because her gut just couldn't handle 'that *modern food*.' What is modern food, Everly? Please explain that to me."

I giggled, a tiny snort escaping as I tried to maintain my

composure. It didn't last and soon we were both laughing hard as we made our way to the hotel for my fancy bridal shower—another must-do on the very long list of wedding requests from Ryan's mother.

At least she was paying for this one.

Sarah had been gracious enough to arrange everything since Mrs. Sparrow was across the country, and as we pulled up to the beautiful historic hotel, I was thankful she had.

At least, if I had to have a shower, it was going to be in a beautiful place.

To my great surprise, the equally frugal Sarah chose to valet park her car. She shrugged her shoulders and tossed a wink over her shoulder. "It's a big day for you," she explained. "Let's go crazy!"

I just rolled my eyes.

I didn't want it to be a big day for me. I hadn't wanted a shower in the first place. All those people staring at me, smiling and expecting me to entertain them. It was too much pressure.

We entered the grand lobby, and before I could wander over to the front desk to ask for directions to the correct ballroom, Sarah grabbed my hand and pulled me to the right.

"You don't think I haven't figured out where I'm going? I've only been here like four times making sure everything would be perfect for today."

I stopped her, grabbing her hand as people began to move around us down the busy hallway.

"Thank you," I said sincerely, emotions tugging at my heart as I realized everything she'd put into this day.

"It's not a big deal," she answered, trying to play it off.

"No, it is. To me, it's a huge deal. All of these people don't mean a thing to me compared to you, Sarah. You are my family. Thank you for this. For everything."

Her lip quivered as she gave a weak smile. "I love you," she said softly.

"Love you right back."

"Now let's get you in there," she grinned, smacking my butt with enthusiasm.

"Ouch!" I laughed as we started back down the hallway. She stopped midway at an open door. I could hear faint laughter and conversation going on just inside.

She turned to me and quickly smoothed out my hair and dress.

"Okay, showtime!"

"You know how you asked me if I was nervous and I didn't answer?" I said, all the words running out of my mouth in quick succession.

"Yep."

"I'm nervous as all hell," I admitted, biting my lip as my eyes widened in fright.

"Would it help if I told you there's booze in there?" she asked, a cool grin tugging at her lips.

"Yes. That helps a ton. Thank you."

I took a deep breath and walked into the lion's den.

* * *

Our tiny apartment had been taken over.

I sat, curled up under my favorite fuzzy blue blanket on the couch with my hands wrapped around a cherished mug from my collection and just stared at it all.

A giant mountain of crap. No shiny mixer anywhere.

"We totally scored!" Ryan exclaimed, looking at the piles of boxes and gift bags with pride. "And this is just the shower gifts! This is just a small fraction of what we'll get from the actual wedding!"

I didn't know how to respond.

Was he more excited about the stuff or the marriage? Because I honestly couldn't tell anymore. I watched him happily dive into the giant assortment that had taken Sarah and me two trips in her tiny little car and more than ten trips up the elevator, as I sat shellshocked from my long, exhausting day.

I'd walked in with enough nervous energy to power a small village. But I'd held my head high and faced my fears, knowing that what awaited me on the other side was a family and a support system that I'd never had before.

Ryan's mother had done all of this for me, after all. She wouldn't have done it if she didn't at least have some sort of affection for me.

As soon as I'd entered, I'd felt like some exotic rare bird at the zoo. Voices dimmed, all laughter ceased, and I was suddenly on full display for everyone to gaze upon. Glasses were put on, steps were taken for a closer look.

I was up for inspection.

It was the weirdest thing I'd ever experienced.

Sarah's comforting hand had touched mine and I'd instantly felt relief. Mrs. Sparrow had greeted me and taken me through the long rounds of introductions.

I didn't remember a single name.

Not one.

But each of them knew me and made it a point to appraise me in some way or another. It was as if I was up for a job interview I didn't know I had applied for. Mrs. Sparrow fidgeted with my dress the entire time, making comments about my high hemline and poor color choice.

By the time lunch was over and done with, I was exhausted. My once beautiful dress felt cheap and trashy and the unique coppery waves that usually set me apart were now reduced to something of concern. My future children were at risk now—apparently red-headed boys were always bullied in school. The old ladies had concurred, shaking their heads in shame as I stared at them in stunned silence.

The whole afternoon was a disaster that had culminated into a mound of presents I didn't want.

We had an entire apartment full of stuff. We didn't need anything else. Wasn't the point of wedding and shower gifts to help a new couple get a household started?

Hadn't we already done that?

I just felt like we were cheating people out of their hard-earned money.

Twice.

As I watched my fiancé riffle through the boxes, a gleeful smile on his face, I wondered where we'd gotten off track.

When had this become more about the wedding and less about the marriage? When was the last time we'd even spoken about our life after that singular day?

Did it even matter to him anymore?

*   *   *

I nearly fell asleep on the couch watching a sitcom rerun as Ryan meticulously unpacked all the boxes and put everything away, making a large pile of things that now needed to go to Goodwill.

Out with the old, and in with the new, he'd said.

I kind of liked our old stuff, but I didn't bother saying anything. He was so happy, and despite everything—a blender is a blender. I might have figured out our old one's quirks over the last two years, knew the perfect combination of buttons to ensure the perfect smoothie consistency, but at the end of the day it was just a thing.

Ryan's smile was perfection.

And that's what I needed to focus on.

The wedding was just a thing. The presents were just things. The marriage—that was what would last forever.

I hoped. I tried desperately to push away the twinge of doubt that seemed to be growing bigger and bigger as the wedding date approached. It was just cold feet.

Everyone got a touch of cold feet. Unfortunately, mine had started to go numb from frostbite.

"Hey, sleepyhead," Ryan whispered beside me. I cracked my eyes open to see him kneeling next to me with that perfect smile I had just been thinking about.

"We have a bed, you know? There's no need to sleep on this lumpy couch."

"I'm not sleeping," I replied, doing a tiny version of a cat stretch as a small yawn escaped me.

"Liar. Come on, let's get you in bed." He held out his hand.

"Okay," I complied. He helped me up and we started down the

hallway, until the doorbell rang. Stopping short, I turned to him with a curious look on my face.

"What, do you think I was expecting someone at"—he looked at his watch— "nine o'clock. Damn, we're old, Ev."

I laughed, rubbing my eyes to try and whisk away the last remnants of sleep as I walked back toward the door. As soon as I turned the handle and pulled it open, I was accosted by shrill, girlish screams.

"Surprise!" Sarah yelled.

"What the hell?" I looked at her with a mixture of horror and confusion as she stood at my front door with Trudy and Tabitha.

"We're here for your surprise bachelorette party!" they all yelled in unison, giggling and laughing between each word.

"Now?" I asked. "But it's so late."

Oh my God. Ryan was right. I really was old.

Sarah laughed, pushing past me along with the rest of the ladies.

"Oh sweetheart, the night is just beginning. Now, follow me… we have work to do." She disappeared down the hall toward my bedroom as I stood baffled and bewildered.

"You might as well just go," Ryan advised. "You know how she gets."

"Did you know anything about this?" I asked, giving him the death stare.

"Nope. You know I can't keep a secret." He laughed. "Besides, I thought we weren't doing these things. Now I'm kind of pissed. Where's my party?"

"You got to go paint-balling today while I had to have tea with your mom's friends," I countered, raising an eyebrow.

"Good point. Go have fun," he replied with a grin.

I joined everyone in my room, feeling a gasp escape my lungs the moment I entered. They'd already torn the place apart. Clothes had been pulled from my closet, shoes were scattered all over my bed. Pink fluffy boas were sticking out of a grocery bag and I swear I saw a plastic penis in there. I was kind of frightened.

"All right, let's get you ready!" Sarah exclaimed, clapping her hands together in excitement.

I was definitely frightened.

She sat me down and started applying makeup while I listened to Tabitha and Trudy chat. I was honestly surprised to see Tabitha. We'd never hung out outside of counseling sessions—that was a rule of counseling or something, right? I was sure she was probably going to break into hives any second at the idea of hanging around not just me, but Sarah as well—also a longtime client of hers. But it meant the world to me that she was here. I'd never told her, but she was the closest thing to a mother I'd ever had.

And now it appeared she was about to see me dressed as a hooker, I realized as I turned back toward my best friend.

"Oh my God, no. I cannot be seen in public in that," I announced as Sarah held up the tiny bits of fabric that made up the dress she wanted me to wear.

"It was in your closet," she reminded me with a sly grin, her arm pushing against her hip in an obvious challenge.

"I got it on sale…and, I thought it looked different in the dressing room," I rambled. I had honestly bought it on clearance, like every other piece of clothing I owned, but I'd had a clear intention when I'd bought it. I'd had this idea of Ryan coming home and seeing me in it and well…yeah, but I'd never had the courage to try out my plan.

"Try it on," Trudy instructed, her words clearly baiting me.

"Fine," I said, caving to their pressure.

Slipping the fabric over my head, I let the tiny spaghetti straps settle in place as I smoothed the thin layers against my skin. The black fabric hung loosely, but the plunging neckline and barely legal length were a deadly combination I wasn't exactly comfortable in.

So much skin.

"Wowza," Trudy said, uttering a catcall as I walked over to the floor-length mirror behind our bedroom door.

"I look ridiculous!" I scoffed, trying to cover up as much as I could with my hands and arms.

Sarah pulled my fingers away from my chest, standing behind me. She straightened my stance, taking my long hair between her fingers. I watched as she combed through it, taming it with her touch.

"Now, look at yourself. Look at that beautiful woman staring back at you."

I rolled my eyes. She pinched my ass.

"Ouch!" I yelled.

"You are beautiful. And tonight, we are going to go out and enjoy ourselves!" She leaned in closer, her lips nearly touching my ear. "Because after today, I know you need it."

I met her gaze in the mirror and she gave me a wink.

She'd asked me a dozen times as we hauled gift after gift up the stairs if I was okay and I'd simply nodded and smiled. I should have known better.

Sarah always saw right through me.

She'd set this up because she knew I needed cheering up.

I love this woman.

"Let's go have fun!" I hollered, holding my fist up in the air.

Everyone clapped in agreement, and we said our good-byes to a baffled Ryan and headed for the elevator, excitement bouncing between us. As the doors pulled open and we entered, I felt a soft hand on my shoulder and turned.

Tabitha gave me a soft hug and smiled. She'd been so quiet since everyone arrived; I'd wondered if she was having second thoughts about coming. "I hope you don't mind me tagging along tonight," she said. "When Sarah invited me, she said you wouldn't mind having an old lady hanging out with you, but I just wanted to make sure. I know it may be a little awkward...considering..." She hesitated before stating, "I don't normally hang out with my clients. I'm sorry, I don't want to spoil your fun."

I took her hand and grinned. "I wouldn't want it any other way," I replied. "And besides, tonight, you're just a friend. Nothing more. Got it?"

"Got it," she grinned.

She opened her mouth as if she was going to say something more, but then just gave me another smile before the elevator opened and we all headed for the door.

"You didn't," I said, looking out onto the street.

Sarah smiled like a damned Cheshire cat. "I did."

Parked outside our apartment building was a stretch limo.

And it was pink. *Fucking pink.*

"I hate you. Times a million."

"Liar," she laughed. I groaned as our chauffeur, also dressed in a pink vest and bow tie, stepped out to help us with the door.

She was right, of course. There was no way, no matter how many plastic penises or pink limos she threw at me tonight, I could ever hate her. Through everything, she was always the one who had my back.

Everyone hopped in, leaving me last. Hoots and hollers welcomed me as I rolled my eyes, a smirk tugging at the corner of my mouth as I shook my head.

"Congratulations," the pink-wearing chauffeur said as I placed a single foot inside. My eyes met his, first in confusion and then I realized what he meant.

Right... wedding.

"Oh, um. Thank you," I answered awkwardly.

"Big day coming up soon?" he asked, a warm friendly smile on his face.

"Two weeks."

"You must be excited. Mine's in a month and I'm about to bounce off the walls."

"Yep... that's me," I answered lamely, adding, "It's a big day."

I quickly sunk into the car, realizing I'd just regurgitated the words Sarah had said to me earlier. My big day. God, I hated those words.

What was wrong with me?

"Okay, here's the plan," Sarah announced, quieting everyone down, including my wayward thoughts. "We've got a VIP table at the hottest bar I could find downtown. We're going to sit back, drink until everything and everyone looks fuzzy, dance our cute little asses off and not come up until the sun comes up. Deal?"

Trudy screamed. Tabitha looked nervous and I laughed.

I couldn't remember the last time I'd been out until the sunrise, and had serious doubts any of us—well except maybe Trudy—would actually make it past two, but I kept my opinions to myself.

Sarah had plans, and who was I to muck them all up?

Sunrise or bust. Sure, why the hell not?

The rest of the ride was a frenzy of talk. Everyone was feeding off the growing energy in the limo, and as we quickly approached the bar, our excitement was mounting.

"Okay, okay...everyone shush!" Trudy yelled, holding her hands up high in an effort to tame us. It looked a little strange, seeing her wave around her arms in a tight red dress, but it seemed to do the trick. She had us quiet and obedient in seconds.

"We need to decorate our bachelorette before we arrive at our designated location for the evening!" she announced, sounding more proper than I'd ever heard her sound before. "May I have the bag, please, Sarah?"

"You may." Sarah grinned, handing off the plastic grocery bag I'd peeked at in my room.

Trudy pulled out a big, fluffy pink and black boa and placed it around my neck as they all clapped and cheered. I looked down at the monstrosity and gasped. Not only was it pink and sparkly, but it also had a penis-shaped shot glass tied to the bottom.

"You're welcome," Trudy smiled widely.

"I don't even have words," I groaned.

"Good, because we aren't done yet."

"Oh goody."

"Tabitha, will you do the honors?" Trudy asked, pulling out a giant plastic tiara. Tabitha grinned and nodded, taking the seat next to me. Her eyes met mine as she carefully placed the pink crown that proudly displayed my bachelorette status across the top on my head.

"There," she said. "Not quite the princess I'd always envisioned you to be, but it will work for tonight."

"Hold on," Trudy interrupted, reaching up and pushing something on my head. Suddenly everyone looked up and became animated once again.

"What?" I asked.

"Your crown—it lights up," Tabitha explained.

"Oh, for the love of—"

"We're here!" Sarah hollered.

Stepping out of our Pepto-Bismol-colored limo was like walking the red carpet at the Oscars. Every single person waiting to get into the bar turned to see what crazy drunk girls would stumble out of it. My awesome friends went first, leaving me for the dramatic finale, dressed to the nines in my boa and flashing tiara.

I couldn't wait until Sarah and Trudy got married.

Payback was hell.

People cheered as I walked past them. They fucking cheered. A couple of guys even offered to buy me drinks once I got inside. Apparently the idea behind a bachelorette party was beyond them.

As we made our way past the line, bypassing everyone because of our VIP status, I peered inside, hearing chants and cheers. There was a woman dressed similarly to me by the bar. Her shiny sash and glittery top hat made it overwhelmingly obvious she was here for the same purpose as me, as did the circle of half-drunken friends that surrounded her.

A shirtless man lay on the bar, his rock hard abs out on full display as the crowd's cheers grew louder. I guessed very quickly that this was not her future husband.

We got our hands stamped and I lost sight of her for a moment as we made our way to our table. As we all sat down, I pointed her out to Sarah and the rest of the girls. She'd gathered her courage now, standing on a barstool, getting ready to take her shot.

"Shot, shot, shot!" rang out through the bar.

"If you guys make me do that, I will never speak to you again," I said loudly over the booming music.

They all laughed, but the message was clear.

No body shots for Everly.

Gross.

My sister in bachelorette-hood bent down, placing her mouth over the stranger's stomach and sucked the liquor right out of his belly button. The bar went wild. She came up laughing as a lime was placed in her mouth. A quick suck and she raised it up in the air triumphantly. The DJ switched up the song and everyone ran to the dance floor.

I could already tell it was going to be an interesting night.

Our own private server came to take our orders—a perk of our VIP table—and we all ordered. Right before she was leaving, Trudy called her back over and whispered something in her ear. I gave her a look and she just shrugged. "What?"

"What did you do?" I asked.

"Nothing!" She feigned innocence as her smile widened.

No one in this group was innocent tonight. Well, except maybe Tabitha. I looked over at my therapist-friend and giggled to myself as I noticed her silently watching the crowd.

Oh, the things that must be running through that head of hers. I could see her gaze slowly stopping at each small cluster or crowd, analyzing and assessing them—not judging like most would do, just deciphering and evaluating. It was almost scientific in its execution, but when you spoke to her she never seemed stiff or methodical.

On our table were request tickets for the DJ. We were seated right next to the booth, and could request anything we wanted because of our elevated status. The VIP area was completely booked for the evening, with many other tables celebrating various other achievements and events. I saw the glittery top hat bachelorette stumble to a table in the back to a roar of laughter. I guess her friends were enjoying her humiliation.

I looked up at mine as they all filled out tickets, laughing about their song choices, and knew they wouldn't leave me to the same fate. If I ever reached that level of drunkenness, they'd haul me back to the pink limo of shame and call it a night.

No one ever needed to be crawling across the dirty bar floor, shit-faced in a blinking tiara.

Our drinks arrived along with a dozen shots. I looked wide-eyed at Trudy who, once again, just shrugged.

"What?" she laughed.

"Are there more of us coming?" I grinned.

"Nope!"

"Okay then," I said, grabbing one of the shots and taking it in one turn of my wrist. Everyone watched in amazement as I slammed the tiny glass down on the table.

"Sunrise or bust, right?" I said.

They all looked at me in confusion and I remembered I'd said that in my head, so I just raised my hands in the air and yelled, "I'm getting married!" figuring that was good enough.

Everyone joined in, each grabbing a shot. I chuckled as I watched Tabitha make a horrible face, her lips puckering together in disgust as the liquid fire burned down her throat.

"What was that?" she asked, shaking her head back and forth as if she were putting out flames in her head.

"Fireball," Trudy answered.

"It's intense." She took a quick sip of her gin and tonic, her face instantly calming.

I wasn't much of a fan of Fireball myself, but I'd had it enough to know what to expect. Looking down at my glass of merlot as the shot of liquor sloshed around in my stomach, I suddenly regretted my drink choice.

"Oh well," I said to myself as I took a large sip. I didn't have to work the next day.

And I was due for an epic hangover anyway, wasn't I?

Good choices. I was definitely making very good choices tonight.

Drinks were flowing, and song choices were in. We were off to a good start. As we waited for our perfect songs to come on to get us into the dancing mood, everyone slowly started pulling out their phones.

I watched as my *Gilmore Girls* nightmare suddenly happened before my eyes.

I was a *Gilmore Girls* junkie. I'd seen every episode, owned all the seasons on DVD. Whenever there was a rerun on TV, I still had to stop and watch it—even though I'd probably seen it a million times before. Lorelei and Rory were the ultimate mother-daughter duo and as someone who grew up not knowing what either role meant, I was always hungry for anything that would feed that gaping hole in my heart.

As I sat there, I saw Lorelei's bachelorette party morph into mine—the episode where she's about to marry...well, I don't remember who honestly, but it's some guy who isn't Luke, and she's at her bachelorette party and everyone there is calling and texting their honeys while she's sitting there, just like me, wondering why she feels no desire to do so.

Sarah texted Miles. That was his name—Miles. I still hadn't met him, but I at least knew his name now. Several months together—that was a record. She was smitten. I could see it on her face as she sent him message after message, while I sat there...doing nothing.

Tabitha texted her husband. I still didn't know his name. After years of knowing her, I realized I didn't know much at all about her. Did she do that on purpose to separate herself from her clients, or was I just a selfish person?

Note to self...find out more about Tabitha.

Even Trudy, the permanently single one, seemed to have someone special to talk to tonight, as her fingers flew across the keyboard and her face lit up in a devious smile. Things must be going well with the waiter.

Good Lord, I hoped she was being careful, or at least using protection.

I looked down at my purse and considered texting Ryan, but what would I say?

We're here...drank a shot of Fireball. Okay, bye.

I'd just never felt that need—that blinding, overwhelming desire to contact him, to run out and tell him everything that happened during my day.

Should I?

There was once a time when I couldn't stop texting August. I'd tell him everything, from the way the trees smelled to the color of a flower I'd seen on a walk. Even my morning cup of coffee could spark a twenty-minute conversation. Why wasn't it the same with the man I'd chosen to spend the rest of my life with?

Looking down at my glass of wine, I realized it was already gone and I was not nearly drunk enough for this train of thought. Reaching across the table, I grabbed one of the remaining shots of Fireball and tossed it back, followed by another, and then one more for good measure.

No one really seemed to notice. Everyone was far too busy, buried in their phones.

Maybe I should have used my penis shot glass. That might have gotten their attention.

"I'm going to the restroom and then I'm going to make a call," I said, grabbing my phone.

"Ah, that's so sweet!" Trudy said, her head tilting to the side.

"Hurry back, because I think our songs are coming up!" Sarah followed up.

"Will do!" I answered, finally feeling the effects of the liquor starting to kick in. I was always a lightweight when it came to alcohol. One glass, two tops, and I was a goner.

As I walked away from the table, my feet wobbled beneath me and I giggled as a plan formed in my befuddled mind.

I should not have been trusted with a phone.

Chapter Eight

August

I was half asleep on the living room couch, watching *Ghostbusters* when the phone rang. It was the second movie—the one with the creepy painting and all the green goo. I personally liked the Stay Puft Marshmallow Man better. You never could go wrong with an original.

Unless, of course it was me.

Clicking off the movie, I looked up at the clock on the small cable box and I noticed the time.

Midnight.

Considering I knew about five people in the city outside of clients, I immediately sat up, feeling wide awake as I wondered who could possibly be hurt or in trouble at this late hour.

I'd canceled on Magnolia. Again.

She'd graciously understood, telling me she would be here whenever I was ready.

She understood everything now that I'd told her the truth. It was a relief knowing I could stretch out our relationship longer, postponing the attachment I knew she was forming, but at the same time I knew she wasn't going anywhere.

There was literally nothing I could do to drive her away. I was like a lost puppy to her, and all I needed was love and a good home and soon enough I would be healed and good as new.

Only, I wouldn't.

Nothing would ever fix me. I was permanently broken.

Grabbing my phone off the coffee table, I saw the caller ID and groaned.

The reason for my brokenness, calling at midnight.

That could not be good.

Don't answer it, I told myself, as my finger closed down on the green Accept button.

"Hello?" I said tentatively.

"You don't love me, and I don't think I love him." Her voice was slurred. Loud music boomed in the background. "One big mess. So messy."

"Everly?" I don't know why I asked this. Maybe I was surprised at her words—her boldness. Maybe I just wanted to make sure it was really her on the other end.

"Yep. 'S me. Why'd you leave, August…Auggie." She laughed. "You don't like being called Auggie. But you probably already remember that. You remember everything now."

She sounded sad about that little fact, but I let that go, focusing on bigger issues.

"Where are you?"

"Bar downtown. We're celebrating me getting married."

My heart sank as her words settled in place.

"You're married?" I whispered.

"Nooooo." Her voice, low and raspy, nearly sung the word as I breathed out a sigh of relief. "My bachelor party," she slurred once again.

Bachelorette party, I interpreted. She wasn't married yet. I shouldn't care, but I did.

When it came to Everly, I would always care too much.

Even when she was some other man's wife.

"Why are you calling me, Everly?" I asked, rubbing the sleep from my eyes.

"I had to pee," she began, pausing for a moment. I could imagine her swaying back and forth in some darkened hallway. I hoped it was a safe one. "My friends were supposed to show me a good time tonight because I had to spend all day with my evil mother-in-law. Evil mother-in-law to-be," she corrected herself. "She doesn't like my hair. Or my pretty dress. Do you like my dress, Auggie?"

"I like everything about you," I answered honestly, knowing she wouldn't remember a damn thing about this conversation by morning. Remembering the few times we'd drunk way too much wine with dinner, I knew one thing about Everly.

She was a horrible drunk. She'd be out like a light in less than an hour and would wake up with a bitch of a hangover and little memory of the night before. It's why she didn't drink excessively. She hated the feeling of losing control.

Me? The way my life was going lately—drinking was the only thing that felt halfway like living.

"No you don't," she sighed. "You hate me, because of what I did—because of what I did to you. You know, I dream of that night sometimes?"

"Me too," I replied.

"I didn't mean to do it," she mumbled. "I didn't mean to hurt you. I just got so angry, and then we collided and you crumbled to the ground. I thought you were dead." She was nearly frantic in her drunken haze as she recalled the events of that night.

"It's okay, Everly," I tried to say.

"No it's not! I should have told someone then what happened. But I was so scared. What if they didn't believe me? What if I went to jail? I don't know why I did it—no, that's not true. I do. I did it because I was scared I'd be taken away from you."

Confusion blossomed in my mind. "But you left me anyway."

"I didn't want to."

"You had to," I said, realizing she'd done what was right. For both of us.

"We were toxic. So very toxic. I thought we could heal—when you came back, and didn't remember anything. But we still fell apart. And now you hate me. And honestly, I wish I hated you too. I want to hate you. It would be so much easier." Her voice cracked, the pain in her words making my chest hurt.

"I know."

"Why can't I hate you, Auggie?"

"Probably for the same reason I can't hate you," I confessed.

"What?" she asked.

"Nothing," I replied, quickly changing the subject. "Shouldn't you be getting back to your party now?"

"Probably," she confessed. "All my friends were texting their guys, making goofy happy grins while I just stared at them dumb-founded. So I got up and peed. And then I called you."

It wasn't exactly a profession of love, but I didn't miss the fact that she hadn't called Ryan.

She'd called me.

"Why did you leave me, August?" she asked, her voice turning serious.

"I didn't. You left me."

She groaned, giving a bit of levity to the serious tone. "You didn't give me a choice. When Trent showed up, you knew I'd never stick around. You basically kicked me out by welcoming him in."

My eyes squeezed shut, remembering that day.

I'd just landed my first placement in an art studio. It was a major step in the right direction for me careerwise and I had been nearly vibrating with energy when I'd arrived home, ready to share the news with Everly.

But I never got the chance.

Trent had beat Everly home, and my whole life had crashed around me.

I had pushed her away, but not because I didn't love her.

I'd have to be dead to stop loving that woman, and even then, I didn't think my soul would ever cease seeking hers.

"Why'd you do it? Why did you choose money over me—again, August? We were almost there . . . almost at our perfect forever. And then you pushed me away, like you always do. Why am I never enough?"

"You'd never understand," I said softly, knowing I could never risk this kind of truth on a drunken phone conversation.

"Do you remember our baby name game?" she asked, her voice heavy with emotion.

"Tell me about it—like before I had my memory. Every detail, Everly," I requested, grateful for her quick change of pace. I feared she'd ask why, demand to know why a man who said he remembered everything wanted such detail, but in her loose, languid state, she just did as requested and began speaking.

I could nearly feel her warm smile against my cheek as she began to slowly speak in my ear, recounting the memory as she recalled it.

"After we moved into our little house with the flower boxes, I would drag you to garage sales every weekend—without fail. You hated it. Garage sales equaled other people's used shit in your opinion, and the faces you would sometimes make as we walked past boxes of used clothes and baby gear would make me laugh like a hyena. But I loved it. It was decorating on the cheap, and in no time, I was able to turn our little drafty house into something beautiful."

I did have a few memories of us in that house, and from what I remembered, it was everything she described. Homey, warm, and comfortable. I hadn't realized the effort she'd put into making it ours and breathing life into it.

Had she mourned its absence from our lives when I'd whisked her away so suddenly and given her something so new and shiny? Had I even considered how that might have made her feel?

"One day," she continued, "we were walking through a typical sale. This one was heavy on baby stuff, but I'd managed to find a few pieces I thought I could repurpose for our living room. Just as I was about to haggle with the man for a lower price, something caught my eye. A baby name book. Picking it up, I turned to you and waved it back and forth, waggling my eyebrow, figuring you would have a stroke and die right on the spot. Instead, you just grinned, snatched it from me and handed the man a dollar, which was twice the asking price, and started flipping through it.

"'Maxim?' you called out, your eyebrow going all crazy again.

'For what?' I asked, thinking you'd gone completely insane. Which you had, by the way."

A small chuckle escaped my throat.

"'For our future little munchkin,' you said. And then it was me who had the heart attack and died."

My chuckle turned into deep rich laughter, and she joined in.

"You were never afraid of anything back then. I don't know what happened."

Me neither, Everly. Me neither, I thought.

"You continued to do this little game all the way home, each name becoming more and more atrocious until I finally caved and gave my opinion. It turned out to be so much fun that whenever we were bored, we'd pull out that battered old book and start going through names, laughing at the terrible ones, highlighting the ones we actually adored, like our own plan for the future, and just enjoying each other."

She paused, the silence becoming thick.

"I never do things like that with Ryan."

I didn't know how to respond to that so I just let silence speak for me.

"I feel like I'm living a life everyone expects of me, August," she murmured. I could hear the tears she was trying to keep at bay.

"Then live the life meant for you," I urged.

"What if that life was supposed to be with you?"

"There's only one bird in that cage, Everly," I reminded her. "Let her run free. Let her find her own life."

"How?"

"Isn't that the first step?" I chuckled. "Figuring out this shit on your own."

"This makes my head hurt."

"No, I'm pretty sure that's the alcohol," I told her.

"Gross. Don't remind me. Speaking of which, I need to pee again. I knew I shouldn't have gone in the first place. Now I'm just going to be peeing all night long."

"Drinking 101—never break the seal. You should have known better," I smiled, hating that our conversation was coming to an end.

"August?" she said one last time.

"Yeah?" I asked.

"When I wake up in the morning, and everything about this night is fuzzy...what should I remember?"

I took a deep breath, letting it fill my lungs as I put my thoughts together.

"Remember that you're a strong woman, that your friends love you, and that more than anything, you should stay away from me, Everly. Stay far, far away from me."

She sighed, a sad sigh full of frustration.

"Okay. Good-bye, Auggie."

I smiled at the nickname. "Good-bye, Everly."

The phone went dead and as I sat there in the darkness, I tried to picture her in the unlit corner of the bar, her hair frazzled and tossed as she made her way back to her friends with the secret of our conversation. I tried to picture what she was wearing, how the fabric would cling to her glistening skin. No doubt she'd have the attention of every male in the room, and not notice a single glance. She never had.

I hoped she remembered everything I told her, about finding something for herself in this life. For once, my motives didn't have anything to do with jealousy. If she found all roads pointed to him and that was where she was happiest, at least she'd know that was where she belonged.

But she needed to take a leap—and no one could push her off that cliff but herself.

*   *   *

"Lucifer?" She laughed, holding the book so close to her face it almost touched her nose. I swore one of these days I was going to get that girl to the eye doctor.

I'd love to see her in a pair of glasses.

Nerdy Everly. So hot.

"Are you crazy? Do you want a demon child?" I grinned, grabbing the book from her grasp. I flipped through it, loving the many highlights we'd done over the last few months we'd had this book. What had turned into an afternoon joke had become one of our favorite pastimes. While we had never actually spoken specifics, we loved the idea of "what if." There were no immediate or concrete plans to have a child or to even get married, but the notion that there could be—someday—sent butterflies to our stomachs and made us just . . . giddy.

"What about Abstinence?" I said, trying to keep my face calm and neutral.

"That is not in there."

"I swear to God."

She snatched the book back from me, and her eyes scanned the page full of "A" names as her eyes went wide.

"No way! Who would do that to a child?"

"An overprotective father. Just think of her teenage years," I

laughed. "No shotgun needed. Guys wouldn't touch a girl with that name."

"Or," she debated, "you'd end up with the most promiscuous daughter on the planet, determined to prove her name wrong just to spite her parents."

"Ouch. Good point. That's dicey. Krystianna is looking better and better day by day."

"I liked Krystianna!" she retorted, throwing the book at me playfully.

"Yeah, I know. But it's never going to happen. Krystianna Kincaid? That's a mouthful."

She climbed on my lap, my eyes roaming her tight little body as our skin came together on the couch.

"What makes you think I'm taking your name, Mr. Kincaid?" she whispered as my hands wrapped around her ass, pulling her closer.

"Because I like the sound of my name with yours," I answered roughly.

Her eyes rounded as her lips softly touched mine. "I do, too."

*   *   *

Sometimes the memories came without rhyme or reason. Sometimes they came because of a certain person or trigger. Often they brought me to my knees, interrupting my day and life, but other times, they came in the form of dreams.

Last night I dreamed of Everly and our book of names.

In the morning I felt refreshed and peaceful for the first time in months. Nothing had changed. Everly was still marrying Ryan as far as I knew. Trent was still around and therefore my life was just as fucked up as it had been yesterday, but I awoke with a calming tranquility running through my bones.

I hoped she took my advice, wherever it might lead her.

All I ever wanted for Everly was for her to be happy and safe. If that was with Ryan, or in cooking school...halfway across the world...it didn't matter anymore, as long as she found her footing in this world.

I knew she'd be safer with Ryan, but I couldn't be selfish. I couldn't keep forcing her into his arms to keep her farther from mine.

I never do things like that with Ryan.

She deserved so much more.

Reaching for my phone, I looked at the time and slowly rubbed my tired eyes. I'd slept through more than half the morning. Good thing it was Sunday, otherwise Trent would have had my ass.

I'd already pushed aside all of my darkroom equipment in the office to move the gigantic desk back into place so I could start working weekends again. Seemed he already had my ass, and I'd handed it to him on a silver platter.

No. Nothing was going to shake my good mood today.

Throwing a shirt over my head, I headed for the stairs and the kitchen, where my coffeepot was calling my name. Hell, I might even attempt a thing or two for breakfast.

Man could not survive on crappy coffee alone.

The sound of the brew dripping through to the large pot below had started when the doorbell chimed.

Brick really needed to learn the art of calling ahead.

Deciding he might want a cup of coffee himself, I quickly added a couple more scoops and water to the pot and raced to the door. The doorbell chime had segued into an incessant pounding, making me wary of who just might be on the other side. Brick might be nosy and perhaps a tad rusty on the principles of social interactions when it came to visiting a friend, but he'd never been outright rude.

Well, not banging-on-the-door rude.

Opening the door, I cursed under my breath. Of course it was Trent—because my good mood couldn't last five goddamn minutes.

"It's Sunday," I said, greeting him with a straight face.

"Yep," he replied, pushing past me as if he too owned the damn place.

I watched him disappear into my kitchen, casually walking in his jeans and henley with a newspaper tucked under his arm.

I guess we were having coffee together.

Fun.

He was already pouring himself a cup and ransacking my pantry for sugar when I joined him, the paper still carefully stowed underneath his arm.

"Didn't have anything better to do this morning?" I asked as I watched him finish fixing his cup.

"Just had some loose ends to tie up," he answered vaguely as he took a sip and blew out a breath, muttering about it being too hot. "And no, I absolutely have a lot better things to do this morning. Several in fact," he sneered, the intent clear in his voice as I tried not to look away in disgust.

I followed his lead, taking a mug from the shelf above, and poured a cup for myself, leaning against the counter in silence as I waited for him to explain why he was here, so he could then get the hell out.

He'd shown up at my door unannounced. He could do the talking.

He made a show of adding more cream to his mug, slowly stirring it as I waited. He must have known I was growing more and more agitated with each second that ticked by because I could see the slight grin that tugged at his face when he finally looked up at me.

"There was a fire downtown last night," he said, as if we were standing around the water cooler at the office and it was a sleepy Monday morning rather than Sunday afternoon in my kitchen.

"Okay." I shrugged my shoulders.

"It's all over the news. Big fire. Such a tragedy." He shook his head back and forth in an attempt to appear dejected. The emotion didn't look right on Trent, and instead he looked more like a villain than I'd ever seen.

It sent chills up my back and warning signs went up all around me.

"Where?"

He reached for the newspaper he'd been keeping a secret since his arrival, and slowly smoothed it down in front of me in a manner that almost appeared loving.

"Downtown Fire Claims Local Art Gallery. One fatality."

My eyes widened in horror as I gazed down at the photo. The small art gallery I'd been in numerous times, meeting with the owner as he graciously agreed to hang my photos on his walls, was gone.

Everything gone. Including Rodger, the owner.

As I sat there, feeling the shock set in, I saw Trent set something else down.

The single photo I'd sold.

When I looked up at him, he just grinned.

"Let me remind you of something, August. You work for me—for our partnership. There's no room for lofty dreams or distractions. Is that clear?"

My portrait, the one I'd taken while Everly and I had walked the streets of San Francisco, covered most of the newspaper heading, but I could still see the flames from the photo, rising around the building as it was overtaken. Had the old man suffered when the fire engulfed him?

You were never afraid of anything back then.

The gallery's address was printed near the bottom, reminding me just how close the art gallery had been to Everly's new home address.

Blocks.

Just mere blocks.

"Crystal clear," I managed to say, the words feeling like sandpaper against my throat.

"Good. Then we're done here," he said, patting me on the back as he dumped the rest of the coffee down the drain. "Oh, and I expect the deal with the Yorkes is still going well?

I nodded, feeling the blood drain from my face.

"Good. Don't fuck it up. Oh, and do yourself a favor and get better coffee, man. This stuff is shit," he said, laughing as he walked away. I could hear his chipper whistle echoing down the hallway as he left.

And then it was just silence.

"Holy fuck," I cursed, my voice breaking apart as I grasped at the newspaper with shaking hands. I'd always known he was crazy—seeing him go apeshit on waiters and pretty much anyone who wronged him—but I'd never had proof.

Yes you did.

Yes I did, a voice deep down echoed as that haunting memory from that fateful night came rushing back. I'd been scared for my life. Scared for both of our lives.

It was why I'd pushed Everly away for so long.

Because deep down, I'd known this day would come. I'd known eventually Trent would show his true colors, and when he did, I wanted her as far away from me as possible.

"When I wake up in the morning, and everything about this night is fuzzy... what should I remember?"

I took a deep breath, letting it fill my lungs as I put my thoughts together.

"Remember that you're a strong woman, that your friends love you, and that more than anything, you should stay away from me, Everly. Stay far, far away from me."

Shaking my head as I pulled the photo up for a better look, I took a deep breath and prayed.

Prayed that she took my advice and stayed the hell away.

I was more dangerous to her than ever now.

Chapter Nine

Everly

"Good morning!" My soon-to-be mother-in-law nearly sang as I opened the door. I wondered what in the world she was doing at our apartment at this ungodly hour. Tightening my robe around my waist and rubbing my eyes once again, I squinted in the direction of the microwave clock, trying to see what time it was.

Eight in the morning.

My last day off before the wedding. The last day I could spend sleeping in, cuddled under my sheets, pretending things like centerpieces and flower arrangements weren't things I needed to agonize over.

Glancing over at Ryan's mother, and the bags and bags she was slowly carting in, one by one into our small living room, I realized my beautiful morning of laziness had come to an abrupt end.

Centerpieces were priority of the day.

Joy of all joys.

"I'm going to start a pot of coffee and go get dressed," I

announced, hopping over several plastic bags to reach the kitchen. I quickly started my much-needed fuel, figuring I'd need an entire pot to myself to get through the morning, and then promptly headed back to the bedroom.

No wonder Ryan had insisted on working straight up to the wedding day. I thought he was just being a workaholic.

Now I realized this had been a strategic move. He was purposely getting out of all of the wedding prep.

I wish I had been that smart.

I'd started out this second attempt at our wedding day with a clear vision. I'd wanted to be involved. I'd let Sarah take over so much of everything the first time around and I'd thought maybe my un-involvement had led to our eventual parting. This time I would be present. This wedding was going to be all about us.

That was, at least until Ryan's mother had gotten involved, and everything simple and easy I'd wanted had flown out the window. Since then, my planned centerpieces, tiny glass vases with a single daisy in each, had been replaced with ginormous crystal things that held mile-high floral arrangements.

I didn't want to know how much each of those cost.

Ryan was now going to wear a tux, rather than a tan suit. No man should be married in something he'd wear to a country club, she'd said.

I didn't quite understand why it mattered, but Ryan had agreed to it, so of course, so did I.

The whole thing felt like someone else's affair. But I kept reminding myself it was only one day.

Just one day of our lives and then we would be married.

Married for the rest of our lives...

Pulling a shirt over my head, I headed to the bathroom and quickly brushed my hair and teeth, trying not to notice the dark circles under my eyes. It had been almost a week since my infamous bachelorette party, which had resulted in my best friends having to nearly wheel me out of the bar and carry me home, and I still hadn't seemed to recover.

The hangover to end all hangovers had passed, and even though most of the night still remained fuzzy, I couldn't seem to return to a normal pattern of sleep.

I'd curl up in bed, fall asleep, and an hour later find myself back awake and staring at the ceiling. Other times I'd wake, panicked, my heart racing full speed ahead to a destination unknown while I tried to shake off the nerves that threatened to take over without waking Ryan.

This was why I'd been looking so forward to a morning alone in bed. Maybe I could actually sleep, because right now, I was seriously starting to look more like the bride of Frankenstein than anything else.

"Everly! We have a lot to do! No time to dawdle!" Sophie hollered. That was her name—Sophie. Although I wasn't supposed to call her that. It was either Mrs. Sparrow or Mom.

Yep. Mom.

That little bomb had been dropped the other night at dinner.

In another world, I would have been overjoyed. I probably would have cried big fat tears of joy. But I didn't. I felt nothing but pressure and guilt that I didn't cry and jump up and hug her on the spot, thanking her for her love and support.

Instead, I just sat there awkwardly as Ryan and Mrs. Sparrow stared at me, waiting for some sort of response.

"Thank you so much," I'd managed to choke out. I'd quickly grabbed my glass of wine like a life preserver.

I'd wanted a mom for as long as I could remember. I used to sit on my borrowed beds with my ratty secondhand sheets, imagining what it would be like to have someone who loved you like that—unconditionally, with no end. I pictured days in the kitchen baking cookies, and hayrides in autumn to find the perfect pumpkin. It would have been wonderful. Me and Mom.

But it was only a dream, and foster kids rarely see the end of the rainbow.

None of it—the sheets or crappy clothes—would have mattered if I'd just had someone to stand up for me, someone to hold me when the kids made fun of my lanky limbs and the scattering of freckles that covered my face.

When I'd first met Ryan and he told me about his childhood and how much his parents had wanted him, I couldn't wait to meet his mother. I thought, if she wanted him, surely she'd want me as well.

But I don't think anyone would ever be good enough for her precious little boy.

Wandering out into the living room, I leaned up against the door frame and watched her buzz around the room for a moment, wondering where all that energy came from. She wasn't in the best of health, having advanced arthritis in several locations and diabetes that constantly gave her issues, but something about this wedding had invigorated her.

I think it was the opportunity to make her son happy. It was what she lived for.

She'd spent most of her life waiting for a child, and when that day finally came, Ryan became the woman's entire world.

So much so that nothing else mattered. She was so blinded by her love for him that sometimes I think she went a little overboard.

Like crazy long to-do lists and mile-high centerpieces crazy.

She meant well, I reminded myself. She really meant well.

"Oh good! You're back! I thought we'd start by assembling the gifts you'll be giving the guests, and then we'll move on to centerpieces."

We're giving them gifts?

"Why don't you take a seat at the table, and I'll show you what to do?" she suggested, waving her arms in that general direction when I didn't appear to be moving fast enough.

"Sure, I'll just grab a cup of coffee—"

"No time! No time! We have too much to do!" she protested.

No time for coffee? Oh God, I might die.

Making the biggest pouty face possible, I slumped down in the chair closest to the kitchen in a desperate attempt to filter caffeine through my system through the scent that had filled the small space alone.

Yes, I was that desperate.

"Okay, here is what we're going to do," she said in a chipper tone, sitting down next to me. Reaching into a bag on the floor, she pulled out several medium candles. They were heavily scented, making me scrunch my nose instantly. I quickly turned and pretended to scratch an itch to cover up my dislike.

"I picked these up at a very upscale department store. The saleslady said giving out candles as your wedding favor is very elegant and she even showed me several ways to present them."

She'd probably enjoyed every penny of her commission too.

"I bought these pretty white boxes, and we're going to wrap a thick silver bow around each like so..." I watched her demonstrate the elaborate bow.

"And for the final touch, I had these beautiful little cards printed. Just attach it with a bit of wire around the knot of the bow and ta-da! Isn't it stunning?"

Looked pretty much like something I could pick up at Target, but like hell I'd say otherwise.

"It looks beautiful," I said with a giant smile. "Can't wait to start!"

She looked completely pleased with herself as she started pulling out the rest of the supplies and dividing them between us. I waited until she began, unsure I could tackle that bow by myself and followed each step alongside her.

It took a few tries, but after a couple of attempts I finally mastered the giant silver bow and moved on to the final step.

"It looks great!" Mrs. Sparrow said with a note of pride in her voice, as I slowly nodded in agreement. Reaching over to my left, I grabbed a tiny card and piece of wire, ready to finish my very first wedding favor.

One down, a gajillion to go.

The silver foil on the card caught my eye and I realized I hadn't even read what it said.

Mr. and Mrs. Ryan Sparrow thank you for spending this special day with them and hope that each time you light this candle, you'll remember true love always burns the brightest.

Everything happened at once. Like a switch on a vacuum, the oxygen in my lungs seemed to vacate my body in one giant pilgrimage, leaving me with a void of nothingness while the air around me grew in density, pushing against me until I felt like I might collapse under the pressure.

Mr. and Mrs. Sparrow...

True love always burns the brightest...

Oh God, too much...must get out.

"Everly, are you all right? You look pale."

"I think I'm going to pass out," I managed to say a second before I collapsed, bringing the entire stack of silver-foiled cards and perfectly tied bows with me as I hit the floor.

*   *   *

After about a hundred vials of blood had been extracted from my body, it was concluded there was nothing medically wrong with me.

As I sat there alone in the emergency room, staring at my bare feet as they poked out of the end of the thin sheet that passed for a blanket around here, I took a deep breath into my lungs, letting it fill every single crevice and shallow space, remembering that staggering, overwhelming feeling of not being able to breathe.

Panic attack.

That's what had happened to me. I'd seen my married name, printed in bold on beautiful white card stock, and I'd gone bananas.

Like passed-out, had-to-call-an-ambulance bananas.

God, I was so embarrassed.

Ryan's mother was in the waiting room, avoiding the germs as much as possible. With her age and her long laundry list of health problems, I didn't blame her. There was no reason for her to be here, anyway.

There wasn't anything wrong with me, after all.

But she refused to leave.

Someone needed to be at my side—even if it was from afar.

She definitely had certain quirks about her—from the way she scurried off when you mentioned the Internet or attempted to speak of anything remotely modern. Or her sometimes smothering approach to wedding planning that made me want to crawl out a window rather than face her once more.

But she did care for me. It might not be the fairytale type dream of a mother I'd always envisioned, but it was something. I realized that now.

Which was why this was going to be all the more difficult.

I took another deep breath, lost in my thoughts, when the door pushed slowly open. Hidden behind a mound of flowers was Ryan.

"I'm sorry it took me so long. Traffic was terrible and the parking garage was full. But I bought you flowers!" he added cheerfully, setting them down on the small tray beside me.

"They're beautiful," I said, my eyes fixed on the small pink roses. "You didn't have to, though."

"Of course I did. You're in the hospital!"

"I know, but only because of a panic attack. The doctor is going to discharge me soon. I just need to follow up with my primary physician in a couple of days," I replied, my eyes unable to meet his.

"A panic attack is a big deal, Ev. It means your body became overwhelmed with stress. The wedding plans are too much for you to handle, which is why I've taken off the next few days and I think you should, too. I realized it's not fair to ask you to do all this on your own. It's our wedding. I should be helping."

Oh, if it were only that easy.

"It's not the wedding," I said in a voice little more than a whisper.

"What?" he asked, suddenly confused.

"It's not the wedding," I stated slowly. "It's us. The panic I'm feeling—it's because of us."

My sad gaze traveled up to his and the words settled in.

"Us? What do you mean?" he asked, coming to the realization. "You don't want to get married?" His voice shook as he spoke and the sound nearly split my heart in two.

"Do you?" I asked, tears wetting my cheeks.

"Of course I do!" he roared back, the fight in his voice vanishing as quickly as it came. He stumbled to the end of the bed and sat, withering before my eyes.

"Think about it," I said. "Why do you want to marry me?"

"Because I love you."

"But, why do you love me?"

His hands threaded his light brown hair, and I heard him blow out a frustrated puff of air. "I don't know. I don't know," he said over and over.

"I don't know why I love you either," I answered.

Several minutes passed before his eyes met mine once more. "We should know," he said finally.

"We should know," I agreed, a single tear trailing down my cheek.

"I remember my mother giving the eulogy at my father's funeral," he began, smoothing the thin white bedsheet beside him as he spoke. "Through her tears, she listed more than half a dozen reasons she loved that man. Some were silly, like the way he always told dirty jokes to cheer her up—that one honestly surprised me. Some were more serious, like the way he never left the house without saying he loved her. When she sat back down, I leaned over and told her what a wonderful job she'd done and glanced down at the sheet of paper she'd been holding. I knew she'd been working on the eulogy for days, but the paper she held in her hand? It was blank. Everything she'd said at that podium was from her heart and completely on the spot."

"You deserve a love like that," I stated, hating that it wasn't me. Hating that I wasn't the woman who would one day fill all the blanks on that sheet of paper he spoke of.

"You do, too," he replied.

"Maybe someday. But for now, I think I want to focus on just one person."

"And who's that?" he asked.

"Me."

*   *   *

Mrs. Sparrow's growing affection toward me turned into white-hot rage when she discovered our impending nuptials had been canceled. I'm not sure what she was more upset about—her grand affair being canceled, or her son.

Either way, I was now the enemy and the reason for everything bad in the world.

Naturally, my red hair was the cause of it. Ryan should have never dated a redhead. They were nothing but trouble. Flighty and unreliable—her words, not mine. She calmed down slightly when Ryan explained our decision to part ways was mutual. Since it had been Ryan's choice, her hatred toward me then only became more justified.

I couldn't wait to be out of the apartment.

My new quest for independence was on hold until I could find a place of my own, however. Until then, I was shacking up with Sarah.

Again.

But this time, it wouldn't be any longer than a few weeks. Because for the first time in my life, I would not be running back to a man.

This time, I was on my own.

Everly the brave. Or whatever.

The breakup was fairly cordial. Besides the snide comments made by Mrs. Sparrow, Ryan and I continued to work well together—proof that we'd become more friends than lovers over the last few months. It was something I think both of us had seen coming, but neither of us had been willing to admit.

Now that it was out in the open, and both of our futures unknown, there was a sense of levity between us. We laughed, joked, and bantered back and forth like grade-school kids.

I felt like a thousand-pound weight had been lifted off my shoulders, and I think Ryan felt the same.

I'd saved us from making a big mistake, and in doing so I think I'd saved something even more precious.

Our friendship.

"Well, I think this is the last of it," Ryan said, dropping the final stack of boxes in Sarah's living room.

"I sure hope so, 'cause damn!" Sarah muttered, looking across the floor at the sea of crap that had slowly accumulated over the last few hours.

I gave her a hard stare, hoping she'd get the hint.

"I'm just going to go into my room and um, yeah... 'bye," she said, making a quick beeline to the back of the apartment.

"She's usually more subtle than that," Ryan laughed.

"Well, I didn't give her much of a choice."

"Ah."

"Listen, I just wanted to apologize for—"

"Stop," he said, interrupting me. I looked up at him a second before he engulfed me in a large hug.

"Good luck, Everly," he whispered.

I squeezed him tighter, my head resting comfortably against his warm chest. "Good luck, Ryan."

We pulled away and I watched him turn, and then pause.

"I almost forgot. I want you to have this," he said, handing me a manila envelope.

My eyebrow raised in curiosity. "I thought we already decided we were sending all the gifts back?" I asked.

"Would you just open it?" he demanded, a smooth grin pulling at his chin. I did as I was told and undid the flap, pulling out a pile of papers and several brochures. It took me a second to register what I was seeing.

"This is our honeymoon," I whispered.

"And it's yours."

My gaze flew up to his. "I can't accept this." I fumbled for words. I kept glancing down as pictures of the Eiffel Tower and Notre Dame filled my head.

"Yes you can," he encouraged. "It's non-refundable and believe me when I say this, I do not want to spend a week with my mom in Paris. So please, go. Take Sarah, enjoy yourself and maybe somewhere along the way, you'll find that one person you've been searching for."

I smiled, remembering my vow to focus on myself for once.

"*Vive la France?*" I laughed.

"Exactly. Now go break the news to Sarah. I need a head start so I can be a safe distance before the ear-splitting screams begin."

"Ryan?" I called out before he turned.

His bright smile met me.

"Thank you," I said.

"No, thank you," he replied before he disappeared through the door.

I was going to Paris.

I looked down at the tickets, my eyes filling with happy tears.

Holy shit. I was leaving for Paris in two days!

Time to make Sarah's day.

Chapter Ten

August

I'd no sooner finished pulling on my suit jacket than the doorbell rang downstairs, alerting me that the driver I'd hired for the day had arrived.

My stomach churned in protest. I did not want to do this.

In the matter of an hour or so, I would be meeting Magnolia's parents, and my plan to win over her father would begin.

I hated myself for even thinking of it. But I knew if I didn't do this Trent would, and he would take them for everything. My only hope was that by being in charge, I could do as little damage as possible and hopefully explain my reasoning to Magnolia when all the dust settled.

Whenever that might be.

I knew it was a long shot—that she'd never forgive me after she discovered my deceit, but when faced with a rock and a solid wall, one tends to choose the easier path. For now, I was going with the rock.

A vision of myself behind prison bars flashed before my eyes and I cringed inwardly, fearing my fate had already been sealed along with Trent's. One could only carry out this type of business for so long before everything crumbled down.

But Trent thought he was smarter, better, and more conniving than so many others that had failed before him.

I shook my head as I made my way down the stairs. I wasn't so sure.

There was always someone smarter and better than you—and they usually carried a badge.

Grabbing the two bouquets of roses I'd picked out earlier that morning, I slid my wallet into my back pocket and opened the front door, greeting the driver who was waiting patiently outside.

"Good morning, Mr. Kincaid," he answered. "Lovely morning for a drive."

"Yes," I agreed, feeling slightly less enthusiastic, but I did agree with him about the weather.

It was beautiful. The morning fog had lifted, leaving crystal blue skies and surprisingly warm temperatures for so late in the year.

A perfect day for a wedding.

I'd been trying so hard not to think of it, but it had been on my mind all week—like an infection, growing stronger as my willpower grew weaker by the second.

Was she getting married today? Had she taken my advice?

I don't know how many times I'd picked up my phone, so tempted to call her and hear the words from her soft pink lips.

But it didn't matter.

We were over. She needed to move on, whether it was with Ryan or not. I was not an option—I couldn't be, and knowing whether or not she walked down that aisle and pledged her life to another man today wouldn't change that. It was the reason I'd deleted every e-mail, declined each phone call, and avoided Brick at every turn.

I knew I'd find out what she'd decided eventually, but for now, not knowing was what kept me moving forward. Either way, whether she married today or not, I knew it would hurt like a bitch and I just didn't think I could handle any more of that right now.

Ignorance was my bliss and for now, I'd drown in it.

The drive to Magnolia's passed in a blur, and soon the driver pulled up to her familiar apartment building. When he politely offered to collect her, I declined, knowing she'd appreciate the gesture of my going up myself.

Time to put my game face on and put my past where it belonged— behind me.

If only it were so easy.

I quickly adjusted my tie in the elevator, and checked my silver cuff links, wanting everything to be in order when I knocked on her door. Magnolia had been raised in high society, and appreciated a man with good taste. She wasn't stuck up like most women with money, but she did gravitate toward the finer things in life.

My outward appearance was a nod to that notion, and I was hoping she'd notice.

I needed all the help I could get. I hadn't exactly been an exemplary guy so far, bailing on dates, forgetting to call. I knew she thought she understood, blaming it all on my past issues. But eventually, even that excuse would be cumbersome. I needed to keep her hooked on me.

For now, at least.

It didn't take more than two seconds before she appeared at

the door, dressed in a gorgeous lace dress and matching mile-high shoes. Her hair was curled and pulled to the side, showing off the massive diamonds that always adorned her ears.

Not a hair out of place or a detail overlooked—that was Magnolia. Always polished and poised, just like she'd been raised to be. But the more I got to know her, the more intrigued I was to meet these elusive parents of hers. Magnolia, the name given to her by her mother, a former florist, carried herself in all the ways a daughter of a prominent wealthy family should. But it was what she lacked that made me curious to know more.

Over the last few months, I'd met my fair share of people who had waltzed through the doors of our company. Most had money and acted like it, demanding this and that and behaving as if the rest of us were simply around to do their bidding.

Magnolia was different, and I had a feeling it was due to a different type of upbringing by eclectic parents who always managed to shy away from media attention despite her father's founding position at one of the country's most lucrative companies.

"You look beautiful," I said, taking a quick glance as I leaned in to kiss her cheek.

"You don't look half bad yourself," she replied, her eyes roaming down the length of my body in slow appreciation. Her gaze left me feeling uncomfortable—exposed. I was used to women looking at me, a sideways glance or a blatant stare as I walked by. But this was personal and intimate, and reminded me of just what I was risking. What I was leaving behind.

"You ready?" I asked, taking her hand in an attempt to hurry her along.

"Yes, let me just grab my clutch."

I had no idea what exactly a clutch was, but a few moments later she reappeared at the door carrying a small purse-looking thing covered in lace and delicate jewels. She tucked it safely under her arm and I waited patiently as she locked the door before we headed for the elevator.

"Is this a new suit?" she asked, her hands sweeping over the sleek, buttery fabric of the lapel.

"Yes," I smiled.

"Trying to impress someone?" Her face broke out into a knowing grin.

"Maybe."

"Good," she answered, leaning in for a kiss, but the elevator dinged, diverting our attention to the doors that slid open to the lobby. Several people stood waiting, and we quickly exited.

I'd only seen Magnolia a few times since that night in her apartment when I'd told her about my past and held her in my arms, feeling her comfort seep into my bones like warm mist. I'd left feeling at odds with myself.

So much so, I hadn't touched her since.

I knew she was growing impatient, even if she said the opposite. Knowing how women worked, she was probably starting to worry whether it was something she'd done or said.

She'd probably even started to wonder if I was gay and had just forgotten, along with the rest of my memories.

If only it were that simple.

"Car service? Fancy," she stated when we approached the shiny black sedan.

"I figured it would give us a chance to relax on the drive down."

"Sounds great."

I followed closely behind as we climbed into the backseat of the car. The driver gently closed the door behind us. The car was spacious and well-kept, offering bottled water and several snacks for the road. There was even a variety of booze if we chose, but considering the early hour, we both declined. Magnolia instead chose a bottled water as the car took off. Shortly after, the driver raised the privacy barrier to allow us to speak freely.

The short hour or so ride down to Half Moon Bay was beautiful, with scenic views of the coast and larger than life treelines. The closer we got to her childhood home, the happier she appeared.

"Tell me something about your life growing up," I asked as the blue coastal water sped past.

"Hmm." She grinned, tapping her finger against her lip.

"What does that mean?"

"I'm trying to decide what might be the least embarrassing story to tell you."

"Embarrassing? Now I'm intrigued."

"I wasn't always so sophisticated," she laughed, making a show at sitting higher in her seat, and folding her hands neatly in her lap.

"No?" I played along.

"Oh no. This is a result of many long years of cotillion and manners classes. Before that, I was all legs and limbs, a tree-climbing, T-shirt-wearing tomboy."

I tried to picture the blond bombshell in front of me covered in dirt and grime, sky-high, dangling from a tree limb.

"I'm having a hard time imagining you as a tomboy," I said, grinning.

"What? You don't think I can climb a tree?"

"I'm not doubting your skills—just your motivation to do so. You might break a nail," I laughed.

"Hey!" She joined in my laughter, playfully slapping my arm. "I was a kid, and I was the best tree climber around. I could also make a mean dirt pie. Drove my mom crazy."

"Hence the reason for the finishing school?" I surmised.

"That was more peer pressure, actually. When my parents were first married, my dad was just starting his company. It hadn't taken off to the level it is now. Their lives seemed to change overnight. They went from working class to one of the wealthiest in the country, in what seemed like a matter of minutes. It was a huge adjustment, and sometimes I think it still is. My parents didn't grow up with much, and being surrounded by those who had was daunting. Certain things are expected, and everyone has an opinion on how you raise a child."

"So a tomboy wasn't ideal for the society pages in the eyes of the neighbors?" I guessed.

"No," she replied. "So, my parents relented and raised a proper young lady everyone expected."

"Do you miss the trees?" I asked, watching her eyes wander toward the ocean.

"Sometimes. Enough that when I have children of my own, I know I'll never hinder them from what and who they want to be."

"Something tells me that even though they took you out of the trees, that feisty tomboy attitude still lives on."

She gave me a sultry wink. "You might be right."

* * *

Half Moon Bay was a short car ride from San Francisco yet it felt worlds apart.

Long gone were the hustle and bustle of the busy city life, replaced by the laid-back vibe that took place by the bay. People were different here. Relaxed and chill. You felt it immediately when you entered the welcoming town, full of eclectic shops and dog-friendly restaurants. People walked everywhere, rode their bikes...talked to each other.

I didn't even know the names of my own neighbors.

As we continued through the town, I noticed the houses—the different shapes and architecture. Not one of them was cookie-cutter or built to resemble the one next to it. Each house stood on its own, from the color of the paint down to the elaborate gardens. I swore I even saw a house that was shaped like a boat.

A freaking boat. This town was awesome.

"It's kind of strange, isn't it?" Magnolia said as we passed through the remainder of the main part of town toward her parents' house.

"What?"

"Half Moon?" she replied. "I always thought it was kind of a silly place to grow up."

"Really, why?"

"It's just so different. I feel much more at home in the city. It's not nearly as friendly, but I do have a Starbucks nearby and I can order a pizza at virtually any time of the day or night."

I gave her a convincing smile, hoping she'd buy it. She did, turning to watch the water slowly reveal itself through the trees.

There were only two things holding me to the city. The love I had for my house, mostly because of the memories it held, and...Everly.

Without her, I was just living in an empty house on the edge of a city that felt completely wrong.

Would everything always circle back around to her, or would my life eventually weave its own path that led away from Everly?

Did I want it to?

Maybe I should just move and make it easier. I could buy a funky house here and never be seen or heard from again. The image of Trent laughing in my face as I told him my grand plan came to mind, dashing the idea instantly. I'd never be able to leave the city. Everly and I would be forever tied together.

And I'd forever be in hell.

"We're here!" Magnolia announced as the car came to a stop in front of a large gilded gate. Magnolia gave the access code to the driver and after a short pause we were on our way again as the gate pulled back and we drove through. Magnolia's parents lived in a gated community of Half Moon Bay. I'm fairly certain with her father's income, they probably could have bought the entire town. Driving in, everything seemed understated to me, for a man of his means.

The houses were massive and definitely screamed money, however. Most were situated next to a pristine golf course that overlooked the gorgeous Pacific coastline. It was all breathtaking. But, again...I had expected more. Twice, maybe three times more.

Mr. Yorke appeared to be a man who did not flaunt his wealth. Or at least not overly so.

If this had been Trent and he'd been the founding member of a Fortune 500 company, there would have been a jewel-encrusted bridge to carry guests over to the house, which would have probably been covered in gold. Trent loved his money, and hated the fact that he couldn't show everyone just how much he had. But that's what happens when you play dirty.

And Trent was rolling in shit.

"There it is!" Magnolia said with exuberance, pointing to the grand house just up ahead. Unlike the rest of the town, this gated community resembled many of the other parts of California I'd visited. The houses were very similar to each other in terms of décor and landscaping. They varied slightly in size and model, but after just driving through town, this area was vastly different.

"Is this where you grew up?" I asked, noticing how new everything looked.

"No," she replied as the car came to a stop. "We lived closer to town. My parents bought this house after I moved to the city. My dad loves to golf and after years of begging, my mother finally gave in and let him move onto a golf course. He's never been happier."

"So, these are not the infamous trees I've heard so much about?" I asked, looking up at the small palm trees as we got out of the car. They were no bigger than me and had probably been planted in the last few years.

"Nope. Those tiny things wouldn't hold me even as a girl. I was a wild child." She gave me a flirtatious smile. "Come on, let's go inside."

I thanked the driver and told him I'd let him know when we needed to be picked up before we began our walk up the driveway. We were no more than halfway there before we were attacked by a barking, licking, crazy dog.

Magnolia laughed as I tried to save my suit, finally giving up to pet the mutt.

"This is Mango," she said, rubbing the ears of the large golden retriever. The dog groaned happily as her tongue flopped out to the side.

"She's cute," I added.

"Thanks. We rescued her a few years ago, while I was still in college. I've always wanted to take her with me to the city, but I know it wouldn't be fair to have her locked up in that small apartment. So she stays here with my parents. But she'll always be mine, won't you, Mango?" Her voice changed, becoming squeaky and high, causing the dog's tail to wag in excitement.

"Looks like she got to you first," a female voice called out. We both looked up to see an older version of Magnolia walking toward us. Dressed in casual black pants and a soft pink sweater and pearls, Mrs. Yorke smiled the instant she saw her daughter, running to meet her open arms.

"I missed you, Peanut," she said happily.

"I missed you, too, Mom."

"You keep forgetting you're just an hour away," Mrs. Yorke commented.

"You keep forgetting how busy I am!" Magnolia laughed, giving her mom a soft tap on the shoulder.

"I know, I know. So grown-up and sophisticated now. Even bringing boys home."

Her eyes met mine with a tiny wink, making me smile.

"Oh my gosh, Mom. He is far from a boy. And please do not embarrass me. Already."

"I'll stop trying if you introduce me to your man friend," she promised, emphasizing the word "man" with a smirk.

I like her already.

"Mom, I'd like you to meet August Kincaid. August, this is my mother, Lisa Yorke."

I stepped forward, offering my hand. She took it and we shook. "So nice to meet you, Mrs. Yorke. Magnolia always speaks very highly of her parents."

"Thank you, August—you can call me Lisa. It's very nice to meet you finally. I've heard a lot about you."

I silently groaned. God only knew what that could mean.

"Let's all go inside and see if we can find that father of yours," she suggested with a warm smile. She turned as Magnolia and I followed, the exuberant dog chasing behind.

The house was decorated just as I'd expected it to be. Warm and inviting, with family touches everywhere. Baby photos of Magnolia adorned the walls, vacation mementos and even a few wedding pictures from years gone by. It filled the large space, making it feel cozy and inviting, rather than the drafty void I came home to everyday.

"It's my long-lost daughter!" Mr. Yorke announced, coming around the corner into the living room, his arms held wide for his daughter. They embraced for a long time and he kissed her head, pulling back to wrap her under his arm.

"Now, who is your friend, Peanut?" he asked, giving me a gentle smile.

"This is August. August, this is my father, Paul."

More handshaking commenced, before he offered us all a seat and a drink. Magnolia came and sat next to me while Lisa took a cozy spot next to her husband.

We spent the next half hour or so making the usual small talk while we nursed glasses of vintage wine. Paul asked me what I did for a living, although I suspect he already knew. I think he just wanted to get a feeling for the man who was dating his daughter, and so I complied, going through the motions of what I did with Trent. I knew Trent would want me to push more, advertise our strengths as a team and really sell our company, but I knew if this was going to work, it had to be done slowly.

Paul Yorke was a complex man. He was a multibillionaire who lived like someone with a fraction of his income, and yet he sent his daughter to manners classes and cotillion so she could compete with others in society. If there was one thing I learned quickly from the short time I spent with Magnolia's father, it was that he was smart. Damn smart.

I had my work cut out for me if I was ever going to broker a deal with him, and a large part of me hoped he turned me down flat. He was kind and loved the hell out of his family.

No part of me wanted to take advantage of this man, or his daughter.

But if I didn't, Trent would do his best and try, and the last thing I wanted was his slimy hands all over this precious family, muddling up their perfect little world. Or worse, putting his hands all over Magnolia.

She deserved better than that—they all did.

Hell—they deserved better than me, but at least I wouldn't leave them destitute, and I was slowly re-learning my skills. I might even be able to do right by them, rather than take them for everything like Trent usually did.

"August, care to join me outside? I was about to start the grill and figured you might enjoy the fresh air," Paul offered as he stood from his place on the sofa. I gave Magnolia a quick sideways glance and her amused grin told me I was going to get the special talk.

The "what are your intentions with my daughter" talk.

Fan-fucking-tastic.

"Sure," I answered, feeling like a worm on a hook, about to go airborne into a lake full of ravenous minnows. Currently there was only one minnow I was worried about, and truthfully, he was looking more like a shark.

Walking through a large sliding glass door, we stepped out onto the expansive deck. Standing here, I could see why Mr. Yorke would want to retire in a place like this. Perfectly sloped green hills, sparkling blue water—it was like a little slice of paradise. With a little bit of golf thrown in.

"Magnolia tells me you had an accident a while ago?" he asked, a blatant attempt for information. I watched him walk around the deck, taking in the panoramic view he'd probably memorized by now as he waited for me to answer.

"Not really an accident, sir—" I began, before he interrupted.

"Call me Paul."

"Okay," I replied, before continuing. "I was mugged," I said, going with the original story. No need to elaborate. "I suffered a head injury and was in a coma for over two years."

He nodded, as if this was information he already knew. "That's a long time."

"Yes."

"And you're still missing bits and pieces?"

"More than bits and pieces," I clarified. "I'd say the majority is still lost."

He didn't ask any further questions, but I could see them on the tip of his tongue as he wandered around the wooden path of the deck.

"I know what you're thinking," I finally said.

He turned to me, his hands casually tucked into the pockets of his tan chinos. "Oh?"

"You're wondering whether I'm stable enough to handle being around your daughter. Whether I'm going to break her heart in a matter of months because I'm too wrapped up in my own mess to focus on anything else."

"Yes, that's exactly what I'm thinking."

"And I wish I could give you answers, but honestly they'd all be bullshit. Right now, I'm just taking it one day at a time, and Magnolia knows that."

"All right." He nodded.

"Letting me off the hook that easily, huh?" I asked as I joined him at the railing overlooking the Pacific.

"Magnolia isn't a little girl anymore—as much as I'd like to deny it. She's a grown woman who makes her own choices and I trust her. If she's chosen you as someone to spend her time with, I've got to believe you're worthy of it."

A lump formed in my throat.

"Thank you, Paul."

Guilt ate at me, gnawing at my gut like maggots.

I wasn't worthy of anything.

*   *   *

"Her first cotillion, she showed up with mud on her tights and dirt in her curls. All the other girls looked at her like she was an alien from outer space," Lisa joked as we dined on grilled salmon and fresh asparagus on the deck.

"Well, who was the one who told me cotillion was on Saturday, when it was actually on Friday?" Magnolia argued, sticking her tongue out toward her mother. "She showed up in my room that night all flustered with a pink dress in hand, words coming out of her mouth so fast I could hardly understand. I think Daddy went out and bought you a PalmPilot or something equally ridiculous the next day to try and keep you organized. You were always getting appointments mixed up."

"Still is," Paul muttered under his breath with a laugh.

"Oh shush, both of you. I figured it out, eventually. And you made it to cotillion on time, didn't you?"

"With dirt in my hair!" Magnolia laughed.

Lisa waved her hand in the air, dismissing the comment as everyone settled.

"Paul, the salmon was fantastic," I commented, placing my napkin down beside my empty plate.

"I'll be sure to get you the recipe before you leave," he offered, leaning back in his chair. His arm relaxed on Lisa's shoulder, playing with the stray hairs that had fallen out of her bun.

"Thank you, but that won't be necessary. I'd hate to destroy a perfectly good memory. I've been told my cooking skills are quite terrible," I replied as Everly's laughter filled my head from when she'd tried to teach me to cook.

"Something you and my daughter have in common then," he said. I looked to my side, trying to shake the memory loose.

Stay in the present, I reminded myself.

Magnolia just sat there staring at the ceiling, pretending not to notice the increased attention.

"Magnolia can't cook?" I asked, remembering the riot act I'd received when I'd arrived late to a dinner date and botched her perfectly planned meal.

"Last I'd checked, she couldn't even boil pasta."

"Oh Daddy, that's not true!" she huffed before crossing her arms in protest. Her eyes darted over toward me before scurrying away.

"Magnolia?"

"Oh, fine! I ordered out!" she admitted. "I can't cook for anything."

Everyone at the table burst into a fit of laughter, including myself. I leaned over and rubbed her shoulder as her eyes met mine.

"Well, I guess we'll have to stick to takeout."

"I order a mean takeout," she said with a wink.

"Just don't let her anywhere near a stove," Lisa joked.

Magnolia rolled her eyes and chucked a napkin at her mom. These were the typical antics of a happy family, and it made me long for more memories of my own mom and dad. So far, very little of those had surfaced—a few fleeting flashbacks, but nothing concrete. I'd spent hours . . . days . . . trying to figure out a pattern to how the memories came back, but there seemed to be no rhyme or reason.

Part of me wondered if it was our house that brought back certain memories of Everly and our life together, which was why I refused to leave it. But often I just believe it was chance or longevity, and that eventually everything would find its way back if I waited long enough.

There was no waitstaff in the Yorke house. Lisa and Paul did all the cooking and tidying up themselves. For anyone else, this seemed like no grand miracle, but for most who had the means to do so, a cook and a maid would have been high on the list of must-haves.

Simplistic billionaires. What a concept. It was something I thought about on my way to the kitchen as I helped Lisa with the dishes and leftovers. Magnolia disappeared into the game room to find a deck of cards. Since I'd never heard of gin rummy—or at least didn't remember hearing of it—she was determined to teach me.

A soft silence settled around the two of us as we worked through the lunch dishes. Lisa rinsed while I piled them in the dishwasher. I made neat rows of plates and bowls and slowly began to wonder if I'd ever done the dishes like this with my own mom.

Would I ever remember it?

"Magnolia tells us you have your own house over the water?" Lisa said, interrupting the quiet.

"Yes, although there isn't a golf course," I said with a smirk.

"Hmm, I might like your house a bit better," she laughed.

"Not a fan of the golf life?"

"It's all right. It makes Paul happy and he's worked so hard all these years, he definitely deserves it. And the view isn't bad."

I agreed with a single nod as I began stacking a few wineglasses in the top rack.

"Do you miss your old house?"

"Of course, but it's just a house. The memories are all right here," she said, pointing to her heart, rather than her head.

"A home isn't about the building, or the wood required to construct it. It's about who's with you inside it. My home can change a hundred times over, but I know those two out there will never change. They're my home, whether we're in a shack or a palace.

"Do you have a home, August?" she asked, turning to me as she dried her hands on a towel.

"I don't know," I answered.

"Well, it's about time you started figuring it out."

My eyes caught Magnolia as she danced into the living room with her dad, and I smiled as a part of me died inside, thinking of Everly walking down the aisle today as a bride.

"I think you're right," I answered. "I think you're right."

Chapter Eleven
Everly

"We're on a plane," Sarah said, nearly bouncing up and down on the seat next to me.

"Yes," I replied, avoiding her bubbly expression.

"We're on a plane, and we are going to Paris!" she exclaimed, so loud that the couple in front of us turned and gave us an amused expression.

"Yep."

When I still hadn't jumped on her happiness bandwagon, she then resorted to grabbing my arm and shaking me violently.

"Everly!"

"Ouch!" I laughed. "You're rattling my teeth!"

"We're going to Paris!"

"I know, you've told me a hundred times since this morning," I exclaimed, pushing her shoulders down so she'd stay seated. A hundred times might be a little shy of the true number, but it wasn't far off. Our flight had departed from San Francisco around noon, but little Miss Overeager had decided to wake up at five in the morning.

Five in the freaking morning.

She'd also decided that she needed company at that god-awful hour. Even after I explained to her that we had the longest flight in the history of flights ahead of us, she was still jumping around like a lunatic, talking about the Eiffel Tower and the Hunchback of Notre Dame and pastries. *Oh, the pastries.*

Hey, I was excited, too, but a girl needed her beauty rest.

And I was starting to believe I wasn't going to catch a wink of it during this entire transatlantic flight. How much was it to upgrade to one of those fancy first-class seats in the front? The ones that reclined fully and came with a three-course meal? I watched as a flight attendant slowly pulled the curtain to the first-class area closed, and I caught a last glimpse of the fancy life. Real plates, fancy glasses... legroom for days. It probably cost more than my entire bank account held at the moment. *Or ever.*

"Tell me you're not excited!"

"I'm not excited," I tried to say with a straight face, but my lips began to curve into a giant smile as my head fell back against the seat cushion.

"Liar! This is going to be the best week ever! Thank you so much for not getting married! I've always wanted to go on a honeymoon! And I didn't even have to pledge my undying love to do it!"

My eyes slanted sideways to give her a dirty look as she made a sour face.

"Oops, sorry. Was that too soon?" She scrunched her nose as if the air had suddenly gone sour. I shook my head in disbelief.

Nudging her shoulder, I replied, "You're welcome, butthead. But you better not complain about a single calorie the entire time we're there."

She opened her mouth to argue, but I caught her mid-breath.

"Not one single word, ballerina girl."

"Fine," she pouted. "But don't ever call me 'ballerina girl' again."

"Okay."

We were cruising somewhere over the Midwest now. Drinks and meals had been consumed and everyone was quieting down. Many had snuggled into their airplane blankets to watch a movie, while others were reading or sleeping. My airplane partner was still staring at me like I was her sole entertainment for the next eight hours.

"What?" I asked.

"Talk to me," Sarah whined.

"About what?"

"Anything. Come on, I'm bored!"

"Didn't you bring anything to do? Books, magazines? What about a movie?" I suggested, pointing to the little screen in front of her. "There are like a million of them."

She scrunched her face in an unpleasant manner. "I don't want to watch TV. I want to talk!"

"Okay, fine," I relented, setting my Kindle down in my lap. I'd been just getting to the good part of the book, too.

Her face brightened and she turned her body to face me, leaning against the window of the airplane. Her knees bumped mine due to our tight quarters in coach seating and her extra-long legs, but I didn't mind.

"So, how are you—really?" she asked.

"Good...fine," I answered, using that word that she and Tabitha hated. She gave me an exasperated look until I finally caved, rolling my eyes in an overly exaggerated fashion.

"Honestly? I've been better. There are times when I feel good—like really good. Relieved, you know? But then, I begin to miss him. And then I start to regret everything. It's wrong, Sarah, so wrong because I know, deep down, I didn't love him the way I should have, but—"

"You still loved him."

I nodded. "And it's weird not having him around. Like, this morning, when I woke up and remembered today was the day we were leaving for Paris, the first thing I wanted to do was turn to my side and wake him up and tell him. But he wasn't there. He was my best friend—besides you, and now I don't know how to act. When we were packing everything up, things seemed great—easy. But I haven't spoken to him since. What if I never do?"

Good Lord, apparently I did need to talk.

"You will. You both just need time, Ev. You were engaged—to be married," she stressed with an impish grin. "It's going to take a little bit of an adjustment period to go from almost being husband and wife to just being friends."

"You're right. As always. It's just—God, when did my life turn into such a soap opera?" I moaned, burying my head in my hands as we both began to giggle.

"Right around the time your ex-boyfriend woke up from a coma. Oh my gosh, you are living a soap opera! Watch out for kidnappers on this vacation!" she joked.

"Hey, you're in my life, too. You could be roped into this crazy circus at any time, too," I warned.

"Oh, hell no. I'm keeping my distance."

"I know, I know. You and your mystery man."

Her smile resembled that of a cat who'd licked an entire bowl of cream completely clean—full and contented. "Yes. Me and my man will stay far away from you and your drama, thank you."

"Well, that's probably a good place to be," I commented with a frown, as memories from my bachelorette party began to resurface.

"What did you do?" she asked.

"What?" I said, looking up at her with a curious gaze.

"The way you just said that—you did something stupid, didn't you?" she prodded, poking me in the ribs.

"Ow! I always do stupid things—isn't that why we're on my honeymoon—without a groom?" I feigned innocence.

"No, this is different. And you're turning red. You always turn red when you're lying."

"I'm pale. I turn red all the time," I defended myself, knowing it was no use. She'd just keep poking and pinching and doing whatever else she could until I confessed.

"Spill it," she demanded.

"I hate you."

"Uh huh. Out with it."

"Fine," I finally caved. Wringing my hands in my lap, unable to look at her, I whispered softly, as if the people around me would care, "I may have called August the night of my bachelorette party."

"You didn't. Everly Adams, how dumb are you?"

"Apparently really dumb," I answered, finally meeting her gaze.

"What did you say?"

"See, that's the thing. I don't quite remember. There were a lot of shots in between my two glasses of wine. But I seem to remember yelling at him, so that's good, right?"

"You shouldn't have called him at all. What does that even mean?" she questioned, looking to me for answers.

Good luck with that.

"I have no clue!" I replied. "I'm out supposedly celebrating one of my last nights on earth as a single woman, and what do I do? I called the one person I shouldn't."

"Do you still love him?" she asked, which resulted in me giving her the death stare. "Okay, wrong question. Do you want him back?"

"No," I quickly answered. "I mean, hell—I don't know. I know a part of me will always want him. How big that part is? That's the question of the century."

"So, what are you going to do now?"

I took a deep breath, letting my eyes briefly close.

"Nothing. Absolutely nothing. I'm going to go to Paris with my best friend, and eat pastries and macaroons until my pants don't fit, and then when I get home, I'm going to finally learn what it's like to be a grown-up. All by myself."

I'd been dependent on others, especially men, for far too long.

I was taking back my life.

But as we settled down into our separate activities for the duration of the flight—Sarah becoming lost in the selection of movies and me finally able to read my book— I knew part of me was retreating back to my old ways.

Because as much as I wanted to find myself—break free from the dependency I'd developed over the years—I knew it was just a front to cover up the real truth.

I was running. Again.

*   *   *

"Whoa," Sarah nearly whistled as our tiny taxi pulled up to the hotel Ryan had booked for our Parisian honeymoon.

Besides agreeing to the location, my involvement in the planning process of our honeymoon could be compared to Ryan's involvement in our entire wedding. Or lack thereof.

When had we left for Europe? Earlier that day...or evening...or yesterday? I was so turned around and jet-lagged, all I knew was that when we left the States, we were to meet a suited gentleman who would be holding my name on a large sign at the airport. Now that we'd accomplished that, I had no clue where this adventure would take us.

And it would be an adventure, because from the looks of the very thick envelope Ryan had given me, he'd planned quite a number of activities for us.

Right now, all I wanted to do was sleep.

And then when we woke up, I wanted to take a shower, and possibly nap again, because wow—whoever could possibly sleep on an airplane deserved a standing ovation, in my opinion. Tiny seats, no legroom, and the constant noise. No thank you. I needed a bed—that reclined and had fluffy pillows and blankets that didn't feel like burlap.

I'd had enough of that crap in my life.

"Whoa is right," I agreed as I attempted to pay the taxi driver with my brand-new stack of euros. It looked like Monopoly money to me, and I had to keep reminding myself that it really was cash and not just printed pieces of pretty paper.

When he handed me change, which included about a dozen

different coins, I definitely had my first American moment but tried to play it cool as I shuffled through them and handed a couple back, making a tip of a few euros. I didn't even know if it was standard to tip in France, but he seemed pleased so I decided it was okay.

I probably should have spent less time shopping for clothes and more time researching cultural differences and how to count euros. Learning a few words in French would have been useful as well.

Oh well. This was an adventure. I was just adding to the mystery of it all.

Yeah, that sounded convincing.

Officially passing my first test with European currency, we hopped out of the taxi as the hotel doorman helped with the baggage. I'd stayed at several fancy hotels with August during our years together, and they all came with the typical doormen. Sharply dressed, always accommodating and happy to assist with whatever you may need. Most doormen were a dime a dozen.

These French doormen, though? They looked like they'd just stepped off the runway for *GQ*. Were all Frenchmen built this way? I gave Sarah a sideways glance as her eyes began to pop out of her head from all the man candy around us.

And the most amazing thing happened. They spoke. *Good God almighty.*

It was like hearing angels from heaven. Their accents were cultured, sophisticated, and made my insides feel like butter on a hot sticky day. That huge manila envelope Ryan had given me, filled with every detail of our trip, was instantly turned into a makeshift fan as we followed two men into the lavish hotel.

We were sorely disappointed to be greeted by a gorgeous young woman at the registration counter as the men bid us *au revoir*. I almost cried to see them walk away, understanding their evil plot completely now.

The tall, dark, and handsome men lured you in, trapping you in their beautiful hotel until you coughed up all your money for a room just in hopes of seeing them again.

"Visa or MasterCard?" the woman at the desk happily asked.

Works for me, I said to myself as I handed over my credit card for incidentals. As she went over the summary of our bill, my eyes nearly bugged out of my head at the amount Ryan had paid for the room. We had originally agreed to each pay for half, but in all the drama of breaking up and getting back together, he'd never asked for my share, and I'd completely forgotten about it.

More than likely that had been his plan all along.

A twinge of guilt settled in my stomach as the earlier feeling of glee fled like a cold breeze in autumn.

It's better this way.

We'll both be happier, I reminded myself.

And we would. In time.

"Your room is ready," the happy Frenchwoman announced after everything was signed and settled. "May I offer someone to assist you with your luggage?" she asked.

We both looked at each other eagerly as a mutual smile grew between us.

That's the great thing about a best friend.

The mutual mind meld.

We could look at each other and know what the other was thinking without words, and right now, I knew Sarah was wondering whether the bellhops were as hot as the doormen.

"Yes, that would be quite helpful," Sarah answered. I covered my mouth, trying not to giggle.

That ride up to the fifth floor was worth every single euro we handed over.

Turned out the bellhops weren't just as hot.

They were hotter.

*   *   *

"It's official," I announced, holding my wineglass in the air. "I'm never leaving!"

We'd just spent our first day in Paris, having narrowly avoided the infamous jet-lag curse. We'd successfully dropped off our luggage in the hotel room without laying down or even attempting to take any sort of nap.

When I'd first asked Sarah about this ridiculous practice, she'd told me it was a traveler's tried and true method.

"You're insane," I'd said.

"No, I'm serious. When you arrive in the morning after flying overseas from the States, you're supposed to stay up all day. No naps of any kind. It helps you adjust to the time difference."

"What about a catnap?" I'd argued on the plane.

"Nope."

"Ten minutes? Please?"

"No! Because ten minutes will turn into eight hours and then you'll wake up at seven at night and be completely turned around."

"Okay," I had finally relented. "You win."

So, I'd done as she'd said, and bypassed the luxury bedding, though it screamed my name as we freshened up in the bathroom,

reapplying makeup and changing out of our wrinkled plane clothing. I put on a comfortable pair of jeans and my favorite pair of
boots, threw a vibrant scarf around my neck and paired it with a
thick wool coat. I was ready to tackle the day.

Or at least I looked like it.

But as soon as we walked out onto the streets of Paris, I'd found
myself wide awake—no coffee needed. Although, I did find some.
Okay, a lot. A girl didn't change just because she was in another
country.

And this girl needed fuel—the caffeinated kind.

As we made our way through the city, I found myself falling
in love with a new side of me—a side I'd never known existed.
Growing up, I was never given the opportunity to travel. Summer
vacations and weekend trips to the beach weren't the norm in my
world, and as I got older, I'd just stayed in my little bubble of San
Francisco.

When I met August, we had spoken of traveling—the what if's
and future bucket lists, but in the beginning we'd never had the
money, and toward the end, there wasn't enough time because August was always working.

I'd always wanted to make time for this—for culture and art.
For people-watching and spending time with the ones I loved the
most. Walking down the streets of that ancient city, I realized an
entire world existed outside my door, and I wanted to discover
it all.

"One day, and you're already hooked on Paris, huh? Are you
sure that isn't the free wine talking?" Sarah joked, replying to my
declaration of love for my newfound home.

"Wasn't that amazing? Table wine! Freaking table wine, Sarah!

For free! Water—eight euros, but table wine is free! God, I love this country."

She laughed at my outburst and I watched her lift the half-empty glass of table wine she'd been nursing since we'd arrived at the local little restaurant recommended to us by one of our handsome doormen. After walking what felt like miles around Paris today, seeing everything from the Eiffel Tower to Notre Dame, we were just happy to be sitting and off our feet for the foreseeable future.

"I could see myself living here," I stated, looking around at the tiny apartments around us. Wrought-iron balconies, flower boxes—it was a perfect space in the middle of a Parisian paradise.

"You say that now, but wait until you see their rental prices. You thought San Francisco was expensive."

"It'd be worth it."

"You'll never leave the city," she said with certainty, grabbing a piece of fresh bread from the basket the waiter had just brought over.

"How do you know?" I asked, hating that she found me so predictable. I was building a new life. I didn't want to be seen as ordinary anymore.

"Okay, let me clarify. I don't see you leaving the city anytime soon." Each word was spoken through a mouth full of bread. For a ballerina, she really was kind of a mess sometimes.

"Why?"

She washed down her bread with a large sip of wine, placing the glass down in front of her. Looking up at me, she just stared as if it should be obvious. My eyes widened as it dawned on me.

"August? You think I'm staying in San Francisco because of August?"

"I think you will," she replied.

"You're crazy," I said, shaking my head as my arms fell across my chest defensively.

"Well, then leave. When we get home, pack up all your shit and move here. Picture it, Everly. Sit here and really picture it—leaving everything behind. You'd never see him again."

"I don't see him now," I argued.

She shrugged. "Yeah, but this would be permanent."

My face twisted in disgust. "I hate you. Why are you even doing this? I thought you hated the guy."

"I hate seeing you unhappy more."

"So you think I should just jump from one relationship back to another—never mind the fact that he doesn't want me anymore."

"You don't know that," she said, before adding, "And no, I don't think you should just hop back into something with August. But I do think you should start being honest with yourself. You didn't walk away from him because you didn't love him, Everly. Those feelings don't diminish overnight. You tried to make things work with Ryan and look where that led you—nearly walking down the aisle with the wrong man. So do us all a favor, take the time to decide what you want. For real this time."

"Okay," I agreed, hating the idea of even dedicating one second of thought toward August. But I knew she had a point. There was a reason I was avoiding the issue altogether. I'd thought I had come to terms with it all when I went back to Ryan, but really it was more like putting a Band-Aid on a seeping wound that was now festering out of control.

A Band-Aid could only do so much before infection set in, and I was definitely starting to spike an emotion fever.

We quietly finished our free table wine as we sat by the window and enjoyed the view. People walked their dogs, carried fresh groceries to their small apartments above the shops, and I heard the remnants of conversations pass by as friends met up for meals. It was so similar to home and yet so vastly different.

"Where do you see yourself in ten years?" I asked Sarah, bringing up the old question I'd once asked August.

"Ten years? Gross. I'd be, what? Thirty-five?"

"I'll be forty!" I laughed, playfully punching her in the arm. "Baby."

"Yeah, but forty for you is totally different. I'll be washed up, clocked out. Hell, even by thirty-five, I won't be able to find a job beyond teaching ballet to a bunch of snotty-nose kindergartners."

"Who says that won't be great?" I challenged her with a tilt of my eyebrow.

"Have you ever taught a bunch of kids?" she shot back.

"No," I laughed. "But how bad can it be? At least it will be in the field you love. And you'll still be dancing, Sarah. Maybe it won't be in front of a packed theater, as a prima ballerina, but it will be something."

"Yeah, I know. And you're right. Maybe I'll even have a couple snot-noses of my own by then," she said with a wink.

My mouth opened and I nearly dropped the wineglass I had in my hand.

"You can't be that serious with mystery man?"

"He has a name," she reminded me.

"Yeah—Miles. That's all I know about him."

"Well, he was coming to the wedding, but—"

"Oh, oops." I bit my lip and giggled.

"It's okay. We'll have him over for dinner when we get back and you can meet him then. All the mystery will finally be gone."

"So, you swear he's not a blow-up doll?"

Her head fell back as she laughed. "No, definitely not. He's... special to me," she explained as her face sobered. "I've never met anyone like him."

"Well, I can't wait to meet him. And all his rubbery parts."

"I hate you," she laughed.

"Right back at you. Can we go to bed now?" I begged, looking down at my empty glass of wine and picking over my plate of food.

"Oh God, yes," she replied, before adding, "Race you back to the hotel?"

"You're on, bitch," I said, throwing down enough euros to cover our bill and a little extra.

I have no idea who made it back first, but I do know I was the first to leap headfirst into the mountain of pillows that awaited us when we arrived.

We were both snoring exactly three seconds later.

Vive la France, indeed.

Chapter Twelve

August

Magnolia turned to me as the gates of her parents' picturesque neighborhood disappeared behind us. Night had fallen, and all I could see through the windows were darkened tree branches as we passed one after another in an endless sequence of twisted limbs. We'd stayed much later than planned and were just now making our journey back to the city.

"Ready to go home?" she said brightly, obviously searching for something to talk about to break the silence.

"No," I confessed, my voice hoarse and vacant.

After visiting someplace so bright and full of energy, the last place I wanted to return to was a home that felt more and more like a tomb with each passing day.

A mausoleum of memories I was desperate to preserve.

"We could go to my place," she suggested, leaning closer to me as her gentle finger grazed my chest, making her intent clear.

"Okay," I agreed as Everly's face flashed before my eyes one last time.

Good-bye, *I silently whispered, giving in to whatever new memories might come.*

But I hadn't made new memories.

Just new regrets.

Spending the night with Magnolia solidified our relationship and gave meaning to whatever was blossoming between us. Now, whatever happened, I knew without a shadow of a doubt I would end up hurting her.

Spending the day with her family, in her perfect world, had made me weak. I'd left that day craving something more, something real that I hadn't had in months, and Magnolia had been more than willing to give it.

Every touch of her skin against my body felt like a betrayal to my heart and mind. She was a beautiful, giving lover and any man would have been lucky to have her.

But my body, heart, and soul had already been handed over to someone long ago. What else was there to give?

"Am I doing something wrong?" she'd asked, pulling away as a veil of timid nervousness blanketed her features.

"No, I'm sorry. It's not you," I tried to reassure her, running a frustrated hand through my hair.

" 'It's not you, it's me'? That's what you're going for here?" she said with a frown.

"I know it's a cheesy line, but in my circumstances, it's true."

She rolled on her side, tucking the sheet around her, giving me space to speak.

"My illness wasn't the only reason I broke things off with you," I confessed.

Understanding blossomed across her face. "There's someone else." She looked down at the pillow as her fingers began weaving an invisible pattern across the fabric. Reaching down, I touched her chin and angled it upward.

"Yes, there was." Taking a deep breath, I added, "Still is, at least for me. I'm still trying to get over it."

"Do you want her back?" she asked timidly.

"It doesn't matter." I shook my head.

A single nod was all I got in response.

I don't know how long we lay together, side by side in bed, each waiting for the other to make a move, or to say something. It felt like an eternity.

"Look, I don't know where this is going to take us, but for now—let's just be this. Okay?" She leaned forward, kissing me long and slow, easing my loneliness with every touch, until I was drowning in her warmth. No other words were spoken.

I didn't think for the rest of the night. I just acted on impulse.

When I awoke the next morning to her hands slowly creeping along my chest, to her asking if I wanted a cup of coffee, I nearly bolted from the apartment and fled to the streets half-naked.

Dear God, what had I done?

I knew logically I hadn't done anything wrong. I was a single man. It was time for me to move on after the breakup. But why did I feel like a married man waking up in the wrong bed?

My heart ached at the memories of Magnolia's hands on me, and as much as that touch had helped soothe my loneliness, it only made things worse in the aftermath.

Because she wasn't Everly.

I hadn't moved an inch since I'd returned home this morning. After declining breakfast, a dickish move on my part but one that was desperately needed, I'd fled Magnolia's apartment and found my way back to my own place by cab.

Seeing her make coffee and attempt to assemble some sort of breakfast for me this morning had just been too much. It made it too real—brought back too many precious memories—and right now, I needed to be back home.

Surrounded by the ghosts of my past.

Magnolia's mom may have said a house is only a building, but for me, it was all I had left. And right now, I needed to fucking drown in it.

Laying back on the couch, I let the memories bury me, collapse over me, one after another. Everly's smile, her laugh as we'd chased each other through the house...the way she'd looked when we made love. The memories were few and far between, filled with expansive gaps, but they were enough.

They would always have to be enough.

Just as my eyes fell shut, the doorbell rang.

Slowly rising, I twisted and stretched, relieving the tension in my back and neck as I walked to the front door. Expecting a long overdue visit from Brick, I didn't even bother looking through the peephole to see who was waiting for me on the other side.

When I opened the door, I was nearly knocked over by shock.

"What the hell are you doing here?" I asked Ryan after rubbing my eyes to make sure I was actually seeing him standing at my front door.

"Wondering what the hell is wrong with you," he muttered, pushing past me.

"Please, come in," I joked darkly, watching him wander down the hallway toward the living room. I followed, still wondering what the hell he was doing here. He wandered around the room, looking at several framed pictures on the walls before settling into the chair on the opposite side of the room.

"Shouldn't you be on your honeymoon?" I asked, trying to sound as neutral as possible, but failing miserably. The venom in my voice was unmistakable as I glanced down at his left hand.

No ring.

"It's not me she wants," he answered, settling into the plush chair as if preparing for a long journey. With a huff, I decided to join him, favoring the couch.

"She left me," I reminded him. "And chose you."

"Only because she thought it was the right thing to do at the time. As did I."

He was dangling hooks, casting them out into the vast sea of my curiosity faster than I could comprehend. I had so many questions; I didn't know which to ask first.

Or if I should even ask them in the first place.

Nothing had changed. I still worked for a madman who burnt down buildings, killing innocent people when he got angry, and who was working on a one-way ticket to the slammer.

No good could come from being associated with me, and yet I still wanted to know why. Why hadn't she married him? Why wasn't she here?

"In the end, we weren't right for each other. We never were. I mistook friendship for love, believing that if you got along with someone well enough, that equated to the same thing as passion. It doesn't. I should have known the minute she left and went straight into your arms, seeking something more. Something I couldn't give her."

I opened my mouth to say something…anything. But all that came out was air.

"She still wants you, August."

"Did she tell you that?" I asked, tugging at that single hook he dangled in front of me.

"No," he answered. "She doesn't have to. It's written all over her face, etched in every movement of her body and fragile line of her soul. She's yours whether either of you know it or not."

"So what's the point in coming here, Ryan? Is this your good deed of the day? Is this your way of making yourself the better man? Again?"

Ryan had always had a way of making himself the hero of the story. I was usually the villain—a role I'd earned on multiple occasions.

"This isn't about me. It's about Everly. I may not love her the way I thought I did, but I still love her. And I always will. She's special, August, and you of all people should recognize that."

"I do," I nearly spat.

"Then why are you sitting around here doing nothing?" he roared, rising from his seat. It was the most anger I'd ever seen from the man. It was like hearing a menacing growl unfurl from a harmless-looking kitten, and suddenly realizing that the tiny creature with the sharp fangs and pointy claws was actually capable of vast danger.

"It's complicated," I replied.

"Then un-complicate it."

"It's not that easy! Look, she walked away from me. She. Left.

Me." I stood up, frustrated by this entire conversation. Didn't he understand that given the chance—a change in circumstances, I would run to Everly in a heartbeat?

"Yes, but why? What did you do to drive her away? She didn't leave because she stopped loving you, I know that much."

"What makes you so sure? I am known to be kind of an asshole," I replied with a touch of dark humor.

"She calls your name out in her sleep."

That one sentence gutted me to the core. I had no witty comeback. Nothing. I just sat there dumbfounded until he continued. I felt myself crumble back to the cushions of the couch.

"She has ever since I've known her. At first I thought it was just a PTSD thing—getting over the trauma of you."

I winced at the mere thought.

"But every so often she'd murmur things like, 'I'm sorry, August...so sorry.' I thought about asking her about it, but I figured she'd been through enough, so I let it go. You were not something either of us wanted to talk about—a big black void in our relationship until you actually woke up, and then it was like this giant elephant neither of us could get around. After you awoke, the dreams increased and suddenly she was calling out to you almost nightly. I tried to tell myself it was just the shock of having you back in her life, but deep down, I knew better. As time went on, it only got worse. Eventually I had to come to terms with the truth—that she was still in love with you. She always had been. I was just a placeholder until you came back."

"I don't know what to say," I answered honestly.

"I'm not looking for an apology," he said. "In a way, I guess we both used each other without realizing it. I wanted a relationship.

I was nearly starving for someone in my life and when I saw her in that coffee shop, I knew she was the one I wanted. I didn't take no for an answer, kept at her until she caved to my demands. I should have known then that we weren't right for each other. You shouldn't have to drag the woman of your dreams into your happily ever after. She should come willingly."

"And that's why you're here now? You think I'm that guy for Everly?"

He nodded, stuffing his hands in his pockets. "Haven't you always been? I mean, I don't know much about you two in the past, and I know things haven't always been easy, but I do know one thing. No matter what happens, you two always find a way back to each other. Eventually, Everly is going to need to find her way back to you. You need to be there when she does."

"What's in it for you?" I asked wearily.

"Knowing she's happy? That's all I need, believe me."

I eyed him with disbelief as we made our way toward the front door. As hard as I tried, I couldn't find any ulterior motive when it came to Ryan. He was a dying breed—the last of his kind. The gentle giant, a class-act gentleman who carried his heart on his sleeve and cared with every fiber of his being. I knew, had he actually married Everly, that he would have given everything to her, simply because of the promise he'd made and the principle behind it. He would have loved her as much as he could have and never wandered. It was just the type of man he was. I remember Everly telling me he'd been raised by older parents and part of me wondered if his blast-from-the-past mannerisms and notions were a nod to them.

Whatever the reason, I respected the hell out of him. Even if I couldn't do any of the things he asked of me.

Despite how much I wished I could.

"So, if you're here, does that mean Everly went on your honeymoon alone?" I joked as we reached the door.

"No," he answered with a smile. "She went with Sarah."

"Ouch," I replied with a shake of my head.

"It's fine. I was happy to give it to her. Especially after I got this," he said, pulling his phone out of his pocket to reveal a photo he had saved. Holding his phone out in front of him, he showed me a photo of Everly sitting in a tattoo parlor, her bright eyes gleaming as she smiled for the camera. All of her beautiful red hair was pulled to the side to reveal her bare shoulder, where a single new blackbird had been etched into her skin. Just outside its cage, the bird's great wingspan in mid-flight was gorgeous as she flew away from her prison.

"She's free," I found myself saying.

"Yeah, I guess she is."

She was making memories and discovering her own path around the world. It was all I'd ever wanted for her.

"That's my girl," I murmured as my face lit up in a smile. "That's my girl."

*   *   *

It was late.

My weekend events had left too many things to do and not enough hours to complete them. Leaning back in the uncomfortable leather chair that had probably cost more than most people's mortgages, I looked across the darkened office, noticing the dust that had accumulated on the equipment I'd once prized above all other possessions.

I couldn't even remember the last time I'd taken a photograph.

After Everly left, I'd lost the will to even touch a camera. What was the point? Photos were to capture cherished memories.

I no longer had any.

My favorite room in the house had become my prison. The one place I'd gone to for sanctuary was now nothing more than another place to push around papers and crunch numbers.

It was my personal form of hell.

Whatever part of my brain that had enjoyed doing this in my former life was obviously gone, lost in the shuffle—that battle of new and old, the modern and outdated me.

Some things remained the same, like the way I wore my hair and the type of toothpaste I preferred, while other parts of my personality felt as if they had become vastly different.

Before my memories had begun to resurface, it had been as if I were starting anew. A completely new model. A new prototype of August. The ancient model of myself preferred chocolate ice cream and loved cream in his coffee. The new me preferred vanilla and my coffee straight from the pot.

Now that the flashbacks had begun, it was like a melding of two lives. I was no longer a new version of myself, just a different version.

August 2.0.

I found myself liking things I hadn't six months ago, simply because I remembered them from the past. Various memories that had surfaced told me I had once had an overwhelming desire for power and wealth—much like Trent. This had been the crack in the perfect life Everly and I had once shared. As my payouts had become bigger and bigger, my need and drive for money had taken off. It became an addiction. At first, I'd done it all for her—wanting to give her everything under the sun, but then I'd lost sight of reality—of everything, really. Life became about money, just like Everly had said.

Those had been hard memories to relive—to see myself so altered, so driven by materialism. It was one addiction I hoped stayed forever in the past.

I didn't know how long this thing Trent had going could last. How long could he go on fooling everyone before the floor fell out beneath him and the precious empire he'd built was exposed for what it really was?

One dirty corruption after another. And unless I came up with some sort of brilliant plan—fast—all of us in that office were going down with him.

Coming up with the cash to buy my way out by swindling Magnolia and her family was growing on my conscience more and more with each passing day.

I'd become attached. Not just to Magnolia, but to her family as well.

If I stuck to my guns, went all in and worked Mr. Yorke like a pro, squeezing every dime I owed out of him, I could hand it straight over to Trent as I watched his smug face fall to the floor.

With my debt paid, I wouldn't have any reason to keep my current position. I could sell my partnership back over to Trent, assuming he'd allow it. If not, I'd just walk away.

I'd be free.

And Everly? I don't know, but I felt like there was something there that hadn't been there before.

Possibility.

But this all hinged on my ability to screw over one person I cared for to gain another.

Was I willing to do that? Could I? And if Everly ever discovered the depths I'd gone through to get her back—destroying other people's lives and breaking hearts—would she look at me in the same way?

My only other option was to do nothing. I couldn't hurt Magnolia and I wouldn't betray what little trust Everly still had in me.

I would find a way to get out of Trent's grasp, but one thing was for sure.

It wouldn't involve hurting others.

Chapter Thirteen

Everly

Sarah's magic cure for jet lag was crap.

I woke up the next morning—if you wanted to call it that—feeling like I'd been hit by a Mack truck.

Everything hurt. I felt at least ninety years old, maybe older.

"I'm dying," I groaned into my pillow, stretching my tired limbs one at a time.

"Rise and shine!" Sarah nearly sang, pouncing onto the bed we'd shared the night before. It was actually two beds, but when I'd called to adjust the hotel reservation from one bed to two, it was explained to me in broken English that we'd have euro beds. I'd just thanked them and laughed, saying no problem.

What the hell was a euro bed?

At the time I didn't care. My wedding had been canceled, my ex-fiancé had just handed me an all-expense-paid trip to Paris, and I was just trying to make sure Sarah and I had beds to sleep in.

We'd soon learned upon our arrival in Paris exactly what euro beds were. It was like a twin, only two were shoved together to make a queen, or maybe a full? I don't know—it was small. It was basically one bed that had a large divot down the middle.

It was a good thing I loved Sarah so much, because that little bed divider meant nothing to her. She was a bed hog and took more than her fair share of the euro beds, regardless of the rather large divider.

"Why are you so damn perky at this ungodly hour?" I whined into the soft fluffiness of my pillow, hoping that if I buried myself in deeply enough, she'd go away.

"It's not an ungodly hour—it's nearly ten in the morning!"

My eyes opened in surprise, but all I saw was the black fabric of my pillow shoved against my face. Rising up onto my elbows, I squinted and looked about with disdain.

"Ten in the morning? How is that possible? It feels like..."

"The middle of the night?" she guessed.

"Well, yes, actually."

"Jet lag, babe. Here, have some coffee. It will make everything better."

"Well, shit—why didn't you just start with that? Everything would have gone a lot smoother," I told her, grabbing the cup of espresso from her hand. I nearly stuck my entire head into the small cup, inhaling the nutty aroma. It was intense and dark, and my mouth was nearly watering as I wrapped my lips around it.

Within minutes, I was already beginning to feel the buzz and things were looking much brighter.

Caffeine is magical.

"So what are we going to do today?" I asked, pointing to the giant packet of information from Ryan.

When Ryan had handed it over, a twinge of embarrassment

seemed to pass over his face. At first I'd tried to ignore it, knowing things between us were still unsettled, but finally I couldn't let it go and I'd texted him, asking what had made him so nervous.

"There are things in there I'd planned especially for you—for our honeymoon. If you decide to not do them because you're with Sarah, or because you think they're corny or lame...just know I won't be offended," he'd written back.

I'd assured him I was fully confident in his abilities to plan a trip. A wedding, however? Well, I wouldn't trust either one of us with that task.

But as I sat there salivating over my cup of French coffee, I pulled out the packet and nearly lost it before breakfast had even been served.

"What is it?" Sarah asked, rushing over to my side.

I just held up a piece of paper, tears streaming down my cheeks.

"Oh, Everly..."

I couldn't even form words. I just nodded, wiping snot and tears from my face. It was gross, but I was a mess of emotions and I'd been deprived of a normal night's sleep.

"He really is the best guy," she said softly.

"I know." I looked down at the sheet of paper she'd handed back to me, confirming a reservation for two at an exclusive cooking school. He'd scheduled an entire day of cooking lessons for me, with a world-renowned chef.

A day of bliss—just for me.

"Shit! We'd better hurry. We need to be there in an hour!" Sarah announced as we both looked down at the reservation and simultaneously panicked.

"I'll take first shower, you take second!" she yelled, darting toward the bathroom faster than I could stop her. I mumbled under my breath but knew not to complain too much. When it came to both of us getting ready in the morning, I knew I was the quickest and most efficient. Even though I hated the feeling of wet hair, I was more or less okay with throwing my crimson locks up in a tight bun or topknot if there wasn't enough time for a blow-dry.

Sarah? She'd rather go out naked than let someone see her without perfectly polished hair. With little or no control as to how she had to wear it for work and performances, I believe she liked the ability to wear it any way she pleased when she was on her own time. Loose braids, wild curls or stick straight—she was always doing something different.

I just hoped whatever she chose today was quick.

After ten minutes, I stuck my head in the bathroom and gave her a five-minute warning as I began brushing my teeth. I heard the water turn off as soon as I finished gargling mouthwash.

We danced around each other as we got ready, and in no time I was showered, dressed, and wearing enough makeup to look presentable to the outside world. Knowing I would soon be covered in flour and sugar, I didn't put too much effort into my appearance.

Sarah, on the other hand, took every precious moment she had, primping, curling, and smoothing every surface until the very last second.

"Oh my God! We are just cooking! Can we go now?" I begged, pulling her toward the door of our hotel room.

"Okay, okay…can I just put a little perfume on?" she asked, wincing as she wiggled from my grasp and ran back to the bathroom.

"What for? Isn't Miles like a million...miles from here?" I giggled at the play on his name.

"Funny. And yes," she answered. "But I still like to smell good." She came racing back to the door, smelling like vanilla and some sort of flower. I crinkled my nose, a little overwhelmed by the smell as we grabbed our purses and headed out.

One of the handsome doormen was more than delighted to hail us a taxi and we were just as happy to sit there and watch him do it. I'd never been much of a man-ogler, having spent the entirety of my adult life in committed relationships, and part of me still felt guilty for standing here doing it now.

But this was the whole point of this vacation. Trying new things, discovering the real me. Maybe the real Everly wasn't meant for long-term relationships and was best suited for something more casual. Perhaps ogling men all day long was exactly what I needed.

Just then I spotted a man walking down the street in a pair of Converse and a button-down shirt, carrying an antique camera, and my heart stopped. His deep laughter was accompanied by a beautiful female's as she tugged on his arm and they happily fled down an alleyway.

It wasn't him. Just another ghost.

Even now, he still haunted me. Even without the suit and the fancy clothes.

Would it ever stop? *Did I want it to?*

"Come on," I said, feeling frustrated as a taxi pulled up in front of our hotel. "Let's get going. I don't want to be late."

The cooking school was outside the tourist areas of Paris and took a decent cab ride to get there. I was surprised by how quickly the scenery changed outside our taxi window as we left the pristine shops and historical landmarks behind and drove through the more lived-in areas of the city. It wasn't that we were entering a ghetto or someplace seedy; our surroundings just felt less grand and opulent. I guessed it would be like if a child stepped behind the scenes at Disney World and those illusions were shattered. Life in Paris wasn't everything I thought it was, based on my narrow view from my touristy hotel windows. People actually lived here, and not the way I'd envisioned—perched above a high-end retailer with beautiful flower boxes and cute little balconies. There were actual apartment buildings and skyscrapers—busy freeways and graffiti. Suddenly, Paris was just like any other city I'd been to. Loud, boisterous, and compact.

"Starting to rethink your move?" Sarah smirked, nudging my shoulder as we pulled up to the curb of the rather understated building that housed the cooking school.

"Shut up," I laughed. "It was the red wine talking."

"I know. Now come on, let's go make lunch, or rather…you make lunch, and I'll stand there and look pretty for our sexy chef."

"How do you know he's going to be sexy—how do you even know it's going to be a guy?" I asked with a grin as I waited for her to pay the driver. We had been taking turns on paying for things, figuring it would all even out at the end. It was her turn to ante up for the cab fare.

"I guess I was just hoping our luck with Frenchmen would continue."

Unfortunately for Sarah, her luck ran out the minute we were escorted inside and introduced to our chef for the day—who was most definitely not male.

Chef Corrine was an up-and-coming chef in the cooking world.

She was also so damn beautiful, it nearly hurt to look at her. After a brief introduction, I was beginning to have serious regrets about my previous makeup and hair choices, and instantly wanted to run back to the hotel for a few more minutes of primping, just so I could feel like I had a fighting chance standing next to her.

"Dear Lord," Sarah whispered next to me.

"I know. It's like staring into the damn sun," I hissed back. We followed Corrine into the first kitchen, where we would assemble the bulk of our meal. No one should look that good in a chef uniform.

It was explained to us that Chef Corrine would assist us with the side dish and main course and Chef Jacques, one of the owners and a pastry chef to the stars, would step in and help us with dessert.

I was nearly panting with excitement.

We were each given an apron with the school logo and name on the front. They'd even gone the extra step and had each of our names embroidered underneath. That, of course, required several pictures of each of us, pointing and laughing at our names, which would later be posted to social media. It was fantastic. I couldn't wait to bring home my official apron and wear it to cook my own meals.

Wherever home might end up being.

New thought. Definitely new thought.

Much of the prep work had been done ahead of time to make the process go more quickly, but Corrine did leave some of the more fun aspects of cooking for us to do. Our side dish for the day was a cheesy Italian risotto and my mouth literally watered as she pulled out the various cheeses we were going to use.

Even if Paris had diminished slightly on our ride here, becoming more of a normal city and less of a fairytale, nothing could take away the love affair I had with its cheeses.

Or bread.

Or food in general.

I could probably just eat cheese, bread, and red wine in this country and be perfectly happy for the rest of my life. I'd weigh about eight thousand pounds, but I'd be really happy about it.

Sarah kept her promise and mostly stood there and watched, enjoying the free wine that came with our lesson. I, on the other hand, became completely engrossed in everything Corrine said, feeling like I was in my element for the very first time.

"You're really very good at this," Corrine mentioned as we transferred the risotto into a display dish.

"Thank you," I answered with a faint blush that slowly crept up my cheeks. "I love to cook at home."

"Have you ever considered attending a school?" she asked in her thick French accent.

I shook my head and then stopped myself. "A few times, but not seriously."

"You should. I think you would do very well."

A goofy, lopsided grin appeared on my face as I caught Sarah staring at me from across the counter. She gave me a wink as I continued to work alongside Corrine, feeling the jitters of something big welling up inside me.

The possibility of more.

The rest of the day was nothing short of amazing. From the risotto, we moved on to braised lamb, and then we were taught how to make the French favorites—macaroons. Sarah actually dirtied up her apron for the sweets and helped make the beautiful lemon yellow cookies. Having the handsome older man in the room didn't hurt, either.

Playing host to many of these private cooking events daily, the cooking school had everything down to a science. Once our cookies were pulled out of the oven, we were seated on a beautiful terrace and everything we'd made throughout our two-hour class was served on beautiful plates with root vegetables and sprigs of rosemary.

"Wow, did you do that?" Sarah asked, looking down at the plate.

I shook my head, laughing. "You really weren't paying attention, were you? No, they made up the plate while we were in the dessert room."

"They handed me wine. What was a girl to do?" she shrugged.

We dove in, pairing the risotto with the perfectly cooked lamb.

"Dear Lord, I'm never going to fit into a tutu again," Sarah moaned, as one of my own followed hers.

"Guess your understudy will have to take over permanently," I joked, knowing she was still slightly bitter over the woman taking her part while she was on this impromptu vacation with me.

"Don't ruin this for me."

We finished up, nearly licking our plates clean, just as our cookies arrived. Our eyes widened as a special dessert was also presented. The chef had made a chocolate torte in our honor, with a tiny sugar decoration on top.

"Our poor little cookies look very sad next to this," Sarah laughed.

I joined her, picking up a tiny macaroon and setting it on the plate with the elaborate dessert. "I bet they both taste amazing, though."

"Only one way to find out!"

We dug in and ended up polishing off the entire basket of cookies as well. Sitting back in our chairs with a final glass of wine, we
made jokes about needing to be rolled out of the school in wheel-
barrows as they took our plates away.

"Thank you for coming with me," I finally said as I took my last
sip of wine.

"Thank you for asking."

"I have one favor, though," I added.

"Anything."

"Can we stop somewhere on our way back to the hotel? There's
something I really want to get before I go home."

"Oh! Is it Chanel?" she asked, her eyes wide with excitement.

I laughed, wine nearly coming out of my nose.

"No. It's definitely not Chanel. I want to get a tattoo."

*   *   *

"This damn thing itches like a motherfucker!" I whined, turning in
the bathroom to sneak another peek at the little bird resting on the
other side of my shoulder.

No longer stuck in that cage. *She was finally free.*

Now I just needed to work on me.

"Well, don't scratch it!" Sarah yelled from the bedroom as I pivoted back around to face the mirror properly. It was late.

Like, ten o'clock at night late. And I'd somehow allowed myself
to be talked into going out to a nightclub.

"What fun is being single if you don't have a little fun?" Sarah
had said, pulling out a sexy black dress I'd shoved in my suitcase at
the last minute.

A last-minute decision I was really starting to regret.

"You're not single," I'd reminded her, throwing my arms across my chest in protest.

"But I'm not dead, either. Now get dressed. We're too young to be going to bed this early—in Paris of all places!"

And that was why I was currently in the bathroom, applying mascara, rather than cozied up in my warm flannel pajamas reading.

With makeup finished and a quick fluff of my hair, I stepped out of the bathroom to a barrage of catcalls and other obscene noises.

"You're obnoxious."

"Just trying to prepare you for what you'll hear when we leave this room," Sarah laughed. "Come on! The doorman—you know the one with the hot ass?"

I gave her a vacant stare.

"Right. They all have nice butts. Anyway, one of them was telling me about a club that isn't too far from here. I want to check it out."

"Lead the way."

"You could try to sound excited," she said, pinching my elbow.

I just sent a glare in her direction.

"Who knows, maybe you'll find some French action to bring back with you?"

My eyes widened as I stopped in the middle of the hallway. "You've got to be kidding me."

"What?"

"That's why we're doing this? To get me a piece of ass?"

"Well." Her eyes batted in feigned innocence. "Not entirely, but if the opportunity presented itself, I wouldn't want you to feel like you had to turn it down. I'd be more than glad to disappear for the night. I'm sure I could find a sofa or a nice chair in the lobby to sleep in for a few hours."

"Oh my God," I said, my hands flying up in the air like a madwoman as I began to pace erratically up and down the hallway. I sincerely hoped the walls around us were either thick or the rooms were empty because I was not even attempting to be quiet as I had my mini meltdown on the fourth floor.

"I can't handle this right now. I am so not prepared. Do you even know when the last time was that I picked up a guy?" I asked her, using air quotes to prove my point.

"Are you afraid your lady parts are shriveled up down there? Because I remember some of the things you said you did with August…and let me assure you," she said with a mischievous grin. "You are definitely not dead."

"Dear Lord, let's just go," I replied, trying not to let my mind wander back.

No cab fare was needed on this excursion, since the club was within walking distance—although several blocks in I was beginning to regret our decision to walk as my feet began to ache in my five-inch heels.

There was a long line of people waiting outside for bouncer approval, and the music could be heard nearly a block away. It reminded me of my earlier days, hanging out in clubs with no clue what I was doing in life.

That wasn't much different from now, actually.

We got in line amidst the glares and womanly comparisons of outfits and hair and waited our turn. We apparently had something going for us because when we got to the front, we passed the bouncer test and got the wave to go in. Looking over at Sarah, I raised an eyebrow wondering how we managed to make it through. She simply smiled and shrugged her shoulders. "I gave him a flirty wink. He must have liked it."

"Did you show him some boob, too?" I asked, wondering why we'd made it in and the half-naked girls in front of us had been ushered away.

She just rolled her eyes as we dodged and weaved our way through all the people toward the bar. The music was reverberating through my chest, a constant mixture of top forty hits I recognized and foreign music that seemed to please the locals.

We bought drinks and managed to find a small table by sheer dumb luck, and began one of my favorite activities in a place like this—people watching. The club wasn't so different from the ones I'd been to in the States. People were divided into large and small groups, all huddled together, laughing and smiling. Couples clung together on the dance floor, nearly making love with their clothes on. I tried not to stare—or let my jealousy show.

"Okay, let's play," Sarah said, waggling her eyebrows.

"Oh come on! Seriously? You get me all dressed up, drag me out at this late hour and this is what you want to do?"

"Well, if I can't talk you into picking up men, then yes," she said, her bottom lip jutted out for effect. "This is what I want to do."

"Okay, fine. But I'm not sure it will work in a foreign country. We've never even tried it outside of San Francisco," I warned.

"I guess there's only one way to find out," she grinned, holding her vodka tonic up in the air for a celebratory toast. Thrusting my drink toward hers, I joined in with a laugh as we set our sights on the crowd.

Ever since we'd become friends, we'd had this little game we would play when out in clubs or parties. Given that we were both avid people watchers, it gave us something to talk about, rather than just sit next to each other silently sipping drinks like losers.

Instead, we were losers who invented weird story lines about the people we watched and laughed over the ridiculous fantasies we created. I didn't say it was a great game—but it gave us something to do during social events when both of us were feeling slightly less than social.

Sarah might act like the social butterfly of the century, but when push came to shove, she was actually quite the introvert. Weighed down by years of self-loathing and constant body image issues, she'd come a long way, but it was still difficult for her to be the first to make an introduction or walk into a room of unknowns. She could be social if surrounded by people she knew, but she tended to stick close to home and those she knew—those who made her feel safe.

"I get to pick first!" she said loudly, over the sound of the music. "What about those two?" She pointed to a couple huddled in a corner booth. The woman was much older than the man, probably by decades, but both were stunning. Their efforts at being discreet were failing miserably as I noticed his hand sneak up her inner thigh. I felt my cheeks redden as I turned away.

"Wealthy cougar?" I guessed as I swiveled the tiny straw around in my drink.

Sarah gave me a less than enthused look. Her eyes slanted downward as she tried not to smile through her frown.

"That was pathetic. Try again."

"I told you this might not work in France," I shrugged. "Cultural differences."

"You're not trying!"

"Fine. How about this? She's a former trophy wife, but obviously things have started to go south as things tend to do after a certain age—even with exceptional maintenance." I coughed, emphasizing my meaning of "maintenance."

Sarah grinned. "Yes, go on."

"Her billionaire husband has lost interest in her, choosing to upgrade to something...newer, let's just say. She's angry, vengeful. She's done nothing but primp and keep herself in pristine shape for him! She's even had her vagina retightened for him!"

"Wait...hold up," Sarah said, waving her hands around as she tried not to spit out her drink. "You can do that?"

"Why do I know these perverted things, and you don't?" I asked, laughing. "Yes, you can do that. We live in a world where almost anything is possible. Why wouldn't that be one of them? You can also have your hymen repaired," I added with a wink.

"Why? Seriously? So people are going in and having their hymens reconstructed so they can be born-again virgins? That's a thing?"

I shrugged my shoulders.

"Okay, moving on. Your trophy wife."

"Right. So rather than leave him, she decides to beat him at his own game. She'll cheat on him! Because who needs maturity when you have money, right? That's when Don Juan Sexy Pants enters the scene. She finds him on Tinder...or whatever the equivalent is here in France and well, let's just say, Mrs. Trophy Wife will be having a grand old time tonight."

I took a sip of my drink and looked up at her, waiting. "How was that?" I finally asked.

"I'm sorry, I'm still stuck on vaginal surgery. I don't think I heard anything past that," she confessed as I burst into laughter.

"My turn!" I announced, searching around the club for our next victim. I found him at the bar, waiting to order. He appeared to be alone as he leaned against the sleek wood, tapping his fingers as the bartender all but ignored him.

"Him," I said, singling him out with my index finger.

"I hate when you pick a loner. They're always so difficult."

I just grinned and sat back in my chair, waiting and watching as she sized him up. He was attractive, wearing dark pants that hugged him in all the right places. A tight knit shirt made it achingly apparent that he didn't have more than an ounce of body fat on his six-foot-plus frame, which was making me seriously regret all the bread and cheese I'd consumed since arriving in Paris.

I didn't understand how the French stayed so thin. It was mind-boggling.

"Okay, I'm ready," Sarah announced, taking a deep breath, as if she were getting ready to do something incredibly impressive, like sing the National Anthem, or give a speech on poverty.

I ignored her dramatics and waited for her to begin.

"I believe our loner friend is on a secret mission. Notice the unassuming way everyone seems to pass by him? He's almost invisible. How does someone that good-looking go unnoticed?"

"It's France?" I wagered a guess. "All the men around here seem to be hot."

"That guy who gave us a cab ride to the cooking school yesterday?" she reminded me.

The toothy, nearly bald man's face came to mind. "Okay, not all the men. But the ratio seems to be more favorable than home."

"Anyway," she said, clearly moving on with her espionage story. "He's here on a secret mission, and his goal is to remain as incognito as possible. Don't arouse suspicion. So that's why he's being so patient at the bar. Raise a hand...call out? Instantly, someone will remember his face, because he was a jerk."

"Your story sucks," I said, giving her a big thumbs down.

"Oh, and yours didn't? Cougar? Really? Try something original next time!"

"At least now you know you can get that shit tightened down under," I laughed.

"Oh please, there is nothing of mine that isn't tight."

"Gross. Just gross," I said, pretending to gag. We were so involved in our conversation that I barely noticed someone else had approached our table until I looked up and saw the loner from the bar making his final steps toward us.

My cheeks flushed instantly, knowing we'd just been discussing him at length without his knowledge.

He smiled and uttered something in French. I giggled like a foolish schoolgirl and replied in English.

"I'm sorry, I don't speak French."

"American?" he asked.

I simply nodded.

"My apologies. I was simply asking if I could buy you a drink."

My belly was instantly a jumble of nerves, as everything came to life, dancing and fluttering inside. I glanced over at Sarah, who was giving me the slightest nod, with eyes that said if I said no, I was an absolute fool.

"Sure, but I do have a rather odd question for you first."

"But of course," he graciously agreed.

"What do you do for a living?" I asked.

He was a bit confused by my turn of phrase, so after a brief explanation, he nodded his head in understanding and answered, first in French as he searched to find the English word.

"Taxes," he finally answered, looking for something more specific. "I'm an...accountant."

I caught Sarah's expression out of the corner of my eye as she shook her head and silently spoke the word "spy." I fought the urge to roll my eyes.

What had I just gotten myself into?

Chapter Fourteen
August

I hated work lunches.

It took all the joy out of the simple pleasure of eating.

Instead of eating at my desk or fleeing from the office like I normally did most days, I'd let Trent pull me in on another one of his client lunches where he made me dance like a pony and did what he did best.

Lied his ass off.

It was enough to make me lose my appetite.

The only benefit to these work lunches was that Trent always paid, and there was plenty of alcohol. Coming back to the office with a healthy buzz always made the rest of the day go by a little faster.

It also helped numb well...everything. And lately I was enjoying the tangible feeling of absolute oblivion. The memories were coming faster, each random and varying in length, but they pushed me further and further down the path of self-destruction.

I'd always known the type of man I was, but now I was seeing it firsthand. I watched memories of my former self fall from grace, my own future fall by the wayside.

The night before, I'd had my first memory of locking Everly up. I understood now—the fear behind why I'd done so. Trent had become less of a business partner and more of an evil over-lord through the years—pushing my paranoia until greed had driven me a bit insane. I could feel the fear running through my thoughts as I'd clicked the lock securely into place and walked away, listening to her sobs as she'd begged for an answer I never gave her.

So many mistakes.

I'd also eventually realized after several long nights, as the flash-backs played over and over in my head, how much I'd neglected my long-lost friends Vodka and Bourbon. They were quiet, didn't ask a lot of questions, and always managed to make me feel better with-out much fuss. They also dulled the memories.

This was exactly the kind of comfort I'd been requiring lately.

It was the only kind of friendship I deserved.

I'd lost count of the number of times Magnolia's number ap-peared on my cell phone as a missed call. I hadn't spoken to her since our single night together. Try as I might to avoid it, I'd be-come the man I had feared—the one who takes and takes with little remorse.

Only, I had remorse. And guilt, regret, and pain.

I'd just chosen not to do anything about it.

I could have answered her phone calls, apologized for not being the man she'd hoped I could be. I could have ended things civilly, with the maturity someone my age should have.

Instead, I dove inside a bottle and drowned myself over and over, wishing I could rewrite time.

Men like Trent, the masters of fortune and fame, thought they owned the world with their riches and ridiculous bank statements. They tossed around cash like it was paper and laughed at others' misfortunes because they couldn't fathom walking in someone else's shoes. Money was the ultimate commodity and they ruled it—owned it and completely dominated it.

But if you looked around, at the old and the dying—visited a man saying good-bye to his ailing wife after eighty years of marriage—there was always one thing people desired more than money.

One thing they would give everything up for in a heartbeat.

Time.

If someone could figure out a way to harness time—to give that dying man an hour or even a day more on this earth with his wife? Or if someone could manipulate time and send them back so they could start all over again?

He'd be a god among men.

I knew I'd surely give every dime I owed and more to go back to the moment when I'd first shook Trent's scaly, double-crossing hand, leaving my comfortable job behind to go work for a shark. What would my life with Everly be like now if I'd walked away from him? If I'd said no and we'd settled into our shabby low-key life?

I guess I'd never know.

Because time wasn't for sale, and no matter how hard you

tried—you'd never get a second chance to go back and fix your wrongs.

Life was nothing more than a series of choices—right or wrong, good or bad. How we sorted through—that mess was the real test, and I guess I'd failed. Miserably.

I shuffled through papers and entered data into the spreadsheet I was working on, not really caring about the work I was doing, as my earlier buzz slowly wore off. My eyes moved to the tiny numbers at the bottom of the screen, noticing the time.

Two in the afternoon. At least three more hours until I could leave.

This wasn't how a life should be lived. Staring at clocks, waiting for time to shuffle on. It was a waste—a horrible waste of a life—and I hated that the man I'd been just mere months earlier had succumbed to this paltry existence.

A tiny buzz against my desk caught my attention and I looked down to see a notification pop up on my phone.

A new text message. From Everly.

My hand shook as I picked up the phone, unlocking it to read the message.

It contained one single word.

"Rutherford."

My eyebrows furrowed in confusion, and I wondered if perhaps she'd texted me by mistake. I don't know how long I sat there staring at that one word, as my mind went through every conversation, every memory, trying to remember something about a person named Rutherford. Finally, as my brain was nearly squeezed dry, empty of ideas, she sent another text.

"Norbert."

And then it dawned on me.

"Do you remember our baby name game?" she'd asked me that night on the phone, her words slurring together in a haze as the liquid truth serum known as alcohol coursed through her veins.

Now that I knew the meaning behind her odd texts, I found myself filled with even more confusion.

What did this mean? How did I even respond?

One final text came in, a plea. *"Please, August."*

After several moments of all-out war with myself that involved serious pacing around my office and several curse words, I finally came to a conclusion.

No good could come from answering those texts.

I didn't respond.

Brick had said I had a choice when it came to Everly. I could choose to involve her in my life, and the choices I'd made, or I could make the mistake of leaving her in the dark.

That was where she belonged.

Darkness kept her safe.

*   *   *

Ignoring Everly became an internal struggle for the rest of the afternoon. It left me irritable and edgy, so much so that I'd nearly leapt toward the door the second the clock hit five, muttering that I'd finish the rest of my work from home.

The crashing ocean waves did nothing to soothe my restless disposition as I settled in for the night, trading my suit and tie for a pair of jeans and a tattered old henley shirt. I downed a second glass of bourbon, feeling it ease my tense muscles.

Looking down, I pressed the button on my phone, checking for alerts for the hundredth time since I'd arrived home. I hadn't let go of the damn thing in hours, clinging to it like a lifeline. My lifeline to her.

She'd contacted me—despite the way I'd acted toward her in the dress shop as she'd stood there looking like a damn angel from heaven. She'd looked down at me with such a raw panic in her eyes. How long had she been carrying that secret with her? What kind of damage did that do to such a pure soul? There must have been a thousand times since that moment that I wished I could have told her I didn't blame her for that night. But I hadn't.

Because what better way to keep her away than fear?

But even fear, it seemed, couldn't keep Everly away.

Now, on my fourth or fifth glass of liquor, I bypassed the kitchen, choosing a liquid diet for the evening, and stumbled to the couch. Flipping through the channels, I found an old movie about a lone detective hired to unveil the dark underbelly of the Las Vegas mob. Slowly unconsciousness took over, and I fell asleep. Reality fell away and I found myself on the gritty streets of a long-ago Vegas metropolis.

Trent had replaced the mob master and I was the detective sworn to bring him in. But no matter how hard I tried, I could never get what I needed. He was always one step ahead, smiling his way to the bank. Nothing got past him and I found myself flat on my face, trying to protect the people I loved.

The woman I loved.

If I could just get him behind bars...everything would be fine.

Everyone would be safe.

I was startled back awake when my phone, still in my grasp, vibrated to life, pulling me back into reality.

Jumping up, I cursed as the ice from my cup fell into my lap. The cold to my nether regions sent another string of obscenities from my mouth as I pushed the ice that had fallen into my lap to the rug and looked down again at the phone.

Everly.

My heart sped into overtime as my muddled, liquefied brain tried to make a decision.

I really should have eaten something for dinner.

That reasonable, level-headed August from this afternoon, who made good, sensible choices, was halfway down a barrel of bourbon now, singing show tunes, giggling about flying elephants.

I picked up the phone and answered it without thinking.

Impulsivity for the win.

"Hello." I staggered.

"You've ruined me," she stated.

"S'cuse me?" I tried saying. "I believe *you* ruined me."

Silence followed as she most likely tried to comprehend my words. "No, no . . . no, no. This is not how this phone call is going to go. I had a plan when I picked up the phone. I have things to say, and I'm going to get them out. You are not going to detour me."

"Okay," I answered, feeling my head sway slightly as I tried to stay upright.

How much had I drunk?

"I went on a date tonight and, ah hell—are you drunk?"

"Yep," I answered rather quickly. "I recently discovered I really like bourbon. Did I always like bourbon?"

"What?" she asked out of confusion.

"You went on a date?" I asked, changing the subject.

"Oh, um…yes. Right, I went on a date," she said, seeming to get back to her point. "And doesn't that sound a bit fucked up to you?"

"I don't know. I've never met the guy," I answered with a tiny shrug. I gave myself a mental pat on the back. Even drunk, I could be aloof. And funny.

"What? No, August. Not the specific guy—the sheer fact that, less than three weeks after I called off my wedding, I went on a date. Not a hookup, or a one-night stand. An actual date. With a guy. Why would I do something like this? Why?"

"Was he good-looking?"

"I hate you," she muttered.

"Good," I answered.

"Why? Why do you want me to hate you?" she pushed, seeing through my drunken state to something deeper, something I knew I couldn't share.

"You shouldn't be dating, Everly," I finally said, giving her the answer she was seeking. "You need to be spreading those new wings you have. Give yourself time."

"You think I don't know this? And how do you know about my wings?" she asked, suspicion tinting her words.

"What wings?" I played dumb.

"Never mind. It's seriously hard to talk to you when you're drunk. Anyway, it's what I've been telling myself since the moment I called the wedding off—I need to be single. I haven't been alone since I was eighteen. I don't know how. I've been dependent on someone else for the entirety of my adult life. And yet, every time I think about being alone in this world, I want to run back to you."

Her tone changed, like a dam cresting over. Suddenly that anger she'd come into the conversation with spilled over, giving way to waves of emotions I guessed she'd been holding deep inside.

"You don't want me. Not really," I tried to convince her. "You're just scared."

"How can you be so sure?"

Taking a deep breath as I tried to steady my thoughts, I stood, making my way toward the wide windows that opened out to the darkened sea below.

"Because I'm a fucked-up mess. Because someday, you're going to meet someone who makes you want to fly—who doesn't cage your beauty or squash your dreams. That partner who encourages rather than holds you back—and when you do, I'll be nothing but a distant memory you'll eventually forget."

"I could never forget you," she whispered, her words shaking.

"Take it from me, even the most precious of memories can be forgotten."

The quick intake of air told me she'd taken my words the wrong way, and I quickly opened my mouth to apologize, but the sobering side of me realized it was probably for the best not to.

"You know," she said in the small voice. "Sometimes I wish it was me—who'd ended up in that hospital bed. I wish it was me who'd forgotten everything—who forgot you."

Now it was me who was speechless and searching for air.

"Why?" I asked.

"Because then I wouldn't feel this never-ending pain each day when I'm not with you. I wouldn't know what it feels like to love someone who doesn't want me." Her voice grew louder. "And I wouldn't remember all the ways you broke my heart." She breathed a long, defeated breath before saying, "Good-bye, August."

She didn't bother waiting for me to respond as I heard the line go dead.

My heart quickly followed as I fell deeper into the blackness.

*   *   *

I called in sick the next morning.

Or at least I think I did.

I remember picking up the phone, punching in a series of digits and announcing I wouldn't be showing up to work that day.

Sounded legit to me.

Frankly, I really didn't give a fuck. Trent could drive his ass over here and drag me back to that prison he called an office if he wanted. It didn't matter.

None of it mattered.

Because, like the good lapdog I was, I'd always go back. Tomorrow, I'd put on my freshly laundered suit, neatly matching necktie, and walk out the front door, ready to do whatever the hell he told me.

This was what my life had become.

For her.

And she wanted to forget—everything.

Every lingering touch, each single kiss that had slowly etched her name to my soul—erased from her mcmory.

"Jesus—did you drink all of that?" Brick's abrasive voice cut through the silence as my dark thoughts ceased and I found myself looking up at the old man from the living room couch I'd slept on all night.

"What's it to you?" I said, my words coming out in quick succession. I tried squinting to stop the light beaming in from the windows from being so damn bright. Raising a hand above my head, I tried to focus on my good friend whom I hadn't seen in ages. He still looked much the same. Khaki shorts had been traded in for a pair of jeans due to the colder weather and his button-down was another version of something I'd seen before.

Good old predictable Brick Abrams.

"I see you're not any more pleasant than the last time I saw you," he replied, rubbing his forehead and letting out a frustrated breath of air. I watched him as he turned, taking a seat in the chair across the room. He settled in, lifting his leg across his knee as he studied me.

As if I was a lab rat.

"I'm not your client anymore, Brick. You can't just show up like this. Why are you even here?" I didn't like when he looked at me like a patient, or someone that needed help.

There wasn't a damn thing he could do to help me. Not anymore.

"You called me."

"What?" I asked in confusion.

"I was still in bed this morning when I got a call from you. Seemed rather odd since I haven't heard from you in months, but I figured maybe you'd turned a new leaf. Maybe you were ready to make amends. But when I answered, all I got was a drunken string of unintelligible words that obviously weren't meant for me."

Realization dawned on me.

"I meant to call my secretary," I clarified.

"I finally got that after a moment or two," he answered.

My eyes flickered to my phone as I realized I'd never actually called the office. I might talk a big game when the alcohol was free-flowing in my body, but the idea of Trent coming here to my home, looking for me, wasn't high on my to-do list for the day.

I mostly just wanted to crawl into a bed with a bottle of Advil and never resurface.

"I called your office," Brick announced, regaining my attention.

"You did?"

He nodded. "I pretended to be you and feigned a cold. Your secretary wishes you a speedy recovery."

"Thank you," I said, the single two words falling from my mouth like bricks as the weight of everything I'd done, or rather the lack of what I'd done, finally crashed around me.

It was a sobering moment.

"I don't know what to do anymore, Brick," I confessed, sitting forward as my head fell into the palms of my hands. "I thought I could push her away. I thought I could keep her safe this way but it's not that simple. Nothing between Everly and me is ever simple."

"Do you want her back?" he asked simply.

"Every damn day of my life," I answered. "Each day I crawl out of bed fighting the urge to race back to her and beg her to forgive me. It's exhausting, Brick, and I'm fucking tired of fighting it. But I will. If it means keeping her away from Trent, I'll keep doing it."

"You could always—"

"No. I can't tell her. She'd never leave my side, and if anything happened to her..." I shook my head as I imagined the possibility—the poor man in that art gallery. Even confessing everything to Brick was a risk, but one I'd taken because I needed an outlet, and when my whole world fell apart those days after Everly left, he seemed like the only viable option.

I should have known better than to spill all my secrets to a shrink. Or whatever he called himself.

"Trent will do anything to keep me on track—to use me as he pleases. I get the feeling that there is something else going on here. Fifty million is a lot of money, and yeah—I get that it's an epic fuck-up on my part, but I just wish I had all the missing pieces of the puzzle. I feel like I'm working with only half of the information, and it's frustrating as hell."

"Would you ever consider hypnosis?" Brick asked, and my interest suddenly piqued. I looked up, my eyebrows raised. "You can do that?"

"Yep," he said with a hint of cockiness shadowing his tone.

"Why haven't you ever mentioned it before?"

He shrugged. "Before, when none of your memories had surfaced, I didn't want to give you false hope, so I focused more on helping you cope with the cards you'd been dealt. After your memories resurfaced, well... you basically shut me out and I wasn't going to force my expertise on you, was I?"

"No," I said, slightly dazed. "I guess not. When can we start?" I asked, rising from the couch excitedly.

"Not so fast, Bourbon King. You need to sober up. And from the state of this living room, I sincerely doubt that's going to happen any time soon. I'll be back in a few days. Try to lay off the booze until then."

"Okay," I answered.

"And August?" he said, before he disappeared down the hallway.

"Yeah?"

"For what it's worth...I don't think you should give up hope on your future with Everly. You've found a way back to each other before; don't doubt that you'll do so again."

He didn't wait for a response, and as I heard the door latch quietly click, signaling his departure, I wondered if he could be right.

Was there a way back to Everly? Or had I burned all the bridges that marked my path back to my happily ever after?

Chapter Fifteen

Everly

A few days after we returned home from Paris, I began to wonder if there was an actual name for what I was feeling.

Did most people feel this type of depression when resuming the everyday monotony of their life after experiencing the once in a lifetime charm only Paris could give?

The streets didn't have the same sense of excitement, the coffee wasn't nearly as exotic, and hell—even the cookies lacked that whimsical color only the French could perfect. Yesterday afternoon, I'd spent hours searching for the right type of brie to satisfy my new addiction to cheese.

I was a mess.

As much as I wanted to blame it all on cheese and wine and the entire French culture, I knew it really had nothing to do with Paris at all. It all boiled down to the perfect date that had spiraled me out of control and sent me running back to our hotel, ready to blame August for every problem I'd ever had.

It had all started out so innocently. A cute guy, a little flirting. It felt good to know I was still attractive to other men, especially to a sexy Frenchman—who had definitely not been a spy, much to Sarah's disappointment.

Leo, the accountant, had sat with us for several hours that night, getting to know us and vice versa. His English was quite good and our conversations carried on very well. When the night came to a close, Sarah had begun to give me the suggestive eye waggle, trying to persuade me into something more with the man sitting across from me. But that just wasn't my style.

I wasn't a one-night stand kind of girl, and I never would be.

Which was why, when he asked me out to dinner the next evening, I leaped at the chance. I was the dateable type—the girl you brought home to your mother. It had seemed like a great plan. At first.

The next evening I found myself in a dimly lit restaurant. Romantic music was playing and my head was beginning to spin.

What had I been thinking? I quickly excused myself from the table, rushing to the bathroom as the air became thin around me. I barely made it to the stall before tiny lights began to flicker around me. My head fell between my legs and I struggled for oxygen.

I was so stupid. So incredibly stupid.

The ink on my shoulder was still fresh and here I was, ready to go out and find Mr. Dependable #3? I'd left Ryan to find myself—to make a life of my own...and I was already scoping out his replacement barely three weeks later.

I'd quickly cleaned my tearstained makeup in the bathroom mirror, then faked a stomachache, asking Leo to take me back to the hotel. He suggested we reschedule, but I never called him again. I didn't need any more complications in my life. I already had a big six-foot-tall one I was doing an amazing job of ignoring.

It had taken the better part of our plane ride home for me to figure out my plan of action, but now I had one. No more floundering, no more waiting. I was going to finally take back my life, starting with fulfilling the one dream I'd always put on the back burner.

With all the lights having long since gone out, I snuck into Sarah's small kitchen and quietly brewed myself a single cup of coffee. She had one of those fancy brewers I loathed. They tended to make crappy coffee and I needed about five or six of those tiny expensive cups to make it through a morning. I much preferred a good old-fashioned brewer.

But for late night sneaking around, it had its benefits.

With coffee in hand, I quietly tiptoed back into my room and pulled up Google to begin my research. I'd had this dream for as long as I could remember, and for now it would remain solely mine until further notice. For all I knew, it could end up flat as a pancake on the side of the road with all the other ideas I'd had in the past.

So for the time being, I typed in "culinary schools in San Francisco," hit enter, and started taking notes.

Career goal research had begun; now I just had to work on everything else.

Easy peasy, right?

Why did I feel like the world was about to cave in around me?

*   *   *

Was there anything better than the smell of bacon?

Maybe bacon with a hint of coffee?

As I lifted my third—possibly fourth—cup of caffeine to my lips, I smiled as I surveyed the kitchen. Bacon was sizzling, the shrimp was prepared and ready to be sautéed. I'd even preheated the oven for the sweet potato biscuits I'd made from scratch.

Everything was turning out incredible.

"You're really outdoing yourself," Sarah commented as she strolled into the living room from her bedroom. She'd spent the last hour and a half primping while I slaved away in the kitchen.

While most people would be annoyed by this fact, I was grateful.

The kitchen was my sanctuary, and I cherished the peace and quiet. Everyone else could stay far, far away... until the dishes were dirty, that is.

"I just wanted everything to be perfect. After so many months of hearing about this guy, I feel like I'm about to meet a celebrity," I confessed as I moved around the sizzling bacon and onions.

"Miles is just a normal guy," she promised. "Which is why I'm so protective of him. Normal guys usually don't end up with me. I'm usually a tractor beam for the weird, insane, or crazy types."

"I'm sure that's not true," I encouraged her. Since we'd been friends, Sarah hadn't dated much. A guy here or there that led to nowhere, or a brief mention of a meal that had ended in disaster, but she'd never given much time or effort to any specific man. I'd just figured she was too involved in her career. I knew athletes were always sensitive about time—or the lack of time they had—when it came to how long they could perform at their peak. I'd just always assumed she was putting off the heavy attachments until she was in a different phase of life.

"Oh, it's true," she countered. "I know I haven't spoken much about my dating past, but I'm a magnet for weirdos. My first serious boyfriend was one of my ballet teachers. I was eighteen. He was thirty. That right there should have been a warning. He took my virginity on the hard wooden floor after class one night. Being so young, I thought it was romantic. God, I was dumb."

"What happened?" I asked, afraid to even ask as I watched her once lighthearted face morph into something full of pain and regret.

"It was little things at first. A little pinch of skin when we were in bed, or a sideways glance as I dressed. Sometimes he'd pull my food away before I finished, reminding me if I wanted the bigger roles I needed to keep my portion sizes small."

"Jesus Sarah, he started it," I said, knowing everything she'd been through over the years regarding her body image.

"No." She shook her head. "I did—I started it. I didn't have to listen to him. But I did. I let him control my thoughts, and soon I began to believe them. It was all downhill from there."

I turned to move, to be there for her, but she held out her hand to stop me and shook her head.

"If you hug me right now I will cry, and I just spent the last hour perfecting my eyeliner."

Smiling, I stayed put and nodded. "Okay, but just so you know. I love you and I will totally tackle-hug you in your sleep tonight—ninja style. You won't even see me coming."

"Well, now I'll be expecting it. You're a terrible ninja."

"I never was good at keeping secrets," I said, but the words made my throat suddenly go dry.

I'd become an expert at keeping secrets. From those I loved—even myself.

I'd hide them away, lock them up, and never think about them again.

Until it was too late.

My late-night conversation with August came back to the fore-front of my mind.

Was it too late?

*   *   *

Thankfully, as the imminent arrival of our guest of honor ap-proached, the mood seemed to lighten up. No more talk of bad boyfriends, and no more dark thoughts of all the horrible things I'd managed to keep hidden over the last few years.

Tonight was about celebrating.

Sarah was happy and therefore, I was happy for her.

After everything we'd both been through, at least one of us should be happy. I just hoped the guy she'd chosen was worthy of her.

She hadn't given me many details to go on over the last few months, but what I did know sounded promising. He was a business owner, made good money, and treated her well. Whenever she spoke about him, she got that faraway, dreamy look girls tended to get when they were headed toward the big "L" word, and now all she could do was pace the floor in nervousness.

"Are you okay?" I asked, closing the oven door. I put the mitt down on the counter and joined her in the living room.

"Just nervous. I really want you to like him," she confessed.

"Why does it matter so much?"

"You and I are like sisters," she explained. "You know I'm not that close to my family. They live so far away and we don't exactly see each other that often. When we were going into your bridal shower, and you stopped and said we were family? That's exactly how I feel, Ev. You are my family, and I care what you think."

"Well, shit—now you're going to ruin my makeup," I cursed, sitting down next to her. "I'm sure I'm going to love him as much as you do."

She opened her mouth to protest my use of the big "L" word, but I moved on before she could say a word. "But, you've also got to realize, it doesn't matter what anyone else thinks as long as you know what's in your heart."

Her smile was a bit smug. "Maybe you should follow your own advice."

Rolling my eyes, I pushed her shoulder with a laugh. "We're not talking about me. Now, go check on my rolls while I fix my makeup."

I quickly ran back to my room, moving around all the boxes I still hadn't unpacked. I'd secretly sent out several applications to culinary schools in the area for the spring semester, and if all went well, I'd be moving into student housing or something similar in the next few months.

No need to get situated here, right?

Plus, the idea of unpacking everything I'd shared with Ryan made me sad. Just another failed life to sort through. Part of me just wanted to toss half of it and start over fresh.

Out with the old Everly, in with the new.

Rummaging through my makeup on top of my dresser, I found my mascara and a small mirror. Falling down on the single bed Sarah had placed in this room for guests, I quickly redid my makeup, tidying up the streaks that had made their way down to the corners of my eyes.

As I was finishing I heard the doorbell, and Sarah's exuberant greeting as she welcomed Miles into her home. I'm sure this wasn't the first time he'd been here, but no doubt it was the first time since I'd moved in. Taking a deep breath, I took one last look in the mirror, making sure I looked cordial and warm. I walked out into the living room with a happy smile on my face, ready to meet Sarah's new man.

As soon as he turned, I felt all the air rush out my body as I struggled to stay upright.

"Oh my gosh, Ev—are you okay?" Sarah asked, rushing to take my hand.

My eyes stayed locked on the man before me. On Trent.

Dear God, why was he here?

She held me as I stood upright, the blood so loud in my ears I barely heard her as she said, "This is Miles. Miles, this is my best friend Everly."

His slow smile sent chills down my spine as he took a step forward. His hand reached for mine.

"So nice to meet you, Everly," he said, meeting my gaze as he pulled me closer, as if to offer a friendly hug.

"Don't you dare say a single word. Do you understand?" he whispered into my ear.

I pulled back, nodding ever so slightly as his smile widened.

"Good, good—this is great. We should have done this sooner. I've been begging Sarah to introduce me to the infamous Everly. She talks about you so much, I feel like I know everything about you," he said with a laugh—a laugh that made my skin crawl.

"Hopefully not everything," I replied, trying to sound calm even though I was anything but. My brain was in a frenzy as I tried to do the mental math. How long had Sarah been talking about this mystery man? Several months...long before I'd even gotten back together with August.

Dear God. Had Trent really been plotting this the whole time? And for what?

"Is something burning?" Sarah asked, turning toward the kitchen.

"Oh crap! The rolls!" I yelled, rushing to the stove. Smoke billowed from the oven as I yanked on the protective mitt and pulled out the cookie sheet. The once beautiful, round orange biscuits now resembled hard lumps of charcoal.

"It's okay, Everly. No one is perfect," Trent commented as his arm slid around my best friend. I watched her head rest on his shoulder. Such love and trust she had given him.

He deserved none of it.

He gave me a wink, making my stomach turn so hard I nearly blurted out the truth right there. But then I remembered Sarah's story—her failures in love. If I came out and told her now, she'd either accuse me of sabotaging her one chance or she'd blame herself for finding another weirdo.

I knew I had to do something—anything to get her away from him, but I couldn't do it alone.

I needed help.

I needed August.

Chapter Sixteen

August

Relax, he'd said.

Take deep breaths, he'd said.

Just let it happen, August, he'd said.

Sixty minutes had gone by and nothing had happened. Nothing at all. Not even an inkling or a single eye twitch that would suggest that I was making progress toward being put under Brick's hypnosis, and the longer we tried the more and more frustrated I became.

"August, you can't give up," Brick said, offering encouragement through his soft-spoken words.

"Maybe this type of thing just doesn't work on me. Aren't there certain people who just can't be influenced? Maybe I'm not made for this," I remarked as I rose from the horizontal position I'd taken on the couch. Sitting up, I instinctively turned toward the windows, looking out at the water, hoping the sight of it would somehow calm my frazzled nerves.

"There are individuals who are more susceptible to suggestion and hypnosis than others. It does not surprise me that someone like you, with a strong will and a stubborn personality, would be a challenge."

I threw a hard stare over my shoulder, letting him know the comment hadn't gone unnoticed.

"But I don't think it's impossible," he added. "You just need to be able to clear your mind—find your center and let go."

Find my center? This was sounding weirder and weirder by the minute.

"And you think the hippie music you're playing in the background is going to help me do that," I said, waving my hand toward the portable boom box as it softly played one of the CDs he'd brought over.

I'd thought it was some sort of joke when I'd pulled open my door this morning and found him standing there holding a boom box and a brown bag filled to the top with groceries and CDs. Who listened to CDs anymore? Did they even sell them in stores? When he'd pulled out freshly baked croissants and began feeding me, though, I'd decided not to rib him over the ancient audio equipment and instead just enjoy the crazy ride.

But now, the sound of the high-pitched flute and that trippy guitar playing on and on were getting on my last nerve and I was left with nothing but frustration.

"I can put something else on if you want. This usually helps, but any type of mellow music will work," he offered. The music cut off and my irritation dwindled slightly.

I was being a jerk, while Brick was offering nothing but kindness.

As always.

I fell back on the couch, my head hitting the pillow as I let the air deflate from my lungs.

Why he kept coming back, I'd never understand.

The doorbell rang at that moment, and I didn't bother getting up. Brick already acted as though he owned half the place. He might as well answer the door, sign for packages, or whatever else was needed. I'd work on clearing my head so we could try again—because I desperately needed my memories.

I needed answers and I was tired of waiting.

With my eyes closed and my breath tempered, I focused on calming myself, emptying my mind as Brick had taught me to do. Errant thoughts kept swirling through my head, causing me to lose focus and become frustrated. The sound of Everly's sweet-sounding voice echoed so loudly between my ears, I could almost swear it was real.

"Why is he laying down? Is he sick?"

My eyes blinked open. That wasn't her voice in my head. Swiveling up and around, I came face to face with her for the first time in months.

So beautiful.

Nothing had changed. She looked just the same as the last time I'd seen her. A bit more covered up, however—wearing a long gray sweater and leggings, she proved she could wear anything and still look stunning. I watched as she took a hesitant step back, as if she were slightly shocked by my abrupt turnaround on the couch.

That, or she was afraid of me. That realization was like getting doused by a bucket of ice water as I suddenly remembered why she needed to be so distant and why I needed to be so cold.

"What are you doing here?" I asked, clearing my throat as I tried to compose myself.

She briefly closed her eyes, but when she reopened them there was a fire in them that had been missing previously. She held up her hand in front of her, basically dismissing me, and turned to Brick.

"I asked you a question," she said, rather pointedly.

He seemed taken aback for a moment, but then a slight grin snuck upon his face. "No, not sick. We're trying to hypnotize him."

Great, Brick, why don't you tell her everything?

Her gaze snuck back to mine, and a mischievous smile spread across Brick's face. He was enjoying this back and forth with Everly and the fact that I was decidedly not involved.

"Hypnotize? Why?"

I opened my mouth to answer, but she *shh*'d me again, still holding up her hand. I found myself dumbfounded by her newfound spunk.

"I'm speaking with Brick right now. Not you," she said firmly, ignoring my attempts to argue.

She was supposed to stay away. I'd done everything I could—broken her heart, put fear in her bones, and ice in her veins—yet here she was.

Brick's eyes briefly connected with mine and in that moment I knew he wasn't going to lie for me.

Not again.

The ruse was over.

"We're trying to get his memories back," he answered. Everly's gaze widened, as the truth of my betrayal became a sudden reality.

"What? But why? What happened to them? He still has them, doesn't he?" she asked softly, her hand finding the arm of the plush chair she'd always found herself in when she'd stayed here. I watched as she settled into its cushions, noticing the way her fingers trembled and the way she tried to hide it.

"I lied," I responded. "In the dress shop."

Her expression fell. "But you knew. Everything. The necklace—that night. You knew," she said, her voice sounding desperate.

"I didn't lie about that," I said, remembering the cold way I'd explained to her how I'd collapsed with the resurfacing of my first memory. Everything I'd told her then was true. Everything but my anger. "I'm recovering fragments—bits and pieces at a time. That night—the memory of it was just the beginning. Since then, I've had dozens of memories push their way to the surface, but I don't have everything—not by a long shot. I'm starting to wonder if I ever will."

It was my gaze that fell then, but I found myself looking into a pair of brilliant blue eyes. Soft, warm, and seeking—they were like pieces of my soul I'd lost somewhere along the way. Seeing her here felt like I'd come home, which only made the pain of knowing I couldn't have her that much worse.

"Why did you lie to me?" she asked.

"To keep you away—to keep you safe," I answered honestly.

"From what?" she asked, throwing her hands in the air as she stood in frustration. Brick, who had been silently watching our exchange, had backed off and stood in the corner with his arms crossed, watching everything from afar.

"It's better if you know nothing, Everly. I don't want you involved."

"Oh my God, you really have no idea, do you?" she said, shaking her head back and forth as she began pacing the floor. She wrapped her arms around her sides and laughter poured out of her.

Pained laughter.

"Did you think this would all just stay with you, August? That by pushing me away, you'd somehow keep it contained? Did you lose your common sense when you went into that coma?"

My eyes narrowed as I stood as well.

"What are you talking about?"

"Trent," she replied.

My vision went red as I nearly lunged for her, gripping her shoulders, feeling the need to check her for physical damage. "What has he done? Are you all right?"

"Not me," she whispered, tears falling freely from my eyes. "Sarah. He's been dating Sarah. For months—to get information, or maybe just for some sick twisted angle. I don't know."

She fell apart in my arms, sobbing as I held her. I tried to be a good person, to keep my feelings platonic as she cried for her friend, but feeling her tender body wrapped in mine was more than I could handle. I felt walls breaking down that I'd thought would never crumble.

"I should have met him sooner—I should have demanded to know who this mystery guy she's been seeing was, but he's been using the name Miles. Why would he do that? This is going to destroy her. She's in love with him."

"Miles is Trent's middle name," I explained. "He must be trying to mess with me by getting to you."

I let out a frustrated sigh. This was probably all my fault as well.

The only problem was that I still didn't know why. Trent was taking drastic measures to make sure I stayed within his grasp, and I needed to know why.

Looking over toward Brick, I took a deep breath. I hugged Everly one last time. "I think I'm ready to try again."

I'd found my center, and it was about time I found some answers.

* * *

"You seem lighter, less disconnected," Brick noted as I settled back down on the couch.

I smiled and let my head be gently cushioned by the fluffy feather pillows beneath me. "Did Everly seem different to you?" I asked, ignoring his comment altogether as I stared up at the ceiling.

She'd left about twenty minutes before. After her tears had dried and her emotions seemed to settle, her mood had returned to something closer to anger.

All directed toward me.

I guess I didn't blame her. I had lied to her—over and over. And for what? Had it solved anything? Trent had still managed to weasel his way in—to threaten the one thing in my life that mattered.

I'd been so naïve, so simpleminded when it came to Trent. I thought his motivations were basic when it came to me. I had no idea he'd go so far to seek his revenge, and now I'd not only destroyed the one good thing in my life, I'd managed to bring the devil to her front door.

I'd fix this. I'd promised her that much before she'd left. I wasn't sure how, but I knew it would end with Trent behind bars.

"She seemed more in control of herself, I guess," he said, using his more official-sounding voice. "Less willing to put up with your shit," he added with a slight chuckle.

"I know," I answered with a grin.

"Okay, in order for this to work, you need to try and clear your mind—just like before. Let go of any lingering frustrations, and just concentrate on my voice."

"Got it," I confirmed, shaking out my legs and tweaking my neck one last time before I closed my eyes. Taking a deep breath, I let the events of the day fade away, focusing on just the sound of the air rising and falling within my lungs.

"Good, with your eyes open—still slowly breathing in and out—find something to focus on. One solid object to concentrate on."

Within my focal range, there wasn't much but a spot on the wall, and a black and white photo. It was one I'd never had the heart to take down—a memory I had yet to experience from a life I had yet to relive. In it, Everly was looking up at me with a happy, radiant smile.

It was the perfect focal spot. Looking at this image of Everly reminded me why I was doing this in the first place.

Talking several deep, cleansing breaths, I narrowed in on the photo and let the world disappear.

"Let yourself relax into the couch as I speak, focusing on the spot you've chosen. Soon you will begin to feel your eyes grow tired and heavy."

His voice was beginning to sound distant, as if I'd traveled away from myself. My eyelids closed and the photo of Everly and me disappeared.

"Good, August, good," Brick's comforting voice praised me from afar. "I'm still here. You're doing great. Keep relaxed, and let me guide you. You can imagine your focal spot if it helps."

It did. Seeing the photo on the wall, even if it was now only in my mind, kept me anchored and calm as I fell deeper and deeper with the aid of Brick's expertise.

"Okay, August," Brick said. I felt myself floating around somewhere in my subconscious. "I want you to imagine yourself in a long hallway, with endless doors. Can you do that for me?"

Fixated on every word, I did exactly what he said. Tattered green wallpaper spread out before me; shabby wood doors appeared on either side. The hallway felt oddly familiar as I glanced around, noticing the blinking light fixtures and stained carpet.

This was where Everly had lived. Long ago—before our lives had collided. I'd never experienced being in this place, but she'd told me about it—described it in detail, and now my mind had somehow recreated it.

"Do you see the hallway?" Brick asked, his voice still calm and even.

"Yes," I answered as my subconscious took a look around.

"Great. Now, each one of these doors represents a memory you have yet to unlock. I need you to concentrate on which type of memories you'd like to revisit today. Focus, August—I know this may be a challenge. When you have the direction you'd like to take in your mind, pick a door and walk in. I'll be here if you need me."

Temptation hit me square in the gut as I struggled to focus. The ability to choose a memory? Any memory? I'd choose one of Everly every single time.

But reliving a lifetime with Everly in my memories wouldn't change a thing. She'd always be a ghost from my past...someone I could see but never again hold within my grasp. Using her like a beacon, however, I reentered and concentrated on exactly what I was hoping to accomplish. Only answers would help me now. With my mind clear, I took a mental leap and opened the first door.

"Come on, Kincaid, shut down that computer and come have a drink!" Trent yelled from the front lobby.

I shook my head, chuckling under my breath. Most companies sent a congratulatory e-mail when you reached an anniversary, or perhaps gave you a gift card or a small cake from the closest gro-cery store. Here, we celebrated with booze. Lots and lots of booze.

Doing as I was told, I closed out the account I was working on and headed out front.

"There's our man!" Trent yelled, even going so far as to stand on top of the receptionist's desk, who had long since left. "My partner in crime—my other half," he laughed, throwing out grand theatrics in spades. I grabbed a highball of scotch, letting him soak up the limelight.

"We wouldn't be here without him. Let's all raise a glass to Au-gust!"

Everyone in the room—the guys I'd brought on to work under me and even Trent's guys I didn't know so well—held up glasses as we toasted a full year of accomplishment.

"Thanks, everyone," I said, feeling awkward from all the atten-tion. I rubbed the back of my neck and tried not to say anything that would embarrass myself. "Make sure to drink all of the scotch. It's all on Trent tonight." I laughed, finishing off the last of my drink with a swift shake of my head.

That was enough for tonight. I had another celebration to get home to and I wanted to arrive with all of my faculties intact.

Everyone dispersed, breaking into small groups, making sure to stop by and congratulate me. Many of these men had been around for nearly as long as I had since we were a new company, but be-cause I was a partner, Trent felt that my anniversary with the firm should be a marked occasion.

And so I just smiled and went with it.

"Thanks for giving away all my liquor," Trent said, coming up behind me, his voice cutting through the noise like a knife. He al-

ways had such a firm presence in a room. Turning, I gave him a smirk as I held up my empty glass. "Not like you can't afford it," I reminded him.

A moment passed between us before his mouth turned upward, a huge grin splitting his face. "True—thanks to you," he remarked, turning to grab the bottle of scotch to refill my glass. I took a deep breath, knowing better than to refuse him and just held my glass as he poured, nearly filling it to the top.

"Thanks to us," I corrected him.

"Well, I can honestly say we weren't doing this well before I took you on as a partner."

I shrugged, taking a heavy sip from my glass as we surveyed the room, watching the men laugh and joke around with each other.

"I don't know why," I said. "I really don't know what difference I make. It's you taking on the big accounts. You're the one making the money."

Something passed through his eyes just then—a glint of malice he didn't want me to see, maybe. As quickly as it was there, it was gone again. "You're doing important work, August. You're bringing people into the practice—getting them hooked. And then, when their greed gets the better of them, I'm there to make them the big cash."

I nodded, understanding the strategy we'd put in place. It'd worked over the last year—just like Trent had said it would. It wasn't something I was all too comfortable with—the concept of capitalizing on someone's greed, but when Trent had come to me, he'd simply stated that that was what we all did anyway. The game of finance was always based on greed, so why shouldn't we utilize it?

We targeted well-to-do business owners—some more so than others, those who hadn't branched into investing for whatever reason—too small, not enough skill, etc. I got them started with just a few small investments, made them some easy money, and then we waited. Sure enough, they'd come back wanting more, and that's when Trent would step in, taking over to earn them even more. Before long, we'd had multibillionaires in here asking us to represent them. Business was booming.

"Oh, before I forget," I said, remembering the client's account I was working on before I'd clocked out. "I was trying to access files on the shared drive today and noticed some of the folders are password protected?"

Trent's jaw ticked before he turned, a slight smile tugging at the corner of his mouth.

"An oversight. I'll have someone fix it on Monday," he said.

"Great."

He held up his glass once again, as our eyes met. I joined in as the sound of our impromptu toast met my ears.

"Keep up the good work," he said, but suddenly each word felt more like a threat than praise.

"Thanks," I answered as I downed the rest of my drink, feeling it burn a fiery path all the way down to my belly.

What had I gotten myself into?

"Calm down, August," Brick's voice came through as I struggled to find my way back. "Take a deep breath, control it, and when you're ready, open your eyes."

My head was pounding as I fought for control. Beads of sweat trickled down my forehead and my chest as I slowly relaxed and finally opened my eyes.

"Was that okay? Did I do all right?" I asked as I wiped moisture from my brow. Brick, who was sitting on the coffee table directly in front of me, shrugged, handing me a cup of water.

"I'd say it went pretty well, considering I've never done this type of thing before."

My eyes nearly bugged out of my head as I tried not to choke on the water he'd given me. "What? You used me as a guinea pig?"

"Not completely—no. I guess I should have clarified. I've hypnotized hundreds of people, but for normal clinical things like weight loss, smoking, depression. I've never hypnotized someone to regain lost memories. It was unknown territory."

"Unbelievable," I muttered.

"But it worked," he said with a smug grin.

"Yeah, but I'm not sure the memory I had was worth it. I already knew I'd worked for Trent. I don't know how much help that was," I said, setting the glass aside as I shoved my hands through my hair.

"Your subconscious brought up that memory for a reason, or at least we have to believe it did. Think, August. What about the memory stood out?"

"I realized Trent was a slimeball," I snorted, "but that's old news."

"But it wasn't then. So, what does that tell you?" Brick pushed, standing up to pace the room.

The memory flashed quickly again through my mind. The toast, the internal thoughts I was having, Trent's words.

"I wasn't working with Trent?" I guessed.

"Good." Brick nodded with enthusiasm. "I don't think you always knew what Trent is so willing to tell you now. What if he brought you in blind? What if, like everyone else in that office, you were just brought in to do a job—another pawn on the chess-board?"

"So are you saying I was an innocent bystander in all of this? Because I don't think that's how this story ends. I locked Everly up for a reason."

"There's obviously more to it, but it's a start."

"When can I go under again?" I asked, looking up at him with desperation and hunger.

"Now you trust me again? Even though I turned you into a guinea pig?" he joked.

"Cut the shit, Brick!" I roared, slamming my hand on the arm of the couch. "This is my life. I need it back."

He held up his hands defensively. "A few days, August. Your brain needs at least a few days to rest. Maybe a little longer. We're in uncharted territory here. Doing hypnosis on you is probably the stupidest idea I've ever had. You should really see your doctor—"

"Don't," I warned.

"I hate the idea of you sabotaging your life. So this is what we're left with."

"Thanks, Brick," I said.

He nodded. "I'll be back. Don't do anything stupid until then."

"No problem."

As I watched his car back out of the driveway, I silently wondered if he would consider my decision to confront Trent as stupid.

Because that's exactly what I planned on doing.

Chapter Seventeen

Everly

Dusk settled, lights flickered on and still I drove. No destination in mind, no interest in time.

For months, he'd lied to me, avoided me and pushed me away.

I'd almost married another man.

Did he care for me at all?

Sick of the swirling thoughts in my head, I found myself swerving to the side of the road. It was time I sought an outlet. She might never speak to me again for this breach of trust, but I needed to speak to someone and waiting until tomorrow wasn't an option.

Looking up the address in my phone, I merged back into traffic and headed to the east part of town. My eyes briefly darted to the clock, and I let out a quick breath of relief at the still-early hour. At least I wouldn't be showing up out of the blue at her doorstep and waking her out of a deep sleep. Although I'd probably be interrupting a meal at the very least. I wondered what Tabitha was like in her private life. Did her house look like her office—with worn, comfortable furniture and cuddly pillows to worry over while you chatted?

Pulling to the side of the road once I'd arrived, I looked around Tabitha's quiet neighborhood, noticing the quintessential narrow houses San Francisco was known for. Several of them had been parceled up and sliced into apartments but it appeared the one Tabitha shared with her husband had remained intact. It was older, the blue stucco in desperate need of repair, but I could see Tabitha's touch everywhere—from the beautiful flowered pathway to the whimsical wind chimes that danced in the evening breeze. It appeared the Tabitha I knew was the same wherever she was.

Or so I thought.

Taking the last few steps to her door, I took a deep breath and knocked. When the door opened I was greeted by the most unexpected person.

Brick Abrams.

Blinking once...twice, I looked around, first at the numbers on the door and then behind me, to reassure myself that the scenery hadn't morphed into something different.

Maybe I'd looked up the wrong address?

But I didn't have Brick's address...

"Tabitha!" Brick called from the front door. "I think you may need to come here, darling."

"'Darling'?" I asked, my expression reflecting my extreme confusion.

His warm smile faltered as he offered his hand. "Why don't you come in and let us explain?"

"'Us'?" I muttered as he ushered me inside. Following him down a long hallway, I couldn't help but notice the long row of photos that lined the corridor walls. Decades passed before my eyes as Tabitha and Brick's life—together, it seemed—was revealed.

"Why didn't you ever tell us?"

"It was never our intention to lie to you," Tabitha said, as she entered the room, joining us in a small parlor. There were books stacked up on the coffee table and old newspapers forgotten underneath a half-eaten plate of cookies. Worn, lumpy couches, perfect for snuggling up on paired perfectly with antique bookshelves and scattered trinkets and treasures. The more I saw, the more I realized they really did live here.

Together.

"But you were both our clients and it put us in a situation we'd never been in," Brick explained as he offered me a place to sit. I gladly took it, trying to digest everything I'd just seen and heard.

"So, you two are married?"

Sitting together on a sofa across from me, they looked at each other and smiled. It was a familiar smile, one that had obviously been developed over time. It was that type of smile couples and close friends have, where words are said but not spoken, and in that moment I could see it.

Their love. The devotion it held.

It all made sense.

"Yes," they responded in unison.

"Did you always know? About August and me?" I asked.

"No," Tabitha explained, her expression warm and open as she held on to her husband's hand. "It all came out by accident, really. I'd had you as a client for quite some time and had never really mentioned you specifically to Brick."

She saw my look of alarm and jumped in to clarify. "Since we're both counselors, we'll sometimes converse with each other about specific clients—no names of course, but sometimes the extra voice helps. It's no different than any other line of work. Sometimes you just need a second opinion."

"I would have thought my rather unusual case would have had you running home to tell Brick all about me," I said, an uncomfortable laugh escaping my lips.

Her head tilted to the side as she leaned forward. "Oh dear no. Don't think that. You grew leaps and bounds in that first year and a half I saw you. It wasn't until August awoke that I began to worry. You closed yourself off, began running from those that cared for you—that's when I spoke to Brick. I needed advice."

I nodded, understanding it all now. "And that's when you realized your clients were connected."

"Yes," Brick confirmed. "It's one of the reasons I stopped charging August and dropped him as an official client."

"But you never stopped caring for him." I gave him a faint smile.

"No," he confirmed. "Someone has to take care of him."

"Why didn't you tell him then? He wasn't your client anymore."

"No, but you were still mine," Tabitha stated. "And honestly, there were so many moments I wanted to tell you, but I just didn't know how. You've grown quite special to me over the years, Everly."

"And the same for you—for both of you. It's still kind of awkward to be sitting here in your house, but at the same time, it feels right, you know?"

They both laughed, "Yes, we know."

"So, how did a guy like you snatch himself a girl like Tabitha?" I asked, helping myself to one of the cookies off a plate on the coffee table.

"Well, it's pretty simple," he answered. "She saved my life."

Cookie crumbs fell from my mouth as I tried to compose myself, looking back and forth from Tabitha to Brick.

"She saved you?" I asked between leftover cookie bits.

"In a manner of speaking," she answered.

"She saved me," he answered with an air of finality. "She saved me from myself, which is exactly what you need to do with August."

"I don't understand."

"Then let me explain," he replied, reaching forward to steal the last cookie before I could. "Maybe August told you I was a spry young boy from the Midwest when I moved here, obsessed with the idea of surfing and not much else. I was naïve. So very naïve," he said, shaking his head.

"It's amazing how quickly a young, naïve boy with little-to-no income can find himself with the wrong type of people. I'd come here for school, but after a week I dropped out. In less than a month, I was stealing cars, picking pockets, and doing just about everything else you could think of to make enough cash to feed myself. I'd come to California to surf, and not much else had gone through my mind—school had been nothing more than a means of getting here. I had no goals for employment, no idea where I'd live. When I got here, things weren't nearly as rosy and hip as the movies I'd watched made them out to be."

"I can understand that mentality," I replied. Memories of the Little Orphan Annie lifestyle I'd lived as a child rushed to the forefront of my mind.

"But that's the thing about hanging out with the wrong crowd; there are always worse things to do. And soon, I wasn't just stealing to feed my belly, I was pocketing huge amounts of cash to feed my growing addiction."

"Oh, Brick," I whispered as my face fell.

"I did say I was naïve." He shrugged. "I was living above a small restaurant in Santa Cruz with a few other surfers then, although we spent most of our time doing anything but surfing. I'd go downstairs and buy the same thing every day—"

"A hot dog and a Coke," Tabitha said with a faraway smile. "I'd always tell you it was bad for you to eat the same thing every day."

"I said it built character," Brick replied. "Somehow she saw through my bad habits and poor choices. Every day, little by little, she chipped away at my grimy exterior, finding the raw center of the boy I'd once been. I don't know how but she saved me, showed me a life with purpose and meaning. I owe her everything."

"And I owe you everything in return," Tabitha answered, grasping his chin as I watched the cherished love radiate between them.

"How bad is it, Brick? How bad is he?" I asked, afraid to hear the answer but knowing I had no choice. I knew the truth now. There was no more running—that's what the old Everly would have done: run away when things got intense and the air got heavy. But that wasn't me anymore—or at least that wasn't who I wanted to be.

"I'm not going to lie, Everly—it's bad. When I found him a few days ago, he'd nearly given up all hope. He thought he had Trent all figured out, but I think he's slowly realizing he doesn't know the half of it."

"No, he doesn't," I confirmed, remembering the way that sleaze-ball had winked at me as he'd wrapped his arms around my best friend.

"He'll deny it until he's blue in the face, but he needs you. I'm helping as much as I can with regaining his memories, but he needs yours as well. He's fighting a battle he can't win right now because he's unprepared. He's basically going in blind. Now that he knows Trent is going after you and Sarah, he might be irrational and in a rush to act."

"How so?" I asked, my panic rising with each word he spoke.

"It's August," he said with hesitation. "He's a swarming mess of emotions. Two different lives converging into one. But the one thing that remains constant is his love for you. He'll do anything to keep you safe."

Memories of being locked behind my own bedroom door threatened to push into the forefront of my mind as I sat there pondering Brick's words.

What if he hadn't been punishing me? What if he'd been protecting me in his own twisted way?

Rising suddenly, I grabbed my purse and bolted for the door.

"Did I say something wrong?" Brick asked as he and Tabitha followed me out.

"No, just the opposite," I answered and bit my bottom lip in worry.

"Sweetheart, where are you headed in such a fright?" Tabitha asked as I briefly turned to bid them good night.

"To find out what August has gotten himself into this time."

A broad smile swept across Brick's face. "Good luck."

"Thanks, but I think it's him who'll be needing luck by the time I'm done with him."

* * *

"Oh my God, what did you do?" I gasped as soon as the door opened and I got a good look at his swollen, bruised face.

"You should see the other guy," August responded, trying to smile, but failing miserably. Instead, he winced at the pain from moving his cut lip. The movement caused it to break open, bleeding bright red and angry.

"Jesus," I muttered, grabbing his hand as I pulled him inside with me. He followed with little resistance as I led him upstairs to the master bathroom, where the small first-aid kit used to be stored.

I pushed him down onto the covered toilet seat and checked out his face, turning it side to side to examine all the damage that had been inflicted.

"Were you going to do anything about this?" I asked as I lifted his chin. There was blood on his collar. I tried not to groan as I came face to face with a black eye that was starting to turn purple and a large gash across his formerly gorgeous cheek.

"Well, I was trying... but you interrupted me," he said. I caught a faint whiff of alcohol on his breath as he tried to remain focused on me.

He was drunk.

He'd gone out, nearly gotten himself beaten to a pulp, and then come back and decided to finish himself off with booze? Brick had been right.

August was in over his head—which was exactly why I was here.

"Ouch! What the fuck?" he yelled as the sting of my slap across his face registered in his alcohol-infused brain.

"Time to sober up, August. Get in the shower, wash off some of that blood. When you're clean and a little more clearheaded, we're going to bandage up what we can and then we're going to talk. And by talk, I mean mostly me...and a lot," I said, folding my arms across my chest as I blocked the door. There was no escaping.

"Since when have you become so bossy?" he asked as I watched his hands reach for the hem of his shirt.

"Maybe I've always been this way and you just don't remember," I snapped, my eyes following his every move. "Since you've forgotten so much."

"Not the important things," he replied, his voice steady and clear as I watched his T-shirt fall to the floor. The sight of his naked chest had my heartbeat racing. I suddenly realized how confined we were in such a tight space.

"I'll just give you a few moments," I said quickly, darting out of the bathroom before my heart galloped out of my throat.

Had he always been so attractive? I nearly had to smack my own hands to keep from reaching out to pet him. Taking slow, small steps, I made it to the bed and sat, waiting for the shower to start. My eyes darted from the still open door to the dresser, back to the door and then down to the floor.

Torture.

This was torture.

I'd come here to help August, not grope him.

Chemistry—the physical connection between us—had never been an issue. It never would be. Every time I looked at him, I felt a spark spurring deep in my belly, telling me this was the man I was meant to be with. But chemistry wasn't enough to keep the fires burning forever. There had to be more.

Sarah had told me my life had become a soap opera, and she wasn't far off in that regard. So much drama had been thrown at my doorstep in the last year, it felt like someone would surely yell "Cut!" and life would eventually return to normal.

But sometimes in life, we don't get to pick what's normal and what's not. We only get to choose how we define ourselves in the process. I would not become the heroine who ran back to her man just because the story was coming to an end. He needed me and I needed him, but there was still so much left for us to figure out.

So for now I'd let the shower water run, and my heart gallop... knowing that hopefully someday I'd join him.

But just not right now.

*   *   *

I'd talked myself off the ledge of temptation, but that didn't mean I wasn't thinking about every bead of water as it hit his rock hard body in that damn shower.

How long did it take for a guy to shower anyway?

Oh crap...

"August!" I yelled, running back into the bathroom, my mind now racing with horrifying images of him lying unconscious and half-dead in a pool of water.

Or worse.

Pulling the curtain back, I found myself face to face with a very alert, very naked August—who was not the least bit unconscious.

His hands were wrapped around a bar of soap, working it into a lather—all over his naked body. Bubbles had never looked so sexy to me in my whole damn life.

A bit of drool fell from my lips.

"Did you need something?" he asked, pausing mid-chest scrub. His amused expression met my horrified one.

"Um, I panicked. It had been a while and I was worried something had happened to you—because of your injuries and whatnot." I blabbered on, the words falling out of my mouth like an overturned basket of marbles.

"So you decided to just barge in?" he asked, the smug grin on his face clearly showing he was enjoying himself.

"I called out your name," I said, huffing slightly as my hand fell to my hip.

"The spray from the water is kind of loud in here," he shrugged.

An awkward silence grew before he tilted his head to the side and said, "Everly?"

"Yeah?" I answered.

"I'm okay," he said, chuckling.

"Right!" I said in a rush, realizing I was still standing there with the curtain pulled back, staring at him. All of him. "Oh God. I'll just be out here. Waiting for you."

I pivoted, rolling my eyes at my extreme awkwardness. When had I ever been awkward around this man? Nervous, scared...shy even, but I'd never acted like a teenage girl encountering her first crush.

It was embarrassing.

And kind of thrilling at the same time.

"Any chance you've sobered up yet?" I asked, throwing a towel over the shower curtain before I stepped out.

"Not even a chance!" he hollered, before a quiet hum filled the bathroom.

This was going to be a long night.

* * *

"Drink this," I demanded, pushing a cup of coffee in his direction as we settled into the living room. I'd finished cleaning up his wounds, bandaging what I could after his shower. He smelled like pine trees and fresh rain, and seeing his hair slick and wet made me want to run my hands through it just to feel its softness against my fingertips.

But recalling the earlier image of him battered and bruised had me resisting, knowing that unless we figured out how to resolve the problem at hand, we'd never be able to move forward.

And we'd be stuck in this revolving pattern of nothing for the rest of our lives.

"You always made the best coffee," he remarked after taking a long sip. The look on his face was priceless, like he'd just tasted the prize-winning pie at the state fair. "Every cup I've made since you left has tasted like shit."

"It didn't have to be like this," I said, feeling the anger I'd pushed away rising to the surface. "You could have told me what was going on. I could have been there, helped you."

He shook his head as he stared at his cup of coffee. "I wanted to keep you out of this. I wanted to keep all of you safe."

"It doesn't work that way."

"No," he shook his head, a note of sadness crossing his features. "I can see that now."

"Are you going to tell me what happened today?" I asked, pointing to his less-than-stellar-looking face.

"I went to talk to Trent."

"Alone?" I jumped up from my chair, hands risen in anger above my head. "Are you crazy?"

"He's threatened you and Sarah. What was I supposed to do?" he replied. His eyes narrowed, full of ire and hate. "I can't allow that, Everly."

"He's dangerous, August. You don't know what you may have started," I said, the fight fleeing my bones as I watched him, knowing he'd sustained such damage for me.

How much pain had he endured for me?

"I've already paid the cost." His expression was crestfallen as he looked up at me.

"What?" I asked, my heart pounding in fear.

"A couple of months ago I started seeing Magnolia again," he began. A slight pinch squeezed in my gut at the mention of Magnolia's name. "It wasn't personal," he added, seeing the discomfort in my eyes. "It was business—at first. I had this idea that if I could make enough off a deal from her family, I could walk away from Trent."

"But you couldn't do it," I said, finishing his thought.

"No." He shook his head. "I couldn't. I'm not that type of man. And, thanks to Brick's hypnosis abilities, I don't think I ever was. Things are still murky, but I'm starting to get a clearer picture of just what I did and didn't do before with Trent, and I have a feeling I wasn't the evil overlord I'd pictured myself to be. Or at least I wasn't to begin with."

"What did you do?" I asked, my eyes narrowing on him. "What did you give him?"

"Me," he said with resignation. His shoulders slumped in defeat. "He knew I wanted out. He wouldn't have it. So, I agreed to stop trying. He wants his pliable, naïve partner back, and that's what I'll give him."

"But you're not that guy anymore, August," I urged. "You can't go back."

"I don't see any other way, Everly."

"Of course you don't!" I said, my voice escalating as the intensity of my anger rose. "Because if there's one thing that's remained the same, it's your damned need to protect everyone—regardless of how it affects you, us, or anything else. As long as we're all safe, it doesn't matter—isn't that right, August?"

His surprise at my outburst seemed to cause a delay, but I could see him stepping up to the plate, ready to argue. Ready to fight back.

But I beat him to the chase.

"You've screwed up everything in your quest to keep me safe. Everything! Don't you realize that? And for what? Don't you understand by now that we're no good when we're apart? All of this plotting and scheming to keep me away—keep me protected from Trent? You broke my damn heart, August. You broke us. I could have been here for you. I could have helped you, but you didn't trust me. That's why you locked me up and never told me why. It's why you let me walk out that door. I came here with my eyes wide open, hoping that with some time and a little healing, perhaps we could mend what was broken between us.

"But now, all I see is a disaster zone. And I'm not sure I'm willing to comb through the mess by myself, just to see it all end in tragedy again. If you can't learn to trust me, this thing between us will always be just a handful of memories."

I wanted to tell him I'd help him—that we could work it out, just the two of us. But I was sick of trying to worm my way into his life.

I'd been the helpless bystander in his world for far too long, standing on the sidelines while he silently fought against Trent, pretending everything was just fine. I wasn't that woman any-more.

I could have done something. I would have done anything, had he just asked.

But he hadn't.

And until he did, I wasn't going to push my way into his life any-more.

August had once said I deserved someone who would treat me as an equal partner in life.

He was right.

As I turned to leave, letting the silence between us serve as my good-bye, I just hoped that August might still be that perfect person he'd described. If not, I wasn't sure my heart would ever forgive me for walking away.

Again.

Chapter Eighteen
August

I let her walk away.

Again.

She'd bled her heart out to me, grieving over all the missed opportunities we'd destroyed—I'd destroyed—and then I watched her turn and leave.

I hadn't done a damn thing about it.

She was right. I hadn't trusted her with the truth. Not because I didn't see her as an equal, but because I knew how she'd react.

And that's what scared me most of all.

Her need to help. Her desire to protect me as much as I wanted to protect her. For that reason alone, I'd lock her up and throw away the key a million times over if I thought it would keep her safe.

But if Trent showing up at her door proved anything, it was that I couldn't shelter her from everything. Eventually, the mistakes of my past would find their way into my future—our future, no matter where we were.

This never-ending cycle had to stop.

But would I ever be able to move past this overwhelming desire to keep her safe, and just live? Maybe she wasn't the only one stuck in a cage.

*   *   *

Opening my desk drawer, I pulled out the bag holding the tiny treasure for the hundredth time since lunch. It had only been three hours since I'd picked it up from the jeweler but my fingers were already twitching, my knees were bobbing, and my nerves were shot.

As the tiny box hinged open, I felt the air vanish from the room.

I'd been searching for the perfect one for months, until I'd finally realized such a ring didn't exist.

There simply wasn't anything on this earth as perfect as Everly. So I'd had one created.

Three carats of dazzling beauty, surrounded by a shiny platinum setting. She'd find it extravagant and outrageous.

It was. It was ridiculous and expensive and crazy.

But that's how I felt when I was with her. Ridiculous . . . crazy and completely out of control.

I knew she found our new lifestyle a bit eccentric. The house had been a huge adjustment and saying good-bye to the place where we'd started had been hard, but this was what I wanted for us.

For her.

Everything.

We finally had the financial freedom to do just that. Life was whatever we chose to make it and looking down at that dazzling diamond, I couldn't wait to begin it.

Glancing up at the clock on my computer, I felt my knees begin to bob again as my patience waned. There were still two hours to go until the end of the day. It was a Friday and I couldn't wait for the weekend to begin. I had serious plans.

Right now.

Fuck it. I was a partner in this firm. I could leave early.

Feeling the excitement welling up inside of me as I slid the tiny black velvet box inside my jacket pocket, I logged out of my computer and headed for the door.

"Leaving early, Mr. Kincaid?" Cheryl asked, looking up from her computer. I smiled briefly, seeing several pictures of her newest grandchild disappear quickly as she pulled up her e-mail to hide it from me. I'd told her a hundred times she could take a break when there was a lull in the day, but she hated the idea. I was glad to see she was at least taking my advice, even if it was done discreetly.

"Yes," I answered, feeling the tiny box in my jacket like a brand against my chest. "Everly and I are taking a little trip to Big Sur this weekend and I wanted to get an early start."

"That's lovely. One of my favorite places to visit on the coast," she said with nostalgia in her eyes. "My husband and I used to take the kids down Highway One and stop for lunch at Nepenthe's. The views from their deck are the best. Sometimes I close my eyes and pretend I'm back there, with all of them." She took a deep breath, her lip trembling slightly.

"Now we're all scattered. And Jack, well he's the most scattered of all."

"You could still go back," I offered. "With your kids, and grandkids."

She looked up and smiled, a look of sadness in her eyes. "Yes. I guess we could. It wouldn't be the same, though."

"Might still be a great memory, though."

"You're right," she nodded. "There's no use in living in the past, when I have so much to live for now."

"Exactly."

"Have a great weekend, Mr. Kincaid."

"You too, Cheryl," I said, giving her a quick wink as I walked away.

One more stop to go and then I'd be free for my weekend with Everly. My stomach fluttered just thinking about it.

Turning the corner toward Trent's office, I opened my mouth to announce my arrival in some sort of rowdy way. A yell, a whoop, or shouting his name. We were rarely polite in this office unless there were clients in the building and then it was jackets buttoned, manners on, and smiles tightened. But on a Friday afternoon, we rarely had anyone in the office, mostly so the boys could have a drink or two at their desks while they waited on the weekend.

As soon as my mouth formed the sound, the noise fell heavy in my chest. I stopped in my tracks.

Trent's office was in the far back corner of the building. It was the largest and it stood by itself, creating a bit of privacy for the creator of our company. Usually it was brightly lit and welcoming. Trent's secretary usually sat out front, blocking unannounced and unwanted guests.

Today the place was dark, as if it had been abandoned. The secretary's desk was unattended and the overhead lights were off, as if to signal a warning to those who entered the area.

Those should have been my first clues.

A faint light under Trent's door burned with intensity, instantly drawing my attention.

Before I had a chance to wonder what the hell was going on, Trent's door slowly opened. Pushing myself against the wall around the corner, I looked over my shoulder to catch a glimpse of him.

He wasn't alone. Another man in a suit joined him at the door, both tossing glances left and right before turning their focus back on one another.

"It's been a pleasure doing business with you again, Mr. Lyons," the suit said, offering a hand.

Trent took it in his tight grasp, grinning. "You too. And I'm going to assume we're good. For everything?"

A tight curve tugged at the man's lip. "For now."

Trent reached up and stuffed something in the other man's pocket. A flash of green and it was gone. "Make sure to keep me abreast of anything you hear. Got it?"

The suit nodded, turning to leave.

My heart pounded as I made my way back to my office, muttering to Cheryl about forgetting something. Shutting the door behind me, I fell against it, feeling the cool hardwood on my back.

Trent had just paid someone off.

Holy fuck, what were we doing here?

The ring in my jacket pocket, sitting against my heart, felt like a ticking time bomb now, rather than a road to salvation.

Touching my chest, I wondered how I could possibly ask Everly to spend the rest of her life with me when I wasn't sure what kind of life I'd created.

I'd wanted to give her everything, but in doing so had I ended the very thing I'd sought to protect?

My eyes opened as my vision swam.

Coming out of a memory never seemed to get easier.

Raising my wrist, I looked at my watch, trying to gauge how much time had passed since I'd been out of it.

Thirty minutes.

Scrubbing my hands over my face, I took a deep breath and rose, intent on one thing and one thing only.

Searching everywhere, I checked every closet, drawer, and cabinet in the house until I thought I might have dreamed the memory.

Maybe it hadn't happened.

The last place I had left to check was my office. Rushing down the hall, I opened the door to the crude mixture of two lives thrown together. Photography equipment was everywhere, scattered over shelves and on the desk, which I had pushed into a corner. I managed to make it to the desk and began opening drawers, moving papers and other random things around...until I found a black velvet box shoved far in the back.

Reaching in with a shaky hand, I held my breath as my fingertips touched the box. Opening it, I saw the truth for myself. There in front of me was the diamond ring I'd seen in my memory.

I had planned to ask Everly to marry me.

Everly...mine. Forever.

Another dream ruined by Trent.

Standing there with the ring I'd never been able to give to the love of my life, knowing if I didn't do something it would just sit in this drawer forever, I knew what I had to do.

I had to let go and trust.

Chapter Nineteen

Everly

He'd let me walk away.

As the tears fell down my cheeks, I climbed into the borrowed bed in my borrowed mess of a room and let the sadness overwhelm me.

When would I be enough? When would I be worth fighting for?

The strong will I'd managed to cultivate over the last several weeks became too heavy of a burden to carry, like an armful of heavy stones. One too many and I was suddenly wobbling back and forth, crumbling under the weight of it all.

I would not fall apart over this.

I would not let this break me.

I had been moving on before all of this had fallen in my lap. I still could.

Rolling over, I pushed onto my elbows and sat up, reaching for the brochures I'd grabbed when I was downtown, touring several of the schools I'd applied to.

This was my future.

Cooking school. But what about Sarah?

"You really should lock the door."

Looking up, I saw August leaning against the door frame with his arms crossed in front of him, as if his being here was the most normal thing in the world.

It was the exact opposite.

Seeing him here, in the apartment I shared with Sarah, felt like a collision and I was the sole victim. There had always been a separation in my life: August, and everything else.

Even after he woke up and I returned to him, I seemed to leave everything else behind. Life became just about him for a short while. Suddenly seeing him here made me realize I'd never fully allowed him into my life.

Maybe he wasn't the only one with trust issues.

"What are you doing here?" I asked, wiping away any leftover tears, knowing I couldn't hide my puffy cheeks and swollen eyes.

"I would have been here sooner but I had a flashback," he said, pushing off the door frame. "Sometimes they overwhelm me—at work, at home. I just collapse and lose consciousness."

"That's not normal," I observed, concern showing in my features as I bit my lip. He edged closer, taking a step into the bedroom. I watched him like a hawk.

"What is normal with any of this?" he asked. "Would anyone even know?"

"I don't know."

"Today, I had a memory of you. Or about you, I guess. It made me realize how much I've given up because of Trent. Because of my need to protect you."

"Tell me—about the memory." I pulled my knees up to my chin and watched him take a hesitant seat on the bed beside me.

"I was going to propose," he said, stealing the breath from my lungs.

"What?" Our eyes met and he nodded, a sad smile on his face.

"Yeah. I don't know the exact day or time, but I remember being so excited to give you the ring. I was going to leave early from work and propose on a weekend trip to Big Sur. I had it all planned."

My eyes closed as I remembered the exact day.

"Why are you canceling?" I asked, confused and furious.

"It's just not a good weekend," he explained, grabbing the back of his neck. He always did that when he was nervous. Or lying. "I have a ton of work and Trent needs me to—"

"Trent needs you," I said, nearly spitting the words. "Then you better go," I said, my voice not much louder than a whisper.

I'd been so bitter. So angry.

We'd planned that trip for weeks, and that morning he'd nearly jumped out of bed, singing in the shower and strutting around the bedroom, talking about how excited he was.

It was supposed to have been our perfect weekend. An escape.

And obviously a beginning we'd never gotten.

"What happened?" I asked, looking up at him as I grieved.

"I went to tell Trent I was leaving early for the day and saw him paying someone off. I think up until that moment I'd only had inklings, maybe a notion or two about some sort of wrongdoings, but this was proof. It was hard to ignore. It spun everything I knew on its axis and suddenly the idea of asking you to marry me seemed like the scariest thing in the world."

"You started locking me up shortly after that," I whispered.

Nodding, he reached for me but stopped himself, as if he wasn't sure how I'd react. If only he knew my body wasn't whole without his tender touch.

"I can't do this anymore," he said, each word on a slow, steady breath.

My heart fell as I looked up at him, knowing it would never beat after this moment if he walked away.

"I can't keep letting him ruin my future. I may have made mistakes and taken wrong turns in the past, but I will not let that govern how the rest of my life unfolds. You were right when you said we don't work when we're apart. It's true. We've tried and failed over and over and each time, both of us end up hurt and even more broken than before. I need you, Everly. I need you now, and forever. I'll always want to protect you, but life—whether it's this one or another—it's not worth living without you."

Without thinking I lunged for him, needing to touch him more than I needed air in my lungs, gravity beneath my feet, or blood in my veins. He was the other half of me—the missing piece I'd been trying to replace for so many years.

But how can you replace something so irreplaceable?

Loving him had always been as easy as breathing. Hating him—that had always been the hard part.

I was done being angry with this man.

I would love him for everything he was, everything he wasn't, and everything we could be together.

Our lips met, as months of separation and a tidal wave of emotions broke forth. Surprise turned to lust, transferring into instant desire and urgency.

I needed him, and as his mouth covered mine, I could feel his growing need for me.

"Everly," he murmured, scattering a scorching path of tender kisses along my collarbone. "We need to talk," he said, the strain in his voice evident as he tried to push away.

My eyes met his and where I expected turmoil for rushing into bed too quickly, or something else equally dumb, I saw pain.

And regret.

"What is it?" I asked, my heart still racing from our kiss.

"I told you I started seeing Magnolia," he began, the confession written so clearly in his mournful eyes that I could almost make out the words hidden there behind his dark green irises.

"Don't," I said, pressing a finger to his lips as I shook my head. I couldn't bear to hear the words, to know the details.

"We weren't together, August. I can't expect anything of you. You didn't do anything bad," I explained.

"Then why does it feel so wrong?" he asked.

I thought about all the times I'd gone to bed with Ryan after my breakup with August. I remembered how it felt—the difference in my heart as I'd made love to another man.

As hard as I'd tried, there was always a part of me missing— something that always separated Ryan and me in those intimate moments. It could have been our drifting...the eventual shift from lovers to friends, but the more I looked back—the deeper I dwelled on those moments, the clearer it became.

I hadn't been making love to Ryan, because my heart was still here with August.

Where it belonged.

"Because nothing will ever feel right except this," I said as his mouth covered mine once again.

We tumbled back onto the bed, our hands and limbs intertwined like vines. Even with my fingers dancing along his skin as I frantically pulled off his shirt, I still couldn't get enough. He was my sweetest addiction and I'd gone far too long without a taste.

"I never thought I'd feel this again…have you in my arms again," he murmured as his lips melted against mine, each word breathing hot air against my skin. "I'm never going to let you go, Everly. Never again," he vowed.

His fingers tugged at the hem of my shirt, pulling it up until the fabric brushed against the back of my head and fell to the floor in a fluttery cloud of purple cotton.

Green eyes drifted over every bare inch of me, capturing the subtle slope of my hips and the sprinkling of freckles along my shoulders. "I would dream of you, of this right here," he said, moving his fingertips along my hip bone as he bent down to place a tender kiss along my skin.

"The way your skin felt against mine," he whispered, as his hands roamed along my flesh. "The smell of your hair as the soft tendrils skimmed my chest when we made love. I remembered it all."

The strap of my bra fell away as he planted hot kisses along my shoulder, moving his fingers toward the clasp in the back. With a flick and a twist, the lace fell freely from my body, leaving nothing but me from the waist up.

"Beautiful," he murmured, his large hands skimming over the sensitive tips of my nipples. I shuddered, my skin pebbling in response to his delicate touch. He bent his head and I immediately felt my toes curl as his mouth closed around my tight rosy bud. Digging my fingers into his hair, I held on as he sucked and licked the taut peak.

"August," I pleaded, writhing against him in need. "Please," I begged.

"Please what?" he asked, his tongue moving out to flick my nipple one last time.

"I need you. Now."

"I'll give you everything you need. Everything," he said. "Right here. Right now." His voice was strong and full of promise as he smoothed my hair back, pushing me against the pillows. "Always."

He rose then, and I took the moment to appreciate his body. Spring, when he had awakened, had long since passed and winter was now upon us. The decline in his body due to his prolonged coma had nearly been erased, and his hard lean muscles, thanks to his love of running, nearly made me blush.

"You're staring," he smirked as he reached for the fly of his jeans. "See anything you like?" His cheesy one-liner caused me to giggle, rising up on the bed to meet him. On my knees, I reached for the denim, pulling him forward until he stumbled slightly.

All playfulness died as his gaze fell, watching my fingers gingerly brush against the rough fabric. The intensity of his gaze never wavered as I slowly undid the loop from the single button. The only sounds in the room were our heavy breaths and the tight grit of the zipper as I slowly worked it down.

August hissed in a mixture of pain and pleasure as my fingers brushed him intimately, working his jeans loose. He was on edge, pulsating with need as he reached for me, pushing me back once again.

Towering over me he readied himself, reaching into his wallet and grabbing protection. I hated that this barrier was needed between us, but time had moved on while we'd been apart. Lives had shifted.

For now, we would come together like this, knowing soon this necessary barrier would be a thing of the past.

Because I knew now that there was no one else in my future but August. No matter how messed up we were together, we were a hundred times worse when we were apart. A single tree in a meadow wasn't any match for Mother Nature's wrath, but give that tree a mate, and together they could wind their branches, combine their roots, and survive even the darkest of storms.

The rest of our clothes drifted to the floor in a cluttered heap, as our bodies slowly came together. My eyes nearly rolled back in my head as I felt his heavy body atop mine, and he deliberately pushed himself into me inch by inch until I was trembling with need.

Our eyes met then, and I gently lifted a hand to caress his cheek.

He winced slightly as my fingers brushed his fresh bruises and I immediately stopped, pulling my hand back.

"Please don't," he said. "Don't ever stop touching me. Even if it hurts. I've had too many wasted memories in the past. From now on, I just want this. Memories of this," he whispered, then bent down to kiss me.

"Yes," I agreed as we lost ourselves in each other. Every thrust he gave, I took. Every moan I uttered, he echoed. We worked together in tandem, bringing pleasure, overwhelming emotions and passion, making love for the first time in what felt like centuries.

This was how it felt to find a soul mate.

My thighs trembled as he continued to bury himself inside me over and over, and I dug my fingernails into his shoulders and pulled my knees to my chest, feeling him sink deeper.

"August!" I cried, beads of sweat dripping between my breasts as I felt my butterflies twisting and coiling deep within my belly. Every breath I took brought me closer to climax and soon I was nearly panting, chasing that invisible finish line.

Through my lust-filled haze, I could see the strain on his face as he raced toward the same finale. His thrusts became more frantic and wild as he bent down, taking my mouth in his as our tongues met in a twisted dance of their own.

I cried out, feeling my core tighten just as he stiffened. A low guttural moan reverberated from his lungs as we came together, falling off the edge together into sated bliss.

* * *

Years could have passed as I lay against his dewy smooth skin, waiting for my breathing to return to normal. He'd collapsed next to me and I found myself curling up into his warm body, even though I felt like my own was on fire.

I could hear his heart racing against my ear, and I smiled knowing I'd made it race with such urgency. I saw his hand move a split second before I felt it brush against my hair, slowly moving between the tiny tendrils as he smoothed them between his fingertips.

"We didn't even close your door," he said. My eyes suddenly went wide. Looking over my shoulder, I realized he was right. The door was wide open, with a clear view into the living room. We were on full display.

"Thank God Sarah has a show tonight," I remarked with a slight giggle, covering my mouth as I did.

"I don't think even that would have stopped us," he commented, rising up on his elbows to gaze down at me.

"I think you might be right," I agreed, loving the sight of him above me. Beside me. With me.

He excused himself to freshen up in the bathroom, taking care of those pesky after-sex things that shall not be spoken of. As soon as he left, I felt the loss immediately. The room became colder; it wasn't as bright and I felt alone.

So very alone.

When he returned, he smiled and snuggled up against me, his heat seeping into my body once again. Closing my eyes, I realized he really was my addiction.

And I was completely dependent.

Sitting up, I took a deep breath and spoke. "There have been so many times we've failed at this, August. I can't bear to go through another round of up and down with you. This time—we need to do this the right way, from the beginning."

"I agree," he nodded. Tiny creases appeared in his forehead as he looked at me with concern.

"I'm not changing my mind, or overthinking anything. Well, maybe overthinking a little, but that's what I do. Or at least, that's what I'm trying to do now."

"Now?" he asked, watching my expression for clues.

"When I walked away from Ryan...from a life I thought I'd wanted, I realized I was living a cookie-cutter existence. I'm thirty years old and I've barely been on my own, or thought for myself."

He turned away, ashamed.

"I'm not blaming this on you, August. I stayed. No matter what went on between us in those years before the coma, I stayed. And it wasn't because I feared what would happen if I stayed. It was because I feared what would happen if I left. I'd thought you'd forgotten about me—that you'd lost interest. What if I left and you truly did forget about me—permanently. What if I was replaced?"

"I could never forget about you," he vowed.

"I know that now, but I was scared. Even then I knew you and I were meant to be. I was just too frightened to know how to reach you. I'd lost you," I said, my voice breaking with the memories of our sad decline.

"You did," he confirmed. "I remember some of it, and even though I told you nothing, you saw so much, Everly. You knew I was headed toward a disastrous path with Trent. You saw the way I changed when money was dangled in front of me, how I'd do anything to keep you safe, even if it meant locking you away from the outside world. I truly was a monster."

"We both have skeletons in our closet, August," I consoled, taking his hand in mine as we faced each other, nestled in the soft sheets of the bed. "And it's time we battle them, together."

"Together," he agreed.

No other words were spoken as he drew the sheet over our heads and pulled me closer, making me forget everything but him and the million ways he could make me fly.

* * *

Eventually, we had enough presence of mind to close the door.

And order food.

As we sipped on red wine and ate pepperoni pizza, we talked. About everything.

August told me about work and how much he hated it. I asked if he still took photographs.

"Of what?" he asked, adding, "My muse had flown away."

"Promise me you'll pick it back up again," I said as my fingers grasped the heavy wineglass and I leaned over to snag a piece of pepperoni from the slice he'd just started.

"I promise. As long as you stop stealing my food, and promise to be my muse again," he said with a wicked smirk, taking the largest bite of pizza possible.

Men really were pigs.

"Absolutely not to the first thing. I will always and forever steal your food, and your coffee. And yes to the second. I will be happy to be your muse, for as long as you'll have me."

His eyes rounded as he looked at me with affection and devotion. "You'll always be my muse," he said. "Because I love you. And that will never change. Not in any memory or lifetime will it ever waver."

Even though we'd already spent hours wrapped up in one another, I felt it again—that undeniable pull toward him. The need to reach out for him, and never let go.

It was intoxicating.

"And I love you," I said, savoring each word as I tilted my head toward his. He tasted like spicy red wine, heat, and passion all rolled in one. I was falling once again under his spell when he pulled back, cocking his head to the side.

"What's this?" he asked.

"Am I boring you?" I laughed, looking over to see what he'd noticed.

"No, quite the opposite, actually. I was about to push the pizza to the floor when these brochures caught my eye. Are you applying to cooking school?" His eyes turned to mine, alive with fire and wonder.

"Yes," I answered, feeling suddenly very shy and awkward, my gaze darting anywhere but toward him.

"Why the face?" he asked, tugging at my chin to capture my attention. "Why do you look so embarrassed?"

Shrugging, I answered, "I don't know. I haven't told anyone yet. I guess I still feel like it's kind of a ridiculous idea."

He shook his head adamantly. "No. Not ridiculous. In fact, I think it makes total sense."

"Really?" My eyes met his.

"Absolutely. You can't cook for me forever," he grinned. Sticking my tongue out at him, I watched as he laughed and continued. "You have an amazing gift, Everly. Don't waste it just because you're scared. I've told you before that I'd be perfectly happy if you spent the rest of your life in that coffeehouse—if that was what you wanted to do, and truly enjoyed it. But if there's something else— something you feel in your gut you must do, then you have to do it."

Giving him a lopsided smile, I remarked, "Sounds like someone is speaking from experience?"

His features fell and I suddenly felt the mood shift. "It's different for me," he answered.

"It doesn't have to be."

"It does. For now," he replied. "Besides, now I have you in my life. I can't be taking risks when it comes to Trent."

"But I can't allow you to sacrifice your happiness," I said, reaching out for him. My finger brushed his shoulder as his eyes tracked its path.

"This is my happiness," he said softly.

"But what if we could have it all? Freedom from Trent, happiness..."

"It's tempting," he admitted with reluctance, as his jaw ticked. "I hate that Trent is involved in any way in our lives, especially when it concerns you. But you've seen what he can do—the way he can manipulate. But that's not all. He's so much worse."

"Which is why we need an out, August. Otherwise, this will all just end in disaster. You know this as well as I do."

"I know," he agreed, his shoulders slumping in defeat. "I just hate the idea of getting you involved with him."

Our eyes met and I could see his insecurity. The vulnerability and fear.

"Trust, remember?"

"Trust," he repeated.

"Good. Now it's time to form a plan."

The front door opened just then and Sarah's voice could be heard from the other side of the bedroom door, humming and carrying on as she made her way into the apartment after a long night of performances.

"We need to tell Sarah, huh?" August said softly, looking at the door as if it were a barrier between our life now and the life we were about to embark on.

"Yes," I confirmed. "We need to tell her everything."

Taking a deep breath, I prepared myself.

In a few minutes I was going to break my best friend's heart.

God give me strength.

Chapter Twenty

August

Sarah took the news better than we'd expected.

She screamed into a couch pillow for about three minutes straight, and then came up with about twenty different, very detailed ways to remove Trent's male anatomy from his body. The entire conversation made me and my own anatomy very uncomfortable and I quickly began to pace the room, rather than sit around just in case her rage went viral.

Sarah on any given day could be slightly irrational and usually beat to the sounds of her own drums. Scorned and cheated Sarah? She was batshit crazy.

But batshit crazy Sarah wanted revenge and we could definitely use that.

"So what do we do?" she asked as she slowly came back down to earth, smoothing out the battered pillow with her hands as she ignored the few angry tears that still drifted down her cheeks.

"I think we need Brick and Tabitha's help," Everly said, sitting across from me now, acting as an anchor for her best friend. Snuggled together, Sarah leaned her head against Everly, looking smaller than usual. Her long lean frame, usually so statuesque and rigid due to years of training, was now droopy and withdrawn from the news of Trent's betrayal.

"Both of them?" I inquired with mild curiosity. I'd never met Everly's therapist and was surprised she mentioned her at all. In the past, when she'd spoken of her, I had always assumed that their relationship was professional and nothing else. Client and therapist.

When had that changed?

"Oh." Everly blushed, smiling as she looked at me from across the room. "I forgot to tell you."

"What?"

"Brick and Tabitha...they're married."

I sat frozen in place, staring at her as I tried to process what had been said. I'd heard the words, understood their meaning, but it was like trying to process something while intoxicated.

"What?" I finally said. "You've got to be joking."

She shook her head, that warm smile still plastered all over her beautiful face. "I went over there earlier today...yesterday, I guess," she said, looking at the wall clock.

I joined her and sighed. Today had felt like the longest day I could remember.

When Brick had shown up at my door this morning with the boom box, ready to take a dive into my subconscious, I'd had no idea this is how my day would end up.

Sometimes it took years or days. Today, in a matter of hours my entire world had changed.

Everly had done that. Everly had changed everything.

"Went over where?" Sarah asked, lifting her head from Everly's shoulder.

"Brick's," she answered, and then shook her head, correcting herself. "Tabitha's. Whatever! I went over there thinking I was going to see Tabitha. I had her address from the wedding invites, and well—I was distraught."

"That's an understatement," Sarah chimed in. I rolled my eyes.

"So, I got there, feeling all sorts of bad because I knew I was breaking some sort of cardinal rule by visiting her home, and who answers the door? Brick! I was flabbergasted. I actually almost turned around and walked away."

"Tabitha and Brick?" I finally said, still trying to process it all. Why had he never told me?

"Yeah. They're cute together," Everly said, that same smile appearing across her face.

"How long?" I asked, needing to stand again. Everly looked at me in confusion, waiting for me to clarify my vague question.

"Sorry. How long have they been married?"

"I don't know an exact figure, but I'd say decades at least."

Decades. And he hadn't told me?

"I can see the questions forming in your eyes, August. They didn't keep this from us because they were trying to be devious. Tabitha was simply trying to uphold her ethical code, which hasn't been easy with the three of us. When Brick found out about our connection, it made things difficult for them. They'd never shared closely linked clients, and had no idea how to handle it. They could have just dropped us both, but they cared for us. So they did the best they could."

I nodded, remembering how Brick had suddenly stopped charging me shortly after we met, but kept close regardless of how many times I'd tried to close myself off from him.

"We do need them," I finally agreed, knowing their two even-tempered minds would help cool down the revenge-hungry flames that burned within all three of us.

"Good, but let's do that tomorrow," Sarah suggested, yawning into her pillow. "I need to go to my room, take a shower, and cry for a few hours first."

Everly wrapped her arms around her. "Just try and sleep."

"I'll do that, too," she promised, rising from the couch. She blew us a kiss and disappeared into her room.

I knelt down next to Everly on the couch and kissed each one of her knuckles as I brought her hand close to my face.

"I'll make this right," I promised, seeing the worry on her face after watching her best friend crumble before her eyes.

"No, we will. Together."

Nodding, I agreed. It still scared the shit out of me, but I couldn't walk away now. She was mine and I was hers, and the only way we could accomplish anything in this world was hand in hand.

Together.

*   *   *

Walking into the house Brick shared with his wife was surreal. It was nothing like I'd expected.

The few times I'd visited Brick's office, he'd given off this hip, cool vibe—sleek furniture, cool, soothing tones, and mellow music to help with relaxation.

The longer I knew Brick, though, the more I realized his office persona was a complete sham.

Although Brick himself was calm and collected, his outward appearance was generally anything but. Wearing everything from brightly colored Hawaiian shirts to khakis and polos, the man looked like a tourist half the time and a professional golf player the rest.

As we settled into the worn, plush couches, I took a moment to look around. Tabitha brought us refreshments. Aged photos dotted the walls, memories of years gone by and two lives forever entwined. Old books lined the shelves, ranging from trashy romance novels to classic poetry and even old college textbooks.

The house felt lived in, warm and inviting. I'd spent so many nights in my own home, the chill of loneliness creeping into my very bones as I longed for the touch of Everly once more. Sitting here, among the years of clutter and dust, it made me eager for the future. Eager for our own future. Where would it take us? How would we fare and what battles would we face?

I knew one thing was for certain: our future might not be possible if we continued to let Trent run our lives. We had to stop him, and today, we would figure out how.

"I know I'm probably not supposed to say this, but I'm so happy to see the two of you sitting here together," Tabitha said as she re-entered the room, bringing a tray of sandwiches. We'd only called them an hour ago to say we were stopping by. When had she found the time to make so much food?

"It does settle my nerves quite a lot," Brick chimed in, rounding the corner behind his wife, carrying several liters of soda and a few bottles of water. Had they been expecting us, or was this just what older, well-adjusted people did—kept food on hand for impromptu guests?

Whatever it was, I was impressed.

And starving.

"Well, anything I can do to settle your nerves, Brick," I joked, eyeing a big roast beef sandwich near the corner of the tray that was calling my name. Everly caught me staring and leaned forward, grabbing the sandwich of my dreams and handing it to me with a grin.

"You guys really didn't have to do all this. We weren't expecting lunch," Everly said. I took a large bite of my sandwich and groaned in pleasure.

"But we really appreciate it," I mumbled, causing Everly to giggle.

"We're happy to," Tabitha remarked, taking a seat next to her husband on the couch across from us. Sarah had taken the single chair, making it almost appear as if she was seated at the head of an invisible table. The observation must have been lost on her, because all her focus was on the turkey sandwich she was dismantling, eating just the turkey and veggies. The bread sat untouched.

Everly had once said Sarah's issues with food got worse when her life was in shambles. I'd never seen her obsess over anything before. Usually she just groaned about the calories, ate small portions, and made several promises to work it all off later.

But today, she was scrutinizing everything, and Trent was the cause of her anxiety.

"We want Trent to pay for everything he's done, and we need your help," I said, setting down my food and getting right to business.

"So, you've finally realized that you can't do this alone?" Brick said, his eyes meeting mine with compassion.

I nodded. "Yes, and I want to apologize. For everything I've put you through over the last few months. All of you, actually. I thought I could handle Trent on my own. He was my problem, and I had hoped by pushing everyone away, I could keep the ones I loved protected. But Trent is far smarter than I gave him credit for, and he's got me on a short leash. He always has. If there's one thing I've learned from my memories, it's that I can't continue down this path. I need help, and I'm hoping the five of us can bring him down. For good."

"How?" Brick asked. "And how can we help?"

We strategized all day, going through the entire plate of sandwiches and several liters of Coke, until Everly put her foot down and went to find coffee to recharge her drained mind. Everything we thought of came down to the same simple problem.

Trent would always be one step ahead of us. He seemed to have ears everywhere, and without knowing how, we could never be too careful.

When I'd pushed Everly away, hoping he'd see I was no longer interested in her and to divert his attention somewhere else, he'd instead followed her, forming a growing connection to Sarah he'd begun just to keep himself in the loop. When I'd gone to Magnolia, he'd always seemed to know what I was doing and in what direction I was headed.

How was I supposed to poke around and get answers when he was constantly breathing down my neck?

"What if I played spy?" Sarah asked, taking a deep breath.

"No," I said immediately.

"But—"

"Absolutely not. You cannot go back to him. Besides, he's got to know we would have told you—especially after I went over to his place the other night and beat him to the ground for hurting you."

"You didn't." Sarah's eyes widened as her gaze fell to my cut lip and black and blue bruises. "I was going to ask, but I wasn't sure I should."

"We had a few words," I remarked, as Everly squeezed my hand. "Besides, even if he was willing to play that game and continue seeing you, I couldn't ask that of you. It would be too much."

She nodded, knowing I was right.

Which left us with only one option. Something I'd left for the last minute if nothing else was on the table. Everly was going to hate this idea.

"What if we bring in Magnolia and I give Trent the deal of the century?" I suggested, afraid to even look at Everly. How would she react to hearing Magnolia's name...knowing we'd been more than casual?

"Explain," she said calmly, her hand still tight around mine.

"I've been trying to wrap my head around this whole thing. Why Trent wanted me back so badly...why he's gone to such lengths to keep me here. I still think the answer is hidden in my memories somewhere, and that's where I need Brick's help. I want to dive deeper into hypnosis and see what else I can find."

"And Magnolia?" Everly asked, her voice strained.

"It's Trent's trigger. Ever since I came back, he's been vying for this deal, even going so far as to burn down the art gallery where my photography was displayed, just to keep me focused."

Her eyes rounded as she turned to me. "You had photos on display? In an art gallery?"

"Yeah," I replied, "I got the call the night Trent showed up. I was so excited to tell you."

Her expression fell as a tear dripped down her cheek. "I wish I could have seen it."

"Maybe you will—someday," I answered, tilting her chin up to find those beautiful blue irises once more. "Which is why we need to do something drastic," I continued.

"You're right."

"Giving him a huge account like that will be like dropping a pile full of cash in his lap. He'll be giddy. I'm hoping this excitement makes him careless, maybe even a little reckless in how he handles things at the office. So far, I haven't been able to get in to any of the locked files, but maybe if I can work on him, make him happy, he'll budge a little."

"It's a long shot," Sarah said, raising her eyebrows in doubt.

"I know it is, but it's the best idea we have. In the meantime, we hope and pray we find something better in my memories. Something solid. Because we have to pin this on Trent and Trent alone, otherwise..."

"You could be charged as well," Everly finished my sentence for me.

"Yes."

"Then let's do it right," Sarah said, turning to Tabitha and Brick for guidance.

Brick took a deep breath, directing his gaze at me. "Are you actually planning on taking the money from Magnolia and her father?" he asked hesitantly.

"No," I answered as I watched his chest fall in relief. "I'm going to be honest. With both of them. They deserve that. I got to know Magnolia's father in the brief time we were together and I'm hoping he'll agree to this little scam we'll work up."

"And if he doesn't?" Tabitha asked.

"Then we think of something else," I said. "Because this has to end."

Everyone nodded in agreement, and we got to work.

After several calls and conversations, I had a lunch date with Magnolia and her father.

Time to come clean.

* * *

Everly and I spent nearly every second in bed up until the moment I had to leave to meet Magnolia. As I dressed in the clothes I'd arrived in two days prior, having made no time to run home to change, I glanced down at her on the bed, feeling my chest ache at the sight.

I'd never felt so conflicted in my life.

Seeing her—being with her, feeling her heart race and her ragged breath as we made love, I'd never been happier. But this risk—this plot we'd planned out to hopefully expose and take down my partner—filled me with dread. Would I be able to keep the ones I loved safe? And was I taking on more than we could handle?

A part of me just wanted to stay here, wrapped up in bedsheets, with her as my prisoner forever. I'd make it worth it. She'd never miss the outdoors.

And she'd be safe. From everything that could harm us.

But I knew that was the old me talking—the one that had lost touch with reality. The August who'd become so consumed by his own self-worth that he would rather lock up his life than solve his problems.

I wasn't that man anymore.

Or at least I hoped I wasn't.

Everly trusted me to fix this, and in turn, I had to bestow upon her the trust I'd never been willing to give.

"Your face looks a little better today," she said as she looked up at me from the bed, her eyes hooded, sleep still lingering in those baby blues.

"Liar," I smirked, leaning down to kiss her cheek. She smelled like us; the woodsy smell of my aftershave lingered on her skin from the hundreds of kisses I'd scattered through the night, but I could also still smell the fruity fragrance of her shampoo, reminding me that she was still her own person.

Still Everly.

She'd grown stronger since the last time I'd seen her. In the months since we'd parted, she'd found herself among the ruins of her relationship with Ryan and the reinvention of herself.

I was just glad I still belonged in there somewhere.

"How long will you be gone?" she asked, sitting up now to watch as I tucked my wallet in my back pocket and grabbed my shoes.

"I'm not sure. Not too long, but hopefully not too brief, either—that would be a bad sign."

She nodded, her apprehension showing in the tiny creases in her forehead.

Placing my shoes next to the bed, I sat down beside her and pulled her to my side. "It was nothing," I said, hoping she'd truly hear me this time.

"I know," she said, sadness still lingering in her voice.

"Then why are you so upset?"

"I don't know," she replied. "It's stupid, really. I was engaged for months. I nearly married another man, and yet I'm sitting here pouting over another woman in your bed."

Clutching her chin, I made sure her eyes met mine. "There will never be anyone but you. In my bed, in my heart, or in my soul."

Tears stung her eyes as her lips met mine. "I love you."

"I love you, too." I smiled back, smoothing away the moisture from her eyelids, knowing there weren't any truer words that had ever been said.

*   *   *

I'd planned on meeting Magnolia about thirty minutes prior to her father showing up. She deserved answers, and it was definitely past time I gave them.

Arriving at the restaurant a few minutes early, I sat watching people converse and mingle at other tables. Families, business associates, lovers—everyone had an agenda for the day.

What was on mine?

Hopefully, a step toward something brighter.

As if she'd heard my silent plea, Magnolia appeared. Ushered by the host, she walked toward me from across the room and smiled politely.

That was a good sign, at least. Our conversation yesterday had been a little less than cordial. "Frozen and brief" would have more aptly described it. I was surprised she'd even agreed to this meeting in the first place. I blamed it on sheer curiosity, but now I was hoping—begging the heavens above—that it might be more.

I'd always been afraid of and intimidated by Magnolia's affection toward me. It was heavily one-sided and made me feel inadequate because I wasn't able to reciprocate feelings for someone so deserving. In a perfect life, the wealthy August Kincaid would have loved someone like Magnolia Yorke. They would have fallen madly in love, with the vast approval of her parents, and driven off into the sunset. It would have been a beautiful, photo-worthy ending.

But life wasn't always what it appeared to be, and sometimes what we saw on the surface was only a false representation of what really lay hidden underneath.

I was not the wealthy, power-hungry man everyone assumed I was. Or at least I wasn't anymore. And this empire I'd helped build was teetering, and I was afraid under the right scrutiny, it would crumble.

Which was why I needed out.

Fast.

And Magnolia just might be my savior.

"August," she greeted me, offering her hand as I stood to take it.

"Magnolia," I replied, taking her hand in mine as I leaned forward to kiss her cheek. It was an intimate greeting, one we'd done many times before. The fact that she was still allowing it gave me hope.

"Long time, no see," I said, suddenly searching for words. I'd had this all planned out in my head, what I was going to say—how I was going to say it—but all the words seemed trivial and contrived now that she was here in front of me.

"Yes, it has," she replied, taking the seat across from me. Our eyes met in awkward silence, as I searched for the right thing to say.

"Look—I just wanted to—"

"Stop," she interrupted, holding her manicured hand up in the air. "Let me talk first."

"Okay," I relented.

"I know what you're going to say. I can see it in your eyes—the apology, the remorse. Let me say, it's not needed. I knew what I was getting myself into when I started seeing you. I knew you were... challenging," she said with a sly grin that seemed to elevate the mood slightly. "And I knew there were no guarantees. When you said there had been someone else, I pretty much knew my efforts were wasted."

"But then why—?"

"Did I sleep with you?" she asked, finishing my sentence. "Because you're not the only one who gets lonely, August. And you're not the only one with issues. I know, after meeting my family, it's hard to believe I could be anything but the rosy, bubbly woman I personify, but we all have baggage."

"You're right," I agreed. "I'm sorry I never took the time to know you better."

She shrugged, tapping her fingers on the table. "You saw what I wanted you to see. And that's my fault. Maybe if I learned to let my guard down... let someone in, then perhaps I'd find the right person."

"You deserve that."

"So do you," she replied. "And I have a feeling that's why you're here."

Our eyes met and I nodded. "Yes, and I need your help."

Chapter Twenty-One
Everly

Meet me at the Cliffs.

That's all the text message had said. August had been gone for hours, and as the minutes slowly ticked by, I'd never wished for the relentless monotony of work more. *Of course it had to be my day off,* because nothing fostered creativity more than boredom, and right now my brain was being very creative indeed.

It was idiotic. Moronic and stupid.

After all the nights I'd spent screaming and crying at him for his jealous, domineering ways—for locking me up when I thought he was just being cruel, or the way he'd corner me in a room if a man looked at me the wrong way.

Now who was crazy?

I'd told myself a hundred times it was a business meeting. It was nothing more than a business meeting. He was going to ask her for help, and that was it. But that didn't stop my mind from reeling and my brain from going haywire at the thought of her anywhere near him.

Parking near the curb, I got out of my beat-up car, noticing how it stood out among the formidable houses that spread down the long street. Thinking about the message again, I looked up at the house August and I had once shared, and decided to walk toward the back, taking his message literally.

The salty smell of the waves crashing below filled me with a flood of memories.

Happy memories, sad memories... but memories just the same.

As I walked along the pathway then opened the gate that led to the backyard, I saw him... standing along the cliffs with his back turned to me. His black T-shirt flapped around in the wind, giving me glimpses of the tanned skin I'd worshipped just hours earlier.

The roaring thunder of the waves filled my ears, making my footsteps seem nearly silent as I approached. As I wrapped myself around him, I felt him tighten and then relax back into my arms. He felt solid, safe, and real.

And mine, finally mine.

"How'd it go?" I asked, having to raise my voice over the sound of the surf.

He turned in my arms, gripping my waist with his firm grasp. "Good," he smiled. "Better than I could have expected."

I swallowed the lump of jealousy that I felt blossoming as he began speaking of his meeting with Magnolia. Seeing his eyes light up as he spoke about her—I knew he was excited about our possibility, our future, but I just wished it didn't have to include her.

"Hey," he said, stopping suddenly. His eyes rounded and focused on me. "What's wrong?"

"Nothing," I answered casually, trying to cover my doubt with a hopeful smile.

"Everly," he warned. "I can see something is bothering you. Please don't shut me out."

Feeling frustrated, I tore my gaze from his. "It's stupid."

"It's Magnolia again, isn't it?" Waves crashed below us as he waited for me to answer.

"Yes."

"This can't just be jealousy. You've never been the overly jealous type."

He was right. That had always been him. Never me. Even in the years when our relationship was rocky, I'd never doubted his faith in us.

There'd never been any other women in his life. It had always been money, and that's what this was about.

"She intimidates me," I confessed.

"Why?" he asked, rubbing his hands up and down my shoulders as the wind rushed around us.

"Because she's everything I tried to be and failed. I guess I just wonder if you picked her because she wasn't me—because she was different."

His arms tightened around me, protecting me from the cold. "I know your fears. I remember the man I once was, and I can see the insecurities in your eyes. But please believe me when I say that this man—past, present, and future—will always want you, as you are. No matter what."

Feeling his protective warmth, I asked, "Is it strange? Remembering the person you were? Is it difficult? I always feared when your memories returned, you'd change...become something different."

His chest rose against mine before he spoke. "I honestly did, too. It was my biggest fear as I quickly discovered just how downhill I'd gone in those last few years. I never wanted to return to that, and maybe that's what kept me from doing so." He shrugged slightly. "Whatever the reason, I've been able to balance it all. I remember, I process, and then I move on. But parts of me still struggle. The old me still wants to protect you from everything, and I'm having a hard time battling that need to keep you from harm."

"What we're doing is right," I said as the wind howled and the waves broke below.

"I know. I just hope we don't fail."

"Me too," I agreed, pressing my face into his chest. "Me too."

*   *   *

"Are you sure you want me to be here?" I asked as he settled down on the sofa, his posture relaxing as he tried to find a comfortable position.

"Yes," he answered with absolute certainty. "It will help me focus."

I gave a hesitant glance to Brick, who smiled and nodded, giving me a bit more confidence as I sat back into the plush chair and waited for things to begin.

After our talk outside by the cliffs, we'd walked back inside, cold from the wind and salty air, and retreated to the kitchen. After I made us a strong pot of coffee, we discussed the details of August's lunch date with Magnolia and her very wealthy father.

"He's agreed to what I asked," August stated as we huddled in the kitchen, clutching our warm mugs.

"Really? Just like that?" I questioned, wondering what kind of man would simply hand over that kind of cash without any guarantee it would come back to him.

"He trusts me," he shrugged, looking down at the floor. "Not that I deserve it."

"You said Magnolia didn't blame you," I said, grasping his arm in comfort.

"No, she doesn't, and I'm grateful. But the fact of the matter is I used her."

"Maybe you needed each other, for a short period of time. She did say she had baggage of her own. Isn't that why she never walked away?"

He nodded in agreement, but I knew he was still feeling remorse for everything. He always would. It was a change I'd seen since he'd awoken, how the weight of the world always seemed to fall so heavily on him. Years ago, when life was all about success and power, August had rarely given a second glance to problems that arose as long as they were taken care of. Now, everything seemed to be the result of something he'd done.

I understood his plight. But I also understood what it meant to forgive yourself and move on. I'd spent countless hours lying awake, dealing with my feelings over the way I'd handled August's coma—how I'd lied to police and made up a faulty story. It was guilt I'd held on to for years.

Guilt, over time, can ruin you, leaving you in an endless revolving pit of shame.

Life didn't run backward. He needed to remember this. I only hoped my presence here reminded him.

As the calming music played on, I settled into the chair and watched as Brick began working with August, talking in soothing tones, barely over a whisper, to lull him into a hypnotic state.

I'd never witnessed anyone being hypnotized. I'd always assumed it was something akin to a comedy hour where the poor moron would fall immediately asleep and begin clucking like a chicken, completely under the spell of the person who'd hypnotized them.

But it was thankfully nothing like that. August seemed to be fully in control as he fell deeper and deeper into a trancelike sleep. I watched as his breathing evened out, becoming slower. The entire room seemed to mellow as he did and I found myself sinking further into my favorite chair, wrapping my arms around myself as I watched the two men work.

The entire process fascinated me—the idea that August could walk through his subconscious and pick out memories still locked up tight and try to reveal them. I knew, if given the opportunity, he'd ask Brick to put him under this process as much as possible. The temptation to retrieve as many memories as possible was immeasurable. I could see it in his eyes the moment Brick arrived at his doorstep, ready to begin. But the process was lengthy and, according to Brick, risky.

Risky.

That word scared me.

None of us knew what we were doing, really. With August's brain injuries so foreign and with the addition of his flashbacks, we all knew we were walking on shaky ground.

What if it was too much? What if his brain couldn't handle it?

Suddenly, my false sense of security was shaken and nothing in the room could put it back in place. I sat up straighter, zeroed in on August, and just hoped wherever his mind was, he was safe.

Now, completely immersed in a memory, he was eerily still. Only slight movements in his face indicated he wasn't actually asleep.

"He doesn't talk them out," Brick whispered, turning slightly toward me, as we both still focused on August.

"So, you just watch him lay there for however long it takes?" I asked, the worry in my voice growing with each word.

"Yes. He knows I'm here if he needs me, but it's his journey. He takes it alone."

"I wish I could be there for him," I said, my eyes narrowed in on his vulnerable frame. Awake—hell, even sleeping next to him—he always looked so formidable, a force to be reckoned with. But now, seeing him like this, with his mind in flux as he fought for the memories he'd lost, I realized how much he'd been through.

How fragile life really was.

I could have lost him.

I still could.

"You are," Brick said softly, his warm gaze filled with heavy emotion. "You always have been."

Just then, August began thrashing violently. His eyes were still locked tightly closed, his back bowed as he fought against some inner demon in his mind.

"Brick!" I cried, rising from my spot across the room to rush to August's side, but stopping short as Brick took command of the situation.

"August," Brick said calmly. "It's just a memory. Remember where you are. Who you're with," he said. I began to pace, not sure what else to do.

I felt completely useless. I wanted to touch him, to mold myself into his body and erase the turmoil it was suddenly experiencing. But what if I did more harm than good? What if my touch caused him pain...brought him out of the memory too quickly?

"Go to him, Everly. My voice isn't getting through to him. Whatever he's experiencing, it's pulled him in deep and he needs help."

He didn't need to tell me twice. In what seemed like a nanosecond, I was at his side, my hand palming his in a soft, rhythmic motion as I watched his face for any signs of change.

Slowly, I saw the pain in his face ease. Each muscle in his body began to relax back into the cushions of the couch as my fingers brushed over his skin. His breathing evened out and soon I found myself staring into the depths of his bewitching hazel eyes.

"I felt your touch," he said, his voice rough, as if he'd just awakened from a long night of slumber.

"I'm glad," I answered. "You had us both worried."

He lifted his head, glancing in Brick's direction. Nothing was said between the two men, but I could feel a silent conversation pass between them. Like a father checking on his son, Brick silently asked if August was okay and he answered with a slight nod of the head.

Other things must have been discussed in that non-verbal conversation as well, because moments later Brick announced his departure.

"I'm going to let you rest for the evening," he said, rising from the couch and grabbing his coat. "We'll talk more tomorrow."

I followed him out, curiosity peaking as I watched him reach for the door handle.

"Don't leave him alone tonight," Brick said softly. "He may want to talk about it...he may not. Just be there for him. Whatever he remembered was difficult and I can see he's still processing. We just need to give him time."

Nodding in understanding, I reached forward and gave the man a hug. "Thank you," I said. "For everything."

His arms squeezed me gently and then he was gone, disappearing into the night. I turned back toward the living room.

August was still in the same position, lying with his back flat against the couch and his head turned away from me. I thought it might be frightening, approaching him after such a turbulent event. Would he be erratic or different? Would he remember things that might change him?

But I slowly realized as I took this journey back to him that none of it mattered. I'd spent so much time trying to hate this man, and all it had done was cause us pain.

The simple fact of the matter was I'd always love him. Despite his flaws and failings. Maybe I loved him more because of them. Without them, he was just another man and I was just another woman. Our flaws defined us in a way, bringing out the very best and worst in us all.

I'd seen all of August. The highs, the lows. And I loved every single moment in between.

"It's all my fault," he said softly as I entered the room. I sat by his side on the floor.

"What do you mean?" I asked, hoping I wasn't pushing too hard.

"That night—the night I ended up in the hospital, in the coma. It was all my fault. I remember why I was so frantic—so worried. God, I was so stupid, Everly."

I could hear the rising panic in his voice, as if he were reliving the memory once again. Moving up, I pushed him over slightly on the couch, making a tiny spot for my body. He immediately shifted, opening his arms as I snuggled in, facing him.

"I never knew what Trent was doing. Not at first, at least. I don't know how blind and stupid I could have been to not see it. All the signs were there, but it's like I chose to ignore them."

"You became greedy," I said, hating myself for the honesty, but knowing I couldn't sugarcoat the truth.

"Yes," he agreed. "I did. I wanted so badly to give us everything and beyond. That was how it started, and then I just became obsessed. It wasn't enough. I needed more—everything. The clout, the status...Everything that went with the money, I had to have. It's a sickening reality to come to terms with."

"It started from a good place," I said, my fingers stroking his arm in comfort.

"It landed us in this mess," he replied, the regret heavy in his tone. "But I was trying," he said, with a long pause. "I was trying to get us out—to fix everything."

My head lifted as my wide eyes met his.

"You were?" I asked.

He nodded. "I remembered the anxiety I felt that night, picking you up, driving to dinner. I was nervous—so incredibly nervous. But I couldn't figure out why. All I knew was I was going to tell you everything, but then it all went blank."

"When I knocked you to the ground," I said quietly, my mind reliving those few seconds, seeing his surprised face as he'd crumpled to the pavement.

"Hey, it was an accident. And, you've said it before—everything happens for a reason. We've got to believe that now. We're moving forward, remember?"

I nodded. "I remember your agitation that night. You seemed off—not your usual smooth demeanor I'd become so used to," I recalled as I settled back into his grasp.

"I was trying to collect information on Trent—to turn him in. But, it was hard—he's careful and tediously discreet. I could see our relationship crumbling. I knew it was only a matter of time before you left me for good, and that scared me more than anything. I'd been keeping you locked away while I sniffed out evidence and I'd become paranoid that Trent was on to me. Every single whisper had me on edge."

My eyes closed as I remembered all the times we'd argued, fought over that damn lock in the bedroom. I'd never understood why he kept me around if he hated me so much.

If he'd only explained.

So many lost chances.

"My fear for your safety had me acting rash. I knew I was good at what I did—so good that Trent had based our entire operation on my skills alone. I knew that if it came down to it, I'd be able to prove my innocence. Every deal I'd done was legit. But I didn't want to be part of his empire anymore. I hated living in fear and I was cognizant enough to recognize the deterioration in myself.

"I needed an out."

"What did you do?" I asked, scared by what he might say.

"I took out the majority of the liquid assets in the company—the real money. Not the fake shit Trent was making up in the books. I was amazed when I figured out just how little cash we actually had. I took it and invested it in something I thought was sure to double overnight. I thought if I could make Trent a fortune, hold the money over his head, I'd be able to walk away."

"You lost the money?" I guessed, suspecting this story didn't end with a rainbow.

"Yes," he nodded. "That night when I picked you up and tried to take you to that horrible restaurant, I'd planned on telling you everything I'd done and hoped you'd forgive me."

"I would have," I insisted.

His lips met mine, softly at first, almost as if he were begging permission. As my mouth opened, granting him the freedom he sought, his hands touched my face. Tracing tiny paths along my cheeks, down my jawline and across my chin, he seemed to be recording me with his fingertips as his mouth dominated mine.

All words, all memories of the past were forgotten as I clung to him, letting his body take mine completely. He owned me, body and soul. He always had.

Whether a monster or a prince, this man would always be the other half of my soul, and never again would I wander.

Chapter Twenty-Two
August

My lungs burned as I ran, trying to get to her, but every direction I turned she disappeared from my grasp.

Harder and harder, my run turned to an urgent sprint as the wind pounded against my face.

Where had she gone?

Gunfire went off and my heart suddenly froze.

"Everly, no!"

"August! August, wake up!" Everly called out to me as I suddenly bolted upright. I blinked, my eyes burning from the glare of the white-hot sun coming through the large skylights above. Raising my arm to block out the rays, I took stock of my surroundings as my heart's gallop settled back down to a healthy trot.

We were still in the living room, blankets pulled up around us on the couch.

Looking down, I saw her worried expression meet mine.

She was safe.

I exhaled, feeling myself calm as her gentle smile greeted me.

"You were having a nightmare," she said.

"It was nothing," I replied, trying to shake off the fear I was still feeling.

"You called out my name."

Running my hands through my hair, I sighed, knowing she'd see through my sorry attempt to fly under the radar. "Just anxiety," I said. "Left over from last night."

"About last night..." she mentioned. My brow rose in interest and I saw her immediately roll her eyes.

"Not that!" she laughed. "I'm trying to be serious."

"Okay," I said, holding up my hands in defeat. My smile was still wide, though, and I caught her trying to look away to maintain her focus.

"You said you were trying to gather evidence," she started, immediately catching my attention.

"Yes," I replied, wondering where she was going with this.

"Well, do you know what you did with it? If you were gathering evidence, you would have put it somewhere, right? A safe place?"

"I guess," I agreed. "But I've looked all over this house, taking down boxes and boxes of things from the attic...clearing out papers from the desk. I haven't seen anything out of the ordinary."

Her features scrunched together in frustration. "Well, then we look harder. It's got to be here somewhere. You must have been collecting things here and there for several years. You wouldn't have put the evidence just anywhere."

"Maybe you can look for me," I suggested.

She smiled brightly and nodded. "Of course. But don't think that you're going to keep me in this house searching for papers for the next few weeks while you're out doing God knows what."

"Wouldn't dream of it," I grinned, shaking my head.

"Liar."

"Shit, what time is it?" I asked, suddenly remembering what day it was.

Monday—the day we began pulling off this crazy scheme.

"Early. I have to be at work in thirty minutes. You have an hour or more," she said, stretching out next to me like a flexible kitten. Watching her made me never want to move from this spot on the couch again.

Her eyes met mine and I felt the heat between us stir. Rising from the couch, she held out her hand.

"Come on," she said, her nakedness from the night before leaving me completely spellbound.

I did exactly as she said, reaching for her outstretched hand and following her as she walked gracefully across the living room toward the staircase. I took a moment to admire the new bird that stretched its wings wide across her shoulder, free of its cage.

I hoped she still felt that same freedom, now that she was here with me.

Silence fell around us as we went up the stairs, and she came to a stop in front of the master bedroom doorway. Until now, this place had been off-limits—a room she only entered with a specific purpose. She hadn't slept here since I'd reawakened from the coma, and had stayed in here for only short periods of time, too burdened with memories of a time long since passed.

"It's time we moved past the memories that have defined us for so long. You are August, and I am Everly...and for as long as I can remember, I have loved you. Even when things were bleak, and it seemed like our future was lost, that was the one thing that remained constant—my love for you."

In one swift movement, I lifted her in my arms, feeling her long legs wrap around my torso as our eyes locked. Carrying her into the room she had once feared, I watched as our bodies tumbled to the bed that had so long ago carried our love and loss.

"You're going to be late for work," I said, my voice rough with emotion as I let my gaze wander over her naked flesh.

"Good," she replied, reaching up to tug on my shoulder. I came willingly, loving the feel of her skin as she pressed against me.

"You'll let me know if—" I began, rising up to meet her gaze.

"Shh, just love me," she whispered, arching her back.

Whatever demons had resided in this room, we exorcised them that morning. With the glistening magic of our bodies, we worked together seamlessly, reminding ourselves that memories were meant for the past. What we had now was worth living for.

"I love you," she said as each thrust of my hips sent her spiraling. "I've always loved you. Even when I shouldn't have, even when I hated you. I've never stopped loving you, August."

Every word from her lips set me on fire, creating an inferno in my heart as I worshipped her body, her soul. No one would ever love her as much as I did. No one. And I would spend every moment of forever showing her just that. Never would she be taken for granted again. She would never have to wonder, or doubt my love again because I would fucking sing it to the heavens if she asked.

She owned me. She always had. I'd known it the moment she walked into that hospital room and I knew it now. Everly Adams was my mate, my true north, and my heart. Two years of lost memories couldn't keep us apart, and I'd be damned if one shifty-eyed crook of a man would stand in my way now.

Rising up on my forearms, I moved deep and low, pushing her knees forward as she moaned beneath me. Her hands ghosted up my chest, teasing the muscles in my abdomen and torso.

"You feel so damn good," I muttered, my voice barely above a hoarse growl as I took her again and again. Soon her muscles began to tighten around me as I struggled to hold on.

"Oh God!" she cried out, her nails digging into my chest as our eyes met. The waves crashed below and I felt my body give way as we both tumbled into oblivion.

Fucking stars. Every damn time.

Our breaths came together, racing in and out as I fell beside her.

"You'll be careful?" she asked, the apprehension in her voice apparent as I turned to face her.

"Yes," I answered.

"Don't do anything risky." Her hand rose to touch my face, as the reality of what we were attempting became very matter of fact.

"I won't," I answered. "I'm just doing a little looking around. Nothing big. He'll never notice."

"He notices everything," Everly warned.

Nodding, I pulled her into my arms, giving us a few more minutes of peace before the real world invaded our little slice of heaven. Soon, we would both have to leave for work, going our separate ways, and I wouldn't be able to protect her anymore.

Soon, I might not be able to protect myself.

*   *   *

I spent the entire morning going through old books, researching anything I could find that was related to my dealings in the company since I'd joined as a partner. If I was going to turn over evidence to the authorities regarding Trent's illegal activities, I wanted to be sure I couldn't be roped in as a coconspirator. I would not go to jail for this asshole.

After hours of scanning through numbers and tables I'd just barely begun to understand, I finally felt sure enough that I really had been in the dark, that my dealings had been legit business as a front for the company.

I had a feeling everything beyond me, though, was absolute crap.

And that's what I needed to discover.

Time to act.

Feeling the nerves all the way down to my shoes, I rose from my office chair and took a deep breath. This was for Everly. This was for our future.

The old me would have hidden. The old me would have lied to the woman he loved.

No more.

I tried to ignore the need to ball my fists tightly as I walked toward Trent's office. For the first time I noticed how separated we were from each other.

Me on one side of the building. Him on the other.

Why had I never noticed that before?

Maybe I had. Perhaps it had been one of many things I'd noticed over the years, filing the fact away in a box of oddities that finally overflowed into a messy pile that couldn't be ignored anymore.

Trent practically lived over here, a world away from me. He had his own guys, his own team, apart from me. I had no earthly idea what they did, or even who they were. When I'd returned after my coma, I just hadn't cared to know, but maybe I wasn't supposed to know?

The memory of Trent exchanging money with the suit came to mind as I moved across the building, smiling at Trent's secretary as I arrived.

"Is he in?" I asked, acting casual and carefree.

"Yes, let me tell him you're here," she said, holding a finger up as she pressed a few buttons on her phone. I didn't pay attention to what was said as I looked around, noticing the expensive artwork that hung on the walls. *How much had that cost our clients?*

"You can go on in, Mr. Kincaid," Alice said, smiling up at me. Her eyes lingered on my blackened one for a moment but she turned away, blushing.

"Thanks," I answered, strolling past her with my hands in my pockets, as if I had all the time in the world. Alice loved Trent. He'd made sure of that, with flirty comments and extra bonuses at Christmastime. She was his faithful servant now, and I couldn't risk one tiny slipup around her. She might not understand what kind of beast she was working for, and she'd protect him if she felt I was in the wrong.

As far as I was concerned, every person in this office was the enemy until I could do something to save them.

Crossing the threshold, my gaze immediately locked on Trent, sitting at his desk like a king residing over his fucking kingdom. He looked pompous and heavy-handed, with his feet resting high on the polished wood. He exuded confidence and class, reminding me of everything I'd once loved but now hated.

Wealth, power... the pursuit of it all.

None of it mattered. It could all be gone in the blink of an eye.

"Nice face," Trent sneered, his expression menacing as he smiled up at me, only giving me partial attention as he glanced at his phone screen.

"Ditto," I replied, nodding in his direction. He might have gotten several swings in, but I'd done my fair share in leveling the playing field. His face was cut and bruised, too, a mangled version of what it had been before we'd fought.

I'd gladly do it again.

"Alice thinks we had a crazy weekend in Mexico," he said, chuckling under his breath.

"Whatever," I answered, not bothering to take his bait. I had bigger issues at hand. Like a multimillion-dollar deal to put in play.

"So, what's up? Come to threaten me some more? Want a rematch? Or are you coming to grovel at my feet? Because I could use some groveling right about now."

"I got the Yorke account," I said through clenched teeth. It took every ounce of control I had not to step forward and show him exactly what kind of groveling he deserved, but I needed to be smart.

He was baiting me as usual and I would not fall for it.

I watched as his feet hit the floor, and his cell phone dropped to the desk.

"You're shitting me. How much?"

His full attention was mine as I took a seat across from him. Grabbing a pen from his organized desk, I wrote a number down on a Post-it and passed it to him, watching his eyes go wide with wonder. I could practically see dollar signs already in his black irises.

The money-grubbing asshole. I had him exactly where I wanted him.

For exactly two seconds.

As quickly as he'd exploded over the news, he seemed to re-evaluate, drawing himself back in. His excitement became contained as he suddenly looked me up and down, scrutinizing every aspect of my demeanor.

This was the Trent everyone feared.

"How?" he asked, shifting back into his seat as he studied me.

Sometimes the best lies are the ones closest to the truth. Working with someone like Trent, I knew I couldn't risk him seeing through me.

Letting out a long sigh, I shook my head in mock defeat. "I just don't want any more trouble," I said, raising my hands up like a white flag.

He eyed me suspiciously, still not convinced, so I rambled on. "Look, I get it. I'm not going anywhere. I just don't want what we do here to keep affecting my personal life. I'm done fighting. I just want peace and quiet."

"What is it about this girl?" he asked, a menacing smile spread across his face.

"Everly stays out of it. All of it," I said, the venom in my voice unmistakable.

"Damn. Okay. You got it," he practically laughed, the dollar signs returning to his eyes before they went dead cold. "But August, remember—one step out of line, and she's fair game. Got it?"

Feeling my heart kick up a notch at his threat, I nodded, acting the compliant servant I was pretending to be. "I told you. I'm done fighting."

"Good. Let's go make some fucking money." He grinned from ear to ear.

It sent chills racing up my spine.

Had I just made a deal with the devil?

*   *   *

With each passing day, I felt my panic rising.

As we dove further and further into this convoluted plot, the fear I felt grew like a cancer. Soon it might be terminal, and I would be plagued with tumors of doubt as they fed on my anxiety over losing the ones I loved.

The man I had once been suddenly felt very real—very raw.

It was so easy to judge him when I was on the outside looking in, given only glimpses and pieces of memories to rely on. But now that I faced his reality, knew his fears, I understood the man he'd become back then.

I understood the paranoia he'd felt. Because I felt it, too.

Meetings were no longer held at the Cliffs, for fear that we were being watched. Instead, we met at Brick and Tabitha's for dinners, hoping that even if Trent was suspicious of my newly compliant behavior, he wouldn't suspect anything of an innocent dinner party with friends.

Every time we gathered, I felt guilty. Guilty for their roles in this. Guilty that they were part of my life and of this dangerous thing we were doing.

It ate away at me until I found myself staring at the ceiling at night, listening to the crashing waves as they beat against the cliffs. I'd hold on to Everly, feel her warmth against me, and let the fear consume me until I found myself waking her with my tongue, my mouth, and every other part of me, just so I could convince myself she wasn't an illusion.

"You're not happy," Everly said late one night after I'd once again awakened her from slumber, taking her fast and hard as my body quaked with need.

Turning toward her, I saw sadness in her eyes. Smoothing back strands of coppery hair from her face, I questioned her words. "Why would you say that?" I asked, my heart still beating wildly from our lovemaking.

"You barely sleep," she began, sitting up in the darkness, taking the sheet with her. I watched the moonlight touch her ivory skin. It illuminated her, making her look almost ethereal under its soft glow. "And when you do, you have nightmares. You call out my name in your sleep."

Letting out a heavy sigh, I reached for her. She came willingly, lying next to me. I tucked her into my side, my fingers slowly brushing over her arm as I spoke.

"I'm terrified I'm becoming him," I admitted, knowing lies would only send us backward. I'd seen what kind of life lies had produced. I had no interest in a repeat performance.

"Becoming who?" she asked, her gaze turned upward toward me.

"The old me," I said. "The paranoid, fearful August who panicked and did rash, stupid things. What if I haven't changed at all?"

She sat up slightly, rising up on her elbows so I could see the powdery blue of her eyes. "When I first discovered you'd lost all of your memories, my first question was what type of person would you be? Would you be different or the same? When I got to know the new version of you, my fears changed and suddenly, I was scared you'd morph back into the old August—uncaring and dominating."

"And now?" I asked, touching her face. She smiled.

"Now you're just you," she said simply. "There is no older version of you, or new improved model. There is just August. You are a representation of your life—past, present, and future. What you've experienced, just like the rest of us, will mold you and shape you, but it doesn't have to define you. Be whom you choose. Be brave. Be loved and be you—whoever that may be."

My mouth took hers. We spoke no more for the rest of the night as my fears dissipated in the deep valley between her breasts.

Be whom you choose, she'd said.

I chose this. I'd always choose this.

Chapter Twenty-Three
Everly

It had been weeks since we'd instigated our little offensive against Trent, and in that time we'd done little to push ahead. Trent was turning out to be smarter than we'd anticipated. Although he was thrilled with August's ability to lock in Magnolia's father for a substantial sum, he was not talking.

Or giving anything up.

We'd hoped that over time, with the Yorkeses' money in play, he'd loosen up and August would be able to dive in and find something—anything—that would get us the information we needed to turn him in to the authorities.

But without solid evidence, we were without a case.

It was literally August's word against Trent's.

If we went in without all fingers pointed solely at Trent, he could turn the tables and claim that August had had his hands in everything. With August's memory so spotty, it wasn't as if he could defend himself against such a charge. Sure, he had solid records and books, but those could be considered fakes.

We needed proof. I would not see August go to jail for the sins of that man.

"Everly? Did you hear that last order?" Trudy asked, turning to me from the counter. Blinking several times, I looked around and shook my head.

Focus, Everly.

Lack of sleep had me nearly seeing double. August wasn't the only one having sleep issues. I was burning the midnight oil trying to come up with new spots to search in the house. I'd all but torn the place apart half a dozen times looking for hiding places.

The evidence August had collected before his coma had to be there.

"Um, can you repeat it?" I asked, feeling the heat rise in my cheeks.

"Sure." She smiled, rambling off the order for a soy latte to me again. I repeated it back and started the process as my plans to investigate closets and rummage through boxes took a back burner. I needed to be present at work; otherwise I'd end up burning something, and I really liked all of my skin and extremities exactly how they were.

Hand-delivering the coffee, I took a moment to stretch my legs and check on creamer and other supplies around the front of the store. It wasn't technically part of my job, which was working the back end, but we all liked to help out when we could, and considering we were short-staffed with the recent departure of Steve, I knew Trudy would appreciate the help.

Our manager had said Steve had left to focus on his budding

music career, but Trudy and I both feared he'd been laid off. Business wasn't booming, and with the tourist season over until late spring, I knew funds would be tight for the tiny coffeehouse.

It made my chest squeeze as I looked around. This place had been my home for three years, giving me work when I needed it and comfort when I'd had none. I'd met Ryan here and even though things hadn't worked out exactly as we'd planned them, my time with him would always remind me just how big a heart could be.

"Hey, can I ask you something?" Trudy said just as my cell phone buzzed in my pocket.

Nodding absently, I pulled it out and glanced at the text message that had just come in from Sarah.

Thick packet came from the Culinary Institute? What's that about?

My eyes went wide and a small squeak escaped my mouth.

"Trudy, you went to college, right?" I asked, momentarily forgetting her question.

"Yep," she answered brightly, before adding, "Well, for a few years."

"Thick envelopes are good, right? For admissions?"

"Oh yeah. Thick envelopes are the best," she agreed, watching me with a speculative gaze.

"Did someone get a thick packet, Everly?" she asked then, nearly singing the words as they gently flowed from her mouth.

I looked up at her, nearly forgetting I hadn't told her I'd applied anywhere.

I hadn't told anyone—except August.

"I think I may have gotten into culinary school," I said, the words still feeling foreign to my tongue as they dissipated into the air.

She slid under the counter, jumping up and down as we hugged in the middle of the coffee shop, in front of the few local patrons, who clapped and cheered for my success.

I really hoped that thick envelope wasn't just a really nice way of telling me I sucked, otherwise later on this moment would be totally ruined.

*   *   *

Turned out "thick" still meant great things, and as I opened the packet in my borrowed room at Sarah's place (that had mostly been cleaned out as I slowly moved back to August's—finally deciding I was never going to live on my own, and was perfectly happy with that conclusion), I fell back onto the bed in amazement.

Staring up at me was the acceptance letter I'd always dreamed of getting. There in big bold letters was my name, under the official school seal. It had even been hand-signed by the Dean of Admissions.

I'd done it. All by myself.

When Sarah discovered my treachery, she scolded me for not telling her and then promptly hugged the crap out of me.

"You did it!" she exclaimed as we jumped up and down, doing a repeat performance of the dance I'd done with Trudy in the coffee shop. "Does August know?" she asked, grabbing the letter from me so she could see it for herself.

"No, I've barely had time to process it," I answered, feeling giddy. "But he knew I applied. And he was excited. And proud."

"Well, he should be. Cooking has always been your passion, through everything. I can't wait to see what you do with it."

Something about what she said struck a chord, and I found my-self repeating her words in my head. "What did you say?" I asked.

"Cooking has always been your passion," she echoed.

"Just like photography was always August's," I said slowly, feel-ing like the pieces of a puzzle were coming together. I'd torn the house apart several times over, going through boxes and boxes until there was nothing left to look through.

Except film.

Hundreds and hundreds of canisters of film.

If he were to hide something, and hide it well…that would be the place.

"Sarah! You're a genius!" I exclaimed, kissing her on the cheek as I jumped to action.

"Where are you going?" she asked, laughing as I grabbed the let-ter from her hands and fumbled around the room for my purse and car keys.

"August's! I think I know exactly what to look for now!" I hollered over my shoulder as I raced out the door.

Film.

The answer was film, and I was going to find it.

*   *   *

The house was eerily quiet when I entered, the slapping sound of my flip-flops echoing around the walls like a wild boomerang.

"August?" I called out in vain, looking around the unlit house for his familiar form. His car was parked outside, and the little bowl by the front door held his keys—all evidence of his presence.

What if he'd blacked out? I'd never seen it happen, but he'd mentioned it occurred every once in a while and when it did, he couldn't control it.

I hollered for him once again, then climbed the stairs two at a time, suddenly feeling frantic.

Turning the corner into the master bedroom, I finally found him. There on the floor, his large body lay in a messy heap, as if he'd fallen mid-step.

"August!" I yelled, rushing to his side. My hands roamed over his chest and his beautiful face.

Breathing. Oh thank God, he was breathing.

His eyelids fluttered and danced as his subconscious forced another memory loose. It was as if he were dreaming. He looked peaceful.

I hoped it was a good memory.

Winding my fingers with his, I did the only thing I could and sat with him. I watched as he lay unconscious before me and patiently waited for him to return to me.

It felt like an eternity as I clung to him, listening to the waves crash in tandem with his tempered breaths. This was how I remembered him—before I'd left.

Before I'd walked away and started a new life.

Night after night, I'd held his hand and tried to will him back into existence with my thoughts alone. But he never woke. And eventually I'd had a decision to make.

Some may assume it was an easy one. Our life together had been anything but easy by then, but still...leaving August had been the hardest decision of my life.

Because no one could walk away from their own soul and not feel pain.

That's exactly what I'd done, and I'd been grieving ever since.

Ryan had eased my suffering, made life bearable again, but we'd both known in the end it was temporary. No one would ever replace August in my heart and the moment he awoke, so did my damaged, embattled heart.

And it only beat for one man.

Sudden movement had me nearly jumping out of my skin as I looked down at August. His breaths became shallow and his fingers twitched with movement.

"Hi," he finally said as his mossy brown eyes found mine.

"Hi." I smiled faintly, still worried—still checking over every inch of him to make sure he was well and safe.

"My memory—it was of you," he said as a happy wistful grin spread across his face.

Standing, I offered him a hand, hating the way he looked sprawled out on the floor. The idea of me helping his six-foot frame up obviously amused him. Taking my hand in his firm grip, he stood, not needing to use my offered leverage at all.

"Tell me about it," I asked as we both sat on the bed, still tossed and messy from our lovemaking hours earlier. Kicking off my shoes, I let my fingers hover over the smooth sheets, loving the luxurious feel against my skin.

His hands found mine, and I looked up to see the tiny crinkles around his eyes as he watched me.

"I remembered the first time I saw you," he said.

My breath caught in my chest and I froze, waiting for him to continue.

"You were the most beautiful woman I'd ever seen. I knew there was something special about you from the moment I saw you."

"You seemed completely out of my league," I confessed,

remembering how my heart raced the second he approached me that night. He'd still been dressed for work, wearing gray slacks and a sharp, checkered tie. I'd felt completely wrong standing next to him as he introduced himself, and I'd tugged at the tight dress I'd borrowed from my roommate.

"I noticed your eyes first," he said. "The milky blue intensity as you looked up at me."

"Your smile," I replied. The nostalgia of that moment surrounded me like a warm blanket. "That's what I remember most. It was so confident and I was anything but."

He laughed, shaking his head. "All a sham. I was terrified. My work buddies had seen me eyeing you and forced me to go introduce myself. I thought for sure you'd turn me down or throw a drink in my face."

"Never."

"Your dress was tattered and frayed at the edges, and I caught you eyeing the food the bartenders brought around several times. I don't know how many times I offered to buy us appetizers, but you refused. I knew you were hungry."

Biting my lip, I turned away, feeling ashamed. "Pride—stupid pride. I didn't want you to know I hadn't eaten that day. It wasn't exactly first date material."

"But I knew anyway. I always wanted to protect you. Save you— even from the beginning."

"I wasn't a damsel that needed to be saved," I said, watching as our fingers slowly intertwined.

"I know that now. I always wanted to give you more—make you happy. But I never stopped and realized that what we had—what was happening between us—was enough."

"It was always enough—even when it was just flower boxes and drafty kitchens," I pressed, hoping he'd finally understand. "Do you remember the earthquake a few months ago?"

"The small one?" he asked, his gaze turning curious as we sat on the bed. Our feet wrapped together under the warm blankets.

"Yes. What were you doing?" I asked.

"I was at work," he replied. "The walls shook and by the time I had a chance to get under my desk, it was over. I barely remembered what to do—having no memory of being in any other quakes."

"Were you scared?"

"For a moment, yes," he answered honestly, our eyes meeting. "I thought of you—where you might be. The moment the ground began shaking, I longed for you, wished for you."

"I was at work, too," I explained. "And I remember Trudy saying something about when it came to the end, she hoped she had someone special to be with. It struck me because in that moment, I didn't think of Ryan. I thought of you. Even then, in the midst of wedding planning and my belief that you hated me for everything I'd robbed you of. I knew in those last moments on earth, you were the only person I'd reach out for."

He pulled me close.

"I'll still always want to give you the world."

"And I'll still only want just you."

*   *   *

"That's a lot of film," he groaned, looking at the many boxes of tiny black canisters we'd collected throughout the house. Most had been tucked away in the closets, long since forgotten after years of dormancy.

But several more had been scattered throughout the house—in kitchen drawers, strewn all over the office. We even found one in the guest bathroom medicine cabinet.

"Do you think I did this on purpose?" he asked, looking down at the monstrous task. "Leaving them everywhere?"

"It wouldn't surprise me," I answered. "You were extremely paranoid, and perhaps for good reason. If you were collecting evidence against Trent, you would have done everything and anything to protect me—including erratic measures, to hide it."

"Well, this is erratic," he said as he grabbed a box. He hoisted it over his shoulder, and headed for the makeshift darkroom.

All of the film had been developed, thankfully, so our task was fairly simple—just cumbersome. The darkroom wasn't necessary to see the film, but the light table August had purchased did make it easier. Plus he owned several magnifying tools which would make the job even simpler.

It was like finding a needle in a haystack. After hours of searching, we were feeling the magnitude of our task.

"What if I'm wrong?" I asked in defeat, sitting back in the leather chair, the sting of my aching back making me groan in pain.

"What is your gut telling you?" August asked, bending over yet another fruitless canister of film.

"That it's here," I answered, "somewhere."

"Then we keep looking."

We ordered Thai food and then continued going meticulously through each roll of film. Sometimes it was hard to keep focused, seeing our past come alive on the tiny black and white film sheets. Every so often, though, we'd stop and I'd share a memory with August: picnics, trips to Muir Woods, and birthdays long since gone.

"What about this one?" August asked eagerly, holding out the magnifying glass for me to use. Bending down, I felt the heated touch of his hand as it rested on the small of my back, gently rubbing the sore spots.

Frowning, I tilted my head sideways, trying to recognize the photos he'd asked about. They were hard to make out, as all exposed film was. But usually I could pick out something in the backgrounds, a scenic location or a familiar landmark that would help me deduce where a photo had been taken.

But these shots were completely foreign to me.

"I've never seen these before," I said, still staring down at the ghostly white figure that appeared in nearly every single frame.

"But they're of you," August said, bending down to take another look.

I appeared to be bent over the rails of the deck, peering out at the bright blue ocean. It was something I'd done a lot in the later years, when there hadn't been much communication between August and me.

"You must have taken them when I wasn't looking," I said, remembering how many hours I would spend out there, with the wind whipping around my face, wishing he would join me—wrap his arms around me and carry me back inside the house.

But he never came. I'd always assumed he didn't care.

I never knew he was right there, wishing for me as well.

What a messed-up life we'd lead.

Now was our chance to fix it.

I don't know how many more canisters of film we found that August had shot of me during our estrangement, when we were basically strangers living in the same house. It made me realize how precious love was—how much it needed to be nurtured.

Without communication, without trust, we were nothing.

"Holy shit, I think I found something," August nearly shouted, grabbing my hand and tugging me to see what he'd unveiled. Rather than scenic landscapes or cheesy photos of us from across the years, I found myself looking at documents. Tons and tons of documents.

"What is this?" I asked, using the magnifying mirror. August was next to me doing the same thing, his eyes narrowed as he tried to read the small print.

"It looks like records of shell companies. The notes I made in the margins...I think I may have actually driven to this one," he said, pointing to the document he'd been reading. I moved over to it and saw what he was pointing at, recognizing his chicken scratch hand-writing.

"We need to develop this," I said, feeling the excitement welling up inside me.

It wasn't nearly as exciting as our last session in the darkroom—and there was definitely more clothing involved, but over the next few hours, we produced enough solid evidence to bring to an investigator and finally...finally, I felt like we might see a future without Trent.

Chapter Twenty-Four
August

Everything was running smoothly—perfectly, I'd even venture to say.

Well, almost perfectly.

The frequency of my random flashbacks had dropped significantly, calming Everly's nerves—and mine, too, if I were being honest. As nice as it was to regain a memory of my childhood or an anniversary we'd celebrated, the blackouts were hard on my body. Never knowing exactly when or where they were going to strike made life slightly daunting.

We'd collected the once hidden evidence, and I'd even picked up my camera again—snapping photos of Everly whenever I could. She was my muse once more, and I never wanted to forget that.

It seemed like life was going our way. Except for Trent. The bastard.

I was getting very little leeway from Trent at work. His fingers were still tightly wound around every aspect of the company. Even with him giddy as a schoolboy on game day over the deal I was working with the Yorke family, I couldn't get him to loosen up on account passwords or any secret drives. So much was still a mystery and it was driving me insane.

He was like Fort Knox and I was desperate to get inside.

I knew he would slip up eventually. He had to. I hadn't managed to gather all that data over the years because he was seamless. He had his faults. I just hadn't learned them yet.

But as time went on, I found myself anxious and eager to wrap everything up in a nice neat bow.

I wanted Trent behind bars so I could finally move on with my life. I'd spent too long pushing my fate away in order to bend to this man's will. It was time he learned what it felt like to pay for his sins.

We finally had mostly everything we needed. The canister of film I'd found thanks to Everly's genius mind had proven a priceless asset to our goal.

I'd assumed that alone would be enough to put him away for years.

Everly and I had happily marched into the local FBI office, presenting our information, and naïvely thought any investigation they might undertake would all be wrapped up by that evening.

But nothing was ever that easy, and if we truly wanted him gone, sacrifices would eventually need to be made.

The FBI was definitely interested in what I had collected, and had actually been alerted to Trent's activities earlier, but like me, they'd had problems placing solid blame. What I gave them absolutely pointed the arrow directly at my former friend; however, after hearing how our little operation worked, they were out for blood.

"We want him to serve time. Lots of it. These people he's

used—taken from—they deserve the swiftest form of the law. But right now, with evidence that's years old and the only eyewitness someone whose memory is well, less than ideal, our case is weak. We want to be able to show beyond a shadow of a doubt that this man is guilty, so that no judge or jury has any choice but to put him away."

"What do you want me to do?" I asked, more than willing to offer any assistance I could to make that happen. I'd seen first-hand the people he'd used for his own personal benefit, including Sarah and Everly. I would do whatever was necessary to make sure he spent every remaining day of his pathetic life rotting away in prison.

"Would you be willing to wear a wire?"

Everly's eyes met mine and I could see the fright—the fear. But she knew as well as I did. We needed to do whatever it took.

"Yes," I answered.

"This could be dangerous," the investigator warned, his hard face taking on a touch of warmth as he spoke.

"I understand."

"Good," he responded, rising from his seat behind his desk. "There's just one more thing."

Everly grabbed my hand tightly, anticipating the worst. I gave her a quick squeeze in response.

"We know you were blind to this from the beginning. I can see your imprint in the legitimate side of the business. I want you to know we are not pursuing you in this case, however—"

My heart skipped a beat as I waited for him to continue.

"Everything you own is ill-gotten. It can be traced back to this company and the fraud Trent Lyons has conducted."

"What are you trying to say?" I asked, wishing he would stop pussyfooting around the issue and just say it.

"When this hits the press—you'll be thrown to the wolves," he said, sadness filling his eyes. "Those families who lost everything—"

Holding my hand up, I stopped him mid-sentence. I understood what he was saying right away. Every penny I had in my bank account was wrong and evil, and suddenly having it felt dirty.

I didn't care about the papers or what people said. But I did care about the people Trent had taken advantage of. When this came out, some of them would be destitute. Businesses would be shut down, houses would be foreclosed on. It would ruin lives.

I couldn't go on living in a palace when others were suffering.

It all had to go.

"Can you be sure Trent will go to jail?" I asked, my gaze pointed at the agent.

"Yes," the agent said without pause. "As long as we can get him on record, like we discussed."

Giving Everly a quick glance, I nodded. "I'll donate every damn dime this second if you can keep that promise."

A sharp approval from the agent and several bank calls later and we were set.

I was officially broke, and I'd never felt better.

*   *   *

This is never going to work, I thought to myself as I stepped into the office the next day.

Underneath my dress shirt, beneath my expensive suit jacket, were tiny wires stretched across my broad chest. I was now broad-casting live.

Agent Martin, the man assigned to our case, had decided this should be our first approach—cornering him at work. I'd tried to explain to him exactly why this would fail, but with the government, even a branch like the FBI, every investigation had to be thorough.

So here I was at the office, wired and ready to make waves, as Agent Martin put it. As I logged in to my computer, preparing exactly how I would approach Trent that morning, I shook my head. This was ridiculous. I'd been riding Trent hard for weeks now, trying to get him to soften up, and I'd barely made a dent. Now this Martin guy expected me to produce miracles in a matter of hours, just because I was wearing a wire.

If there was one thing I'd learned about Trent, it was how methodical he was. In the office, he was rigid and safe, never saying more than he had to and always playing a role.

It was when he was outside these walls that he slipped, and that's when I needed to catch him.

But for now, I'd do as I was told, because it wasn't my ass on the line.

And I definitely wanted to keep it that way.

Not wanting to appear overeager, I took my time that morning. I started up a conversation with Cheryl about her grandkids, knowing it would take at least a half hour to get away. I made myself a cup of coffee, then a second. I fucked around on my computer, purposely prolonging the moment when I would go speak to Trent.

Maybe I was prolonging the inevitable.

Maybe I knew something would go wrong.

Whatever the reason, it was nearly noon before I took that fateful walk over to Trent's office. Each step closer, I tried to remember how many times I'd walked this path over the last year. How many times my feet had taken this exact same route, wondering if I'd ever find a different one.

Some might say I was a pushover when it came to Trent. Some might say I could have fought back, battled him for control.

All of these things are true.

But when something more precious than your life hangs in the balance, you find yourself being overly cautious, maybe to the point of extremes. And that's exactly what I'd done. From the moment I'd met Everly, I'd wanted to take care of her—to give her the life she'd never been given.

It was a noble concept, wanting to give someone you love everything. But love wasn't material. It wasn't something you could grasp or hold between your fingers. It was felt, in the quiet moments when I held her, or the way I made her laugh in bed. It was the whispered moans as we made love...the contented sigh she made when we kissed. Those moments couldn't be bought, and somewhere along the way I'd lost sight of that.

In my own way, by donating the money, I was protecting her once again.

From myself. Never again would I become the man she'd hated.

Never again would I become the man she'd feared.

We might never have an ocean view again or a kitchen quite as grand for Everly to cook in, but we'd make do. As long as we had each other, we'd make do.

Trent's secretary was missing when I arrived, and the door to his office was firmly shut.

Knowing I'd already wasted enough time, I knocked once

and pushed my way through, hoping to catch him in the act of something...anything...that would end this cat-and-mouse game. But luck was not on my side, and as I waltzed in, cool-headed Trent just smiled up from his screen and greeted me.

"What's up?" he asked, leaning back casually in his chair.

"Just checking in," I said, suddenly realizing in all our preparations I hadn't come up with any reason to be here.

"Aren't you the dutiful employee," he said, punctuating each word.

"Partner," I corrected, feeling my fingers curl inward as I fought the urge to retaliate.

"Right, right." He smiled again. "It's just that you're so helpful all of a sudden. Always willing to lend a hand. Kind of like a dog. Obedient, you know?"

Something was wrong.

He was pushing just a bit too hard.

"I told you," I replied, keeping my expression neutral. "I don't want to fight anymore. I have more important things to focus on now."

"Everly." He nodded. "Everything always revolves around Everly."

He said this almost like a question, and even repeated it to himself under his breath as I watched him rise from his seat and begin to pace.

"It does make me wonder. If you and Everly are back together, how did you manage to grab the Yorke account so easily?" he asked, his gaze turning cold. "I thought you and Magnolia were quite the pair for a while. Wasn't she a little put out to discover she'd been replaced?"

"The deal was with her father," I pointed out.

"And he didn't mind you screwing over his daughter?"

"He knew we could make him money. It's all he cared about. I did my job." My jaw was clenched and nearly every word came out at a lower pitch as my voice began to resemble the sound of churned-up gravel.

"Now why do I think you're lying?" he asked, suddenly in my face. His usual cool and collected exterior had slipped, revealing an edge of panic I didn't recognize.

"Why would I lie?" I asked, trying to stay calm. The wires against my chest felt heavy and large as he stepped into my personal space.

"Why wouldn't you?" he shouted, shoving me to the wall. "You've been a pain in my ass since we started this business. If I find out you fucked up this deal, August, I will—"

"What? You'll what?" I asked, baiting him, begging him to say more.

His hold on me loosened and I watched him transform. His eyes went dull—lifeless—as his demented smile slid back into place.

"Nothing. Nothing," he replied, brushing my jacket with his hand and straightening my tie. "Just get it done. No more delays. Get him in here to sign the paperwork. Close the deal."

"Fine," I answered, turning toward the door.

"And August?" he called as I was about to be free.

"Yeah?"

"Don't disappoint me."

I nodded, hearing the silent threat loud and clear.

Unfortunately, silence was not admissible in a court of law. So far, we had nothing.

*   *   *

"Trent is on to us," I said as my pacing commenced. Back and forth through the living room I went, holding my cell phone while I spoke to Agent Martin on the other line.

"I think if you just give us a few more days," he began, although his voice resonated with doubt.

"No," I said swiftly. "You heard him today. He's holding back. We need to do something bigger. Something drastic."

I heard a sharp intake of breath and I turned in time to see Everly enter the room, her car keys still dangling from her hand.

"What do you suggest?" Agent Martin asked.

"Let me get back to you."

I didn't give him a chance to respond before I ended the call, dropping the phone on the couch as my gaze narrowed in on Everly.

"What are you going to do?" she asked timidly.

"I don't know, but I'm sick of waiting. He's like a loaded weapon, ready to explode. I saw it in his eyes today. We need to act. I can't stand the idea of him being in the same airspace as you, let alone the same city. I want him gone."

Her keys dropped to the floor with a *thunk* as she ran for me. My arms enveloped her as her legs wrapped around my torso in a tight grasp, the sound of her sobs making my heart ache.

"Shh," I soothed. "It's going to be okay."

"Everything is changing so fast," she cried. "What if something goes wrong, August?"

"Then we'll deal with it," I said. "Just like we've dealt with every other obstacle that's come our way." Tilting her chin upward, I stared into those beautiful blue eyes I'd fallen in love with so long ago. "Look at everything we've overcome—everything we've managed to face together. Don't doubt what we can accomplish now."

"I won't, I promise."

Carefully carrying her upstairs, we spent the rest of the night exploring each other slowly. Each kiss lingered. Every touch brought passion in its wake.

"I love you," I whispered as our bodies moved together over and over under the moonlight.

"I love you," she echoed as the waves crashed below.

Love was precious. We knew this more than most, having lost each other more than once over the years. But it remembered.

Love always remembered.

Later, after we'd showered our sweat-slicked skin and I'd washed her hair, we eased back into bed, tired and content from our time together. It was late, the slivered moon high in the sky, as I wrapped the blankets around our naked bodies.

"I'm going to decline my acceptance to culinary school," Everly said, her voice cutting through the happy silence like a jagged steak knife.

I froze, turning toward her in the darkness. Her eyes caught the faint light above, reflecting sadness and remorse.

"Why?" I asked, confused.

"There's too much going on," she said quietly. "I would have to start in two weeks, and—"

"And what?"

"I don't think we can afford it," she admitted sheepishly.

The statement hit me hard, like a punch to the stomach. She was right. Besides this house, which was only ours at the moment to keep up appearances for the sake of the case, we were downright poor.

I didn't have a single cent to my name.

Before I knew what to do, I was laughing.

Doubled over, rolling on the floor.

"Do you seriously think this is funny?" Everly asked, her expression contorted in complete bafflement as she flicked the table lamp on to get a better look at me.

Grasping my sides, I tried to contain myself.

"No, I'm sorry. I don't think you quitting school is funny. In fact, I think it's the opposite. And it's not happening. However, the fact that I am broke—the former Mr. Moneybags himself? Yeah, I find that kind of humorous. Don't you?"

I watched her process what I'd said, and suddenly her eyes went round and laughter burst from her mouth.

"Can you imagine what the old you would have done? All of those watches?"

"And the suits? Dear God, the suits. And the shoes. My precious fucking shoes."

My life had been consumed by material goods for years as I collected meaningless crap. Years and years' worth of stuff that meant nothing.

In a blink of an eye, it could be gone.

And what would I be left with? The memory of a nice watch?

No thanks.

"We'll figure out how to pay for your classes," I consoled her, pulling her into my arms.

"How?" she asked, the worry evident in her voice.

"How do normal people do things, Everly? School loans, financial aid, good old-fashioned hard work. It's your dream. We'll make it happen."

"Thank you," she said, her arms wrapping tightly around me as my eyes closed and peace settled around us.

For once, I didn't listen to the sound of the waves that night.

No, it was something else entirely that drifted me off into dreamland.

Something I knew I couldn't live without.

The rhythmic sound of Everly's heartbeat.

*   *   *

"We're all set?" I asked as the wires were placed back on my chest.

"Yep, we're ready," Agent Martin replied as he watched the other men in the black van finish me up. I was given the thumbs-up, and I quickly rebuttoned my shirt, feeling antsy in the enclosed space.

We'd selected a neutral, public space for this next push.

Less risk of things spiraling, Agent Martin had said. As I said good-bye to Everly, giving her a long hard kiss, I had to agree. I didn't say the words, but I knew she felt them. I could see the promise in her eyes as the lock slipped into place and my heartbeat stilled slightly. She was safe, and that was all I needed to know.

"Okay, you've got about fifteen minutes to get to the meeting point. We'll be around the corner. If anything happens, we'll be there. Got it?"

I nodded once, hopping out of the van into the bright afternoon sun. San Francisco was well into winter, which meant a higher than average number of sunny days. The proximity to the bay made the seasons almost reversed. Summer brought fog. Winter brought sun.

It pissed a lot of tourists off, but for us locals, it was like a little secret we never intended to share.

Despite the slight chill in the air, many city dwellers were enjoying the sunny day. People sat outside, enjoying warm cups of coffee and sandwiches. Laughter could be heard as I walked through the streets, approaching the small plaza I'd chosen to lure Trent.

I didn't know what to expect when he arrived, but I was planning on him being something close to livid.

About an hour ago, I'd sent an e-mail to his work address containing several snapshots of the documents I'd collected over the years.

In the e-mail, I'd written, "Looks like I was the smart one all along. Meet me in an hour."

The address had been attached and the FBI nerds Agent Martin had been corresponding with had monitored the e-mail to make sure it had been read. When I'd called him this morning, this was the plan I'd given him—to go all in with guns blazing. Thankfully, he'd agreed.

I don't think I was the only one who was getting antsy.

The location I'd chosen was in a popular shopping area. Boutiques and upscale eateries lined the streets, and in the middle, a small fountain trickled audibly as children threw pennies from their mothers' purses in hopes of getting their secret wishes fulfilled.

Reaching into my pocket, I pulled out a single quarter I had left over from a toll road. Feeling nostalgic, I walked over to the fountain, seeing in it the glimmer from a thousand wishes at the bottom. I held out my tiny offering.

"What are you going to wish for?" A little girl asked me. She had strawberry blond hair and bright green eyes. Tiny freckles dotted her porcelain complexion and she wore a bright pink shirt that proudly displayed the words "Daddy's little angel" with tiny devil horns holding up the halo.

She couldn't have been much older than five, but I'd never been good at telling ages—especially in children. I was an only child, and with most of my memories still under lock and key, children were still very much a mystery to me. This was something I hoped to change.

"I don't know yet," I said, smiling down at her. "What do you think I should wish for?"

Her face scrunched together as she looked me up and down, taking in my faded blue jeans and messy hair. Her eyes went to my hand, checking for a wedding ring I assumed, and then she frowned.

"Are you married?" she asked.

"No, but I have a girlfriend I love very much," I replied, checking my watch. I still had a few minutes.

"You should get married," she advised, putting her hands on her hips in a very womanly fashion. It caused me to smirk, and I couldn't help but ask why.

"Because then you can ask for a kid."

"And that's what you think I should wish for?"

She nodded with enthusiasm.

"And what's so great about a kid?" I asked, wrapping my arms around my chest in mock defiance.

"My daddy says I'm what love made. He says he and my mommy had so much love for each other that it made me! He says when he looks at me, he sees me and my mommy shining back at him."

She glanced back at a man about my age who was holding an

infant in his arms at a nearby table. He waved back at her and she smiled.

"Your daddy seems like a smart man."

"He is," she said proudly.

"Well, I don't know if Everly and I are ready for someone as cool as you yet. But why don't I wish for happiness?"

"That sounds good. My daddy says my little brother and me bring him happiness, so maybe you'll end up with everything?"

"Yeah," I smiled. "Maybe I'll end up with everything."

I helped her up on the fountain ledge and with her helpful hand, we tossed the single quarter into the water. I watched as it floated to the bottom, sparkling with promise among the other wishes and dreams.

I said good-bye to my new friend and watched her skip back to her father. It made me wonder where I'd be in five years. Ten, even. Would I have a similar life? Baby bottles and life lessons with a toddler?

Only time would tell, and Everly and I would finally have plenty of it soon.

At the thought of time, I suddenly lifted my watch to my eyes, seeing the specified meeting time had passed. Not knowing what to do, my gaze shifted around the plaza, searching for Trent.

He was nowhere to be found.

Having been so sure Trent would take my bait and meet me, we hadn't spoken of a Plan B. I had no idea what to do. Did I wait? If so, for how long?

Pulling my cell phone out of my pocket, I contemplated what to do. Before I had the chance to decide, it began to vibrate with an incoming call.

Trent.

"You're late," I answered, each word spoken through clenched teeth.

"Now, why would you say that? It seems you are the one who's late, my friend," he replied, that cool calm edge to his voice back in place.

"What are you talking about?" I asked, looking around the plaza but still coming up short.

"How'd you like to say hello, sweetheart?" he said, the phone's sounds becoming muffled, and then I heard a sharp female cry.

Everly.

"August!" she screamed, as more shuffling commenced and I began to run. Darting through shoppers and smiling children, I sprinted until my lungs burned.

"Where are you?" I asked, looking around at the crowd. I felt useless, utterly useless. There were too many people and he was nowhere to be found.

"You threatened me," he said. "That's not cool. I just stopped by your house to try and solve the matter—man to man. But you weren't home. It was so very nice of Everly to let me in, though."

My car. I had to reach my car.

"If you touch one fucking hair on her head, I swear to God—"

"You'll what? Do nothing? Come on, August. You're not really going to do anything—you never do. That's why you're you and I'm me. Because I get shit done and you sit around and take orders. Now I gotta give you kudos for this e-mail you sent me. It's great—really. I can't imagine how you managed to collect all that over the years. But what exactly do you plan on doing with it?"

I knew we already had what we needed. He'd threatened Everly...broken into my home. He was going away for a long time. Now I just needed to keep him there long enough to get home.

And keep Everly safe in the process.

"I just wanted out," I lied as I hopped into my car and started the engine. I had no idea where Agent Martin was. He'd said if anything went south, he'd be there. But this was completely north of what we'd planned and I wasn't taking any risks.

Not when it involved Everly.

"I figured this was my ticket."

Cars flew by as I sped down the road, inching closer and closer to the Cliffs, thankful we'd chosen someplace close by. I only needed another minute and I'd be home.

"Was this something you'd planned all along? Were you going to try to rip me off again and run?"

Rip him off?

He thought the fifty million dollars I'd lost was a failed attempt to steal from the company?

"That money, Trent," I said calmly. "It was for you, I swear. I was just trying to leave, and I knew your money would help, but I'd never done a deal that big. I got in over my head and lost it all."

The car skidded to the curb right behind Trent's flashy black Mercedes. I didn't even bother parking in the driveway, and I barely took the time to slam the driver's-side door as I raced toward the front door, still wide open from his forced entry.

The small table we used for keys and whatnot had been knocked over, the glass bowl I'd bought at a small antique shop smashed into a million pieces. Tiny jagged chunks of glass caught the sunlight, twinkling in the chaos of Trent's destruction.

"Is that you, August?" His voice rang through the house. "Come to teach me a lesson?"

Laughter followed, then whimpering.

Everly.

Following the sounds of their voices, I took quick but careful steps into the living room and felt my heart drop. There on the couch where we'd made love a dozen times, the place where we'd shared countless meals and endless memories, the love of my life sat with a gun pointed at her head.

She trembled with fear as tears trickled down her beautiful face. Trent sat next to her, looking passive—as if he was getting ready to go grocery shopping or mow the lawn.

Except for his eyes. I'd almost missed those. Usually steely and ice cold, the windows to his soul were on fire today. Maniacal.

And they scared me to death.

This was not the man I was used to—the one who kept everything and everyone at arm's length. This was not someone who had everything under control. This was what happened when you capped a volcano too long. It stewed and boiled beneath the surface until there was only one way for the lava to go—up.

Trent was about to explode, and he was planning on taking Everly with him.

"Do you have any idea what I did for you? What I gave you?" he said, his voice shaking with intensity. My eyes were glued to the gun he held. Every movement, every shift or careless jolt had my breath catching, my body rooted to the floor in absolute horror.

"Just put the gun down," I urged, holding my hands out like a white flag of surrender. "And we'll talk this out. No one needs to get hurt. Nothing needs to happen. We can all walk away from this."

"What's going on with the Yorke deal?" he asked, the words spilling out of his mouth like liquid venom.

"It's fine, I swear," I lied, my gaze shifting to him and then back to Everly.

"You lie. You fucking lie! About everything!" His hold tightened around Everly as he stood, and I watched as her eyes filled with panic.

"You think I'm stupid, August? You think I haven't figured all this out yet?"

I honestly didn't care what he'd deduced from this. All I wanted was that gun as far away from Everly as possible.

"You don't think I've caught on to your plan? You were never going to give up Yorke. You were just going to dangle him over my head, distract me while you took the money and ran. Then while my head was still spinning, you'd turn over that evidence to the authorities and play the poor innocent partner who didn't have a clue. Well, fuck that, August! I'm on to you. You may not have had any idea what was going on in the past, but you do now. If I go down, you sure as hell will be going down with me!"

Each word was louder than the last. He was livid, rage and spit flying from his mouth, sweat pouring from his temples. With one arm wrapped firmly around Everly's waist and the other tightly gripping a 9-millimeter, he made me feel like I was out of options.

I couldn't play it safe, and I couldn't hide from this danger. Not anymore.

I inched forward as he rambled on incoherently.

"You're always fucking me over. I should have known. I should have known a spineless little asshole like you wouldn't be worth my time. And now look at us. We're so fucking screwed, it's not even funny. And it's all your fault."

"What do you mean?" I asked, trying to keep him talking as I made my way slowly across the living room. His focus was everywhere. He'd gone completely off the deep end, and because of that, it made my pursuit that much easier.

"I'm bankrupt!" he yelled, finally looking directly at me. I froze.

"All the money we have in the company? Fake. Totally fucking fake. I've been grasping at straws for the past couple of years trying to pull shit together while you wasted away in a fucking hospital bed. You and your fifty-million-dollar mistake. I told you our money was liquid? Well, nonexistent is more like it now. I needed you to keep us afloat, and instead, you ruined us!"

Several pieces of the puzzle settled into place all at once. Memories of him needing help in almost every financing class. His pursuit of me after I'd gotten out of the hospital, the almost stalker quality it had. How he'd seemed to insert himself into my life in every way.

He'd been out for revenge, sure. But that hadn't been the only reason.

Desperation. He'd lost everything.

Trent was destitute and the only person he'd thought could turn the tide was the one person he despised. The one person who had deceived him and cost him everything.

Me.

Greed made people do all sorts of things. It created a neverending hunger that would never be fulfilled. I had no doubt the investment blunder I'd made right before my coma had added to the financial distress of the company. However, seeing Trent now—his need, the way he seemed completely desperate—I knew he was the ultimate reason for the downfall.

Fancy boats, multimillion-dollar houses...living well beyond our means. It had all finally caught up.

And now it was time for him to pay.

As soon as he turned his head, distracted by his own deteriorating mind as it poured forth an intangible string of words, I acted, jumping for him before he had the chance to react.

Two things happened simultaneously. The gun went off and Everly let out a blood-curdling scream.

Chapter Twenty-Five
Everly

A shot went off and everything happened at once. All I could do was watch in horror as August and Trent wrestled for the gun. I screamed at the sight of the blood covering both of them, not knowing which man it belonged to.

August took a swing, his face pale, and Trent fell to the floor. As soon as he went down, the entire house erupted in noise. Men outfitted in SWAT gear swarmed the house, guns at the ready.

Both of us held up our hands, unsure what to do, but their focus was all for the man on the floor.

It was over.

Oh thank God, it was over.

I managed to lock eyes with August from across the room, seeing his relieved expression moments before I noticed the blood soaking his shirt.

"August!" I screamed. His fingers touched the bullet wound

above his heart, near his left shoulder and his gaze traveled back to mine in shock.

And then he collapsed, crumpling to the ground like an oversize rag doll.

"No! Oh God! No!" I cried, rushing to his side.

"We need an ambulance!" one of the men said into a walkie-talkie as they handcuffed an unconscious Trent. His head bobbed to the side as they pulled him to a standing position. Slowly, he began to regain consciousness, and that's when I saw red.

"You fucking asshole!" I yelled, pushing past several large men to get to Trent. "If I lose him because of you—I swear to God, there won't be a jail cell deep enough for you to hide in. I will find you!"

His sneer was the last thing I saw before they took him away.

Three of the men stayed behind. While two of the men secured the area and provided communication, the third stayed by August's side, applying pressure to his wound as I knelt beside him, praying to every deity I could think of to not take him away from me.

"It's a clean wound," the man said, his gaze strong and true. "Clear exit wound. It must have gone through muscle only." He pointed to the back where several makeshift towels had been applied, soaking up more blood than I'd ever seen outside the human body.

"Will he—" I couldn't even say it.

Before he had a chance to answer me, the EMTs stormed in, rushing into action. I was asked to step back as they did their job. I watched from the sidelines as they tended to August, feeling useless as they tried to keep him alive.

My hands shook and sobs quaked through my body.

"I'll take her," Agent Martin offered, reappearing just as they lifted August into the ambulance. Knowing his situation was far too dire for me to accompany him, I silently nodded and watched as they drove away.

Oh God, what if I lost him?

Again.

The trip to the hospital was quick. So much of the experience took me back—to the last time I'd sat in a spot just like this, waiting, wondering...worrying. After a long while, I was allowed back to a room and found him asleep. He looked so much like the man I left all those years ago. I still remembered holding his hand, wondering if I'd lost him for good as guilt had clawed at my belly.

If I had only kept the door shut like I'd promised. Perhaps none of this would have happened.

I knew that wasn't true.

Trent wouldn't have given up. He never would have given up.

And this time, neither would I.

* * *

I stayed by his side all night, and through the following morning.

Seeing him in a hospital bed again was like taking a walk back in time.

Even though the doctor assured me he was not in a coma, the fear was still there.

What if he never woke up?

What if he did, and he didn't remember? Had he hit his head when he fell? I couldn't recall.

Everything would be better when he woke up.

August...please wake up.

The news of August's injury reached our friends quickly, and the outpouring of support was massive. Looking around the room at the scattering of flowers and cards, it filled my heart with warmth and love. What a difference a year made.

What a difference *we* had made.

Together.

Around midnight a nurse snuck in to check his vitals, seeing my unchanged position from the last time she'd been in the room. Fifteen minutes later, she reappeared with a tray of food and a soda.

"Eat, sweetheart," she urged. "And try to get some rest."

"I can't bear to look away," I confessed, looking up at her with tears in my eyes. "What if he needs me?"

Her caring smile warmed slightly as she took the seat in the corner, letting her feet rest for a moment. She had those funny white shoes nurses often wore, the ones that look like a cross between clown shoes and something you'd see in Holland. There were tired, dark circles under her eyes, probably from working the night shift, and her gray-brown hair had been neatly pulled back into a severe bun. Her Hello Kitty scrubs made her seem young, though, reminding me of something a child might wear rather than a nurse who was probably pushing sixty.

"I heard what happened to him," she said, her eyes moving over his still frame. "It's a brave thing he did."

I simply nodded. It was all I could do to keep the sobs at bay.

"He'll be needing a lot of help over the next several weeks. Bullet wounds take time to heal."

"I'll be there for him," I said.

"Good. Then eat," she pressed. "He'll need his strength. But so will you. You can't take care of a great big guy like that with no food in your belly. Rest while you can, so you can take care of your man. Got it?"

Looking down at the tray of hot food she'd brought, I heard my stomach growl, realizing it had been over twenty-four hours since I'd last eaten.

"Yes ma'am," I replied.

"All right, then. I'll be back in here to check on both of you," she said, rising to her feet. She stretched languidly, several of her bones cracking as she moved to the door. With a quick wink, she was gone.

I don't know how many hours passed after that. They all seemed to mesh into one another. After eating several nibbles off a bread roll and some lasagna, I fell asleep, waking every half hour with a jolt—the memories of the day before rushing back with a vengeance.

My hands would skim over August, making sure he was still there—still in front of me, within my reach, and then I'd drift off again.

Soon, we'd be together again.

"Soon," I whispered to myself as my eyes closed once again.

*   *   *

Daylight filtered through the hospital window as my eyes slowly fluttered open, taking in my surroundings. Just like every other time I'd awakened since Trent's break-in, my mind went back.

Back to the moment he rang the doorbell.

Back to the moment he'd threatened August if I didn't answer.

Back to the instant he'd fired the gun, sending a fiery hot bullet into August's chest.

Panic.

It all came back.

"Shhh, I'm right here." August's voice came through the noise in my head. I looked up and saw his beautiful hazel gaze looking back at me.

"You're awake." I breathed a sigh of relief.

"Yeah." He smiled weakly. He still looked pale, with dark shadows around his eyes. His voice was hoarse, as if he'd spent a night at a concert screaming over the loud noise rather than lain unconscious in a silent hospital room.

But none of this mattered.

Because he was alive.

So beautifully alive.

"August," I said, my voice cracking as tears fell down my cheeks, following the same path so many had before them. I'd cried a lot of tears in the past twenty-four hours.

These were tears of joy. Tears of relief—because we were finally free.

"You scared me," I whispered. "I was so scared."

"You never have to be scared again."

And that was the simple truth. Through the years, we'd lost each other over and over—to greed, loss of trust, and a thousand memories scattered in the wind. But our love had never surrendered. We'd never given up on each other and here we were.

We'd been lost to each other so many times over. But now, we were found.

At last.

Epilogue
Everly

Three years later…

"Hey, boss lady! We need more peanut butter brownies up front!" Trudy yelled from the front counter as she went back to softly humming a popular top forty song to herself. Her large belly bobbed and bounced as she danced, bringing a smile to my happy face.

We'd done it.

Just as this place I'd called home for years had been facing foreclosure, I'd been able to do the impossible. It had taken time, a whole lot of savings, and it had meant putting off several things, including the possibility of a family, but it was one wish I could officially strike off my list.

I was my own boss.

The coffee shop I'd loved for so long was now mine, and since taking over, Trudy—now general manager—and I had made some major changes, including the addition of a new kitchen—

complete with the fancy stainless steel mixer I'd always wanted. We no longer counted on anyone else to make our food, which meant I had the freedom to use my pricey culinary degree to its fullest.

Within months of announcing new ownership, we'd been recognized in papers and food blogs all over the city for our ingenious salads, delectable sandwiches, and to-die-for desserts.

Business was booming, and I couldn't be happier.

Carrying out two orders of Cuban-inspired sandwiches, I delivered them to a couple sitting near the window, thanking them for their business as they checked out our funky interior and original artwork.

"Do you sell these pieces?" the woman asked, pointing to a black-and-white framed photograph of the Golden Gate Bridge.

"Yes, we do." I smiled, looking at the photo with pride.

I wasn't the only success in the family.

"Ever since August got that feature in the *Chronicle*, we've barely been able to keep the walls covered," Trudy said with a wide grin as I walked back to the counter, grabbing a pot of coffee. She watched with lust as I filled a cup to the brim, grabbing the brownies she'd asked for so she could refill the to-go case. As she began, I leaned against the counter and enjoyed a few moments of bliss as I sipped slowly from my "I'm Awesome" cup. I knew drinking coffee in front of a pregnant woman was mean, but what else could I do?

It was my fuel. I needed it to function.

"I know," I agreed with a small shrug as I looked at the walls we'd decorated with my husband's vibrant prints. "But he won't sell them anywhere else. At least he's in the paper for his artistic ability and not because of the trial."

When the media had caught wind of Trent's arrest, the story had swept through the Internet and newspapers with gusto. August was sought after for interviews—exclusive and everything in between—especially when it was discovered that every penny that had once filled his very large bank account had been handed back to help the victims of Trent's fraud.

He was touted as a hero, and although I agreed, he hated every second. All he wanted to do was melt into the background and live our lives in peace. And he eventually got his wish. Trent was prosecuted on several counts of embezzlement, and after a few tips regarding the gallery fire had come in, a trial for murder was becoming a real possibility. He'd spend the rest of his useless life in a jail cell.

Away from us, away from those he could hurt most.

Life had finally moved on.

Looking out at the café, I noticed the changes—the fresh coat of paint and the updated tables and chairs. We'd done a lot since taking over and it showed—even changing the name to Flower Box Cafe—a nod to August's and my humble beginnings. Although some things had been modified, we'd still managed to keep the feel, and that was why when I gazed out into the sea of people filling the small café, I saw many of our old patrons, still occupying the same spaces they had for years, drinking the same coffee, because I hadn't changed the beans or the way we made it. We'd even kept their favorite cups.

It had been hard work. Every penny we'd spent on this place had been earned, borrowed, and bled for. I wish I could say when we left the hospital all those months ago, things had been rosy and our road paved with nothing but promise.

But there were hard times. Like everyone else in this world facing financial problems, we'd struggled. Even our wedding had been done on the cheap—a small ceremony overlooking the ocean with those who were closest to us. Brick officiated—another one of his talents—and Sarah planned a small meal at a nearby restaurant. It was intimate and romantic, and we had about a dozen rolls of film for every second that had passed.

We found a small apartment near the school. August worked two jobs while I was in classes, doing anything from working in restaurants to brushing up on his skills in the financial world. He'd hated every second. But at night and on days off, he'd pull out his camera and shoot pictures—anything and everything that caught his eye. I was still his muse, but his lens eventually widened as he began to see a world beyond my ginger red hair and blue eyes. Every once in a while, he'd send out feelers to galleries but would rarely hear anything back.

Then, when we heard the coffee shop was having difficulty, we knew what we had to do. The money we'd been dutifully putting into a savings account every month for two years, hoping to buy a house one day, turned into a down payment on a much smaller piece of property. With the acquisition of a business loan, and some much needed help from our friends, we took on the role of business ownership—knowing full well if we failed, we'd end up broke.

Again.

But sometimes you have to take a risk to find your heart.

And that's what we'd done.

"Oh boy, look at the hot young things coming in here," Trudy said, a slow smile spreading across her face.

I turned to see the two men who'd forever altered my life walk in side by side. Smiling and sweaty, August and Ryan ambled in, fatigue showing on both of their wind-burned faces.

"Good run?" I asked as I went up on my tippy toes to offer August a kiss, purposely putting a safe distance between me and all his stinky sweat.

A mischievous smile spread across his face as his arm slinked across my back and hauled me against his wet T-shirt.

"Great run. Too bad Sparrow slowed me down."

I turned, completely happy with my sweaty fate now as his muscled arms wrapped around me. Ryan was cozying up to his wife, bending down to kiss the child growing in her belly before he turned around.

"When Everly's pregnant and asking you to go out in the middle of the night for McDonald's, because it's the only thing that will possibly make her happy again, then we'll talk about who's slowing who down," he said, with laughter in his voice as he turned back to wrap his arms around Trudy.

I don't know how many times she'd tried to get my attention, stop me at work to tell me about her and Ryan, before she'd literally grabbed me by the shoulders, sat my butt down in a chair and said, "I'm dating Ryan!"

She'd been nearly shaking, so fearful I would be upset with her.

I'd risen from the seat, taken her in my arms and cried. Not out of sadness, but of joy. Because I knew in that moment, Ryan had found the one.

Trudy was everything he'd been searching for. She was kind and giving, sweet and tenderhearted. For gentle Ryan, they were the perfect match. As I watched their love blossom, I knew this was exactly how our lives were supposed to end up.

Friends. All of us.

In a few months, August and I would stand up in a church and be named their daughter's godparents and tonight, we were all attending Sarah's first ballet as a choreographer. She was even bringing a date to the after party... and this time he wasn't a mystery to us all.

So much joy. So much happiness, and it was just the beginning.

All because two people didn't take no for an answer.

We'd fought for this happily ever after, and in the end, it had finally found us. Our own little slice of heaven. With coffee.

Lots and lots of coffee.

Bonus Scene
Sarah

I saw him again today.

He wore the same crisp black suit that always seemed to hug his lean body so perfectly. He carried that same crooked, beautiful smile that had haunted my dreams since the day I walked away.

Yes, today I saw him.

Only today it wasn't a nightmare. Today it was real.

* * *

The People vs. Trent Miles Lyons had finally begun. People from all walks of life had gathered at the courthouse, hoping to catch a glimpse of the man who was now known worldwide as a financial tyrant and an all-around bad guy. Witnessing the crowd below was like watching a scene out of a movie. Photographers fought for higher ground, hoping to get a money shot as Trent was hauled in, avoiding eye contact with the crowd as if his life depended on it.

As I listened to the near-deafening cries of hatred and malice, I thought maybe he wasn't far off. Maybe it did.

After news got out regarding the substantial money he'd stolen over the years from various families and business owners all over the world, and the attempted murder on August's life, he was now one of the most hated men in the country.

As he and his lawyer struggled through the crowd and I watched the way he seemed unaffected by it all—as if he were just another celebrity, working his way into an exclusive club, rather than a courthouse where he might be convicted to life in prison—I couldn't help but agree with my fellow man.

It was time Trent paid for his sins.

And there were plenty to go around.

Standing near the second-story window of the courthouse, watching my former lover march inside the building as people yelled and jockeyed for a place in the crowd to see his cold hard face, I suddenly felt my body fall into a sheer, blinding panic.

It was something I'd come to recognize well. As this day grew nearer, the number of times I'd almost blacked out from panic attacks had multiplied as I'd worried myself sick over the idea of facing him. My heartbeat fluttered erratically. Beads of sweat lined my temple and my stomach instantly soured as the room slowly closed in on itself.

He was here. In the same building.

I needed to leave.

Now.

Turning abruptly, I headed for the door and fresh air, and nearly knocked into Everly who was slowly pacing the room, taking deep audible breaths through her nose and out her mouth.

"You okay?" she asked, her eyes growing sharp and keen as they took in my wary appearance. No doubt she'd already come to the same conclusion I had.

"He's here," I managed to say, my voice no more than a croak. *When had I become so weak and vulnerable?*

With nothing more than a slight nod, she reached out and took my hand. It was warm and solid. In all my life, I'd never had a friend like Everly—except maybe one. She was the sister I'd prayed for late at night when my mother and father waited for their little ballerina prodigy to cash in. It had started out so innocently— my love for dance. After all, what small girl doesn't want to take ballet lessons? My father had scoffed at the price tag, but Mother had insisted it was good for discipline—something I desperately needed.

The moment my feet touched that floor, I'd felt as though I'd found a best friend in the wood beneath me. It cradled me, loved me, and comforted me as I'd become more and more infatuated with the art of dance. Weekly lessons became daily, and even then it wasn't enough. Like many friends in life, the dance floor and I had growing pains and challenges, but it was the only true constant during my childhood. Until Everly.

I knew the minute I saw her, sitting in Tabitha's waiting room that we shared something more than a therapist; we had something immensely personal in common. I could see the same brokenness in her that resided in me. Her leg bobbed up and down nervously as she stared absently at an outdated magazine about the hottest men in Hollywood. I'd probably looked similar on my first day, and knowing that I offered her a smile and words of encouragement, and the rest was, as they say, history.

Most of our shared history since then had been good, but some... well, some had been just downright bad.

But I was hoping to put all that behind us today.

A click of the closed door had me spinning around on my heels, the fluttering sensation in my chest kicking into high gear once again at the slightest noise.

I needed to get my shit together.

Peeking his head through a small opening, Brick looked around at the three of us and gave a kind smile, most likely hoping to break the tension that was floating around the room like a thick black fog soaking up any rational thought and replacing it with pure dread.

"It's time," he announced.

August, who had been the quietest of us three, rose from his chair in the corner, straightening his suit and tie as he made his way to Everly. They had been told by their lawyer to present a united front, believing America might still be confused on August's involvement with Trent.

Sometimes lawyers can be incredibly dumb.

Telling August and Everly to present themselves as united was as redundant and unnecessary as telling a child the sky was blue.

As long as there was breath in their lungs and days left on this earth, Everly and August would be by each other's side, no matter the reason. Their long-awaited reunion had not only solidified them as a couple but grounded them as individuals. August's memories had begun to return quicker and with less of a shock to his system, thanks to Brick, and Everly no longer needed weekly counseling sessions with Tabitha. Although the three of us did still meet for coffee quite often, but now as close friends. Tabitha had grown into the motherly figure we'd both missed out on in our early years, and I knew, like Everly, she would always be there for us.

Our lawyer had also underestimated the public's need for a hero in this crazy story that had become our lives over the past year or so. It is a simple fact of human nature—whenever there is a villain, a person will always seek out a hero. And that hero was August Kincaid.

Once word had gotten out of his heroic deeds to save Everly's life, topped with the news that he'd given his entire fortune to help those who had been financially destroyed by Trent, there was no need to try to spoon-feed, or sell, anything to the country regarding August's involvement, or the way he felt about Everly.

The people loved him, and it was well deserved.

As the three of us exited our tiny sanctuary provided to us by our lawyers in an effort to keep us away from the crowds, I took Everly's free hand and squeezed.

"It's going to be all right," she said softly. I wasn't sure whether she was trying to encourage me or herself in this statement, but nevertheless, it helped.

We'd all been through hell and back because of the man downstairs and now it was our chance to see that he paid for the many wrongs he'd committed. August and Everly had lost nearly everything, and me? I was still trying to piece together everything he'd taken from me.

Brick waited outside the door, standing close to his loving wife, Tabitha, who had come to support us in this endeavor. Neither Brick nor Tabitha had been called to testify. With the three of us, our lawyers were fairly certain they could win this case in record time. I hoped they were right. As the noise downstairs escalated, reaching our ears as we took the stairs toward the courtroom, I wasn't sure how much of this I could take.

I hadn't seen Trent since the night before I discovered who he really was. I'd never had the chance to confront him about all the ways he'd hurt me, and now that I was mere feet from him, I was ashamed to admit my knees felt like they would buckle at any moment. I didn't love easily. When it came to rough starts in life, mine had been far from an after-school special. My parents were both alive and well. They took care of me, kept me clothed, and paid for every single dance lesson I took. To most, I would have been considered one of the lucky ones, but as I grew I began to realize I was far from fortunate.

At my first dance competition, I was given a solo. It was a great honor and one that wasn't handed out to just anyone—especially someone as young as I had been. I'd practiced nonstop, giving every available second to dance. I wanted to make everyone proud—especially my parents. As I went onstage and took my starting position, my fellow team members yelled and cheered for me, making me feel like an instant star.

The music began and everything was a rush of adrenaline, nerves, and absolute joy as I owned every inch of that stage. There was no doubt in my mind as I ran off the stage that I'd secured a first-place trophy, and when my name was called during the awards ceremony, my fellow dancers knew it, too. I was going places. Fast.

As I rushed off the stage with adrenaline still carrying me, I found my parents in the crowd and hoped today would be the day I saw them smile.

It wasn't.

As my friends' parents lifted them, cheering and congratulating them on their success, I was simply escorted out of the building like nothing had happened. When I asked if they were proud, my mother simply replied, "Yes. Well done."

That was it. No celebratory ice cream. No pat on the back.

I'd done what they'd expected and now it was time to move on.

Tabitha had once said I was a cautious lover, a holdover from the lack of affection I'd been given as a child. I'd always assumed this just meant I wasn't a pushover. I gave my love to those who truly deserved it and wasn't willing to settle.

When Miles, aka Trent, entered my life, my entire world shifted on its axis. He shook up my life and restored my faith in love. I'd never fallen so fast and so hard since my teenage days. He made me feel giddy and young. Looking back now, it's as if I were under the influence, a victim to some sort of mind control or crazy drug—but no, there was no one to blame but myself.

I'd fallen victim to his game. Me, the cautious one.

And now, it was time to repay the favor.

With more conviction than I'd had in weeks, I took a deep breath and walked into the courtroom ready to face him once and for all.

Game over, Trent. Game over.

Don't miss the first book in J.L. Berg's Lost &
Found series—the powerful story of a man and a
woman searching for their happily ever after...

Please see the next page for an excerpt from
Forgetting August.

Prologue

Sound roared in my ear like a freight train as I fought against the rushing tide.

I clawed, gripping and pawing my way to the surface. Where it led, I didn't know—only that I needed to get there. Somehow.

In the distance, I heard an echo of a laugh. Soft and feminine, it disappeared like a feather drifting and dancing in a violent windstorm.

Sharp colors and fuzzy images danced around my head, confusing me, enticing me—motivating me to push ahead.

Where *was I*?

The sound of a siren blared in the distance as a murky green light seemed to move in and around me. It flowed like water and pulsated through me like it had a purpose. The color looked so familiar. I reached out to touch it and suddenly everything stopped, making my heart stop in its tracks.

I need to get out of here.

The woman's voice called out once more and I instinctively chased after it, determined not to lose it.

But once again, like everything else, it faded and I was left alone in a dark tunnel with nothing but myself.

Sometime later, the soft green light returned. I watched it intensify, swirling and changing until it morphed into a single stone. It fell to the ground with a solid clink just as I glimpsed a wisp of red hair around a corner.

"Wait!" I yelled. "Come back!"

My lungs heaved and my body ached as I tried to catch up.

"Don't leave without me!" I begged.

One tiny plink, then another. I looked down to find several green stones hitting the earth. As I looked up to the heavens, it began to pour. Thousands of stones fell from the sky like rain, filling the streets as if they were a giant glass bowl. I tripped and stumbled over them until I fell face forward and hit the ground. Reduced to a crawl, I still didn't give up.

"August!" the woman yelled.

The stones piled one on top of another, surrounding me until I was choking and nearly gagging on the dazzling brilliance as each stone slowly buried me alive.

"Please," I cried, clawing my way to the top as the stones began to cover my head, "Don't leave me here."

My next breath broke the surface and I opened my eyes.

I was awake.

Finally.

Chapter One
Everly

I saw him again today.

It was at the mall this time.

He was wearing a gray suit and it was just seconds this time before he disappeared around a corner and my life returned to normal once more.

It had been two years and yet I still saw him. Everywhere.

The day after that fateful night, I saw him in our neighborhood walking a dog. Months later, he was next to me at a stoplight when I went out for groceries. Two weeks ago when Ryan got down on one knee and placed a dazzling diamond ring on my left hand, I swear I saw his face the minute I said yes.

He was like a ghost—my own personal poltergeist.

I knew it wasn't really him. My therapist had reminded me of that simple fact over a thousand times, but that didn't stop my heart from skipping a beat or my lungs deflating of air every time I saw someone that looked like him pass in my direction.

It could be the color of a person's hair or the way someone laughed that set my body on edge.

Today, it was simply a suit.

Tailored, dark gray with a small pinstripe. The style had been his favorite, and even though the man who wore it looked nothing like him, I still found myself frozen in the middle of the food court.

Still as ice, unable to move.

Because life really didn't move on from a person such as August Kincaid.

No, you simply learned to adapt and above all, you survived.

And that was what I had been doing for the last two years.

Surviving.

"Hey, you went blank again. Are you okay?" Sarah asked.

I looked around, and the world suddenly shifted back into focus. Children cried and begged for ice cream, teenagers laughed and flirted as they walked by us. The smell of cinnamon rolls and cheap Chinese food mixed and mingled, as people pushed and shoved their way around to get in ridiculously long lines. Life went on around me as I returned to the land of the living.

"Yeah, I'm fine," I assured her. Concern was written all over her beautiful, trim face. Her hand lifted briefly as if she were going to offer a hug, but quickly decided against it.

"Okay," she answered, defeat clearly written all over her face. She knew I wouldn't talk about it.

I never did.

There were certain things that just didn't need to be shared.

Specific memories of my past were one of them.

She already knew I was a nutcase yet for some reason became my friend despite this. I guess we had that specific trait in common.

We'd met in the waiting room at my therapist's office. She was a re-covering purger, or at least that's what she called it. Since the time Sarah was barely old enough to vote, she'd been suffering from a variety of eating disorders. She attributed her illnesses to a dance mentor who'd never thought she was thin enough to be a ballerina.

"When all you want to do is be the Swan Princess in *Swan Lake*, you make sacrifices," she'd told me that day in the office very matter-of-factly. Sarah was at peace with her issues. She'd gone through years of counseling and this year would finally be the swan princess she always dreamed of being—fully in control of what she considered her "livable flaws."

Me?

Well, I guess we all had issues that lingered. Some had visible flaws they could see in the mirror, touch with their hands… measure on a scale. Others, like me, had memories that woke us from sleep and haunted our waking hours, making normal, well—different.

I doubted there would ever be any glorious end of the rainbow moment that would somehow magically cure me of all my flaws.

But, I was working on it and Ryan had made a world of dif-ference in my once bleak outlook on life. Now I saw possibilities where there once was only darkness. He brought hope to my sad-ness and light to my life. There wasn't a day that went by that I wasn't thankful for his persistence in seeking me out.

I'd been a hard one to nail down, or so he told me.

"So, are you ready?" she asked, grabbing my hand and moving away from the frozen yogurt and fried food.

"As I'll ever be," I sighed, taking one last longing look at the exit.

"Oh come on. Most girls are excited to do this. Hell, I've been excited for this day for weeks!"

"Then say you're me," I begged, as we turned the corner and my eyes spotted the brightly lit sign at the end of the walkway. I could feel the groan already forming, the deep rumbling sound vibrating through my lungs as it made its way up to express my displeasure.

"Everly Adams. You will not ruin this for me! This is your day and you will enjoy it!"

"I thought *my* day was several months from now," I joked.

"As the blushing bride-to-be, you will have lots of days between now and then. Get used to the attention."

I groaned again, looking at the floor-to-ceiling windows that displayed more tulle and sequins than I'd seen in my entire life.

"We should have eloped."

* * *

"This is horrid, Sarah," I whined, shuffling out of the dressing room in a gown that could only be described as a cross between the Little Mermaid and that scary Alfred Hitchcock movie with all the birds.

"It's beautiful! And so fashion forward," she practically squealed, clapping her hands together like a happy toddler who had just been given a lollipop for supper. "Look at the way the fabric gathers together, making it look like tiny feathers at the bottom of the skirt. So dramatic."

"That," I said, pointing to my calves, "is also where my legs are supposed to be able to move back and forth. It's called walking. I look ridiculous!"

"Walking is so overrated. Besides, how much walking are you planning to do in this thing?" She rolled her eyes, kneeling down to play with the skirt some more. It resulted in the tulle or whatever the puffy stuff was called doubling in size.

"There, perfect."

"I'm not wearing this," I said firmly, trying to look anywhere but at the three different mirrors all reflecting my ridiculous reflection. "Pick another one. And for the love of God, pick something less...well, less you!"

I once again attempted to walk back into the dressing room, doing more of a waddle than a walk. Once there, I was joined by an attendant to assist me. There was no way I could get out of this monstrosity by myself.

"Your tattoo is lovely. Quite unique," the bridal attendant said, as she stood behind me and removed the clamps that held the dress in place. My thin, boylike frame never did fit into sample sizes well. The lack of hips and boobs kept me in sizes most women would die to wear, but the lack of aforementioned body parts sometimes sucked. A lot.

Especially when trying on wedding dresses. Or anything remotely feminine. I felt more like a prepubescent boy trying on drag than a beautiful, curvy woman.

"Thank you," I answered awkwardly, as my hand instinctively reached behind my shoulder to touch the piece of me that I rarely shared with others. The walls of mirrors put my body completely on display, highlighting every rough curve and jutted angle, exposing the harsh black lines of the branch as it wove up my back and around my shoulder.

"Why doesn't the bird fly away? She's free," she said absently, her head cocked to the side as she stared at the birdcage etched on my right shoulder. It was intricate and beautiful as it hung on the barren branch, the door swung wide open for the world to peer in on the tiny bird inside.

"Maybe she's not ready yet," I answered quietly, looking away.

"Okay, I've got another one, Everly! And I promise, you're going to love it!" Sarah's singsong voice seemed to break the spell hovering above us, giving us both a startle. The attendant straightened, turning quickly as I retreated into the corner to grab the satin robe. I'd just fastened it around my waist when she opened the door to let Sarah in.

"Tell me you love me," Sarah said as she waltzed into the room, holding up a simple ivory-colored empire-waist gown with a small amount of beading around the neckline and not a single bit of organza or tulle in sight.

"I think I love you," I said as my eyes widened at the understated elegance of the dress. Simple and understated. Everything I wanted to be.

"Let's try it on," she suggested, handing it to the attendant, who motioned for me to come forward.

Nodding, I agreed, knowing it was unnecessary.

It was perfect and as I glanced around the room, I caught a glimpse of that tiny bird on my shoulder. The one too afraid to jump out of her cage and discover the world outside.

Soon, I would be perfect, too.

Or as close as I could be to the word.

*　*　*

"You are mine, Everly," he whispered. "Mine and mine alone. I own every part of you, every inch of your body...every breath in your lungs. You. Belong. To. Me."

"Everly," another voice murmured. "Everly, wake up. You fell asleep right at the good part again." Ryan laughed.

My eyes cracked open as the glow of the TV made me turn my head toward the comfort of his warm chest.

"Hey, sleepyhead," he said, pulling me tight against his body. "You'll never know who the winter soldier is now," he joked, his head leaning forward just close enough that I felt the heat of his breath against my neck.

"I saw that plot twist ages ago," I answered, covering a quiet yawn with my palm as I stretched in his arms.

"You always do."

"I can't help it. The story lines are always so obvious."

"And if you had written the story," he said, pulling back slightly with a boyish grin lighting up his face. "What would you have done differently?"

"I don't know—I'm not a scriptwriter," I answered with a shrug.

"Maybe you should be." His brow arched, challenging me to answer.

"Who's being the obvious one now, Ryan?" I asked with a huff, rising from my comfortable spot on the couch in order to create some much needed distance. "And seriously? Scriptwriting? Pick something a little less insane next time. When have you ever seen me pick up a pen? Or sit in front of a computer?"

Whenever the subject of where I was going with my life came up, I needed space.

Unfortunately our apartment was only so big, and right now a football field or two didn't seem large enough.

"I don't want to start an argument, Ev, but I just want you to think about it."

"I have been thinking about it," I answered, stepping into the kitchen as the lights flickered on. I pulled open the refrigerator and grabbed a bottle of water. Roughly twisting the cap off, I upturned the bottle and chugged half the contents in one gulp. Water was definitely not my first beverage of choice, but right now I didn't have the patience for anything else.

"And what have you decided?" he asked cautiously, rising from the couch to take a seat at the kitchen island across from me.

"That I'm still deciding." I held my head high, avoiding his eye contact.

I was not in the wrong here.

He sighed long and slow, and I let the silence settle between us, setting the half-empty bottle down on the counter in front of me. A quick glint of light caught my attention as I turned my head and I swiveled back around toward my left hand, noticing the way the overhead lights reflected on the small diamond centered in the middle of the thin gold band.

Three weeks ago he'd asked me to marry him and I'd said yes.

Despite everything I'd put him through—the cold indifference and the numerous rebuttals to his advances, he'd loved me. When I'd told him there would always be a part of me unavailable...that I just couldn't share, he'd accepted me. For who I was.

And what I was willing to give him.

"I'll look at the brochures again," I said, offering up an olive branch as I stepped forward and held out the rest of my water bottle.

His warm smile returned as his fingers encased mine around the plastic.

"I just want to see you succeed. In whatever you choose, Ev. Hell, you can major in basket weaving for all I care. I just want you to feel like you have a purpose in life beyond working at that coffee shop you refuse to quit."

"I know, and I love you for it," I replied, feeling the deep gaze of his eyes settle on mine. Needing to be closer to him, I walked out of the kitchen and walked into his arms at the counter where he sat.

He pulled me into his large frame, where the world felt safe and measurable again.

"I do make a mean cup of coffee," I said, my lips curving into a smile.

His fingers cupped my chin, tilting it toward his dark brown eyes.

"I know. Why do you think I kept coming back every damn day? It wasn't your charming personality."

"I thought it was my ass," I laughed, shaking it as his hands closed around each cheek and squeezed.

"Ah yes. The ass of a porn star and the mouth of a mime. No matter how hard I tried, I could never get you to talk to me."

"Such a sweet talker, and besides—I was told to never speak to strange men," I said, quickly hating myself for saying it. My face slipped slightly as my stomach turned, rolling and churning as my mind replayed unwanted memories from my past.

I never, ever want to see you speaking to another man again. Do you understand me, Everly?

The words rolled around in my head as I tried to shake them out. In the last two years of my life, I'd had a thousand moments like this. A glance, a turn of phrase—anything could bring them on. I'd learned to recognize the symptoms and process the reaction quickly.

So quickly that Ryan didn't even seem to notice anymore.

"Well," he said, grinning, his hands slipping underneath my shirt, "I finally did wear you down. And now you're mine."

A weak smile spread across my lips, seconds before his mouth touched mine.

No matter how much he loved me.

No matter how much I loved him in return.

I would never, ever belong to another person.

For as long as I lived.

*   *   *

The movie had been long forgotten, as had our clothes.

They were strung out all over the apartment, leaving a trail toward the bedroom. Little breadcrumbs of debauchery.

"Hey, it's still early; do you want to order a pizza?" Ryan yelled from the shower as I took a long breath and snuggled deeper into the covers on our bed.

"Does it require me to get out of this bed?" I whined, moving my legs back and forth against the smooth sheets. Ryan always said it looked like I was swimming in bed when I did this.

Growing up, I never had nice sheets. Hell, sometimes there were foster homes that didn't even give me sheets—just a blanket and a dirty bare mattress.

Luxuries like Egyptian cotton sheets were things I would never grow accustomed to, no matter how many times my legs touched them. Every night, I'd sink into bed and run my legs back and forth against the smoothness, loving the way it felt against my skin.

Like Ryan, it brought me peace and made me feel safe—two things I'd struggled with the majority of my life.

"Please, babe. I'm hungry. So very, very hungry," he said, sticking his head out the door of the bathroom. His lips turned downward, making him look years younger. I laughed, unable to resist his boyish charm.

"Okay, okay," I said, stretching one last time before I rose to grab my robe.

"On second thought, I might need to work off a few more calories first," he said, stepping out of the bathroom in just a towel. His tanned skin was slick and wet from the shower, and I couldn't help but lick my lips as I watched a tiny drop of water skate down his chiseled chest.

Who knew nerds could be so hot?

His gaze turned heated as he stalked forward and I watched the towel drop to the floor. I stepped backward, feeling the edge of the bed hit the backs of my knees.

Our bodies met once more as his hand cupped the back of my head, tilting it upward. "I love you, Everly. I love you so much," he whispered, touching his lips to mine. I moaned into the kiss, feeling every hard inch of him press into me.

Always aware of my needs, he was gentle as he lowered me to the bed. As my head touched the pillow, I heard the sounds of a cell phone ringing throughout the apartment.

Ryan's head dipped forward, shaking back and forth.

"Just ignore it," he said.

I was already pushing at his shoulders, begging him to let me answer it.

"It can't be that important, Ev," he said, his eyes dancing with amusement. "I'm right here."

I rolled my eyes, grabbing my robe as I raced to the living room.

"It could be Sarah," I said. "She had her first rehearsal tonight."

I picked up the phone, not recognizing the number, and paused.

"Babe," Ryan said, standing in the doorway of our room. "Come back to bed. Whatever it is can wait."

I didn't listen. Instead, I answered and heard the words I had begged God to never allow to come true.

"Miss Adams?" a woman said on the other end.

"Yes," I answered.

"This is Doctor Lawrence from St. Marcus Hospital."

My heart began to beat frantically as my hand sought out something solid to hold me up. I knew it was coming. Like a freight train in the middle of the night, I could see the light off in the distance...I knew what was coming.

Who was coming.

"He's awake."

The phone hit the floor seconds before I did, and then the world went black.

Acknowledgment

Writing a book is like releasing little pieces of your soul to the world. You do so knowing not everyone will understand or appreciate what you've created, but you hope that maybe...just maybe somewhere out there, another soul will connect with those tiny slivers of theirs and make magic.

Making magic isn't a singular job, and in my life, it often takes a village. I don't know how I'd ever make it through from one novel to the next without the help of my family, friends, and support team.

Although there have been many fictional men in my life, there has only been one real life man, giving me enough memories in the last twenty-three years to make an endless supply of gallant, amazing book boyfriends. Chris, thank you for being my soul mate and best friend. You are the reason I'm able to write amazing love stories over and over.

My children manage to keep me balanced. When life gets crazy, a hug from an eight-year-old never gets old. Thank you to my azing me with their love,

ay without a great set
erything you gave us

a thick skin and a
ige thank you to
l Tanya Turner
ladies.

to spell my
ys ℓ.. kful for an
.t team. To my a... .he ..milton at
..iral, thank you for everything you do to make sure my
...s are amazing. Jill Marsal, thank you for being agent extraordinaire! You always have my back, and to Jill Sava, the world's best personal assistant, I have no words. You are my rock. Tara and the rest of my InkSlingers family, thank you for everything you do to keep my publicity rolling so I don't have to worry about it. Ever. It helps me sleep at night.

Lastly, I'd like to thank my readers. Thank you for giving this lifelong dream of writing wings to fly.

About the Author

J. L. Berg is a California native living in the South. She is the author
of the self-published Ready series. When she's not writing, you can
find her with her nose stuck in a romance book, in a yoga studio, or
devouring anything chocolate.

Learn more at:

JLBerg.com

Twitter: @AuthorJLBerg

Facebook.com/AuthorJLBerg